Praise for Kevin Baker's

Sometimes You See It Coming

"A winner. . . . Put this one on the shelf with Bernard Malamud's *The Natural.*" —*Time* magazine

"Ingeniously seductive. . . . An entertaining debut."
—*Entertainment Weekly*

"An offbeat search for the deeper meaning of the game. . . . Contains some of the best play-by-play game descriptions we've ever read." —*Playboy*

"A bona fide four-bagger." —*Milwaukee Journal*

"Baseball as it's meant to be." —*Kirkus Reviews*

"Ranks with Jane Leavy's sadly underrated *Squeeze Play* as the best baseball fiction in the last couple of decades. . . . For those who know the game, there are more layers of meaning than in *The Name of the Rose.*" —*Philadelphia Inquirer*

"A smart, funny first novel." —*Cleveland Plain Dealer*

D0004003

Ellen Abrams

About the Author

KEVIN BAKER is the author of *Dreamland* and *Paradise Alley,* and served as chief historical researcher for the *New York Times* bestseller *The American Century.* He has been published in *Harper's, American Heritage,* the *New York Times,* and many other publications. He lives in New York City.

Sometimes You
See It Coming

Also by Kevin Baker

Dreamland

Paradise Alley

Sometimes You See It Coming

Kevin Baker

Perennial

An Imprint of HarperCollins*Publishers*

First Perennial edition published 2003.

Library of Congress Cataloging-in-Publication Data

Baker, Kevin.
  Sometimes you see it coming : a novel / Kevin Baker.—1st Perennial ed.
    p. cm.
  ISBN 0-06-053597-0
  1. New York Mets (Baseball team)—Fiction.   2. New York (N.Y.)—Fiction.   3. Baseball players—Fiction.   4. Baseball teams—Fiction.   I. Title.

PS3552.A43143S64 2003
813'.54—dc21   2003040701

03 04 05 06 07 RRD 10 9 8 7 6 5 4 3 2 1

To Ellen and to my family, with love

1

To see the talent is as much a gift as to have the talent.

—REGIE OTERO

The Color Commentary

The only one who was there from the very beginning, the only one who is always there in the middle of everything, was The Old Swizzlehead, aka Rapid Ricky Falls, who was the closest thing John Barr ever had to a friend. And even his account must be taken with a healthy dose of incredulity—not only because of Falls's renowned propensity for obfuscation, exaggeration, and outright deception—but also for the simple fact that *no one* ever got that close to Barr, the greatest if not the most beloved player in the game.

He was grudgingly accorded the former title by the writers, the green flies at the show as the players liked to call them, who knew his honors and statistics. By the end, the flies and the fans could duly recite all the batting titles, the home-run crowns, the gold gloves, and the Most Valuable Player awards. They could list for you the long string of division championships, league pennants, and World Series titles he had won for the New York Mets since that day he had first walked onto the Shea Stadium field, fresh off two years in the minor leagues and before that God only knew where, and proceeded to tear off four straight line drive hits. And after that a thirty-one-game hitting streak, and after that thirteen years of unremittingly battering the small white ball around one ballpark or another.

He was the kind of instant phenom they all should have loved. Tall and lean, hawk-faced and loose-footed, looking every inch the ideal, baggy-uniformed ballplayer of the thirties that still bedeviled their psyches. He played hard, worked on his game, stayed alert, took extra batting practice. He was even duly modest and diffident about his tremendous talent, just like the old-time ballplayers were supposed to be. John Barr let his bat and his glove speak for him, and they were eloquent.

He could do everything on a ballfield; that was beyond dispute. In an era of designated hitters, platoon players, spot starters, short relievers, and middle-inning relievers, Barr could play the whole game. Better still, there was a certain quality of danger that attached to him. There have been great players who never had a great moment; men who went on year after year, running up formidable statistics, but were no more fearsome than anybody else in the few, crucial moments of their careers. They popped up or flied out in key at-bats, or did not even fail that spectacularly. They simply singled when they should have homered, cut the ball off from going into the gap when they should have made the diving, sliding catch. They played on no great teams, took part in no immortal moments, and passed quietly and respectably from the game, vaguely admired by all.

This was not the case with John Barr. His very presence at the plate seemed to jar things loose. It caused the opposing pitchers and fielders to proceed in jerky, tentative movements. His appearance at the big moment almost always guaranteed that something would happen, and usually something that entailed a ball whacked viciously into the furthest reaches of the stadium, and his opponents sent stumbling desperately after it.

And yet—by the end he was still no more than a redoubtable shadow to the flies, the fans, even his own teammates. You could not say he was loved, except perhaps by Ricky Falls or Ellie Jay, Queen of Sportswriters, who loved him not so much for the raw talent but the dedication that she perceived. For Barr played wrapped up in himself, in the narrow devotion of hitting the ball. There were never many color stories on the man, no quotes that went beyond a few, monosyllabic words, no glowing or lurid accounts of him from former teammates. Nothing to say where he came from, other than the name of a small New England town with a funny name. No visible family, friends, women, or interest of any kind outside of a ballpark.

The only one who got more inside on him was The Old Swizzlehead, or again possibly Ellie Jay, who divined in him something that not even Falls could quite discern, after all his years with him. Something detached from the workaday problems of run-of-the-mill, superstar, millionaire athlete gods. Something truly not normal.

Yet it *was* Falls who saw him through his entire career, right from the first moment he set foot on a professional ballfield. Or so he claims. It is The Old Swizzlehead who can better describe the true essence of the great man than anyone else alive—or so he says.

The Old Swizzlehead

He was the best.

I know how the flies like to throw that word around. These days somebody makes a good relay throw, he becomes the best player in the game ever. But John Barr was the best, for real.

You have to think about how unusual that is. Maybe Ellsworth Pippin, The Great White Father, is the best owner and general manager of all time. Maybe the Rev. Jimmy Bumpley is the best TV evangelist. Maybe even Dickhead Barry Busby is the best sportswriter. I don't know.

But I doubt it. And I know John Barr was the best.

Where I grew up, we used to shoot hoop on the outdoor courts on Amsterdam Avenue. We used to play day an' night, nonstop, an' we thought we were pretty bad. But we all knew the best player in the project was my cousin and homeboy, John Bell.

He could two-hand dunk behind his back, every time you gave him the ball within three feet of the basket. We knew he was the best player in the city, best player anywhere. Had to be.

One day we decided we was so good we would go down an' play in Riverside Park. There was a guy down there three inches shorter than John Bell, who could start at the top of the key, take one step, an' jam it through with just his left hand. He blew by my cousin like he was standin' still, an' he rejected everything he put up. He musta scored two hundred points over John Bell that afternoon.

That was when I knew. At the next court there would be somebody even better. An' the same thing at the next one, an' the one after that. Until you get down to the courts in the Village where even the pros come to play. But even then there was maybe better players someplace: out in Bed-Stuy, or up in the Bronx. Or maybe down in D.C., or Houston, or anywhere else, all over the world.

You don't usually get to see the best. An' even when you do, most times you don't *know* you're seein' it.

But I saw John Barr. And I knew.

Dickhead Barry Busby

You'd ask him, "What'd you hit?" just trying to get a quote. And he would stare up at you with those dead eyes he had, like you'd just asked him the stupidest goddamn question in the world. Like he wanted to make you afraid, the son of a bitch.

The Old Swizzlehead

We used to call 'em his drowned man's eyes. You messed with him in any way, that's what he'd give you.

He'd go into second base, spikes high, lookin' to rip the short-stop's balls off. Even on a nothin' play, with us up five runs in the eighth inning, he'd do it.

Anybody else did that kind of shit, there'd be a fight. But with John Barr the shortstop would just curse an' dance around for a while. Maybe he'd make a mistake an' say somethin' out the corner of his mouth.

Barr would give him those drowned man's eyes. Dead an' grey an' lookin' right through you. He'd shut up, look kind of cow-eyed toward third base, an' throw the ball back to the pitcher.

Ellsworth Pippin, The Great White Father

John Barr is a great ballplayer. As far as that goes.

The Old Swizzlehead

He'd stand up there every time, with that perfect stance. Every time, exactly the same. Legs planted like a bulldog. Elbows out, bat cocked up high behind his ear. It was like somebody painted in the spots where his feet were supposed to go.

Every time. The only movement was when he would roll that bat around a little bit in his hands, like a big lazy cat swishin' its tail. Then the pitch would come in, an' it was like somebody pushed a lever. His whole body would turn on it. Legs an' knees an' arms an' head, all moving together.

Perfect, every time. He would turn on that pitch and drive it, be off up the line, bat dropped behind him, not botherin' to look where he hit it. He *knew.*

He looked like he didn't even have to think about it. I told that to him once, an' he looked at me an' almost smiled:

"I think about it all the time," he told me. "Every time I'm up there. But it ain't the stance."

He never had a real slump. Not one, in all the time I played with him down in the bushes and in the major leagues. Not until that last year.

Charlie Stanzi, The Little Maniac

There used to be better ballplayers when I played. They had to work at it harder. One year when I was still a busher I got a job workin' construction in the winter. They had a foreman who hated my guts, and one day he threw sand in my face while I was carryin' a full load of bricks. You can bet your ass I didn't drop a brick. An' I came right back there the next day, too. I had to support my mother an' my two sisters, an' you couldn't do it with what you made during the season.

That's why he could never be as good as they used to be, I don't care what the writers or the statistics say.

The Old Swizzlehead

But he was.

He was the kind of ballplayer who wasn't supposed to exist anymore.

He lived for the game. He had every detail down perfect, an' not just the hittin'. He was the best rightfielder in the game. He could throw a strike to home plate from the corner. He wasn't that fast, but he would steal a base every time you didn't keep him close. *Every* time—whether it was a close game or not.

That was how he played the game. He was the kind the flies all said they loved. The gung-ho, white-boy ballplayer. Not afraid to get his uniform dirty. Didn't know any other way to play the game. Played with the small hurts. An' all that shit.

But they didn't like him. They were afraid of him. An' he wouldn't give 'em anything. Not a quote, not a smile. Not the littlest indication at all that he was even human.

It was the same thing with the fans. Usually they go wild every time some white boy runs out from under his cap, even if he misjudged the ball to start with. They always think a black ballplayer like me makes it look too easy.

But they never warmed to John Barr, good as he was. Everybody in the ballpark paid attention when he was at bat, but that didn't mean they liked him. Sixteen years I played with him, includin' the minor leagues, an' he never made one gesture on the field that even looked human. Until the end.

The Color Commentary

Which Rapid Ricky Falls was there for, too, just as he was there for the very beginning of John Barr in the game. Though you have to keep in mind the source: The Old Swizzlehead, the original trickster, whose whole game is a deceit. Walking up to the plate like an old man carrying wood—bent over, bat balanced precariously on his shoulder like it was too heavy for him. Still bent over when he got up to the plate, knees buckling, bat propped up on one hip barely above his waist. Until the ball came in, and he would slash at it and be off around the bases like a dark streak, throwing everything into confusion.

The Old Swizzlehead, whom the media people would cluster around like flies after honey (his teammates used another word), waiting for whatever outrageous thing he might tell them next and laughing nervously because they could never tell whether he really was a character or just having fun with them. And surely his version of John Barr was the most outrageous story of all. Though it still might be true—

2

I could use a few phenoms.

—ED BARROW

The Old Swizzlehead

I met up with John Barr my first year in pro ball, down in Hell's Gate, West Virginia, where I was playin' in the Coal-an'-Coke League. We used to call it the Hole-an'-Joke League, on account of the fields an' the lighting down there. It wasn't more than a few dead mining towns strung out along a cement highway. Class-A ball at its finest. Our leftfielder fell into an abandoned mineshaft up to his waist one night, goin' for a fly.

"I don't know why the hell anybody bothers to come out here," our manager, Ol' Cal Rigby, used to wonder, slappin' at the bugs an' the sweat slidin' down his old turkey neck.

"It's the lightin'," I told him. "They like the subdued, cocktail-lounge ambience."

Hell's Gate was the worst town in the whole league. People were gettin' out fast. Every day you'd see another hillbilly family takin' everything they owned down to the Greyhound bus station. For promotions, the team used to give away free bus tickets to Miami. We'd have whole hillbilly families sittin' in the stands with their cardboard suitcases, just hopin' they'd win the grand prize in the seventh inning an' get out of town.

They say it used to be called Coventry, or Clovertown—some

nice name like that. That was before they had the big fire underground in the mines. It started burnin' down there an' it never stopped. I talked to one old miner, said he'd been down there an' seen it.

"It was two miles down the main shaft," he told me. "A whole sea of fire. But I just got a quick look, before it smelled the oxygen an' come up the tunnel after me."

They hadda shut down all the mines, but that didn't stop it. You could smell the sulphur burnin' all day long, an' the sky was full of smoke. Late at night me an' some a' the other Hellions would take the local talent back up to Broadfoot Park. We'd sit up top the bleachers, sippin' Jack Daniel's an' watchin' the flames come up out of the ground, all around the town.

"It were one thing with the cave-ins an' the strikebreakers an' the black lung," that old miner told me. "But when hell comes right up after us, it's time to leave."

Not that I did'much talkin' with most of the locals. They had all the black ballplayers on the team livin' in a house together, a block from the park. We used to call it the Jungle House. If you was a black ballplayer who came down to Hell's Gate, you just went there, that was all. When any of us left that house, there'd be a police car cruisin' along behind within ten minutes. They wouldn't stop you—just kinda cruise behind you a half-block or so.

It was like that all over. I'd walk into the 7-Eleven down the street an' the peckerwood behind the cash register would slide his arm under the counter, where he kept a sawed-off shotgun. Every time, I'd come in an' that swizzlehead would reach for it, like a nervous twitch. He was a ball fan, an' he got to know me eventually. He'd even smile when he saw me come in. But that right hand would still twitch toward the gun. It just wouldn't go all the way under the counter anymore. The length of that halfway twitch was as far as civil rights got in Hell's Gate.

It focused you, livin' like that. Every one of us over at the Jungle House got up the ladder to Double-A ball, at least. There wasn't much else but baseball for us to do in that town. I used to go out to the ballpark every mornin' we was home, an' somebody else from the Jungle House would always come by an' throw me some battin' practice. That was how I happened to

be there one Sunday mornin' when I found John Barr, greatest
player in the history of the game, sleepin' in the locker room
of the Hell's Gate Hellions.

It *was* a locker room, too. Not like what you call a *clubhouse* up
in the major leagues, with the carpet on the floor, an' the whirlpool bath, an' the big open wood lockers. In Hell's Gate, where
we dressed looked like any high school locker room, only worse.
It had a bare concrete floor an' banged-up metal lockers, from
all the frustrated high school phenoms findin' out they couldn't
cut it even in the low minor leagues.

John Barr was sleepin' on one of those little bitty aluminum
benches in front of the lockers that are barely wide enough to
hold your ass. I don't know how he could sleep on it, but there
he was. In his street clothes, with a jacket bunched up under his
head an' a copy of *The Sporting News* laid over him.

He looked like a bag person. Back in high school, a couple
used to get into the gym every morning an' we had to throw 'em
out before we could shoot hoops. I figured this swizzlehead was
some sort of new West Virginia bum. So I give him a little tap on
the leg an' said, "Hey, Jack, time to rise an' shine."

That was when I first saw those drowned grey eyes.

I only seen eyes like that a few times before in my life. On
the subway, maybe, when there'd be one of the mean crazies
you didn't mess with, standin' in the corner of the car tryna
start somethin', givin' everybody that same look. You knew he
would just as soon look at you as fight you, kill you, kill hisself—anything.

"What is it?" he says. "What do you want?"

"Why, nothin', sweetness. Nothin' at all," I dissed back at him.
"I just wanted to give you your wake-up call an' ask if you wanted
sugar an' cream with your morning coffee."

He eased his back down off the lockers an inch then an' lowered those eyes a little.

"You a ballplayer?" he asked me.

"No, I'm the goddamned nigger towel boy. They got 'em all
over the place down in A-ball. Who the fuck are you?"

"You been heah long?" he asked me, right like that.

"Two months, same as everyone else. What you think?"

"I don't know. Maybe you been heah from last year, too."

"What the hell do I look like to you?" The kid was beginnin' to annoy me, makin' out I needed two years to get through A-ball.

"I'm leadin' this league in hittin'. Not to mention hits, walks, stolen bases, an' runs scored. That look to you like I been here since *last year*?"

He kept lookin' at me cautious, like he expected me still to jump him any minute. But then he did somethin' else that surprised me. He picked up his *Sporting News* an' goes through it till he gets to the minor league averages.

"You must be R. Falls," he says. "Three-fifty-eight. Not bad."

"Thanks. Means a lot, comin' from you."

"Seventy-five runs scored already."

"You here for my autograph?"

"No. I came to play," he says with a straight face. "I'm here to try out."

"Try out? You 'didn't get assigned?"

"No."

"How'd you get here?"

"I thumbed. Didn't have the money for the bus."

That was when I stopped gettin' on at the fool. I just told him to lay back on the itty-bitty bench an' get some more sleep, while I went off to get Ol' Cal Rigby. I figured the boy could use a little more sleep before it was time to wake up.

The Color Commentary

It wasn't possible that there was still a ballplayer—a *real* ballplayer—out there anywhere who hadn't already been discovered, inspected, and signed or rejected by Ellsworth Pippin's scientific scouting machine. Not in the jungles of Venezuela, or the dirt-road sugar-cutting towns of the Dominican Republic, or even the rice paddies of Japan. Certainly not any white kid who had gone to high school and played organized ball anywhere in the United States.

This wasn't some kind of old-time organization, built around the famous bird-dog scouts scouring the dusty backroads in their fancy cars that brought the farmboys running and staring. It didn't depend on wise, wrinkled faces and steady eyes picking out the talent on a sandlot ballfield, working the stop-watch with one hand and a scorecard pencil with the other. Wiring back to New York at the next one-horse town and getting permission to offer a five-hundred-dollar bonus to the next Babe Ruth.

No. Pippin had put it on an advanced management basis, designed by one of the best business schools in the country, and the other teams had naturally followed suit. This was a system carefully divided into districts balanced by computer analyses of ball-playing demographics per percentage of the population, complete with separate scouts to study every aspect of the game. One man to study pitching, another hitting, another speed alone—all of them arriving with their mechanical gadgetry like some kind of scientific research team. As soon as the game was over, they were gone, too—back to feed into the computer their electronically measured data on fastballs, bat speeds, times running to first base. Which all made its way in the blink of an eye back to New York and The Vacuum, the apex of the whole pyramid, which carefully sifted and balanced it all and within seconds spit out a ranking of each and every prospect in the world, what his percentage chances were of making the major leagues, and how much money he should be offered under current market conditions.

Pippin had originally built The Vacuum to look as big and complicated as a computer from an old science fiction movie, complete with extra dials and levers and gauges—the better to intimidate the other general managers. In fact, the information in its data base would fit into any good desktop terminal—like the one in his oak-lined office, deep in the bowels of Shea Stadium.

Nevertheless, he had the best information. The best information anywhere, on any boy who played the game, and the only reason any real prospect might not be tagged, signed, and invited to a spring training camp somewhere in the Mets' vast organization would be if by pure bad luck somebody else had happened to sign him first.

It couldn't be that there would be anyone left out there, any-where, who was still worth signing.

But there was.

The Old Swizzlehead

I always thought that was why Ellsworth Pippin hated Barr so much, right down to the end. He never could believe he missed him. I didn't believe it either, I got to admit. Not that first morning. Nobody did. Particularly not Ol' Cal Rigby.

It took me a while to get him up an' around, as usual. Cal had been in the game fifty years, an' he lost some parts along the way. By the time he got to Hell's Gate he was missin' his left eye, his right leg, an' all his teeth. The bushes took 'em away, he said. Maybe it was all them long bus rides, just jarred 'em loose. Fifty years in the game, an' he never had got close to the money, either as a player or a manager. Now he was just waitin' out the string until The Great White Father picked out some third-string catcher an' talked him into takin' a cut in pay an' goin' down to Hell's Gate to start a brilliant new managing career.

Ol' Cal had got blind drunk the night before in his boardinghouse, like he used to do every Saturday night down there. It took him ten minutes to figure out which leg he hadda put on, an' he wasn't too pleased when I told him about our newest phenom.

"You woke me up for that? Jesus. You come an' get me for some kid who watches too many movies?"

But he got his clothes an' his spare parts on an' got on back down to Broadfoot Park with me as fast as he could. Ol' Cal didn't like the idea of that kid waitin' down at the ballpark any more than I did.

"You say he just got off the bus?" Ol' Cal asked me, lightin' up a cigarette as he limped on down there.

"Uh-uh. He ain't got money for a bus. He hitched the whole way."

"Jesus." I noticed his hand was shakin'. "Well, we'll see if we can't get some money from Pippin's tight ass, send him back by bus, anyway. I don't care if they take it out of my own goddamned salary. I just want him out of here. Somethin' like this could be bad luck for a ball club."

I was hopin' he wouldn't even be there still when we got

back. I was hopin' he realized all of a sudden he'd come all the way for a pipe dream, an' get cold feet an' just slink his ass outta there.

But he was still in the locker room, on that scrawny bench, but lookin' up now, all alert. Ol' Cal shook his hand an' squinted at him, an' asked him if he was sure he hadn't been assigned, tryna hope against hope that he could get out of this one. But the boy looked at him like he didn't know what he was talkin' about.

"No," he said. "I came to play."

So Cal got him changed out of his street clothes into the only spare uniform we had, which was number 13, for obvious reasons.

"Jesus, even more bad luck," Cal groaned. "We'll be lucky we don't break three legs in the mine holes tonight."

We didn't even have any spikes for the boy, an' he hadn't brought none himself. He said he didn't even own a pair, which almost made Ol' Cal give up an' kick his ass out right there.

"It ain't the shoes," was all the boy said.

Cal wanted to tell him to go home, but I saved the day, I got to admit. I put into motion the whole chain of events, right down through John Barr's whole career of unparalleled greatness to the last play of that last, strange year. Which you can thank me for or not, but I just wanted to point that out.

"Let him go ahead," I whispered to Cal. "Get rid of him easy that way."

"Okay, kid," Cal told him. "Let's see your fielding."

We went out to the field, an' Ol' Cal brought a ball an' a fungo bat. He didn't want to wait for one of the pitchers to show up an' see if the kid could hit a curveball. He figured he would just hit him some tough flies, tell him, You can't even catch the ball, how you gonna play in the major leagues?

"You sure you're ready?" Cal called out to him.

"Uh-huh," the kid said, out among the potholes in center field. I thought he'd be lucky if he didn't fall through to China.

Cal started hittin' flies. He hit everything. High fly balls, line drives. Dying quails an' Texas Leaguers. He hit 'em in front of the kid an' over his head an' right at him.

An' the kid caught everything, even in his street shoes. He ran down every ball Cal Rigby hit to him. He picked 'em off his ankles an' he pulled 'em down off the fence. And every throw back to me, standin' next to Cal, was straight an' hard an' on the line, until my hand ached from it.

The more he caught, the harder Cal made the fly balls. But the boy still ran 'em down, no problem, like it wasn't even a workout for him.

"Shee-it," Ol' Cal said. "Whattaya think? Prison?"

"Maybe a mental hospital," I guessed.

"Yeah, but if that boy can hit, we might be able to use him."

Which is like sayin' a dog can hunt if it's got a nose. You can teach most anybody to field, at least a little. Hitting is what makes you a ballplayer.

It's impossible to hit a baseball, when you think about it. They even had some scientists figure it out. The pitcher is sixty feet six inches away, an' if he's a professional he can throw the ball hard enough to kill you at that distance. He won't do that, but you can't know it, which is where the problem lies.

He can make that ball come right in at your head—then curve out over the plate at the last second. He can make it come in straight an' fat—an' then fall away like it rolled off the end of a table. You have to hit the ball before you see it, if you know what I mean. An' if you don't, it don't matter anyway, cause you'll never be a ballplayer.

Cal kept the kid busy while he waited for some of the pitchers to get to the ballpark. He ran it like a old-time tryout, hittin' some more balls to the kid, timin' him runnin' the bases. Even without the stopwatch, you could see he ran like a professional ballplayer already. He made the turn the right way every time. Hit the bag with his right foot, and when he got to second he made a perfect hook slide, halfway around the base.

"Who is this guy?" Cal said out loud, an' I could tell he was already startin' to get hopeful. "He looks like a finished ballplayer already. You sure he didn't get cut from somebody else's roster? What is he already? A drug addict? A child molester?"

"He says he never played the game for money before."

"Goddamn," says Cal, an' spits on the ground an' bites his lip. Usually he only did that when we got a few men on base, in the late innings.

"I gave up expecting anything out of this game," he said. "This game'll kill you with hope. Inning by inning, year by year. Hoping you can pick up a game on whoever's in first. Hoping you can score the runner from third. Hoping you can get ahead on the goddamned count. This whole game is lousy with hope.

"But if this kid can hit—"

The Color Commentary

And when they came, of course, he hit everything they threw at him, usually straight back at them. Sometimes he would get hold of one, and launch it way past the plasterboard fence in deep center field. Sometimes they got so frustrated at this boy, hitting everything they threw, that they hurled a couple at his head. And every time he got up again, without any expression in his young, serious face, and hit the ball again, straight back through the box, making them skip rope.

The Old Swizzlehead

He was in the lineup three days later, soon as Ol' Cal could get permission from the big club. He woulda had him out there sooner, but Pippin insisted on doin' a background check.

But he couldn't come up with anything. Barr hadn't been in a prison, or a mental asylum. Pippin even ordered him to go through a whole day of tests. But there were no drugs, no alcohol. He was in perfect shape, which you could see for yourself. Pippin finally had no other choice but to let him play an' hope he was all a mirage.

Barr kept the first uniform Cal gave him. Grey, like every other uniform in the Hole-an'-Joke League, set off only by the hat with a blue, orange, and white flame on the front. It was number 13, an' he kept that number the whole rest of his career.

Another ballplayer had to give up his spot on the roster, of course. Another former high school star, who found all of a sudden he couldn't get his battin' average off the I-95, which is what we call somebody battin' below .200 in witty ballplayer talk that don't sound too good when you're the kid gettin' back on the bus.

That poor Jonah sat over on the end of the bench in his street clothes for the first game. It was bad luck havin' somebody who was cut on the bench. But Ol' Cal allowed it, since even he couldn't quite believe John Barr was for real.

That kid sat down there an' watched John Barr hit two line-drive singles, an' run out a triple into the corner, an' make an over-the-shoulder catch out by the fence in right. By the fifth inning that boy knew Barr wasn't no illusion, an' he was vanished off the bench, disappeared down the runway to the locker room, an' out of the game forever.

Somebody had to make way for John Barr. He hit an even .444 that year. Even with missing the first two months of the season, he led the league in hits, runs batted in, doubles, triples, home runs, an' outfield assists. The only reason he didn't lead in runs scored was he batted me in so many times.

His average was so high, even if it was in the low minors, that they brought down a national TV crew to do a story on him for the game of the week. A lot of minor-league ballplayers might fall right apart with a swelled head after somethin' like that. But not John Barr. He didn't even watch it. The day it was on, he was out there takin' extra batting practice, same as always.

He wasn't much given to sensation. He went out drinkin' with some of us a couple times, only it wasn't like he drank anything. He just sat there with one beer in front of him the whole night, watching everything around him, an' didn't say a thing. You didn't exactly get the idea that he was unfriendly. He just didn't know how to act around other people.

He never joked around in the locker room. Some fool tried to give him a hotfoot once—an' Barr gave him those eyes an' slowly stamped out the fire with his other shoe, like he was stompin' that swizzlehead hisself. After those first couple times, he never went out with any of us again. We never saw him anywhere except at the ballpark. It was like the fire in the ground spit him up every night just for the game.

At first I thought he was lonely, missin' his momma an' the rednecks back home. I got picked to room with him on the road trips, since I saw him first an' Ol' Cal Rigby figured I had some kind of special rapport with the boy. He wanted me to take care of him, get him to fit in with the team an' feel at home. But he made it clear he didn't need no takin' care of.

"I'm stayin' in tonight," was all he would say, in a voice that made sure you knew he didn't need any urging. I even stayed home to watch him an' confirm it for my own eyes. The swizzle-head didn't even read, or watch TV. He would eat dinner, then he would take a few swings in front of the mirror an' go to bed. He didn't call his momma, didn't sit up an' sip bourbon. He just made sure his stroke was perfect every time, an' when he reassured hisself of that fact he went right into bed.

There was some nights he might take a walk around town. But usually that was *all* he did. He would walk hard an' fast with his head down. I got to following him for a while. There was one night he stopped in at a X-rated movie theater. But he even came out of there after about ten minutes, walkin' faster than ever. He didn't stop for a drink, didn't try to chat up the local girls. Sometimes his eye would catch the lights in a window or on a porch, an' he would slow down to an amble an' crane his neck at it. But then he would move on.

You never woulda thought he was a phenom. But the TV crew came down all right, and more important, John Barr got a couple of the big New York writers and even Ellsworth Pippin hisself to visit Hell's Gate. There was Dickhead Barry Busby, from the *Post-News*, an' Ellie Jay, who had just started to cover sports for the *Times*.

Dickhead Barry was his usual self. He come down there dressed in a all-white linen suit, expectin' I don't know, mint juleps an' darkie stableboys or somethin'. It was a dry town, Hell's Gate, but he found some young scotch somewhere in about ten minutes, an' curled up to sleep in the bullpen.

Ellie Jay, though, was somethin' else. Bunch of kids like us, we'd never seen anything like *her*. We never even knew there was such things as lady sportswriters. We said stuff, made as many rude remarks as a bunch of eighteen-year-olds could think up. She was the most beautiful woman we'd ever seen, in her designer clothes, with her dark eyes an' her long black hair runnin' down her back. Her breasts were like two fine pillows for the heartsick, promisin' all the comfort of home, but we couldn't get near her.

She seemed much older than us. She already had a way of looking at you through her cigarette smoke with her eyes narrowed— like she could see exactly what you were and what you'd be. She knew the rest of us were bushers, an' she paid as much attention to us as the grass. Right from the start, all she wanted to know about was John Barr.

"He is a specimen," she said when she saw him. "I wonder where he came from. Where did he say?"

"Up north, I think. Or maybe south."

"He thumbed? On what highway? That's all I need."

That girl was curious as a one-eyed cat, once she got the scent up. She knew as soon as she seen him, there was somethin' that didn't make sense about Barr, an' from that day, she wanted to track it down. But there was one person even more curious than she was, an' that was The Great White Father.

It was the first time I ever saw Ellsworth Pippin. He was one of those old men who tries to keep himself immaculate. Every one of his white hairs was slicked down in place, an' he smelled like peppermint and hair tonic. He wore hand-tailored pearl grey suits, with special double cuffs on his shirt sleeves, an' gleaming black shoes you could comb your hair in.

We all froze up with The Great White Father in the stands. We couldn't do a right thing. But not Barr. The first night Pippin come down, he hit two doubles an' a three-run shot, an' stole a base. The next night he hit three triples an' threw out the tyin' run at the plate.

I watched The Great White Father watchin' him. He was sittin' above our dugout, so's he could call Cal Rigby over from time to time the way you'd call a waiter. He'd put one finger up in the air, an' Ol' Cal would have to go limpin' over.

"Have him bunt," he would say. Or, "Does he always run like that?"

An' Cal Rigby would tell him, an' Pippin would nod his head like Cal was dismissed now.

But mostly I noticed his face. He almost never changed expression. The only time I saw it happen was when John Barr hit his third triple, in that second game. I scored ahead of him, an' comin' in it occurred to me to look up at Mr. Pippin.

He winced. His whole face curled up like he was in pain. Just for a half-second, an' then it was gone, an' he looked very serious again, just like The Great White Father.

He knew he couldn't keep John Barr down in the Hole-an'-

Joke League for long. But he still brought him along slower than he needed to. He brought us all up together, me an' John Barr an' Ol' Cal Rigby. He told the flies he didn't want to rush us before we were ready, an' they wrote what a genius he was. But I don't think he ever got over the fact that he didn't find Barr hisself.

We were all glad just to get out of Hell's Gate, though—especially Ol' Cal Rigby. He clung on to John Barr like that boy was a life preserver, all the way up to the big manager's job in New York. Barr was his big find, though Cal was the first to admit he didn't have much to do with it.

"That boy was ready to play in the big leagues the moment he walked into my locker room," he told me once. "But I'll take bein' a genius good as the next man."

A few years back, I drove by Hell's Gate on my way down to Florida. The whole place was gone. The land swallowed up the houses, the ballpark—even the bus terminal. There was just a great big hole in the ground, like it had never existed.

3

*Not Fortune in any sense I had known before, but Fortune as a
trickster, glazing my eyes and soul with the romance of things, so
that I would be blind to the certain sorrows that awaited me.*

—SADAHARU OH

The Phenom at 16

The boy could tell it was spring by the smell of the earth. It was
a wet-clay smell, driven from the woods by the weird spring
breezes, and the water. With the first thaw, countless rivulets
would pour out of the woods and through the backyard. They
would bring the detritus of spring: the black wet dirt, the molded
leaves entombed since the previous autumn, the muddy slivers of
ice formed deep in the woods creeks.

The boy would stand near the end of the yard, back by the
decrepit toolshed, and breathe it in. He thought he could see and
hear every moving thing in the woods: the rustling of the birds in
the rolls of brier; dogs snuffling through the leaves. The woods
were stripped of their underbrush, and everything seemed pre-
ternaturally clear: the dark wet bark of the trees, the little rows of
teeth on each thornbush branch.

His mother thought he had a cold again when he stood there,
sniffing at the air. He had one nearly all winter, staying out for
hours in his thin, worn jacket. She would see him sniffing and
think of the jacket, and start worrying again about how they could
afford anything. She would want to call him in out of the cold, to

some warm snack in front of the open stove and a bath after that to make sure he didn't come down with anything. But she knew it would be likely to cause a bloody scene, full of explosive shouting from her husband about his rights, and his wishes, and why they were never respected. Spring was the worst time for her—when the decay became clearly visible again—and she would withdraw silently to the house.

But the boy didn't mind the weather and he barely noticed the colds. There was a crazy edge to the wind—something blowing that wasn't really cold or warm yet. There was a restlessness in it that made him want to run on into the woods, mindless of the freezing mud and water that would seep up through his shoes—

Instead, he would go up to his room in the skinny wood-frame house, and pull the glove out from underneath his bed. It was where he had carefully placed it after his birthday the previous October. He had rubbed it black with oil, then wrapped it up with the ball wedged into the pocket and strapped tight there with twine and rubber bands. All winter he had wanted to take it out and see how it was coming along, but he had resisted. Sniffing the air now, he knew it was right.

Outside, in the garage by the toolshed, he could hear the clanking as his father worked away at his latest car. He knew he would be called for soon, and he slipped back downstairs and stood by the woods again, in expectant obedience.

"Son, get me that wrench theyah," his father's nasal Yankee voice ordered the boy a few moments later, stern but not unkind, simply expecting his son to attend him as he clubbed the old auto.

The boy looked in, saw his father's head poking out from under the car, and cringed despite himself. His father possessed a naturally foolish face, pinched and vacant-eyed, with a long, sharp nose. No expression really seemed to suit it. Whether angry or laughing, the round pale eyes still blinked dumbly, the thin mouth still dropped slightly open. It was worst when he was concentrating. Then his brow would actually furrow, and his eyes roll upward like runaway windowshades in the cartoons.

Usually when that happened he was thinking about his schemes. The car was one of them. Evan Barr was obsessed with finding "bahgain" cars. He always counted the old junks he brought home as just such bargains because he bought them for only a hundred, two hundred dollars, or less than anyone he knew paid for any car.

That his junk cars were still worth nothing, nothing at all, and were thus no bargain to anyone never occurred to him. That was the way he thought, and he was widely ridiculed for it. He professed that to be fine with him. He despised most of the other men in his small town who congregated at the barbershop. He called it "The Bah-Bah Shop," and cursed them for old women, and his creed ran instinctively against their clichés. He believed, for instance, that he *could* get something for nothing—believed it with the firmness and unyielding passion of a religious faith.

He had thought this out after years of reading stories in *The Reader's Digest* and other magazines featured in the same Bah-Bah Shop. They were stories about "investment millionaires." Or, as he described them to his wife while she sat silent before him, "men without any brains, or any talent, or any gumption more than us that I can see, but with the right money at the right time and the right idea."

Evan Barr had determined to start with a car.

"I know what I'm doin'," he would assure his wife, and himself. "They used to make cahrs better then, you know. So I fix this old one up, it'll run better than anythin' brand new, an' I can sell it for ten times what it cost me."

Which could even have made some little sense, had he known anything at all about fixing cars. Evan Barr consistently overestimated his own skills. He made what living he did posing as the handyman at a local hotel in the summer. There he could barely handle some minor carpentry and plumbing work, and occasionally cajole an electrical circuit into working, at reckless disregard to his own life and those of the guests.

But such triumphs gave him the confidence to spend hours under his derelicts, lavishly covering himself with grease and banging away with his tools. Until finally he would pull himself up with a broad grin, cock his thumb at the boy, and pronounce the car fixed.

In the end they always had to take it to the garage. There it would cost at least twice what he had paid to get the thing running at all, and selling it to anyone was out of the question. The boy's mother would always insist on sitting in the backseat on these occasions, and scrunch down as if trying to hide. The boy would sit up front and listen while some leering man in blackened overalls told his father why he was a fool this time.

"Yah, ya put in a whole new camshaft, but didn't ya see these cylinders was all cracked anyway?" they would say. "Cost ya twice what you could get for her to replace 'em." Or: "Ya replaced the flywheel all right, but ya can't do it with one from that model, ya wrecked every piston in theah. Might as well junk it."

The boy's father would stand outside the car listening to them, his face turning white at first with his usual indignation. Then he would regain his old confidence, nodding his head up and down, acting like it was just what he had expected.

"I would have done it anyway," he always said. "Needed to get some work in on a camshaft. Just wanted to make sure you couldn't do nothin' for those cylinders."

It was always like that, and the boy soon saw through the lies. There was always the excuse of some grand, visionary experiment his father was trying out—as if he were some great inventor of the past, like those the boy read about in school, probing about in the darkness of the car engines for the secret of electricity or sound waves or pasteurized milk.

"I would have done it anyway." That was always his excuse, a vain defense for his small-town neighbors, who counted no fool bigger than the one who tried something and failed—particularly if it cost money. They must have seen through him as easily as his own son did, and the boy knew it, but still Evan Barr clung stubbornly to this fig leaf. Working at home, with only the boy as his witness, he would use it even if he made some obvious mistake. Once, after accidentally piercing a fuel line, he had burst up sputtering from under the car with the same poor excuse on his lips: "I would have done it anyway." He was working toward some greater destiny.

Meanwhile the car would, with luck, run for a few more months before breaking down for good, beyond anyone's capability to revive. No one in the town would have dreamed of buying a car from him anyway, and the needling got so bad that he quit going to the Bah-Bah Shop altogether.

Yet by far the worst car was the monstrous green and brown

station wagon he was working on that spring. It was a behemoth left over from the baby boom, and thus hardly practical either to sell or to use for their family of three. But he had got it fixed up enough to drive, and insisted on driving it—even though neither he nor anyone else could figure out how to fix the small but steady leak in the gas tank.

His strategy was to use it for short trips, calculating beforehand just how long each errand would take, then filling up the wagon with gas from cans he kept stored in the basement. The boy would watch him tear frantically around to the driver's door, the empty can tossed off behind him, the gas already starting to drip from the tank. His sparse hair and the tails of his old corduroy jacket would be flying out behind him, his long, bony limbs splayed out in all directions.

The boy thought the worst thing of all, though, was his father's face. He would be blushed red with the excitement, wide-eyed and giggling as he raced for the front seat. It was obviously the best car he had ever had.

4

Charlie Stanzi, The Little Maniac

I had a fight every day at school. After school, before school. I wouldn't take anything from anybody. Some kid come up to me, I'd pop him before he could even say anything, sometimes. Pow! Just like that, get it over with.

I lost a few, but they finally let me alone. It took a long time, but they got tired. They knew even if I lost I wouldn't make it easy for 'em. I came up like that, the hard way.

The Old Swizzlehead

He was mad the minute he walked out on the field. You could see it in his face, all scrunched up around the mouth, like he ate a grapefruit in one bite. An' this on the first day of spring, with the birds singin' an' the annies gatherin'.

"Oh-oh, here comes trouble," says The Emp'ror, Maximilian Duke. We'd been gettin' our first loosened-up of the year, throwin' the ball around an' talkin' nothin' in a loud voice.

"Tightest anal cavity, manager, first day of spring training on," The Emp'ror whispered to me behind his glove, which is how our team stats man, Dr. Roscoe T. Jones, likes to talk.

Charlie Stanzi always looked like he was walkin' into a wind. He moved bent over, with his hands in his pockets, so he looked shorter. Uniform saggin' off his shoulders like he was wearin' a bag. He was nearly six feet, but the flies all called him a little scrapper. He liked to make hisself *look* small. The fans still liked to talk about the fights he used to get into, an' how one time in the World Series he made a nice catch on a pop fly. When you're a little white guy, you can make a whole career on that.

"He's a tough white scrapper, a real cock-snapper, swings at the ball like he sittin' on the crapper," The Emp'ror sung out just loud enough for me to hear, tryna crack me up.

Charlie Stanzi, The Little Maniac

I had less talent than half the guys who never made it. The Yankees bought my contract, they had those great teams then, an' a great farm system. There were guys who could run faster than me, throw better than I could, hit with more power.

They used to give rookies the whole goddamned treatment in those days, too. We used to take turns throwin' batting practice, an' the vets thought it was funny to stand up there an' throw me screwballs, knuckleballs—any kind of junk stuff, so I couldn't get my eye. First time it was my turn to throw, I chucked three in a row, right at their heads. The coaches finally had to break it up.

DiMaggio was still on the team then, an' I used to be in awe of him. One night he had me up to dinner in his own private hotel room. He ordered up two steaks, but I sat across from him hardly eating a thing, I was so in awe. He tells me, "Kid, you're a Yankee now. You got to behave with some class." I was so ashamed, I didn't say another thing the whole rest of the dinner.

The next day I went into the locker room with a ball and a pen, an' asked DiMaggio to sign it for me. He went to write on the ball, an' the pen squirted ink all over his nice new hundred-dollar suit. They beat the crap out of me then, but I didn't care. He was really gonna sign the ball, too, like he was some kind of goddamned hero and I was a little kid. Who the fuck was he to tell me how to behave?

The Old Swizzlehead

It all started the year before, when we were sittin' around
Ol' Cal Rigby's office after the World Series, drinkin' champagne in secret an' waitin' for The Great White Father to call.
Woodrow Wilson Wannamaker, the great baseball commissioner from Harvard, ruled we shouldn't have champagne in
the clubhouse so's not to make a bad impression on all the
kids watchin' at home.

I don't know how many kids were watchin' at home anymore,
since the commissioner scheduled all the games for prime time,
an' they didn't get over until one in the morning with all the beer
commercials. But it didn't matter to us. We'd won the goddamned World Series before. It woulda been the same to us if
we'd just gone back to the hotel an' rounded up a few annies.

Still, we hadda make it look good for the TV, so ten guys took
shifts whoopin' an' hollerin' an' squirtin' ginger ale at the flies.
The rest of us sat around off camera, in the manager's office in
our underwear, drinkin' the real champagne. 'Cept for John Barr,
of course, who left after the last game like he did every year, without so much as a handshake or a word to anyone.

"Is he gone already?" Ol' Cal asked. "I wanted to say good-
bye."

"He'll be around next spring," I told him. "So will you, now
we won the Series."

"We'll see," he said.

We'd finished second to the Cardinals the year before that, an'
we were second again through August, a steady five games back.
That wasn't what you might call a plane crash, but it was unusual
for us. The twelve years John Barr an' me an' Ol' Cal Rigby been
up, we finished out of the money three times. Dickhead Barry
Busby used to say the old Yankees played like that, but I don't
know about them. I only know in twelve seasons, we took nine
division titles, seven pennants, an' five World Series, an' nobody
wins like that anymore. Even the three times we didn't win anything, we came in second.

It was mostly John Barr's doin', with a few contributions on the side from the game's outstanding lead-off hitter, Rapid Ricky Falls. I led the league in runs scored eight times an' stolen bases six times, but even that was helped by havin' John Barr behind me. He was the force in the lineup, what made everything else work.

I don't just mean the statistical stuff. Everybody knows about that: the ten batting titles he won, the three triple crowns, all the gold gloves. John Barr'd already been Most Valuable Player seven times in those twelve years, an' he'd a' won more if any of the writers had *liked* him. He deserved it. Every year he was in the league, he was the best ballplayer there was.

The key to John Barr, though, was the sheer fear factor. A player that great, he becomes even greater because they know what he is. The other team's pitchers, they get just that little bit more nervous, worryin' about John Barr comin' up. They get so intent on keepin' the bases cleared for him that they're more likely to walk a batter, or hang a curveball. When he's on first, the second baseman an' the shortstop get that little bit more nervous about him stealin' second all of a sudden, or just barrelin' down on them if there's a ground ball. Even the other team's hitters throw themselves off tryin' not to hit the ball to right field, since they know how much ground Barr could cover in the field.

A player like John Barr, the other team's constantly aware of him. It's like he's always up at the plate, because even when he isn't, they're thinkin' of him. I suppose there have been some teams in history bad enough to have lost with him anyway. Baseball's not like other sports, you can get eight guys out there bad enough to lose with Jesus Christ Hisself—and make Christ look bad enough so the sportswriters start wondering what's wrong with Him.

We were a good team in those years, even without Barr. I got to admit it, we were built along the lines Ellsworth Pippin always liked: power hitting, a good glove at nearly every position, and a lot of strikeout pitchers. That's the classic combination, it's hard to go wrong when you got those three things, an' we had a little speed, a few high-average hitters, an' a lot of attitude thrown in as well. The other teams used to hate us for that. We'd come into some big game down the stretch where we thought we could intimidate them off the field, we wouldn't hesitate to do it. We would pull out all the stops: lots of high fives after every run, pointin' at guys when they struck out, throwin' at people's heads. If a fight broke out, then we would really get a chance to beat up on them. If it didn't, we knew we had 'em.

Barr never fought much, 'cept for one memorable occasion down in the minor leagues. Usually he would just kinda walk over to one side, lean against the tarpaulin or the stands, an' watch everybody else throw themselves in a big pile. He would sit there with his arms folded, his glove still on his hand if he was in the field, an' wait for it to be over. The game was his thing, that was all he was interested in, an' when the fight was over he would go back to playing like nothin' had happened.

Those big games down the stretch were always his finest. A couple years we got out of the gate good an' never looked back. But you can't sustain that, it takes too much energy. Most years we'd just keep pace, hang in there while we got over the usual slumps an' injuries, an' found our groove. Whoever was leading the division would have us just over their shoulder. They'd be lookin' back the whole season to see us there, never more than three, four games back, just hangin' in there. Then we'd get into a streak, and the next thing they'd know, we'd be blowin' into town for some big series in September. It used to terrify teams to play us then. They'd pretend it didn't, but we knew better. We could see it in their faces. We were a veteran team, an' we'd come in expecting to win.

We'd expect it too because of John Barr. Nobody did better in the money games. If there was any possible way to win a ballgame down the stretch, John Barr would do it. He always played hard, but in the last month of the season it was like he reached a whole new level. He hit the big home run enough times—gigantic ones, 'taters that reached the upper deck, or broke scoreboards. But just as likely, he was quiet an' deadly. He'd drive in the go-ahead run with a single, break up a double play with a hard slide, or throw out a runner trying to stretch his hit.

If we could get close by the last two weeks, we all felt we would win. But The Great White Father didn't trust us anymore—not after we had crapped out an' finished second the year before. He saw we was gettin' a little old, an' he wanted to make sure nobody blamed him for the demise of the dynasty, as Dickhead Barry put

it. He put out the word through Busby an' his other friends in
the press that if we didn't win the division at least, Cal was gone.

He had Cal all set up, but we surprised him. We pulled out the
division on the last weekend of the season, then we swept the
Giants in the league playoffs, an' the Tigers in the Series. The TV
announcers started sayin' Ol' Cal was a genius again, an' they put
the camera eye on him whenever he limped out to home plate
or the pitcher's mound.

Pippin still didn't call to renew his contract, even after we were
up three games to none in the Series. Even after everything Cal
had won for him over the years, The Great White Father still
wouldn't give him more than one year at a time, and then only
after the last game of the season.

It didn't seem to bother Cal none. He kept packin' his stuff
after we won the last game, like he did every year. He folded all
his clothes away, then reached up top his locker to pull down a
big box that rolled an' clicked like it was full of marbles.

"What the hell is that?" some rook asked.

"My eyes."

Cal had one of every different color, just to impress the annies.
He'd have blue eyes he'd wear for nights out, green eyes he'd
wear for road trips. He'd stick with one particular color for a few
days if we got hot, bein' superstitious like everybody else in baseball. An' he wore a patch over it for big games.

The whole Series, he'd been jawin' with the umpires, an' particularly Ronnie Beluga. Ronnie was the biggest and the best umpire in the game, but Cal was tense that last Series, an' he didn't
like anything Ronnie was callin', even when we were winnin'.

The last game, Ronnie was behind home plate. Ol' Cal come
out to give him the lineup with his patch over his good eye, and
Ronnie didn't notice. When Ol' Cal got up to home plate, he
started rubbin' the glass eye real hard.

"Damn, this one's shot, too," he said, an' popped it right out
an' handed it over to the ump.

"Here, you take it," he said. "It's still gotta be better than the
two goddamned ones you have."

The ump was so shook he forgot to throw Cal out. He had no
idea what it was he was callin', whole rest of the game.

"First goddamned fun I had this season," Cal said when he got back in the dugout, and we all tried hard not to look at the smooth, dug-out place where his old eye had been.

We scored seven runs in the first inning, an' won the last game goin' away. But the phone still didn't ring until nearly an hour after the game was over, an' Cal limped over quick to pick it up, with a little smile twitchin' up around the ends of his face.

"Uh-huh, sure. Right away," he said, an' hung up.

"That him, skip?" I asked. Ballplayers call a manager "skip" when they like him. Makes him feel like Casey Stengel.

"Yep. Wants me to come up an' see him."

"Shit, let him come down here," Jack No-Hit Hitt said.

"No," Ol' Cal said. "It's his ball club. He's got a right."

Ol' Cal went up to see The Great White Father an' come on back down about ten minutes later. He didn't look at any of us, just kept chewin' his tobaccy chaw an' puttin' body parts into his suitcase.

"What happened, skip? What'd you get? One year again?"

Ol' Cal grinned an' spat a flow of that chaw juice between his gold teeth, all the way across the room.

"He did all right. One year, for a even mill."

"Jesus, he gave you that?"

"I told him I wanted two mill. I told the son of a bitch I won seven pennants an' five World Series the last ten years, an' I wanted two goddamned million, same as the last can't-miss busher he brought up from Double-A to hit .250."

"No shit!"

"I told him I wanted two million dollars. An' three years."

"You told him *that*?!"

"What he say?"

"He said okay. He didn't like it, but goddammit he said okay."

"Three years, goddamn!"

"An' then I said," he continued, grinnin' through the brown tobaccy pieces on his gold teeth, "that he could shove it up his ass. Best moment I ever had in this game."

No one said a thing for a long while, until Skeeter Mesquite recovered enough to ask about one relevant topic.

"What about the money, skip?"

"You get to be my age, it feels good to turn down that kinda money," Ol' Cal said. "I'll never spend what I got already. Think about it. When else in your whole life do you ever get to turn down money like that? I spent my time in this game crawlin' after a buck, takin' all their dust. I might as well leave it on my two hind legs.''

Which was all right for Cal, he retired to his houseboat in the Florida Keys, an' went fishin' an' got drunk every day. Two months later, Pippin went out an' hired Charlie Stanzi. That was when the madness began, as they like to say on the Saturday-morning wrestling shows.

We knew he won a lot of games over in the American League, for what that's worth. He'd take some young team an' convince 'em they could win before they were old enough to know any better. The fans always loved it.

But he wrecked teams. He'd destroy the pitchers' arms, ruin the hitters' confidence, just tryna win one more game. He'd get in another bar fight. He'd fight with the players, fight with the owners, fight with the umpires. He'd leave the team all worn out, not knowin' what happened to them. Baseball is a game you gotta play by the year, or even longer. They said Stanzi always wanted to win *now*, that day, an' it was so. He came out now on the first day an' walked to the pitcher's mound. He put on his shades, crossed his arms over his chest, an' stood there just lookin' for someone to do something. That's when I knew there was gonna be trouble. An' that was just the moment John Barr picked to make his first appearance of the spring.

The Color Commentary

He would work methodically around his property all winter, gloveless and bareheaded, with an axe in his hand to trim back the waste. Replacing the rocks that had fallen from the balanced stone walls. Clearing away the dead brush for his fire. Breaking the ice in the well and drawing up the water every morning.

Somehow it came to him in those daily labors, like some inner clock. He would lock up the house, throw a few clothes in a bag, and get into his jeep and drive. He would go for two days and nights straight, without sleeping or talking to anyone other than to order food and gas. He would drive straight down to the Mets' spring training complex, right past the little company town of Fort Pippin. He wouldn't even stop at the team hotel.

He would simply take his bag and go directly from the jeep to the locker room, and come running out of the dugout ten minutes later, in full uniform and with a bat in his hands, ready to hit.

The Old Swizzlehead

You never knew with him. Some years he wouldn't come down until we were already playin' exhibition games. Other seasons he'd be waitin' for us, hitting all day from the pitching machine.

The Great White Father never got used to it. He tried puttin' fines on him at first. He came up with big-money bites: thousand, two thousand dollars a day, every day Barr was late to camp. He did that the first year, an' Barr paid up without sayin' a word. The next year he was down there two days ahead of everybody else.

Pippin thought he taught the boy a thing. Then the next year was one of John Barr's late years, an' he come down when he was good an' ready, same as always. Pippin put the fines up to ten thousand a day. Barr paid again, an' still never complained.

But it wasn't enough for Pippin. Even he knew enough about money to know it has no purpose if it can't get people to do what you want. He tried sendin' telegrams up to Barr at that place he had up in Prides Crossing. He even sent up assistant general managers—just tryna find out *why*. Barr never told 'em a thing.

"I'll be down when I'm ready," was all he would say.

Pippin gave up on the fines. He gave up on tryin' to get Barr to do most anything he didn't want to do. Barr traveled by himself on the road, an' he didn't have a roommate. The team rules didn't apply to him, an' that was all right with the rest of us. We couldn't dispute that he was the best, an' he deserved it.

But it wasn't all right with The Great White Father. Every year, one way or another, he tried gettin' Barr to come around. He'd even offer him *more* money incentives to come down early, travel with the team, behave just like a normal human bein', etc.

None of it worked. Barr just did what he pleased. I remember one time Pippin wanted to put in a artificial field, cause he thought it would look nicer. Barr didn't even bother to talk to The Great White Father. He just told Ol' Cal Rigby that if he didn't have a natural turf field, he would go somewhere else the next year. Pippin came down to the field hisself to talk to the man while he was takin' batting practice.

"But think of how it would help you," he pointed out.

"It's bad on the knees," Barr told him, hitting one frozen rope after another past second base.

"Artificial turf could add twenty points a year to your average. You could hit .400 with it."

That was the only time Barr even looked back at him.

"It ain't the field," was all he said, and then he whacked the next pitch into the leftfield corner.

The old turf stayed. Pippin was out for him after that. But he couldn't even find anything to really complain about. Barr would show up every spring ready to play. Some of the Stiff Legs, the serious guys on the team, they would spend the whole off-season pumpin' weights, runnin', doin' special exercise programs. They would still come to spring training an' need a good month, maybe part of the season, before they got into a groove.

But not John Barr. He come out there with the bat in his hand, an' he was ready to hit right away. An' this last year was one of his earlier ones. He was only two hours late for the regulars. But it was exactly what Charlie Stanzi was lookin' for. His eyes lit up when he saw John Barr come out on that field late, an' right away he called everybody over.

"Okay, men, listen up," he says like he's talkin' to a high school football team. "The first thing I want you people to know is that I got one rule, and one rule only on this team. It's my way or the highway."

We all snickered a little over that one, an' that was when he decided to make an example.

"You," Stanzi said, pointin' his finger at John Barr, who was squattin' down in front, his face blank as always.

"You're late. You know that?"

Which was what the highway cops like to call a rhetorical question. He wasn't expectin' any kind of answer. And especially not what he got, which was John Barr raisin' hisself slowly up an' turnin' those drowned man's eyes full force on Charlie Stanzi.

At first The Little Maniac wanted to call the whole thing off. You could tell. You could see it in his face. I know he had never seen those eyes of John Barr's up close before, an' he took a step backward, an' even raised his arms a little.

He had to know that if Barr wanted to whip him he could, an' if he wanted to walk right off that field an' ignore him he could do that too. But Stanzi had a fool's reputation to protect. He made hisself stand there an' look right back at Barr.

"Ten laps," he said. "Foul pole to foul pole. Right here, right now."

Barr just stood there. The rest of us almost laughed out loud. We were all waitin' for Barr to do somethin'—to punch out The Little Maniac, or walk off the field, or just laugh an' go get into the battin' cage. But Barr didn't walk off, an' he didn't punch anybody. Instead he gave a shrug, an' turned an' started running out to the rightfield foul pole.

He ran big an' easy, like he always did, faster an' faster with each lap. He didn't take the poles straight, but ran the whole curve of the outfield in those long strides of his. It started to rain; one of those fine, warm Florida rains. But John Barr kept on running.

I don't think even The Little Maniac hisself could believe it. He kept this tight little grimace on his face, but in his eyes there was relief. Barr kept goin' till he done all ten laps, and then he come runnin' back into the dugout, not even breathin' hard. The moment he came in, we all got busy like we was doin' somethin', the way we'd act if somebody just popped up with the bases loaded. But he didn't seem to care. He walked right on past us into the locker room with his head up, an' his face blank as ever.

Charlie Stanzi had stood hisself right by the clubhouse entrance, so's Barr would have to walk by him. He didn't say anything to him, but there was a little smile on his lips an' it got bigger an' bigger as Barr walked by. Barr didn't even look at Stanzi. He walked right on down to the clubhouse like he was through with his regular workout, same as any other day.

"It's gonna be a long year," I told The Emp'ror that night, back at the hotel. "He gets Barr to go like that when he says the word, it ain't gonna be good for any of us," I told him.

"Barr doesn't want to start anything yet," Duke said. "You

know how Dickhead Barry and the rest of them would come down on him. 'Fiery little manager beaten up by overpaid ballplayer who can't carry Joe DiMaggio's shoes. Working public incensed.'"

We had somethin' on that night, first action of the new season. It was supposed to be somethin' Terry White, our rook third baseman, had set up for us. He said they were in town with the Gorgeous Ladies of Wrestling, an' we weren't too sure about the whole thing. We were expectin' maybe a couple girls built like a 'frigerator with a head, like the song goes. But in comes these two Japanese girls wearin' black body leotards an' leather jackets with the words FLYING KAMIKAZE ANGELS on the back. They were identical twins, with faces like two little hearts, an' they couldn'ta been five-three. They looked kinda shy, an' stood against the wall.

"Well, hello, ladies," I said, but they just giggled. "Can we take your coats? Get you somethin' to drink?"

They just giggled some more. Just then Maximilian Duke comes out of the bathroom, tuckin' in his shirt.

"Who's my date?" he says with a big grin.

One of the Flying Kamikaze Angels yells somethin' that sounds like "*Huh-Wah!*" She goes ten feet through the air an' hits him feet-first in the chest. The Emp'ror hits the floor with a *oomph* sound, an' she jumps on his chest an' pulls herself up to his face. I look over at her sister, an' see she's grinnin' at me.

"Oh, my," I said, but my throat was too dry to get anything else out.

Later that night I was lyin' in my bed, wonderin' if I had broken my back, when I got thinkin' about somethin' I noticed when John Barr was runnin' those laps, foul pole to foul pole.

Right before it started to rain, I looked up into the grandstand. Ellsworth Pippin, The Great White Father hisself, was standin' way up where the old folks like to go to sun themselves durin' exhibition games. Up there so far you could barely see him. But I saw. I saw him watchin' John Barr the whole time, watchin' that boy run.

5

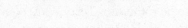

I wouldn't throw ice cubes for that kind of money.

—SATCHEL PAIGE

The Old Swizzlehead

Ellsworth Pippin never cared much for my face after The Great Stirrup Controversy, the first year I come up to the majors—

Ellsworth Pippin, The Great White Father

I never felt an obligation to indulge stupid people. I realized sixty years ago that I was smarter than the men who play this game. It happened when I was eight years old and I saw a player on the St. Louis Browns throw up in left field.

The Browns were owned at the time by Augustus LaForge, who was a friend and business associate of my father's. Mr. LaForge was a gentleman of the old school. He wore a pince-nez and carried a walking stick in one hand and a pair of white kid gloves in the other. My father had taken me along with him on a business trip to St. Louis, and Mr. LaForge invited us to sit in his box. He had the game rescheduled to the morning, and closed the park to the general public. Only my father and I, the sportswriters, the ushers, and Mr. LaForge himself were allowed in.

No more than a few hundred fans would have attended; the

Browns were only playing the Washington Senators. But on that morning it was just us—waited on by every usher and vendor in the park. Anything I wanted—hot dogs, peanuts, soda pop—was brought to me immediately. What I remember most of all, however, was the muffled sound of Mr. LaForge applauding with those little white gloves whenever the Browns did something good.

This was not a frequent occurrence. By the time we arrived, most of the players were already out on the field, running sprints to work off their hangovers. I was so surprised to see that they didn't look much like athletes. They were large, flabby men, most of them, wearing old grey sweatshirts and sweatpants. I remember thinking they looked no different from the men who loaded my father's trucks.

They changed before the game began, of course, and looked more like the real item. But then a particularly obese player called Fuzzy Mitchell chased a ball into the leftfield corner, halted abruptly, and vomited on the outfield grass.

"It is more his diet than the drink," Mr. LaForge told us rather apologetically. "He eats everything—candy, cakes, ice cream. He's like a child."

I will always remember watching that man kneeling over on the grass, vomiting repeatedly. I realized then what ballplayers are.

The Old Swizzlehead

When I first come up, Pippin made out like he was my friend. Unlike John Barr, I was the one he *did* discover an' sign, and he played me up to the flies as proof of his own genius. He even had me up to his big mahogany office at the top of Shea Stadium, to talk about how to invest my money wisely an' stay away from "bad actors," as he liked to call 'em. He used to tell me to come up an' see him personal if I ever needed anything.

That was when I started callin' him The Great White Father, an' the name stuck. I didn't take too sincerely his paternal affection for my black ass, but I thought at least he might be good for a touch from time to time. My first year up, I was livin' too large an' got behind with the bookies on my horseflesh debts. So I decided to take him up on his word. When I told him what I needed, he just stared at me for a few minutes, like I'd said somethin' about his mother.

"You know, I could turn this all over to the league office," he told me.

"That mean you won't give me the advance?"

He threw me out of his office for legal reasons, an' had a detective follow me the rest of the season. He never wanted much to do with me after that, an' he stopped toutin' me to the flies. But that was all nothin' compared to The Great Stirrup Controversy.

It started when some guys, mostly brothers, pulled their stirrups up high. I never knew why they needed the stirrups in the first place. You already got a pair of socks on. Why do you need another pair, with the team colors and the heel and the toe cut off, to go around the first pair?

But if you're gonna wear 'em, they look best pulled up. That's just fashion sense. Not everybody wore 'em that way. John Barr, of course, used to wear his stirrups low an' his pants folded down over the top. He thought it made it harder for the ump to tell where the bottom of the strike zone was, an' gave him another one of those little advantages he was always lookin' for. It was the same way he had his shirts made too big, to make the strike zone look smaller up top.

The rest of us put more of a emphasis on lookin' like a human being out there. But Pippin started gettin' suspicious when he saw us wearin' the high stirrups. He didn't know exactly why, but he knew it bothered him. He got the other club owners to pass a league rule that forbid any player to wear his stirrups more'n three inches high. The league office even sent a memo around to every clubhouse, sayin' you was supposed to measure 'em before you went out on the field.

Everybody ignored it—the players, the managers, even the umpires. When The Great White Father saw nobody was payin' attention to it, he started tellin' the flies it was a black thing. That set it off.

The next Sunday there was a big "What's the Buzz?" column by Dickhead Barry Busby, makin' out that we were runnin' some kind of Black Power protest. It was all over the sports radio stations. You couldn't turn on your radio anymore without hearin' some swizzlehead from Queens callin' in to say he was furious that they didn't make the goddamned overpaid players obey the rules and wear their socks low.

After that, it *was* a race thing. You wore 'em high if you were black or you wanted to show solidarity. Then brothers would get into arguments with umps who they thought were callin' 'em out on strikes just because their stirrups was high. Guys on the same team wouldn't talk to each other anymore, on account of how high their socks were.

Finally The Great White Father announced he was gonna fine anybody wearin' a high stirrup one hundred dollars a day. I went back out there the next game with my stirrups up, an' sure enough, that payday my check was a hundred dollars short.

"That's my money he's messin' with," I told the Emp'ror.

"What's it worth? What're you going to do, take him to court over it?"

"You'll see," I told him.

That day we were playin' San Diego, and the first player up for the Padres hits a single that bounces right in front of me in center field. By the time I could stroll over an' pick it, the batter was standin' on third base. The next guy hit a routine fly that I kinda waved at, an' then there was a hit off the wall that managed to roll all the way back to second base before I could get to it.

By the time we got back to the dugout, there was a messenger there from Pippin with an envelope. Inside was one crisp hundred-dollar bill. And it was the last thing we ever heard about our goddamned socks.

The Color Commentary

The two men sat drinking in the fuchsia dining room above the Florida field. They sat straddle-legged around their chairs, allowing for the girth of their old-men's middles. One of them had an old manual typewriter on the table in front of him, with a string of yellowed clippings taped along the top and a wilted piece of paper rolled into the carriage. The liquid in their glasses was the same color as the amber evening light flowing over them; they both blinked absently into the sunset, trying to remember.

"The best part was that long center field. That's what made the Polo Grounds."

"Oh, yes. It must've been over five hundred feet out there. Shaped like a horseshoe."

"The clubhouses were out there, way at the end of the center field."

"Yes, oh, yes. A whole row of windows, way out there. With a staircase running down each side, so you could see the teams come out and walk all the way across that field. Like they were matadors, walking out there."

"And that big clock, over everything out there—"

"Mays was all the way back to the wall when he made that catch in '54—"

"With his back to the plate!"

They were an incongruous pair, one in a quietly lush business suit, white hair gleaming with oil. The other, in front of the typewriter, a little seedy, wearing a bright orange jacket and turquoise tie, his high, frizzy shock of hair poking up in all directions. They both stopped abruptly, though, when they saw the woman in the elegant red dress moving across the room toward them.

"Goddammit, here she comes," Dickhead Barry Busby said, his voice thick with bitterness. Ellsworth Pippin gestured helplessly.

"What the hell makes a woman want to be a sportswriter anyway?"

Ellie Jay was tall and handsome, with sharp Semitic features and thick dark hair that was pierced by a few strands of white. She moved with an athletic grace that even the high dress could not hide. It was a stunning dress, bright red and etched with black oriental patterns, running from her neck to her knees and boldly traced over her figure.

She usually dressed exotically, to rub it in. The few other women who appeared in the press box looked carefully sedate, in imitation business suits with grey skirts and matching jackets, or in asexual pants suits. She tended instead to bright designer dresses, miniskirts, high black heels, and dark stockings. Anything to throw it in their faces that she was a woman, doing their job.

"Hey, guys, how's it hanging?" she greeted them, and could barely fight back a smile at the looks on their faces. Dickhead Barry Busby tried to ignore her, and primly hunted down and pecked a few sentences into the typewriter:

" . . . Informed sources say Maury Proust's constant complaining disrupting Montreal club. . . . Insiders with club say Proust can't fit in with rest of clubhouse, moans constantly about suspect headaches that keep him out of lineup half the time. . . ."

"How's the slander game going, Barry?"

"You mean, what's it like being a real reporter instead of the Dragon Lady?"

"Oh, yeah. I can see you're hard at work right now." She seated herself insolently in a free chair, and signaled for a waiter.

"Is there some reason why you are here?" Ellsworth Pippin asked, exasperated. She ignored him, ordered a double scotch, and stretched out in her chair, hands behind her head.

"Just wanted to find out what's going on with your new manager and John Barr," she said, accepting her scotch with thanks, and downing it in one long gulp. She could tell without looking what their expressions would be now.

"Nothing," said Pippin, a little smugly. "Nothing but a manager enforcing discipline on his team."

"Oh, hell," she said, waving in another scotch. "You gentlemen care to join me?"

Goaded, they hastily downed the rest of their drinks and ordered up. This one Ellie Jay sipped smoothly, running it up and down her tongue as she perused Ellsworth Pippin.

"How come anybody has to discipline John Barr?" she asked him.

"He arrived late for the beginning of spring training," Pippin asserted sternly.

"He's been arriving late for the past thirteen years. Or sometimes early."

"Maybe it's about time he got in step with the rest of the team."

"That's horseshit," she said, enjoying the effect her vulgarity had on them. Still after all these years, she thought. It's like Pavlov's goddamned dogs—

"Excuse me—"

"You know that's horseshit, Ellsworth. Barr doesn't drink, doesn't take drugs, doesn't get into barroom fights, and doesn't knock up teenage girls. He doesn't even smoke, for God's sake. And you're gonna tell me he's gotta be disciplined for showing up ten minutes late to practice? Gimme a break."

"No player is above the rules."

"Sure they are," she snorted, looking him in the eye. "The best players always are. You know that as well as I do. And John Barr is the best there ever was."

"That's not true!" Busby interrupted agitatedly. "DiMaggio was a better player! Willie Mays. Ted Williams. I've seen a dozen better players!"

"No, you haven't," Ellie Jay said, smiling blandly back at him.

"For my money, Lou Gehrig was the greatest ballplayer I ever saw," Pippin chimed in stuffily. "He was a fine athlete, and a fine citizen. He did whatever he was asked, and never let the team down."

"You're wrong, and you know it," she told them. "You both know there's never been another player like Barr. Maybe he's not a team player. Maybe he shows up late for spring training every now and then. But he's the best."

"The hell you say!" Busby sputtered. "No ballplayer today could *possibly* be the best. They don't have the desire."

"They don't have the discipline—"

"They don't know what it was *like*," Busby tried to articulate. "The—the—the old baggy wool uniforms! All those great old ballparks! The style, the *class*—"

"It's all gone to hell," Pippin burst out. "The game's gone to hell. We lost control of it."

" 'S the union," Dickhead Barry Busby slurred confidently. "The goddamned players' union."

"And the Supreme Court!" Pippin was barely able to contain himself. "Don't forget their role in it!"

"But," Ellie Jay added ruthlessly, "Barr is still the best. You just don't want to admit it because you didn't find him."

"How *could* I find him? He didn't play anywhere for two years before he showed up in West Virginia—"

"Arrogant son of a bitch. Where the hell *did* he come from?" Busby wondered.

"It doesn't matter if he came out of a hole in the ground," she told them. "You've never seen a ballplayer who can hit or play the field like that. And game after game, year after year."

"That's the trouble. He thinks he's the game."

"He thinks he's *better* than the game."

"Why don't you just admit that things change?" she sighed, and shook her head. "And sometimes they maybe even get better. He's the best, and you've got him right here, and you don't see it."

"Nothing's better than it was. Nothing!"

Ellie Jay finished her scotch with another quick swallow and rose steadily to her feet. Busby thought despite himself that she still looked damned good despite her years in the game. There were the white hairs, a few scotch lines in her neck and face, but she was still young, vibrant. What the hell was she doing in the press box? he thought with a shudder.

"Gentlemen, I'd love to stay and talk about the good old days forever, but I have a column to write," she said.

"Yeah, it's tough having to work for a living," sneered Dickhead Barry Busby. He tapped out, ". . . Cincinnati sources say Al Dreyfuss reason for that club's drug woes. . . . Course, but way things are these days, drug abuse practically ticket to Cooperstown. . . ."

"Everything I said is off the record, of course," Pippin added quickly. "Except that I stand by my manager. One hundred percent."

"Ellsworth," she said disgustedly, "what makes you think you said anything else worth putting *on* the record?"

She strode off, waving one hand behind her at them. They both watched her go despite themselves.

"Goddammit, it's no place for a woman."

"Everything's changed, they got ahold of everything and wrecked it. At least I can still hire my own damned manager."

That said, they had wound down again and were quiet for a moment. Then Busby brightened.

"Do you remember that Abe Stark sign at the bottom of right field in Ebbets Field?"

6

Skills can be taught. Talent can't.

—AL LaMacchia

The Phenom as a Young Boy

He knew something was wrong from the start. Sitting on the floor in a room full of angular grey and white forms, something moved too fast. Something fell—an object, or a body. There might have been a cry, or some other harsh noise.

He could never be sure. A few years, still only five or six, he realized that it had become a memory of a memory. That sudden, violent motion was like a grainy black-and-white photograph with suggestive but undecipherable shadows.

It didn't much matter. Even as a young boy, he thought he understood what he had witnessed. He saw the same motion again one afternoon, sitting at the kitchen table munching contentedly on a cookie his mother had given him. She was talking casually on the telephone, preparing their lunch with her free hand. Then his father strode into the room and asked in a loud and peremptory voice, "Who is that?"

Misreading his tone, she waved him off impatiently, trying to hear. The boy knew it was a mistake; he could see the whole thing unfolding, but could only brace himself in his chair. His father walked over, shoved her forcefully out of the way, and jammed down the hook. He then made as if to tear the whole phone from the wall, though it didn't seem to the boy that he could get a good grip on it. His mother, speechless at first with surprise and still holding the receiver, came back at him.

"What do you think—" she started indignantly. Before she could say another word, one hand flew off the phone, backhanding her in the face.

It was not a very hard slap—not hard enough, anyway, to shove her away again or snap her head back. It was more the insult of it, he knew, that caused her to burst instantly into tears. She dropped the receiver and put up her hands to her face. But his father still stood there between her and the phone, as if she owed him an explanation.

"Who was that? Huh? Who was that on the phone, callin' you in the middle of the afternoon?"

She shook her head, sobbing fully now, unable to get any more words out.

"Slut!" he said, his face red with rage. "Bitch!"

He stood there for a moment while she cried, looking away from him. Some of the tension seemed to slip from his body then, and he slid down into a seat across from the boy, looking surprisingly normal. The angry red color was already drained from his pale, slack face, and he smiled affectionately at his son.

"Hey there," he said warmly. "How yah doin' today?"

All the boy could do was answer "Fine," and sit there, still eating, ashamed of himself. For he knew who it was his mother had been talking to. He was already an observant child, and he knew from her casual, easy tone that it was one of her few friends, a woman they often saw in the supermarket.

He still didn't dare to say anything. Across the table, his father was slurping loudly from the bowl of soup his mother had laid out for him, and beginning to hum one of the tunes that he liked to half-sing, half-whistle and purr around the house. The boy recognized it from the broken snatches of words his father put to it: "She's my curly-headed baby / Likes to sit on Daddy's knee. . . ." He loved to hum this bit of a song when he was feeling plainly amorous toward his wife. He would mumble it while grinning sloppily, and wave her over to him, pointing to his own knee. He would sing it before he went up behind her in the kitchen while she was doing the dishes, to give her a tight hug.

The violence was always like that, the boy had noticed. It was almost never directed at him, just his mother. It came and went suddenly—often bracketed by his father's lush admirations.

"Your mother's a helluva woman, did you know that?" was one of the first things the boy could remember him saying. Another time, sitting in the grass, he remembered them both looking at her, far across the lawn, hanging up the wash in a white dress. "There's no woman like her," his father said.

He acted as if he could not contain this passion. One day, when she had taken the boy to Boston on an errand, they had stepped off the return train and been offered a ride home by a passing neighbor. He had not noticed Evan Barr, waiting a few feet away in his car. His mother had hastily shaken her head no, as if in warning, but it was too late.

The neighbor had scarcely turned away before Barr, stepping quickly and quietly from the car, was upon him. He drove his fist up hard into the man's stomach, and the man went down, then bounced up again like a spinning top, sidling quickly away from Evan, his mouth open in astonishment.

More ugly, guttural words had followed, but the boy had been fascinated. He had never seen violence like that between two adult men, outside of a television screen. It hadn't quite seemed real, even while it was happening. His parents' fights back home were nearly as abrupt and shocking. His father would start quietly, then escalate suddenly to uninhibited fits of anger.

"I'm tired of you going around behind my back!" he would yell in a voice that was almost a scream. "You don't think I know what's goin' on?"

She never fought back against these accusations, just wept or exclaimed, as if thereby to expose how ludicrous his claims were. But they fought about almost everything else, as well—about cutting the grass or doing the dishes, spending less time in the bathroom or more time with the boy himself (not that *he* wanted it). She would fight back then, particularly when they argued over money, asking him again and again when he was going to get another job, or when his cars were finally going to pay off, even after he became visibly angry.

"Goddamn you, goddamn you," she would pant, nearly out of breath in her fury. "Goddamn you to hell, you useless man."

Dinner was always the worst time. Carried away by their arguments, either one might get up from the table and pace around the room. They were liable to seize upon anything in their path; he had watched his father throw at his mother a pan of soup, a coffee cup, and at one Christmas dinner an entire turkey. He had seen her throw wine in his face, slide a plate of spaghetti into his lap, and strike him over the head with a wooden spoon so hard that it broke in half—unaccountably sending both of them into gales of laughter.

The boy didn't understand their hilarity, just as he didn't understand their rages, but he always saw them coming. He was a constant witness to their crossed purposes. He could always tell what each one would say that was over the line—could even discern, after a while, what each one *wanted* to hear instead.

That was the worst part for the boy. His parents seemed to possess an uncanny ability for setting each other off, but he believed that if he could just inject the right word, even change the *tone* of the thing said, then he could put everything right. It seemed to him that it was all a big mistake, that he had the power to set their marriage right by just opening his mouth.

Yet he never could do it. Somehow, when the time came, he could never actually say the right thing. It was the way he felt watching other kids make errors in their daily schoolyard pickup games. He could see the whole thing slowly unfolding before him, but there was nothing he could do about it.

He was too insignificant in the face of his parents' anger, especially his father's. Once he had actually gone to his mother, sobbing after a bad fight, and had tried to tell her: "Mom, maybe if you had told him—" But she had only waved him off, without a word, as if he didn't know what he was talking about.

Outside the house, everywhere he went, he tried to anticipate. He tried to be ready for anything and everything that could go wrong. In school, he was constantly alert to the teacher's demeanor, her tone of voice, even when he didn't understand what she was saying. When she was called out of the room, he did not join the other kids in yelling anything, as loud as they could; he knew that the teacher could hear them down the hall, would return and be angry.

His caution would have made him unpopular if it had not been for his skill at games. Already, before he was halfway through grade school, it was clear how much better he was than the other boys. He was tall and developed for his age, could run faster and react more quickly than the others. But part of this skill, too, was mental—it was conscious anticipation. He was as quietly alert on the ballfield or the basketball court as he was at the dinner table, seeing everything before him, his natural empathy tipping him off to the moves of the other players before they made them.

Naturally, they respected his talent—the way he could hit a baseball all the way to the schoolhouse steps, how he could make any ball seem to explode out of his hand. He was immediately the best at any game he tried: baseball, football, basketball, hockey, tag. He was chosen first by the schoolyard captains and deferred to once the game had started. When he came up, the other side's outfielders would automatically turn and run far back, to the very edge of the field they played on.

Despite the near worship of the other boys, though, he had no close friends among them. Once the games were over, he could not invite them back to the dilapidated little house he lived in near the woods. He knew how ashamed his mother was of the place, was afraid of the sudden scenes that might occur; his father was not a man to restrain himself.

He in turn received no invitations from the other children. There had been other incidents in public like the one with the man at the train station—sudden flashes of anger, fists jutting out, his father's slack fool's mouth suddenly twisted up tightly, teeth clamped together. His father might realize how this seemed afterward, when he was almost instantly calmer again, but he would excuse his own behavior with his usual rationale:

"I would have done it anyway," he would tell his wife. "That son of a bitch had it comin'."

Yet like everything else he did, the boy knew his display provoked not so much fear as derision. The reason he was not welcome at the other boys' homes was that their mothers thought Evan Barr was addled.

The boy had been forced to conclude that his mother was not considered very attractive. She was certainly not flirtatious. When most other people—male or female—greeted her on the streets of their small town, she barely acknowledged them. After Evan

Barr's jealous rages became well known around town, the men from the bah-bah shop would play a little game when he wasn't around, stopping to greet her effusively, removing their hats and half-bowing. That was the only attention she really received out in public.

Nobody looked at her longingly or desirously. Not even the men at the toolworks in Granitetown, who liked to sit in front of their factory during the lunch hour and make lascivious comments half drowned out by the crashing and pounding of the great iron hammer behind them. Every woman who passed by drew some remark—except his mother. She was simply too severe. Except to her son she was a cold person, wrapped up in her long coat and long skirts, her tightly braided hair pinned up hard against her head.

The boy could see that even at his age, and even if his father could not. It made the fights, the jealous rages, all the more incomprehensible. Watching them build to a fight, he felt the same frustrated helplessness—but became gradually aware of a vast anger within himself. Always alert and anticipating, it made him afraid that he could be like that, too. Sometimes when he watched them start their fights, he only wanted to smash them, to pound on them with his fists, to make them shut up—especially his father.

One evening during his last year in grade school, his parents were preparing to go to an open house at his school. His mother was upstairs getting dressed; his father remained down in the living room, ready in his usual crumpled brown jacket. He paced about impatiently waiting for her, his hat on his head, giving unsolicited comments and bits of advice about his mother to the boy, who sat silently in a chair.

"Where the hell is she? Well, she's a pearl, that one, and it takes a pearl some time to dress herself up." He half chuckled, and banged his pipe bowl hard against an ashtray.

"Yessir. Prettiest woman in this town. How long does it take her to put on a dress, anyway? What's she do up there? What's she do all day, anyway?"

The boy remained silent, unable to answer, and unsure that any answer was called for.

"You should watch her, you know," his father said, pointing

the stem of his pipe at him. "You should always watch a woman like that. Don't let anyone snatch her away from you. You should watch her for me when you're around. See if she acts funny."

He went on like that for another ten minutes—pacing, sucking on his unlit pipe, making rambling comments that the boy could not quite distinguish. Finally his mother walked downstairs in a moderate black skirt that fell several inches below her knees. His father took three great strides across the room and ripped it off her right there, leaving her standing in the living room in her stockings and a modest off-white slip.

"That's what you think you're goin' out in? Who're you dressin' up for? Who're you plannin' to see down there?"

She ran back upstairs, crying. The boy's father stomped outside, most likely, he knew, to buy a bottle and go rambling drunkenly through the woods. He wasn't sure if his father had torn off her skirt out of his impatience at waiting, or because he didn't want to go to the open house, or because he had actually convinced himself again that his wife was the most wanton and irresistible woman in the town.

The boy was ashamed of the whole scene, but not just because of his mother's humiliation. He was ashamed of himself, too. He knew that besides his fear he had felt a thrill of anger on his own. He had felt a violence growing in him throughout his father's rambling interrogation, had felt something that had been gratified when his father's heels resounded across the floorboard, when the fabric tore and the skirt was yanked away.

The next day, in a schoolyard football game, the boy played with his usual grace, quick and alert, gently overpowering the other boys. But when one of them tried to stop him by twisting a little too hard on his leg, he instantly ran him down, knees banging up fast and hard against the boy's face and chest.

He returned apologetically to help him up, and no one held it against him. It was part of the game, and years later the boy's high school coaches would be pleased to find that kind of fire lurking under his gentle aspect. He seemed like the perfect ballplayer to them, obedient and willing to learn, disciplined yet hard and spirited. They considered it competitive courage; to them he was nearly a man already. Only the boy knew differently.

7

He has a great pair of hands.

—WARREN BROWN

Lonnie Lee

I made it to the major leagues because I accepted Jesus Christ as my personal Savior. It was only Jesus who got me through all the bus rides in the minors. I'd be up sick to my stomach all night, watchin' the black misery go by outside the window. The club kept me on because I had soft hands and a good arm, but I couldn't put my game together.

I was just married to Brenda, livin' out there in California in a tiny house the real-estate man called a bungalow. One bedroom and a combination kitchen–living room, and we couldn't get up to turn on the TV without bumpin' into each other.

We didn't know anybody out there. We didn't even have enough money for her to go to the movies when I was out of town. She'd be lonely when we had away games, an' we'd fight when I got back. She accused me of foolin' around and sometimes I have to admit she was right. But I yelled at her like I never yelled at any woman, I'm ashamed to admit it.

It felt like my whole life was comin' apart. I could feel myself suffocatin' those nights, lyin' beside her in bed. I was sure I wasn't gonna make the major leagues, an' I thought I was gonna lose Brenda in the bargain, and where would that leave me but adrift?

I didn't yet realize that everythin' was going to be all right because Christ had already died for my sins.

The Old Swizzlehead

In the spring, Cookie Cochrane used to drive us around Florida to our exhibition games. He was a fat little man with a face that looked like it been dragged through gravel. All the flies used to say he was a character. They said he was in the major leagues himself, a long time ago, and that he even got some big pinch hit in the World Series and wasn't it a shame he was reduced to drivin' a bus.

I hated the son of a bitch. He used to cozy up to the veteran ballplayers, try to tell us about when he was in the show. Try to tell us all about his big pinch double, forty years ago. But when some rook got cut, he used to hold out his hands like he had a machine gun an' pretend he was mowin' the kid down.

"Gotcha!" he'd say, an' laugh.

"It's just the international shitting order of baseball," Maximilian Duke used to tell me. "Owners shit on the managers, managers try to shit on the ballplayers, ballplayers shit on the hired help. *They* have to try to shit on somebody."

I never liked those Florida bus trips anyway. Nobody I knew did, 'cept for John Barr. He loved everything about travelin'. During the season, if our charter was delayed, he would go over by the airport window an' just stand there watchin' the big jets land an' take off.

On the plane, he would sit all by hisself up front, an' he wouldn't read or listen to music or pinch the stewardesses. All he would do was look out the window, like he couldn't get enough of the clouds, or the land passing by underneath. Even when we traveled at night, and there wasn't a cloud in the sky, he liked to just look out the window and watch the darkness go by.

It was like he just loved the idea of movin'. It was the same way on the team buses. He would sit up front an' watch the highway go by. Charlie Stanzi noticed it right away, of course. He sat up there with him durin' the exhibition season. I don't know if he thought he could get friendly with him or just get under his skin, but he would sit up there an' try talkin' with him about all kinds of things.

"You looked a little slow gettin' around on Thibeault's fastball today," he would say. Or, "You sure you gotta play so far in on Aspesi? I thought you mighta had that Texas Leaguer." All kinds of shit like that. Or he would ask Barr what he was makin' these days. "How many tax shelters you got? Tax shelters—I knew ball-players good as you, they never once visited an accountant their whole careers."

No matter what he said, though, he couldn't get a rise out of Barr—until he got around to pussy. He would try talkin' about hittin', an' the horses, an' the flies, but all Barr would do was grunt back at him, or answer in yes an' noes. But when he got on-to pussy—an' Stanzi always did—John Barr would shut up en-tirely, an' even move back in the bus on the excuse of talkin' to somebody else.

"Hey, Barr, you shoulda seen the dolly I picked up at the hotel bar the other day," Stanzi would start in deliberately after a while, an' Barr's head would jerk back from the window, an' he would have to go find his glove or somethin'. Stanzi noticed it all right, an' the dirtier he would start in, the quicker John Barr would move away.

"How about that?" he'd say, grinnin' that evil smile of his an' watchin' Barr take off. "What's he so scared of?"

"Maybe he just don't like picturin' you undressed," I said, but if I'd wanted to I coulda told him Barr had always been like that. Everyone in baseball likes to talk about women, even the queers, but not John Barr. Whenever the conversation got around that way in the locker room, you could tell he was uncomfortable. He would walk away, or turn up the music. He never said why, an' we never saw him around with a woman. We always figured it would interfere with his hittin'.

The Little Maniac might have got on him more about it, but he had enough on his hands that spring—especially after what happened with Stillwater Norman an' the tragic Dead Clam In-cident. Up to *that*, we still had the best team in baseball, despite all Stanzi's best efforts. The Reverend Jimmy Bumpley was makin' a lot a' noise for his all-Christian Angels team out in California, but they'd only won the division last year, an' besides, that was the American League.

"Statistically speaking, it's impossible for this team to lose the pennant," Dr. Roscoe T. Jones told the flies, wavin' his charts an' graphs at them. Dr. Roscoe used to sit behind the dugout, writin' down every pitch with his long, bony fingers, like he was God hisself figurin' up the score. He was a tall, skinny, bald guy, with a big brush moustache that twitched when he got excited about some number.

"We were the leaders in most runners driven in from second base, after seventh inning, with two out, National League," he'd say, twitchin' away with satisfaction. "Most runners driven in from third base by base hit, eighth and ninth innings, National League."

Every year he'd tell the flies how great we were, just so Ellsworth Pippin could be sure we got the blame if anything went wrong. We *were* a solid team, still. All veterans, comin' off a championship season—but nobody too old yet. Like the flies used to say, we knew how to win, an' we had our strengths at every position.

At first base we had Jack No-Hit Hitt. He was usually on the I-95 at the plate, as you might guess from the name. But he could turn the 3-6-3 double play better than anybody in the game, and if you tried to lay one down, he'd be up your ass before the ball hit the ground.

Hitt was all right for a Stiff-Leg, too. He did the usual Stiff-Leg shit, of course. When we were on the road he was always runnin' up to the hotel room after dinner so he could call his family before the kids went to bed. He'd work out all winter, an' pay attention on the bench, an' before every home game he'd be out on the field with some crippled child, filmin' a charity commercial. By the time we got out for batting practice, there'd be No-Hit Hitt with some big-eyed little girl, sayin', "Please—buy this kid some hair," or somethin' like that. Then at the end of the year he'd get a plaque from the Moose or the Elks namin' him Man of the Year. Maximilian Duke used to stand up in the clubhouse an' say, "Please—buy this man some hits." An' No-Hit Hitt would look up an' smile like he knew he was supposed to take his kidding for the team's morale, just like a good Stiff-Leg.

We were strong up the middle, too, with Lonnie Lee at short an' Roberto Rodriguez, who we all called Bobby Roddy, at second base. Bobby acted crazy, like a lot of the Latins I know in the majors. All he would ever say was "Fuck you." Didn't matter if he booted a ground ball or hit a triple into the corner. He'd still come back into the dugout an' look at everybody an' say, "Fuck you."

We didn't know if it was an act or what. The only time we ever heard him say anything more was once in L.A. when Skeeter Mesquite, his roommate, was gettin' duded up for some big date. He had on a rose-colored suit with a silk vest, an' he spent two hours at the mirror puttin' on cologne an' fixin' his hair. The whole time, Bobby Roddy was standin' next to him, shavin' at a sink with a cigar stuck in his mouth, not sayin' a word even in Spanish. When Skeeter was finally ready to head out the door, Bobby Roddy looks up with the shavin' cream all over his face, pulls the cigar out an' says,

"Hey Skeeter. Just remember—you're still a speeeek!"

Lonnie Lee

It was one night we were in Bakersfield, an' I was just walkin' around because I didn't have the money to go noplace else. I turned down one street by pure chance—or maybe not—and I heard the singin'.

It was comin' from this Spanish evangelical church—just a little *iglesia* built into a storefront, with folding chairs for pews, an' a table with a cloth over it for an altar. I had never seen a church like that before. But I went in an' they made me welcome. They smiled an' sat me down an' handed me a hymn book.

It was all in Spanish, but I started singin' anyway. About halfway through the first song I started cryin'. The Holy Spirit must have filled me, because I felt like I was at home in that Spanish church whose language I didn't speak and with all those people I didn't know.

The Old Swizzlehead

Lonnie Lee is a Jeebee Jaycee, which stands for GBJC, which stands for Good Book Jesus Christ. A Jeebee Jaycee is a Stiff-Leg, only with religion. Lonnie likes to organize chapel before the Sunday games, an' reads Bible verses out loud, an' talks about his personal relationship with God a lot. Every team has at least one, an' some have a lot more, like the Rev. Jimmy Bumpley's Angels.

Every time a Jeebee Jaycee hits a foul ball he goes on TV thankin' Jesus for it. Lonnie's the same way. He'd save a game with a good throw, an' come in tellin' the flies it was really Jesus Christ who made it.

"Goddammit, Jesus can really go into the hole," Spock Feeley used to rag him.

"You know what I mean," Lonnie would say.

Baseball's a game where you live on such a thin edge that you have to find somethin' to account for it—whether it's Jesus, or what you had for supper, or if you touch your helmet before you realign your crotch when you get up in the batter's box.

Except for John Barr. I never saw him with a crucifix, or a lucky charm, or anything else but his bat. He didn't have any peculiar habits, and if he believed in Jesus he kept it to himself.

"I never seen Jesus get any hits," he said one time when Lonnie Lee asked him about it.

"It's Jesus Who makes everything possible," Lonnie said, but Barr just snorted at him.

"I'm the one up there," he said. "It's me an' nobody else."

Sometimes he even went out of his way to break superstitions. No ballplayer likes to step on the foul lines when they run on or off the field. That's just obvious bad luck; you won't see a ballplayer do it, whether he's a Christian, a Muslim, or a Hindu Indian.

John Barr did it, though. He would step on that line on purpose, crush his spikes right down on the chalk. He'd make sure we all saw him, an' do it real slow an' deliberate, like he was enjoyin' hisself. Until that last year, it never brought him any bad luck that I could tell. It seemed to me like he was the only one who really had the game beat.

Lonnie Lee

When I got back off the road, Brenda was waiting for me at the screen door. I opened the door and took her hand and pulled her to me. I knelt down with her right there on the porch, an' asked her to pray with me.

Brenda had a religious upbringing, but she was confused by my behavior at first. But she trusted me, she was a loving wife. I asked her if she had ever accepted The Lord Jesus Christ, an' she said she wasn't really sure if she had. So we held hands an' prayed, an' right out there on the porch that night, she let Christ into her heart, too. It was the most beautiful thing I'd ever seen, watching her with bowed head and humble heart accept the Lord into her life. I loved her more than ever after that night. From then on I was confident in the knowledge that Jesus had a plan for my life, and wanted me to use my God-given talents to the fullest.

The Old Swizzlehead

Most of the infield could pick it, but between Bobby Roddy an' Lonnie Lee an' No-Hit Hitt we didn't have one man who could hit his way out of a paper bag. It was the outfield where we got the hitting, an' which made us a great team.

In center there was yours truly, still the fastest man in the game, no matter what they might say about Good Stuff Goodson on the Angels. In right we had John Barr, who was the best, and in left there was The Emp'ror, Maximilian Duke. He'd been All-Pac 10 in baseball *and* football at Stanford, and he could've been a pro linebacker in the NFL. He hit thirty, forty homers a year an' played the best left field in the league.

We had some pop behind the plate, too, with Spock Feeley. That was his favorite TV character, Mr. Spock. Everyone's got their own favorite shows to kill the time when we're on the road. Some guys like the cartoons, the Jeebee Jaycees all got their favorite TV preachers, an' most of the rest watch the stories. They act like they're just watchin' the ladies on those shows, but they get mad when we have a weekday afternoon game an' they have to miss a day of the stories. They hang around the batting cage with the guys on the other team, askin', "Hey, you see what happened to Jessica yesterday?"

But Spock Feeley always liked "Star Trek" reruns, an' he tried to be cool an' silent like Mr. Spock. He wasn't the kind to bring along a young pitchin' staff. Some young swizzlehead be out there losin' the strike zone an' all Spock Feeley would do was walk to the mound, get into his face, an' say real calm an' quiet, "Throw the ball over the fucking plate."

That was okay with the veteran starters, though. They liked that he would never put too much padding in his glove. Pitchers like to hear a big pop from the catcher's glove when they're throwin'. It lets, 'em know how hard they're bringin' it, and it intimidates the hitters, too, hearing the ball come in like that. Some catchers like to put a little padding in, to save their hands, but Feeley never did. His glove was so thin it sounded like you were throwin' against a board, an' every batter up there thought he was hittin' against goddamned Sandy Koufax all of a sudden.

Moses Yellowhorse was our number one starter, an' he really could bring it. He was half-Jewish, half-Indian, from Butte, Montana, an' Dickhead Barry Busby liked to call him things like "The Kosher Comanche." He also called him "an old-fashioned ball-player," which I guess meant he never opened his mouth except when he wanted a drink.

I never knew if that story was true about Moses takin' the sample cologne bottle the girl offered him in Macy's an' drinkin' it. Nor do I know for sure if he handed it back to her when he was through an' said, "Not bad." But Moses never denied it. He never denied anything about his drinking. Every start, he liked to weave out to the mound an' throw his first warm-up pitch ten feet over Spock Feeley's head. Then he'd chuck the next a couple feet higher than that. With his reputation, it kept the hitters from diggin' in.

After Moses, the starting staff was a little shakier. We had Buddy Lucas, who could give us the innings but who wasn't spectacular, an' then we had Big Bo Bigbee, who was spectacular but didn't like to be out there actually pitchin'. Bo had the best stuff in the league when he was on, but there was always somethin' goin' wrong with the man.

"I can't pitch tonight," he used to tell Cal Rigby ten minutes before a big game when he was scheduled to start.

"Why's that, Bo?" Cal would ask him.

"I got a bad sinus headache," he would say. "And besides, my left arterial tendon feels a little strained."

Bo knew more about the human body than most doctors. If there was any piece on him he could name, it would get strained, sprained, or inflamed. Ol' Cal would push him out there anyway, an' Bo would give him six, seven good innings. Then it would get down to the last couple, with the score still close, an' Bo would develop a limp, or a blister. Cal would keep his seat in the dugout, an' on the next pitch, Bo would start clutchin' his arm. They'd have to bring the stretcher out before he was through.

At least we had the strongest bullpen in the league, between Skeeter closing from the right side an' Al The Fade Abramowitz with his fadeaway pitch from the left. Nobody ever did figure out how he threw that pitch. I batted against it in spring training, an' it was the damnedest thing to hit.

You could not follow his ball when it was on. They even tried trackin' it with cameras an' infrared, but nothin' picked it up. Nobody could even describe it, precisely. That thing would float up to the plate big an' slow as a beachball. The next thing you knew, it was gone. I don't know if it dropped or curved away, but it wasn't there. I asked him how he made the ball do that once, an' Al The Fade looked at me with this little smile around his lips, so I'd think he was kidding.

"The trick is, Swiz, that the bawl actually disappears for a moment. It's a secret of the Kabbalah."

He said it, an' he gave me that smile. But I knew he really meant it. That's the goddamned thing about ballplayers. I knew he really believed it.

The Little Maniac didn't have any superstitions as such, but he wanted to ward off the evil eye, too, in case we suddenly got old and fell to pieces in his first season. So every day down in Florida, he was out there tryna whip us into shape. It was a fool idea, seein' as how you can't whip a baseball team into anything, 'cept maybe a mess.

Stanzi had us workin' on rundowns an' double steals an' pick-off plays every day, like we were still in high school. He kept us doin' sprints an' sliding drills until our legs were covered with strawberries. He had us runnin' through tires like a goddamned football team—instead of just lettin' us hit and get our eye back. Ol' Cal Rigby came up from his boat one afternoon, red as a lobster, an' he couldn't believe it.

"He's even got the goddamned pitchers out there. You shouldn't worry if your pitchers can pick their nose right, long as they can bring some heat.'' But Charlie Stanzi was runnin' the team his way now, an' Ol' Cal went back to his fishin' an' his whiskey, shakin' his head.

"There's no reason why everyone—*everyone*—on this team cannot be a complete ballplayer," Stanzi would tell the flies, an' they'd all nod, even though there wasn't more than four or five really complete ballplayers in the whole league. It was another code word. When you hear somebody talk about a complete ballplayer, what they mean is a white boy who slaps singles into the opposite field an' keeps his mouth shut.

The only real complete ballplayer we had on the team was John Barr, an' I could see The Little Maniac was lookin' for a chance to get on him again. He was followin' Barr through the drills with those little slit eyes of his, waitin' for him to mouth off or let up even for one minute. He wanted some chance to get after him, and show us and the flies and Pippin how tough he was again.

But Barr never complained, he never even frowned. He ran through all the sliding an' bunting an' running drills, and he did 'em better than anyone else. He even seemed to *like* 'em. He would go back an' do extra sets, without crackin' a good sweat. Stanzi had nothin' on him, an' you could see the frustration growin' around his puckered-up evil mouth.

The more he did, the more it almost seemed to put John Barr in a good mood. I even saw him give a tip to a rook one afternoon. It was nothin' much; Barr an' the rook was both out shaggin' flies one day, an' Barr goes over to this green kid, just up for a look from Double-A, an' shows him how to catch a ball so you get a good runnin' start on a throw.

"You do it like this," was all Barr said to him, an' ran it two or three times under flies that Old Coach Plate hit. But it was enough to leave the rook's mouth hangin', an' mine, too. I never seen him do anything like that before.

"You makin' sure you get remembered kindly in history?" I asked him, an' Barr almost smiled back at me.

"Skip wants me to be a good team playah," he said, an' loped away over the field, shaggin' a few more balls. In the twelve years I'd already played with him in the majors, I never seen him treat a rook like that before. I'd never seen him look twice at one before.

These days, some rook comes up, long as he's not a major threat for somebody's job, he gets treated all right. But not by John Barr. I seen him order rooks right out of the batting cage, 'cause he wanted to get his licks in.

"I'm not here to walk 'em through life," was all he'd say. "I got here, an' I didn't ask for any help doin' it."

John Barr never was what you would call a team player—not that it really matters much in this game, no matter what the flies tell you. Still, I played with a lot of different rightfielders an' there's some who play it soft, an' back off an' let you have everything, an' then there's some who play it hard, an' try to pretend they're the centerfielder and take everything they can get away with. Barr played it exact, that's all.

It was like he had a perfect picture in his mind of right field, just like he had a perfect picture of the strike zone. It took me a while to learn it, but I caught on. If a ball went one foot beyond where he thought right field ended, it was mine. If I went one foot beyond where he thought *center* field ended, I could expect to end up with an elbow in my face, no matter how loud I might be callin' for the ball. He'd rather let a ball drop in there and cost us a game than go over his own personal borderlines.

Anyone else besides John Barr, I wouldn't have put up with it. He was like that all over. He'd rather take a walk than hit the ball out of the park—if it meant swingin' at a pitch a quarter-inch outside his own personal strike zone. He could lay down a fine bunt; sometimes he'd do it if the other team played some super shift on him and swung their infield around. He would lay one right down the chalk line, and with his speed he might make it to second. But he would never lay one down or hit-an'-run on orders.

"That's not what I get paid for," he told me one time. He was right, no manager in his right mind wanted to have the best power hitter in the league up there bunting. Still, there was one time, down in Double-A, when Ol' Cal Rigby put the sign on, an' Barr just ignored it. He hit away an' banged a double into the corner, an' when he came back to the dugout, Cal asked him if he'd missed the sign.

"I *did* my job," was all he said. A lot of guys might've pretended they just didn't see the sign, but not John Barr.

Cal Rigby didn't like that much, but he knew enough not to disrespect success when he saw it. It was typical of Barr, too. At times it didn't seem like he even knew he was on a team. I don't think it really mattered much to him whether we even got into the World Series. He was out there playin' for himself.

That's why I couldn't figure out why he was all of a sudden helping Double-A rookies. I thought maybe he was just bein' smart, finding ways to keep The Little Maniac off his back.

Stanzi was determined that he had to mess with *something*. He told the flies, "I'm going to leave my mark on this team," an' what that meant was he had to have a project. He needed some likely-lookin' rook who he could declare hisself the sole creator of. Then he could announce that this was his bobo, an' he was gonna make a major-league player out of him. A lot of managers liked to do that. It was a good way of stayin' employed, have some kid with your name on him. It made the owners think you really knew the game, and if you were lucky the kid would be so brainwashed that he'd tell the flies, "I owe it all to my manager."

The Little Maniac decided on Terry White, a big blond kid we had up straight out of Southern Cal. He'd broke lots of official NCAA batting records with his little aluminum bat down there, an' now Stanzi convinced himself he could make the boy a major league third baseman.

"He has the most natural talent I've ever seen," he told the flies. "But it's raw. He has to be molded into a big league ballplayer."

The flies ate it up. It was just the kind of story they liked: manager turns raw kid into superstar. White was pretty good at pullin' in the annies an' roundin' up some good blow, I'll say that for him. But we all knew he wasn't a major league ballplayer yet. Every now an' then in batting practice he'd get ahold of one an' knock it five hundred feet with his ripply bronze Southern Cal muscles. But mostly he just moved around the jetstream with his big empty swings. And his fielding down at third was what the flies liked to call "suspect."

"Yeah, suspect," The Emp'ror used to say. "It's suspect the way you might call the Boston Strangler suspect."

"Whiff Dick," I told him, which is what we say for White Folk Don't Know, or WFDK.

"Definite Whiff Dick, but they're all going to get behind this one," The Emp'ror said. "The flies, and Pippin, and the fans, and especially Stanzi. They see a big, white-boy star."

They planned a big coming-out for him, in the first exhibition game we had against the Expos. Stanzi had benched Stillwater Norman, who'd been our regular third baseman for the last seven years, an' penciled in Terry White, battin' in the three spot. The flies were five rows deep behind the dugout, an' Stanzi hung around on the top step, leanin' over from time to time an' tellin' 'em how good he was gonna make the rook.

"I believe in taking a chance with a talented kid like that," he said, an' all the flies nodded their heads.

First inning, some swizzlehead for the 'Spos up from Double-A throws a sweet fat pussy fastball down the middle, an' the college boy hits it out past the palm trees behind the centerfield fence. Stanzi leaps right back out to the top step of the dugout to tell the flies what they just seen.

"The boy's somethin' else, isn't he?" he says, pattin' his heart. "We're at the start of something big here."

But White still had to take the field. Bottom of the first, lead-off hitter for the 'Spos hits a ball that hops once, twice, right into his glove. He picks it, sets his feet just like he's supposed to—an' throws the ball ten rows up into the stands. Stanzi's back out of the dugout before all the flies are even through ducking.

"It'll take him a little time and effort to get control over it," he says. "But what an arm that kid has!"

"Sure. The guy in the wheelchair back there isn't even dead," Ellie Jay says.

"It's okay, it's okay, it's okay, that's just one," Lonnie Lee sung out to the kid, tryna calm him down.

"Fuck you, fuck you, fuck you," Bobby Roddy said, in a en-couragin' kind of voice.

Montreal had caught on to the boy, though. Next man up laid a bunt down the third-base line. The Little Maniac still had his back turned, lookin' up at the press, an' he never had a chance. Old Coach Plate Pasquale had to help the ambulance men take him down the runway to the clubhouse.

The Little Maniac didn't get out of the hospital for a week, and in the meantime Stillwater Norman got his job back. He always was an okay hitter, with a little power, an' he could pick a few down there at third. But now he had his best spring in years, an' we were glad to see it.

Everybody liked Norman. He was a good old boy from Oklahoma, an' he thought the best thing that ever happened to him was becomin' a ballplayer. He looked a little bit like Elvis Presley, an' he was popular with the annies. He loved baseball, an' the ladies, and his penis, which he was always very proud of.

He was also the dumbest man alive. The flies loved him cause he was the only guy in the clubhouse who could make 'em think they asked a tough question. They'd say, "How'd you feel after that home run you hit in the sixth?" An' Stillwater would look at 'em, an' frown an' run a hand over his forehead. Finally, he'd just look up an' grin at 'em.

"Gee, pardner, I don't know," he'd say. "That's a good one."

Stillwater's real first name was Bradley. But he got to be called Stillwater because Dickhead Barry Busby decided the man was really a genius. "Remember," he wrote one time in his column, "What's the Buzz?": "Still waters run deep."

Other people thought Stillwater was on drugs, but we assured 'em he was just stupid. One day in Cincinnati he run straight into Maximilian Duke goin' after a pop fly into short left. The Emp'ror was okay, but Stillwater went down hard. By the time our trainer, Doc Roberts, got out there to him, his eyes were open and he was sittin' up, but still looked out of it. Doc grabbed him by the chin an' looked into his eyes, an' asked him who the president was.

"Uh-uh. He wouldn't know that anyway," Maximilian Duke said.

"What town are we in, then?"

"That's no good," Lonnie Lee told him. "He just goes by the uniform colors."

"Okay," Doc tried again. "What day is it?"

Stillwater just sat there lookin' at him.

"Ask him if that was a natural blonde last night, an' what he had for dinner," No-Hit Hitt said. "He'll get that."

Stillwater could tell a good story on hisself, too. Just the night before the tragic Dead Clam Incident took place, he was entertainin' me an' The Emp'ror an' Skeeter Mesquite. We were sittin' around analyzin' about our investments. Maximilian Duke was talkin' about his collectors' cars, while Skeeter was stressin' the need to stay liquid an' I had the third race lined up.

"Hey, Swiz, what're you investing in these days?" Skeeter asked me. "What looks good to you?"

"I got some things goin'," I told him.

"Yeah, you have a feeler on the number-five horse tonight. With maybe a little dip into the quinella, for diversification."

"Nothin' wrong with the horseflesh," I told him. "I hit a six-to-one shot the other night. It's money in the bank, when you play it like I do."

"It's a sucker's game, Swiz," The Emp'ror said. "It's no fun gambling unless you're betting more than you can afford to lose. And then you're crazy."

"You got the wrong attitude about money," I told him. "You can't hang on to money. Money hangs on to you, if it wants to."

"Like with that restaurant?"

"That was a good idea, that restaurant. They put my name on it an' everything. It looked good."

"Ah, shit, Swiz," The Emp'ror snorted. "You should only invest in a restaurant if your name's McDonald."

"How 'bout you?" I called over to Barr, where he was finishin' gettin' dressed and ignorin' us. "What you into these days?"

John Barr looked at us like we asked him to sing a few pieces from *Carmen.* Everybody knew already he was the cheapest man in baseball, an' there's some cheap people in this game. It wasn't like the international shitting order of things. Barr would tip the clubhouse guys an' the bellhops okay. He just wouldn't spend a dime on hisself if he could help it.

"Banks," he said, gettin' up to go. "I put my money in banks. That's where it's safe."

That brought a cackle from Skeeter. "You certainly don't spend it on suits," he said.

Which was obvious. Barr's clothes always looked like he bought them out of a catalogue somewheres. His jackets looked like they were one thread away from comin' completely unraveled, an' he used a paper clip for a tie clasp. He looked raggedy, but it was just that he didn't care. I don't think he even thought about clothes.

I was surprised to hear that he even put his money in a bank. John Barr didn't have any *use* for money. It was like he didn't quite understand it. He never went out to eat anywhere nice, never picked up a round of drinks for everybody, never bought big fancy cars to impress the annies. All he spent it on that I could see was his jeep an' that little farm he had up home. Neither one of them could've cost much—not nearly as much as he made, anyway, with those one-year contracts renegotiated every season with Ellsworth Pippin.

"Best suit a man ever wears is when he's buried," was all he said. He didn't care what we thought of it; didn't even mind us laughin' as he walked out. Barr never acted like he was desperate to save up his money, or afraid somebody else was gettin' more. It was just an irrelevance to him, since it didn't require a bat an' ball. It took people like Stillwater Norman to put it to creative uses.

"I invested in somethin' once," Stillwater said, comin' out of the shower, wearin' a big fool grin on his face an' rubbin' his balls with a towel. He always took delicate care of his equipment. He'd soap his pecker all up an' down in the shower, over an' over, then he'd work on it with a towel until that thing was clean as a whistle. He claimed that was how to avoid disease an' unwanted pregnancies.

"You? When did you ever invest in anything more than a steak dinner?"

"That first year I was up, when we beat the Twins in six games. I took my check from the Series an' cashed it an' went right back home to marry Loretta, my high school girl. We got a ranch house way off in the middle of nowhere for our honeymoon, an' shacked up there for six weeks.

"I mean this place was *isolated.* There was nobody around to bother us, an' we didn't get out of bed for more than ten minutes at a time until this little salesman dude shows up. We were ten miles from the nearest highway, but this dude found us anyway. He drives up in the biggest, whitest Cadillac I ever seen in my life. It were the color of smooth cream right from the cow's tits, even after he drove it for ten miles over the prairie. This little man with a cowboy hat and a suit the color of the Caddy gets out, lookin' serious as a county undertaker.

"I asked him why he came all the way out in that fine car an' he said it was important. An' he don't laugh, an' he don't joke or act like any other salesmen I ever seen. Just stared at me real solemn through these big fish-eye glasses. Then he told me he was sellin' a new microchip that was gonna save the free world."

Stillwater laughed some more just thinkin' about it, an' went up an' down the whole length of his thing with the towel again.

"I thought maybe a microchip was somethin' like Pringle's, but Loretta explained it to me. She tried to talk me outta the whole thing. She told me, 'Bradley, at least go call your agent first.' But it sounded good to me, an' I didn't want this dude in his fancy car to think my woman was tellin' me what to do.

"I said, 'Loretta, I never invested in a computer. I think it's somethin' I gotta do, now that I'm in the major leagues.'

"She points out, 'Honeybunch, you never even *seen* a computer,' which I hadda admit was right. But it made me mad at the time because I wanted it to look like I was a experienced businessman. Loretta finally got me to call up my agent, Ollie Balf, in New York. He tells me, 'No, don't do it, listen to Loretta.' He tells me to call up the county sheriff an' have the man arrested. I said I can't do that, he's a guest in my house. Ollie starts coughin' for a while, then he says to hang on, don't say yes or no, an' he'll catch the first flight to Houston an' drive up direct, just so long as I wait."

"So didn't you wait?" Maximilian Duke grinned at him. But we had to hold up on the story while Stillwater took out some baby oil an' patted down his cock, as gentle an' smooth as if he was greasin' his best duck-hunting gun back home.

"I told him I wasn't interested, but the next thing I know we was havin' a beer, an' Loretta's standin' in the corner with her arms crossed, tappin' her foot. That little sales dude was sayin' he was gonna get serious now. He could talk a streak, that man. He told me this microchip could shoot Russian missiles right out of the sky, an' if the Russians wasn't really our enemies no more, it was still good to keep it out of the hands of the Japanese, and besides, we could always use it to keep the Arabs in line.

"It sounded like a good argument to me, but Loretta was a stubborn woman. She said, 'Bradley, that sumbitch is a con man, sure as he's sittin' there.' An' you know, I suppose in the back of my mind I knew she was right. But I was thinkin' too that even if he was a con man, he hadda make a living, didn't he? And I was kinda flattered, him comin' all that way out there for me."

Stillwater paused for reflection then. With his thing all ready an' serviced, he powdered it with talc like a newborn baby, an' tucked it tenderly inside a pair of red hot bikini briefs, with the letters TCB and a lightnin' bolt on them.

"I was still waverin', though, when he walked out to that cream car an' brought back a piece of paper. That was how he sold me, just on that single piece of paper."

"On a piece of paper?"

"Oh, but it was a fine paper! I still got it down home. It had angels an' cupids an' flowers all over the sides, an' on top there was railroad engines an' airplanes an' ocean ships and even little microchip missiles blastin' off after the Russians. He said it was the official stock certificate for the microchip company, an' he wanted me to know what a easy million looked like.

"Well, I woulda paid the money just for that piece of paper. I bought fifty thousand shares of that stock, an' then the man said he would throw in his car, too, if I'd buy another fifty thousand. I took one more look out the window at that cream bitch, an' I said all right. It was cheap, too. Hundred thousand shares, it only cost me forty-five thousand dollars, which happened to be every cent I had left from the World Series winner's share. I paid the man his money, in cash, an' he handed me that beautiful piece of paper an' the keys to that cream-colored baby, an' he just went walkin' out over the prairie in his shirt sleeves, carryin' his white suit jacket over his shoulder."

When he was through with his piece, Stillwater worked on his hair, strokin' the pomade through it again an' again, until it was black an' wet an' fat on top like Elvis's. He was grinnin' again. It might've been the story, but Stillwater Norman never could resist lookin' at hisself in a mirror.

"After that, Loretta was all over me. She went on for hours, tellin' me to go after that salesman, bring him back an' get my money. I had to explain to her that for a man a deal's a deal, but she wouldn't leave me alone. She said then she realized she married a fool an' she was leavin', an' I told her fine, I would drive her in my new car."

"Uh-huh."

"Yeah, you guessed it. The moment I turned the key in the ignition, things started to fall off that car. First the hubcaps. Then the fender. Then the wheels themselves. I swear to God, by the time we got two miles out on the prairie, there wasn't one thing left attached to another on that car. Even the ashtrays came off the door handle. We were sittin' out there on a pile of junk.

"Loretta got up an' walked away, without another word. But I still have that piece of paper. I figure lots of people got stocks. But nobody else got a piece of paper worth fory-five thousand dollars."

When he got his hair done, we all drove back to the Swamp Meat Hotel together, an' he stuck his head out the back window like a great big dog, testing his pomade. We were goin' over to a little thing Terry White put together with a few annies, an' Stillwater had a big grin on his face the whole way. It wasn't nothin' more than a party we were goin' to, like a couple hundred parties we'd have on the road all year. But he still couldn't get over it.

"There's gonna be girls there?" he asked us.

"Sure."

"Lots of 'em?"

"Sure."

"Most of it, hanging out of his pants, seventh inning on."

"Most of mind, percentage, on pussy, one head."

But Stillwater just kept grinnin'.

"Don't bein' a ballplayer beat all?" he said.

But Stillwater Norman's nemesis was just around the corner. I saw her in the doorway first, but it was hard to miss her. She was tall, with red hair, standin' in the doorway watching the long, tan things from the local junior colleges like they were fishbait. She had on only a halter top, a pair of high heels, an' a itty-bitty red skirt, but she stood there like a queen.

She looked over the whole room, an' then her eyes landed on Stillwater. She made her way across the room toward him with a lighted cigarette held out off one hip, to clear a path through the college girls dancin' an' jigglin' all over the place. He never even saw her coming. All of a sudden she was standin' there in front of him, smokin'.

"Hey, baby," he said, which was his standard line, an' which he was proud of.

"My name is Rita," she said, an' put her arms around his neck, an' started to sway back an' forth with him. "Let's dance."

"Gimme your lips, sugar," she said then. She sunk her teeth into his bottom lip, an' rubbed up close against him. Then she took another deep drag from the cigarette she still had danglin' from her long red fingernails, an' put her mouth over his. When she finally let go, Stillwater looked like he could use some oxygen. He opened his mouth an' a little cloud of smoke came back out.

"All right," she says, an' leads him into the bedroom by his belt buckle. "Time for the national anthem. You gotta stand up an' salute, honey."

The next day, me an' Maximilian Duke hadda carry Stillwater out of his room to make the team bus in time. Rita was still there on the bed, naked as the day she was born, smokin' another cigarette."

"That's a bad habit," The Emp'ror told her.

"Uh-huh," she said. "That's my only one." Then she threw her head back an' laughed. She didn't look quite so good in the morning light. Her mascara had ran, an' you could see the lines in her face an' in her neck, even through the tan. She had a gold tooth in the front of her mouth, an' you could make out the brown roots in her hair. But she was still some woman.

She lifted herself slowly up off the bed, one leg at a time, then walked over, still naked, an' picked up Stillwater's TCB bikinis. She twirled 'em around on one finger, an' stuck em in her pocketbook. Then she blew on her finger like it was a sixgun.

"Best in the West," she said, an' walked into the bathroom.

It might've been just a pleasant interlude for Stillwater, too, like one of them ships that pass an' such in the night. That is, if it hadn't been for The Great White Father an' his goddamned promotions. Every day we had off in Florida, there was another club appearance. Then everybody, even John Barr, was bused out to meet the Kiwanis, or the Rotary Club—or in this case the goddamned Greater Central Florida Association of Bait Dealers. We had to be out to the park by ten o'clock, an' on the bus for a three-hour ride. Cookie got lost, an' the bus air conditioning broke down, an' by the time we got there it must've been a hundred degrees out in the sun. That cheap bastard Pippin was holdin' the event out in a flat tar parking lot, and it was so hot you could feel the tar liftin' up under your feet.

Most of us were still hung over from the night before, an' we had to swallow hard when we saw the tables full of raw clams an' pitchers of beer swimmin' through the heat. Then before we knew it we were surrounded by hundreds of little crackers wearin' caps with truck names on them an' all tryna tell us at once why no modern ballplayer was as good as Ty Cobb.

But there was one in particular who stood out. I spotted him on the edge of the crowd a little while later. He looked just like one more little redneck, with pop eyes and a bowlin'-ball gut, an' some big ugly warts on his neck. But he seemed to be starin' especially hard at all of us, like he was tryna make somethin' out.

At first I thought he was just another citizen awed by greatness, an' didn't pay him no more mind. But when I looked back in his direction, he was makin' his way through the crowd like he had a purpose all of a sudden. I thought maybe he just found his favorite player, but somethin' about the way he was movin' made the hairs go up on the back of my neck.

"Check this out," I said to John Barr, who was standin' nearest to me. But he had seen it before I did, the way he never let nothin' get by him, an' he was already jumpin' over tables, tryna head off that redneck. 'Cause by then we could see he was headed straight for Stillwater Norman.

Stillwater never saw him coming. He had a good appetite that day, same as he always did. He was standin' by one of the tables, suckin' down his clams an' beer an' laughin' with the bait dealers, when the little redneck came up to him.

"You Stillwatah Nahmon?" the little popeyed guy asks him.

"Stillwater! Watch yourself!" I screamed over to him, 'cause I could see now the little man had somethin' in his hand, behind his back. But it just distracted Stillwater.

"What's that?" he said, takin' his eyes off the redneck for a fateful second, an' suckin' another clam out of its shell.

"Well, Mistuh Stillwatah Nahmon, I don't suppose you evah heard of the Bible?" the popeyed little man says, an' whips a marlin pike as long as a man's arm out from behind his back.

He wound up to take a full swing at Stillwater with the thing, but John Barr got there ahead of him an' got one hand on the redneck's arm. It threw his aim off, but he still got Stillwater's shoulder an' sent him flyin' back over a clam table.

All of a sudden there was blood everywhere, an' everybody was pushin' an' runnin'. Bright red blood, like in the movies, squirtin' out all over Stillwater's white shirt, an' over the clams an' into the pitchers of beer. The little popeyed bait dealer's still swingin' that marlin pike around, an' everybody else was knockin' each other over tryna get out of the way. But before he could get another swing in on Stillwater, me an' John Barr were able to get ahold of him an' pull the thing out of his hands.

It turned out to be Rita's husband, Ray, who somehow got wind an' decided to come down an' do somethin' about it. Pretty soon he was disarmed an' cryin' like a baby, but it took another half hour or so to break up all the fights that had started between the rest of the bait dealers. By the time everybody was calmed down again, Old Coach Plate noticed that Stillwater was still missin'.

Lonnie Lee found him, behind the same table he fell over. The bleeding from his arm was stopped, but he wasn't movin' at all, an' his big black eyes were starin' straight up at the sun.

"He shouldn't oughta be that blue," Lonnie Lee said helpfully.

Old Coach Plate tried givin' the boy mouth-to-mouth until the ambulance came, but it didn't do much good. The last time he tried, he come up choking himself, an' then he reaches into his mouth an' pulls out the clam shell Stillwater had been sucking on.

"Son of a bitch," he said. He even spat out his tobacco chaw when he saw that.

"I knew I shoulda stayed away from those clams," No-Hit Hitt said.

To my surprise, John Barr took exception to that remark. He looked like he was gonna slug Hitt right there, an' he hadda go walk around the parking lot for a few minutes before he calmed down. I went over to where he was still stompin' around, his hands on his hips, an' I could see he was really upset. The man looked like he either wanted to cry or beat somethin' up. It surprised me 'cause I never knew he cared that much about Stillwater, one way or the other.

"You okay, bo?" I asked him.

"I should've seen it!" he bursts out, which really surprised me. "I should've seen it comin'!"

"Nothin' more you could do, one way or the other," I told him.

"I should've seen it," he kept repeating. "I should've got there in time."

It took him another half hour to calm down. I didn't know what else to say to the man, I was so surprised. I thought maybe he was just gettin' sentimental about his teammates in his old age, but that didn't seem much like John Barr, either. You'd a' thought he stuck that fishhook in Stillwater hisself.

Nobody else acted that upset. There wasn't anything we could do, 'cept leave Stillwater's body out there among the clams on the hot tar pavement, until the ambulance arrived. The rest of us made sure to stick to the beer an' the corn on the cob after that. There was a few jokes, too, 'bout Stillwater bein' the prettiest thing Old Coach Plate ever kissed, but they didn't mean anything, that was just the way ballplayers are when they are truly shocked. The Little Maniac came over, too, to shake his head an' make some tsk-tsk noises before the ambulances got there.

"Well, he was always some kind of competitor," he said.

I read the same words in Dickhead Barry Busby's column, "What's the Buzz?," a few days later. "Manager Stanzi tribute to late Stillwater Norman: "He was some kind of competitor"—ultimate kudo in this man's game."

"If that's the best they can do for me, they don't have to bother," I told The Emp'ror when I put the paper down.

"Whiff Dick, for sure," The Emp'ror said, shakin' his head. It was the last day of spring training, an' we were ready to go play for real. The clubhouse boys would finish packin' up our bags, an' the players would give 'em ten, fifteen dollars tip for the spring. Bunch of millionaires handin' out a couple little bills to middle-aged men for washin' their jocks.

On the bus to the airport, there was Cookie Cochrane again, mowing down all the reassignments to the minor leagues with his fake machine gun. He put out his hand when all the veterans came by, as if he wanted to shake it. But it was really there so we could slip a few dollars in it. He'd say "Jeez, have a good year, fellas. I wish I was playin' nowadays, I'd make a few bucks."

I was gonna do it, too. I gave the clubhouse boys a couple hundred each. But when I got up to Cookie I just gave him a low five. He looked like somebody kicked him in the mouth, but he didn't have the guts to say anything about it.

"Hey, Swiz, have a great year. Your contract's up this season, right?" he said, like he was hopin' I just forgot an' this was the best way he had to remind me. "I hope you get a big one."

"Thanks, Cookie," was all I said, an' went to sit down next to The Emp'ror, who was waggin' a finger at me.

"It's the international shitting order," he said again, but I didn't give a damn. Cookie was already back to machine-gunning the rookies.

"Gotcha!" he'd laugh. "Changin' planes in Atlanta! Might as well take the bus all the way."

But he didn't shoot down Terry White. The boy hadda go to New York with us, now that Stillwater Norman was dead. I was just as glad we sent Stillwater's coffin on back to Oklahoma already, 'cause no doubt Cookie would've machine-gunned that, too.

"I got a bad feeling about this season I can't shake," I told The Emp'ror. But he shrugged it off.

"How much worse can it get already?" he said.

8

When I think of a stadium, it's like a temple.

—JIM LEFEBVRE

The Boy

The monster station wagon Evan Barr had bought that spring was too much for him, just like all the other cars before it. He was never able to fix the hole in the gas tank, and this time he didn't have enough money to take it to the garage.

"They'd just rob us anyway, damned thieves," he said, damning their petty, limited ambitions above all. He had joyously continued trying to beat the leak home.

One night he miscalculated. He had driven down to the old ballfield by the railroad yard, to take his son home from the American Legion game there. He might have made it, but the game went into extra innings. It had gone on and on, into the long summer dusk, while the gas dripped away under his car.

He didn't care. As he watched, it became a great game—tightly played, the players full of the nervous energy of knowing that one slip, one break would decide it. The longer it went on, the better it was, with each team playing well above what should have been expected from teenage boys. The longer it went on, the longer they seemed to want it to go on—one player after another coming up with a quick, crisp play in the field to keep it going. Evan Barr sat up in the stands with the mothers and the retired men all chuckling softly and making small talk, trying not to show how excited they were by this child's game.

Finally, in the top of the twelfth, the boy had put his team ahead. Squinting to pick a pitch out of the gloaming, he had driven it on a line to the edge of the woods in center field. He had raced around to third on the hit, and come storming home when the next pitch went wild, squirting past the catcher. It went rolling somehow even past the backstop, stopped in the end only by the rail tracks for the Boston & Maine, the catcher slogging back after it in his heavy shin pads and chest protector while the boy ran alertly home and the pitcher slammed his glove on the plate in frustration.

In the bottom of the inning he had saved the game, too. He had come charging down the steep hill that passed for right field, plucking the little white dot off his knees. In the stands, his father had jumped up to watch him make the play: a small, blurry figure, slipping down the ridge with a grace that should not have been possible for his age. He grabbed the ball, then let himself fall effortlessly, rolling over and over, to the bottom of the hill— where he came to his knees and held the ball up, not triumphantly, but simply with a professional flourish so the umpire could see it.

When they got back to the car, they both could see from the size of the gas puddle that it could not make the six miles to home. The boy didn't say anything, not wanting to embarrass his father. But Evan Barr refused to admit his mistake, even when they got in and the gas gauge pointed to less than empty.

"Come on, we can make it," he said, shrugging and grinning at his son. "There's always more than they tell you. That's the beauty of the old cars."

When the motor coughed, then sputtered out, still a full mile and a half from their home, he cut the ignition and let the car glide down a long decline. The boy would always remember that smooth, silent ride. They sailed down the black tar road—past the houses sleeping behind their neat little lawns, and stone walls crowned with fragrant clusters of lilacs and blackberries. They coasted down through the unmatched stillness of a small New England town after nine o'clock at night, asleep way out in the middle of nowhere. They rode as if they were on air, the only sounds the lapping of waves on the rocks, the faint ringing of the marker buoys out by the edge of the harbor—and the whoosh of their own tires along the tar.

In the car he watched his father's face, looking skeletal (but still foolish) by the light of the streetlamps. Alternately lighted and foolish, and in dark, solemn silhouette, grinning at him, looking back at the road, grinning at him again like it was the greatest fun in the world.

The car finally came to a stop in front of the small, bleached chapel that the boy's mother took him to every Sunday (Evan Barr disdained the church as yet another one of the town's servile conventions, and was anyway usually too hung over to get out of bed). The boy had worried that his father would fly into one of his furies over the car's indisputable demise. But instead he saw that he was still smiling.

"Here, give me a hand with this."

The boy got behind the wheel and steered as his father pushed it over to the side of the road. It was one of his favorite things to do. He had been steering broken-down cars while his father pushed them since he was seven years old, and was proud of the trust his father placed in him.

"There, that should do it."

They left the car on the side of the road, not bothering to lock it. Nobody in the town stole cars that worked, let alone anything owned by Evan Barr.

They took a shortcut home, following a thin path made by rail tracks to a quarry in the woods. The quarry pit had flooded out long ago, and the tracks had been torn up for the scrap metal. They had left behind only the railbed impression through the brier woods. The remaining path was called Mosquito Lane, and the two of them hesitated before they entered, thinking of how they would itch. Finally the boy's father shrugged his shoulders and went ahead.

"C'mon." He grinned foolishly back at his son. "Can't be too bad. It's too cool for 'em tonight."

They walked on sandy, sunken earth, under a canopy of tall trees. It was dark, and his father stumbled a little along the uneven path. But he moved calm and unhurried, staring up at what could be seen of the sky through the treetops.

This surprised the boy, for Evan Barr was not the sort of man who noticed the scenery, or the weather. But he even spoke gently as they walked, and not about his latest scheme to make money, or those questions about his mother that always confused him so much. Instead he told him stories about the games he had seen at Fenway Park in Boston, decades before.

"I seen Williams play, plenty of times. When he was at his peak, too, right after the war. I seen him the last game before he went to Korea. They gave him a night in his honor. They gave him a standing O, every time he came out on the field.

"He had a great night, too, hit a couple home runs. But he never tipped his cap for 'em. Nevah did. Not even the last game he ever played, when he hit a home run his last time up in the major leagues."

The thick briers and the tall oaks along the trail gave way to stunted tree trunks, then high grass and reeds. They were passing along the edge of a swamp, and soon they were both swatting vigorously at their arms and at the high, whining noise in their ears. The boy's father let his arms fall to his sides, as if the mosquitoes weren't there at all. With a great effort, the boy lowered his arms, too.

"He wouldn't give 'em the satisfaction," Evan Barr continued. "And why should he? He was bettah than all of 'em put together."

"Did you see the time he threw the bat?" the boy asked.

"Nah, I didn't see it. I was still a kid then. I remember hearin' about it, though. Hit the top of the dugout, bounced up an' hit Joe Cronin's cleaning lady in the head. Cronin was the manager, but he forgave him for it. So did the cleaning lady. But that's when they started to turn on him. They wanted to run him out of Boston for that.

"He was just mad about strikin' out, that's why he threw it. It was just a foolish kid thing to do. Hell, they shoulda been happy that he cared that much.

"But they never forgave him. Not until the end. That's why he used to spit at the crowd. They turned on him, even though he was the greatest hitter in the game."

The boy already knew all about it. He had read every word he could find about Ted Williams, after he had come across an article in *Sports Illustrated*. It was called "The Art of Hitting," and on the cover was a picture of Williams staring out at the pitcher with cool menace. Beside him was drawn in a colored grid to show the exact dimensions of the strike zone.

"Better than Yaz. Better than anybody except for maybe Di-Maggio," his father was saying, shaking his head like he still couldn't believe the fans had turned on him.

"You saw DiMaggio play, too?" the boy asked, eager to keep his father talking about baseball. In fact he had only a vague idea of DiMaggio, as a dignified, white-haired man who did coffee-machine commercials on TV.

"Sure, I seen him play. Cuss, by then he was gettin' old. His legs'd started to go. He could hardly run some days, but he'd still come in an' kill the Sox. They would get off to a good start every year, build up a little lead. Then DiMaggio an' the Yankees would come into town an' just kill us.

"You know, his brother Dom played center field for the Sox, an' all those bums sitting out in the bleachers made up a little song they'd sing to Joe, thinkin' they were wicked clever."

The boy's father stopped in the middle of the woods and tilted his head back. He cleared his throat, then sang in an unexpectedly high and wavering voice:

> *"Better than his brother Joe—*
> *Dom-in-ic Di-Magg-i-o!"*

"Like that. But it wasn't true. They just made fools of themselves with that song. Dom was a good ballplayer, all right, but Joe was better. No question. He could hit for power, an' average, an' he was the best centerfielder you ever saw. He could do more things than Williams.

"But no one could hit like him. No one could ever hit like Ted Williams."

His father held one hand out, palm up, as if he were weighing just how good a hitter Williams was.

"He could hit the ball anywhere he wanted to. There was this guy out in the rightfield seats who used to ride him all the time. He called Williams everything in the book. He was a bigmouth, you could hear him all around the ballpark.

"One day Williams started hitting balls at the guy. Right in the middle of a game. He must've sliced ten, twenty foul balls within a seat or two of that bigmouth out there. Any one of 'em could've been a home run if he had wanted to put 'em a few feet to the left, on the other side of the foul pole, but he didn't. The pitcher started gettin' mad when he saw what Williams was doin'. He started throwin' outside the strike zone, tryna throw things he thought he couldn't hit.

"But Williams still got hold of 'em. And he hit everything right at the bigmouth. The bum finally hadda move his seat an' go sit up under the roof, with the pigeons, where you couldn't hear his big fat mouth so good anymore."

His father laughed just to think of it, and the boy laughed with him. He had listened without interruption, glad to hear him talk. He knew the story, of course. He knew everything about Williams. About how he had 20-10 vision, and a perfect picture of the strike zone in his head. How he never swung at a bad pitch. How he was a war hero, a fighter pilot, a great outdoorsman, and how he liked to come back with his gun in the off-season and kill the pigeons, shooting around the empty park.

He knew all the strange-sounding nicknames: Teddy Ballgame. The Splendid Splinter. The Kid. He liked that last one the best. The Kid. He used to pretend it belonged to himself at night, when he sat up in bed with a flashlight, poring over that old issue of *Sports Illustrated*. It was from the town library, and it was the only thing the boy had ever stolen in his life. He hadn't been able to get enough of it, of the story of Williams, and all the pictures inside.

"Yah, we seen some good ballplayers, you an' me," his father was grinning at him in the darkness. He put an arm around his shoulders, and the boy looked up gratefully at him, and the row of mosquito silhouettes dancing on the back of his neck, unnoticed, at least in pretend.

"The players are bigger nowadays. Faster, better athletes. But they don't have the intensity like that."

His father took him to one game a year in Boston, for his birthday. They would catch the Boston & Maine in the late afternoon, or early in the morning if it was a Sunday game. It was the only time the boy got to ride on a train, and he would sit up in the green patent-leather seats with his face to the dirty windows all the way into North Station, watching the towns go by.

His father walked him all around the park, every time. First they would stand on Landsdowne Street, watching the nets billow out over the top of the great leftfield wall, then they would circle around to the rows of souvenir shops on Van Ness. The street was filled with men moving slowly into the park. The evening air was thick with their cigar smoke and the smell of charcoal from the vendors selling roasted peanuts and soft pretzels. They moved on through the graceful brick archways and the old-fashioned turnstiles of the park—and then, suddenly, there would be the green, electrified field. They would walk up the ramp to their seats and it would burst out before them: the field of perfect grass, glowing under the rows of rooftop lights.

It made him feel heady, like those first sniffs of the crazy spring breeze out in his backyard. His father would let him go down and hang around the rail by the dugouts or the bullpen, thinking he wanted to beg autographs, or be close to the players' languid warmup tosses and pepper games.

But what he really looked at was the field. The players were exciting, too—much bigger in person than they looked on TV, their uniforms immaculate and richly colored, movements big and easy, yet amazingly quick and powerful. But he spent most of his time gazing at the perfect field, every inch of it groomed and raked: the fine-cut grass, the straight white foul lines of chalk—even the carefully combed warning-track dirt.

Every game was exciting, even when the Sox lost. The most amazing thing to him, even more than the field, was the way his father was treated as an equal by the men around them. He would talk in slow, solemn tones with them about the game being played out in front of them now, and about past games and past players. The boy was surprised to see the other men listening to his father, and nodding somberly and respectfully at his opinions—as if he were anyone else.

Walking along in the woods now, he was seized by a desire to ask his father why that was. He wanted to know why he could seem smart enough somewhere else, but could not keep his foolishness from shining through in town. He wanted to know if it was something his father could manipulate at will, or if it was just this small place that he could not stand.

The boy could not find the words he needed, though, and the

conversation soon devolved into his father's usual questions about how he was doing in school, and on the team. They were casual questions, for his father maintained only a sketchy interest in what he was doing. He was vaguely proud of his successes in sports, vaguely urgent that his son get his grades up.

"Can't have too much education," he said, as he always said when anything regarding school came up.

"I never had the chance at a good college education. 'Course, I would've done what I done anyway. I was always too independent to be cooped up in a classroom, some company boardroom."

Inevitably he turned the conversation around to women.

"You're not datin' anyone yet? You got a sweetheart?"

The boy shook his head, embarrassed. There were a number of girls hovering in the background, particularly after the games. But he had been too shy to ask any of them out, to do anything but go out with large groups of other boys to hang around the mall out on Route 128.

It didn't matter. His father was not terribly interested in his answer anyway. He much preferred to turn the topic quickly to his wife.

"Your mother an' I started goin' out when we were juniors in high school. It's a long time, you think you get to know somebody after that long," he said, turning the conversation down a path that always made the boy uneasy.

"You never know with women, though. You think you know 'em, but they don't let on everything. They're mysterious."

The boy could only nod his head helplessly at the mysteriousness of women. Their walk together had begun to go sour, and he was glad to see that the woods were coming to an end.

"That wasn't so bad," his father said, rubbing a hand lightly over his neck. "They don't itch if you don't scratch. Take your mother, now. Whattaya think she's been doin' tonight while we're gone? Huh?"

The boy shook his head again.

"That's the thing. You can't really know. I tell ya, though—if I ever caught anybody—"

He clenched his fists to complete the thought. They had reached the end of the woods path, and came out onto the narrow strip of the old highway that was the last short stretch to home.

They walked down the middle of the road, along the white divider. This route had long ago been bypassed by a wider, more direct highway on the other side of the town, and was now used only by local teenagers for their drag races. The boy could hear them when he lay in bed at night, their motors first audible from very far away, heavy metal music throbbing from their radios. The engines roaring harshly as they passed the house—then dying away again down the road, where he could see the skid marks all running together the next day.

The boy's father continued to talk about the wiles of women, but got quieter and quieter the closer they got to the house. Their home stood back from the road, down a long dirt driveway, and when they reached it he wondered out loud, "I wonder what she is doing, right now. I wonder if she's expecting the sound of the car."

They trod softly up the driveway, the boy trying to match his father's careful footsteps, though he was not sure he should. But out in the dark, with his father, he felt unsure of everything. The wild thought occurred to him that there might even be something going on inside, with his mother. When they came up to the house, the boy started loudly, defiantly up the front steps. But his father hung back again, scraping at the ground with one foot and keeping his head turned away from his son.

"No, you go on in," he whispered to the boy. "I'll be along in a minute. I want to check something."

The boy did as he was told, turned slowly back toward the door and started inside. But then he stopped, and looked back out around the side of the house. He could make out his father running crouched over. Every now and then he would stop and peer up, as if he were trying to make out something through the darkened windows. The boy had a sudden urge to follow him.

Instead he turned away and ran upstair to his bedroom, past the light shard that cut into the hallways from his parents' room. He made only a perfunctory response when his mother called to him, and slipped quietly out of his soft grey uniform with the red numbers she had sewn on the back. He let it lie where it dropped to the floor, instead of carefully folding it like he usually did, and slid into bed under the top sheet. He closed his eyes tightly, thinking that he could make himself go to sleep within seconds if he tried hard enough.

He was still awake a few minutes later, when his mother opened the door of his room. He could feel her cool hand as it caressed his cheek, could hear her pick up his uniform and place it over a chair. He kept his eyes shut, tight. But he was still awake when he heard his father come up the stairs and go into his parents' room, closing the door behind him.

9

No one can stop a home run. No one can understand what it
really is unless you have felt it in your own hands and body.

—SADAHARU OH

Dickhead Barry Busby

I started out as a copyboy with the old *Mirror*, then I caught
on with the *Herald-Tribune*. It wasn't much to start out—I covered college swim meets, some track and field. I tried to jazz
'em up. But it's hard to write great copy sitting in your over-
coat by a swimming pool that's like a sauna. And they would
just chop it up anyway, put in just who won and by how much.
Still, it teaches you to learn your trade that way, from the bottom up.

I was just starting to get better assignments when the war comes
and I do four years in the Navy. I get out, I'm pushing thirty and
still doing features on college divers and boxing undercards. I was
still sleeping on my mother's sofa in the living room.

Then I got a break. End of spring training, 1947, the regular
guy we got on the Giants gets acute appendicitis and I take his
beat. Here I am covering Opening Day, my first major-league ballgame! I stayed up the whole night before in my mother's kitchen,
memorizing the players' names, their numbers, their statistics. I
was gonna be goddamned prepared.

The Old Swizzlehead

I never did like Openin' Day, even before The Home Run That Wasn't A Home Run.

The flies like to talk about how all the teams are even, and anything can happen. But that's the problem. Anything *can* happen. You can't get a good grip on the game yet. A whole season can get away from you in April. Which is why we should have expected something exactly like The Home Run That Wasn't A Home Run to happen on Openin' Day, guaranteeing The Little Maniac a place forever in the hearts of the Shea Stadium faithful.

I got the first nasty surprise of the season, though, when I was headin' up to the field to loosen up. It was my wife. Wanda was standin' behind the visitors' gate, wearin' a round little hat with the official colors of Africa on it.

"That looks nice on you, sugar," I told her. "Black, green, yellow, an' red. Matches with everything."

"Don't sugar *me*, Richard," she said. "You know why I'm here."

"I meant to call you, sugar," I said. "It's just with the season startin' an' everything—"

"Should I let her in, Mr. Falls?" the clubhouse attendant asked me.

"Not just now, thanks," I told him. "You want a pass to the game, honey? I'm sorry I forgot to leave one at the gate."

"What's this?" Wanda said, wavin' a bunch of canceled checks at me. The woman had a one-track mind sometimes.

"Who the hell is Mary Lu Gondrezek?"

"She's just one of the ballgirls down at Fort Pippin," I told her. "Eight years old. I was just givin' her a tip."

"A five-thousand-dollar tip? She's one rich eight-year-old. Don't bullshit me. I know what balls that girl was takin' care of and what tip she got."

"Look, honey, just 'cause you got this check—"

"No, Richard. I don't just have a check." She pulled a whole stack of credit-card receipts out of her purse.

"Eight hundred dollars for flowers. When I called down there, the man told me it was for gardenias. *Gardenias?* You wearing a lot of gardenias these days?"

"That was for my grandmother in Georgia. She *love* her gardenias—"

"Isn't granny drinkin' too much these days? You got another one here, seven hundred ninety-six dollars, Fort Pippin Fine Wines and Liquors."

"Can I help it, I got fine tastes—"

"When we got married you thought a Colt .45 was champagne."

"It was just for a little party with the guys—"

"Oh, yeah. All guys, I know. Any woman come in there, you beat her away with a stick. And this one's the best. Nine hundred forty-two dollars and sixty-eight cents to one Tenille Dunston. Why sixty-eight cents? Another tip?"

"I gotta go, baby. It's time for infield practice—"

"You're an outfielder. You've been in the major leagues twelve years. I know everything, an' I'm tired of this bullshit. I'm tired of you spending your money on every whore in the National League."

"Gotta go—"

"Richard!"

I ran on up to the field, thinkin' about Bruce Emerson, who was goin' for the Cardinals, an' about how I was gonna keep my date with Wanda sniffin' around. Last week of spring training I met this accountant named Lisette who was down there on a cruise vacation. She was a sweet thing, an' I gave her a pass to Opening Day an' told her we'd get to know each other better after the game.

I thought I'd get around Wanda by not tellin' her the season had started, but I shoulda known she'd figure it out, bein' a professor an' all that. At least we had a good club secretary, who spread the free passes out all over the park. The last thing you wanted was to have 'em all in one section, so the wives could look over an' pick out the leading suspects. There used to be some wives on the Phillies who would bring binoculars, just so they could check on who was blowin' kisses to their husbands from the freebies.

Dickhead Barry Busby

When I got to the Polo Grounds, I pushed back the glass from the press-box window and breathed in the air. I took it all in: that strange park, shaped like a giant horseshoe with the short porches in right and left, and the center field that went back forever. I'd never even been to the Polo Grounds before. I was a Dodger fan, an' we didn't go up there to Harlem and they didn't come down to Ebbets Field. And now here I was, my first time, as a god-damned genuine sportswriter, up in the press box.

I put my Smith-Corona portable right up against the open window, and I typed my notes during the game, inning by inning. I put in everything—what the count was, where each ball was hit. The other writers thought this was extremely funny. They kept looking over my shoulder and laughing.

I didn't care. The Giants were pounding the Cubbies, and I thought it was a great game. They had some hitters—Johnny Mize the Big Cat, and Walker Cooper, and Sid Gordon, who all the Jews loved. I thought how great it was gonna be to cover them all year—if I could just write it up enough to keep the job away from that poor son of a bitch who got sick down in Florida.

They finished the seventh inning, and the Giants had a big lead. I had just finished writing up the inning and put the new sheets down, when this little spring breeze comes and blows every single one of my notes right out the window. There hadn't been a puff of air all day long, but this one breeze takes all my notes. Every goddamned page floated down to the field, or off into the stands.

There was some old reporter from the *World* sitting next to me, I remember, and he just laughed and laughed. He said, "Wel-come to the big leagues, kid!" and then he called all his pals over to show 'em what happened. He thought it was the funniest god-damned thing in the world.

I wrote up the game all right, even without the notes. I got the beat, and I covered the Giants until they moved out of New York. That first Opening Day makes a good story now. I tell it on myself. But then I wanted to punch his big slob face in.

The Old Swizzlehead

I heard the voice over by the first-base dugout. I just ignored it
at first. There's always somebody in the stands tryna get your attention, to get your autograph or yell somethin' nasty at you. But
this one kept callin', over and over again, soft an' respectful:

"Ricky," it said, "Ricky. Ricky."

I finally looked over despite myself an' that's when I saw John
Bell, my cousin an' homeboy from the projects. He was standin'
by the dugout holdin' a little girl in his arms, an' there was a boy
not much bigger by his side.

"Ricky. Hey, Ricky."

"How you doin'?"

"Fine, man. Just fine."

I went over an' shook hands with him. I didn't want to, but I
thought it was the least I could do.

"You're lookin' good, look like you're still in shape," I told
him.

"Yeah, well, I still get down to Riverside most weekends. I gotta
play with the older guys, though. Kids too quick for me now."

"I don't believe that."

"It's true," he told me, an' the side of his face lifted up in a
half-smile, maybe. "But I make up for it. I play 'em dirty. Hey, I
been meanin' to tell you, thanks for the passes."

I got his letter back in January. Nice, respectful letter, written
up on the typewriter, askin' if I could get him a couple tickets,
just for his kids. I passed it on to the front-office people, but I
kept intendin' to get back to him myself.

"No problem, man. You sure I got enough? They good seats?"

"Yeah, beautiful. Marla woulda come, but she hadda stay home
with the youngest. She's got a bad fever or somethin'."

"That's too bad. How many you got now?"

"Still three," he said, puttin' an arm around his boy. The kids
both looked at me with their mouths open.

"Eddwena here, and Jamal, an' the baby, Lorynne."

"That's great, man," I said, not knowin' what else to say.
"They're gettin' big."

"How 'bout you, Ricky? You an' Wanda got any kids yet?"

"No, not yet."

He didn't seem to know what to say then, either. John Bell faded back like a man who had walked through a door he wasn't supposed to open.

"All right, I'll catch you later," he said, movin' back up the aisle with his kids. "Come by sometime when you're in town. Me an' Marla'd love to see you."

"I will, I will."

"Friend a' yours?" asked Dickhead Barry Busby, naturally stickin' his nose in everyplace it didn't belong.

"That was the best natural athlete I ever saw," I told him.

"Oh, yeah? Best natural athlete I ever saw was Jim Brown. All-American in football *and* lacrosse at Syracuse. Now there was a man."

"What you want, anyway?" I asked him. "You been pumpin' the DC lately?"

"Funny," he says, adjustin' the collars on his plaid leisure suit. "Fooling the reading public like that."

Barry hated me an' Maximilian Duke since we pulled the great DC drug investigation on him a few years before. It didn't even start out to be a practical joke, though he always took it like that. It was just one day me an' the Emp'ror was messin' around with the words. He was gonna go get a Diet Coke, an' he started talkin' about goin' to pump some DC. Dickhead Barry Busby was down on the field, an' he hadda ask about it.

"What's that?" he says. "Is that street talk?"

We both started laughin', but Barry wouldn't let it go. He was sure he was on to a big drug story.

"Sure it is, Barry," I told him. "It's black slang. But I can't tell you any more than that. I might incriminate somebody."

The next day he put it in his column—at the top of "What's the Buzz?"—callin' for an investigation of players pumpin' the DC. We never let it go. Ever since, when he walks into the locker room, somebody says, "Hey, Barry, you been pumpin' that DC?"

"Keep it up," Dickhead Barry tells me. "You guys are gonna be laughing out of the other side of your mouth before Charlie Stanzi gets through with you."

"Maybe Swiz can laugh out of one side of his mouth, and I can laugh out the other," Maximilian Duke says, comin' up to see what's goin' on.

"We'll see who's laughing in a few months. And you'll see what it's like to have to play hard a whole season again—"

But just then Ellie Jay come over to us, an' he was distracted from his usual lecture about how nobody can play like they did forty years ago.

"How's it hanging, Barry?" she asked him, an' he made a face.

"I'm surprised to find you out here," he said. "I thought you'd be in the locker room, exercising your constitutional right to look at the colored guys' peckers."

"I've already seen them all. And you know what? You wouldn't even make the injured reserve list."

"This is a reporter now," he says, shakin' his head. "I used to cover baseball with Red Smith."

"Red Smith hated your guts, Barry."

"Yeah, but you could respect him for it. He was a real baseball man."

He walked off then, an' Ellie Jay shook her head.

"What makes him so miserable?" she asked.

"Forget him. Let's just talk about you an' me, babe," I said, snakin' one arm around her waist. "We got our whole lives ahead of us."

"Sure," she smiled, diggin' her elbow into my stomach. "You can join the Marines, I'll go into the Navy, and we'll each learn a valuable job skill."

She was accustomed to usin' her body to fight men off by now—ballplayers, other flies, even owners. She knew how to use her elbows, her high heels, even her teeth, to keep guys off her.

"My first trip to Chicago, I walked into the Cubs' locker room and they were all standing there stark naked with Halloween masks on, rubbing their penises," she told me once. "All the other writers let me go in alone, too. They thought it was a big joke. I think they would've really enjoyed a gang rape."

"What'd you do?"

"I looked at them and said, 'Which one of you little pricks struck out with the bases loaded in the seventh?' That cracked 'em up—except for the one who did. Guys always love anything to do with penis size.''

Some ballplayers never could get used to her in the clubhouse, even ones who were cool about everything else. They'd snap her butt with towels, or throw buckets of water on her chest. She gave it back to them, one way or the other. It's what she had to do to cover this game, an' she never complained about it.

We got to be friends, despite her strange resistance to sleepin' with me. She always got her quotes right, she didn't ask too many stupid questions, an' she didn't talk all the time about how great Babe Ruth used to be. She still looked fine, too, after all these years, still had that dark flare in her eyes, an' I told her so.

"Thanks, Swiz," she said. "But you're full of shit. I look my age, and I know it."

"What's that? Twenty-three, twenty-four?"

"I've put in too many years following one team or another around the country to look young anymore. Too many years drinking with those other idiots up in the press box to show them what a man I am. And too many years of you guys, Swiz."

"What about all the admiration you get from us, angel?"

"I don't even mean all the arm-wrestling I still have to do to get through a locker room," she said. "It just doesn't mean much anymore. You guys have a career year one season, and the next you stink, and the year after you're busted for coke. You don't even stay *on* the same teams for more than two years in a row. Always bitching and whining about everything, while you all become millionaires—"

She stopped herself then, and laughed. She had a nice, deep laugh, full of cigarette smoke an' whiskey, and it came easy.

"Goddammit, I *am* getting old. I'm beginning to sound like the rest of those old drunks up there. Next thing you know, I'll be talking about Walter Johnson."

"It ain't such a bad life," I told her. "For anybody."

"It's just that I sat down to write my usual Opening Day piece yesterday. You know: 'Spring comes to a former ash heap in Queens.' I got halfway through the lead, and I wanted to cut my wrists. I started thinking about the columns and all the game stories I've written over the years. About all the games that didn't mean a thing, and all the great controversies nobody remembered ten minutes later. All those words about nothing, and who is ever going to read them again?"

"You do a good job," I said, and meant it, though I was already wondering if there was other ways I could console her.

"I know it's just a game. I told myself that when I went into it. But it gets harder every year. Except—"

"Yeah. Except when you see *him* play."

That girl was still soft on John Barr. She'd been hooked the moment she laid eyes on him, down in Hell's Gate, an' she never got over it. It was the one weakness she had. She never got the nerve to say anything to him about it, not after all this time. It was in the way she looked at him, the way she talked about him. An' he never gave her any indication back that he cared, 'less you consider his not quite gruntin' so much as he did with the other flies.

"I just love watching him play the game—"

"Oh, yeah. It's love on a kinda higher plane."

"There's got to be something more to him. Something to make him play like that, year in and year out."

"How can you be sure? Maybe he's just a robot. Maybe there's nothing behind it at all."

"You don't think that, Swiz."

"No. No, I don't," I told her slowly. "But what else could there be? You tried checking it out already."

That first year down in Hell's Gate, Ellie Jay had tracked down where Barr was from, just like she said she would. She was set to find out all about him. The problem was that nobody would say a thing to her.

"A guy like that, puts the whole place on the map, and nobody would say a thing. Hitler's hometown talked more about him."

All she could find out was that Barr went to the local high school, an' that he was a three-sports star into his junior year.

"Then he just stopped playing. A real prospect in baseball, football, and basketball, and he just quit. He stayed in school and everything, got his diploma. But he didn't pick up a bat or a glove again until he walked into Hell's Gate. And nobody will say a goddamned thing about it. I couldn't even get ahold of his family."

"So what makes you think you can do it now?"

"You're gonna help me, Swiz—"

"Oh, no—"

"It's a book idea, actually. You know him better than anybody, Swiz. I want you to tell me everything you know. I want you to watch him, to keep track of everything that goes on this season."

"I'm not rattin' out anybody in no book. Besides, is this about him or me?"

"Both. And everything else, too. I see it as a thinking man's guide to a typical baseball season—"

"With a few lurid stories thrown in for color."

"All you have to do is talk into a tape recorder, tell me about what it's like being a ballplayer today. Who knows, maybe it'll help you get a broadcast job someday."

"Oh, yeah. That's what I wanna do. Sit there an' talk about pitch selection, an' desire."

"It's really not about the book, Swiz," she said, givin' me a look. "I want to find out what he is, exactly. I want the whole man. I think that's the key."

"You might be disappointed," I said, as I started back to the dugout. "We all might be."

I didn't think the unpleasant surprises was ever gonna end by the time I went in to look over the lineup, but the nastiest one was still waitin' for me. There was already a whole crowd around the card Stanzi had posted, starin' at it like they was paralyzed.

At first it looked just like the same lineup we had for the last ten years. Me leadin' off, followed by Bobby Roddy second and The Emp'ror third. The bottom four slots were the same, too: Lonnie Lee battin' sixth, Spock Feeley seventh, No-Hit Hitt eighth, an' the pitcher Moses Yellowhorse hittin' ninth.

The trouble was in the middle. For the first time since his first month up in the major leagues, John Barr wasn't batting fourth. The greatest hitter in the history of the game, an' Charlie Stanzi had moved him down a notch. And in his old position was the Third Base Phee-nom, Terry White.

"That's my lineup," Stanzi says, comin' up from the clubhouse just then. "Anybody got any problems with that?"

He had his arms crossed over his chest and he tried to sound hard. But a grin was leakin' out from his scrunched-up little mouth, an' you could tell he was lovin' it. It was like he was daring us to do something.

"Has Barr seen this?" I asked The Emp'ror.

"He's still down in the clubhouse, taking his swings in front of the mirror," he said. "Shit, can you imagine what I'm going to hit this year with that rook behind me in the order?"

"It won't ever happen," I told him. "John Barr comes up here, sees where he's hittin', an' that's gonna be the end of Charlie Stanzi."

But Barr never even looked at the card. When he came up, he just went through his usual routines before a game: rubbing his hands down with rosin to make sure he had a good grip, swinging a couple bats together to get used to the weight, checking the centerfield flags to see which way the wind was blowin'. It disappointed The Little Maniac most of all. He thought maybe John Barr just assumed he was hitting fourth, an' he went right over to him to make sure he knew.

"I got you in the number-five slot today," he said, standin' real close to the man, the way he did when he was tryna goad the umpires.

"Yah," said Barr.

"I know it's different from where you're used to hitting," Stanzi tried again. But Barr didn't say a word, just picked up the tar rag an' ran it smooth an' careful down his bats.

"I think he might get careless with the kid," Stanzi said, like he was almost apologizin' for it. He knew how it sounded, an' it just made him madder. His whole face was beginnin' to turn red, but Barr wouldn't give him the satisfaction. He just stood up an' looked at him with those drowned man's eyes.

"It ain't where I hit," he said, an' turned back to his bats. Stanzi's face puckered up again, an' he went to take his lineup card out to the ump.

When they finally got around to startin' the game, it didn't feel right, just like I expected. The first pitch comes in an' all of a sudden you're playin' the new season, just like that.

We were too tight, an' it showed. Moses Yellowhorse was sober, but he was all over the plate anyway. He walked the first two Cardinals he faced, an' one run scored when Bobby Roddy an' Lonnie Lee messed up a double-play ball between 'em. They got another when Terry White let a ball roll right through his legs. Moses wouldn't have got out of the inning if John Barr hadn't made a nice running catch in the rightfield corner.

It was Barr who got us back in the game right away, too. Emerson decided to challenge him with the fastball, an' Barr hit it four hundred fifty feet on a line. It went right out, over deep center field, an' by the time the fans even realized it was out of the park an' started clappin' he was halfway around the bases, running quick an' hard just like he did on any other hit. They were on their feet by the time he reached home, but Barr didn't tip his cap, or look up, or do anything else to acknowledge 'em. He popped straight down into the dugout like he always did, an' sat there on the bench, waitin' for the fans to settle down an' the game to start again.

The home run helped steady us, an' Moses began to find the plate again. He kept us in the game, but he threw a lot of pitches, an' Stanzi pulled him after the sixth for Skeeter Mesquite. We didn't exactly like that either, since Skeeter was supposed to be the right-handed closer, just used for late innings when the game was on the line.

"He keeps bringing him in by the sixth like this, and Skeeter won't have an arm left by August," The Emp'ror said.

But we could tell The Little Maniac really wanted to win this one. He was treatin' it like a World Series game. In the seventh, No-Hit Hitt got thrown out on a close play and Stanzi was right out of the dugout, tearin' into the first-base ump. Like anything else in baseball, you got to pace your ump raggin', or they'll call 'em against you out of pure spite. But Stanzi did his whole routine. First he kicked up dirt all over the ump's shoes an' pants legs. Then he made his patented move of turnin' his cap around, so when he was yellin' in the ump's face he could get close enough to really let the spit fly on him. He stopped just as the home-plate ump was walkin' up the line to throw him out of the game.

"You can't let 'em think they can get away with anything," he said, an' winked at Old Coach Plate as he walked back to the dugout. But his face was all red, an' I couldn't tell if he'd really been in control or not.

"Can't any of you pussies hit the ball?" he burst out at us when his pinch-hitter made the first out of the eighth. He was ballin' his pants legs up an' down in his hands, kneadin' 'em back and forth across his thighs. It looked to me like he wanted to win that one game more than any he ever managed, and I wondered how he was ever gonna last the whole long season.

We knew we could take this game if we could just get to Emerson. By the eighth, sure enough, he was starting to tire, an' the Cards didn't have a pen. I legged a triple into the left-center gap, Bobby Roddy drew a walk, an' the Cards yanked Emerson—too late. The Emp'ror hit the new boy's first pitch into left for a single and one run, to tie it up. Terry White fanned for the fourth time on the day, but Barr hit another one to almost the same place he hit his home run.

This one just nicked the top of the centerfield fence, an' stayed in the park for a double. But it scored two runs, and on the next pitch Barr stole third an' drew a high throw that bounced past the third baseman and on down the line. We were up by three with Al The Fade Abramowitz out on the mound for the ninth.

But Al was tight an' cold like everybody else. He didn't have the fadeaway workin' yet, an' the Cards waited on it, since they couldn't see the ball anyway. He got two outs, but he walked the bases full with Tom Big T Paradee comin' up. An' that was when The Little Maniac decides he has to play genius an' come out to the mound. Spock Feeley tried to cut him off, but he was already out there an' strategizin' before he could do anything.

"Oh-oh," Maximilian Duke calls to me from over in left field, when he sees Stanzi walk out.

"Whiff Dick."

"What do you suppose he's telling him?"

"Prob'ly to throw the super-duper pitch," I told him. "Prob'ly to throw the unhittable pitch to win the game."

But The Little Maniac had a even more complex strategy, as Feeley related to me later.

"High an' inside, Al," he tells The Fade. "High an' inside all the way."

"He throws one pitch," Feeley told him. "Let him throw the fucking thing."

"High an' inside," was all he told Al The Fade again.

"But it doesn't *do* that!" Al The Fade protested. "It just fades away down off the inside or the outside corner."

"You got a fastball, dontcha?"

"I guess so," Al The Fade said, adjustin' his glasses an' lookin' down at Big T Paradee, pumpin' his thirty-six-ounce bat at him. Paradee was the kind of ballplayer you could see the hair on his chest 'cause of all his muscles. They kept him from closin' his shirt all the way.

"Then throw him your fastball high and inside."

"It ain't very fast."

"I don't care how fast it is. Just throw it now."

An' here Feeley said The Little Maniac even winked at Al The Fade an' smiled to reassure him.

"Throw it. You'll see. He won't be expecting it."

The Little Maniac was wrong, as usual. But even being wrong, the next pitch was what got him in with the fans for the rest of the season. It was so even though Al The Fade's high, inside fastball sailed in there big an' slow as the Number One Broadway Local, an' the Big T Paradee hit it into the upper deck in right field for a grand-slam home run an' four runs.

That should've been it, but it wasn't. Instead it was the making of The Little Maniac, Charlie Stanzi. I saw it happen. I saw it all right in front of me from center field, like some bad hop that rolls slowly up a shortstop's arm and off into center field before he can find the handle.

I saw the big white bat come floatin' down from the stands, just as Al The Fade was about to start his windup. At first I even thought it was real, since you never know what the fans will throw on the field. It turned out to be only a balloon, of course. One of those big inflatable things they sell at the souvenir stands. That explains why it came drifting down so slow, just settling on the field by first base.

I saw it. But Al The Fade didn't. He was lookin' at the plate, an' the Big T Paradee standin' down there, eyein' him like his next meal. He couldn't hear nothin' either, not with the crowd all clappin' an' stampin' for the last out. He went into his motion, pulling his arms back, an' starting to swing his right foot forward. The Big T wiggled his bat—

That was when I saw the bat—an' I saw Stanzi. He was walkin' out of the dugout, wavin' his arms, with his mouth open. I couldn't hear what he was yellin'. But the ump at first base was still wipin' his face from the tobacco strands Stanzi'd spit on him in the seventh, an' when he sees The Little Maniac comin' out, he jumps back an' waves his arms for time out.

Al The Fade didn't see either one of 'em. He goes ahead an' pitches, an' throws that high an' inside fastball. The Big T Paradee slams it into the upper deck in right field an' starts to lumber around the bases with a big grin on his face. The fans all go quiet as death, instantly.

Only slowly do they start to breathe an' yell again, because they spotted The Little Maniac walkin' out toward first base. He was walkin' slow an' confident, not even botherin' to shout an' wave his arms this time, an' they all got to their feet 'cause they knew he was gonna do somethin' to save the game.

An' the umpire stood out there at first base, holding that fat white souvenir bat limp in his hand, an' lookin' kinda sad. Because he knew now that he had to make The Little Maniac a hero.

It was a fool move for Stanzi, callin' time like that at the last second. If Al The Fade had seen him calling for it an' pulled up short he might've tore up his knee, been lost for the year. But he didn't see him. And it didn't really change a thing. It didn't affect the play at all, an' if the ump had called time himself an' nobody else had seen it he would've been just as glad to swallow it an' let the runs stand.

But Stanzi had seen him. He'd been lookin' right at the man when he called it, an' the ump had to go over an' tell the Cardinals that the runs didn't count, an' would they just please go back to the way things were before. It was The Home Run That Wasn't A Home Run.

Everything broke loose after that. The Cards went nuts, but there wasn't nothin' they could do about it. They bitched so much the umps finally had to throw out their manager an' all their coaches, even after givin' 'em some consideration for their temperament. They threw out the Big T Paradee, too, after he chucked all the batting helmets, the bat rack, the water cooler, an' most of his uniform up on the field. The Cards said they were playin' the game under protest, an' takin' it to the commissioner, an' threatened to walk off the field right then an' there.

But of course they didn't. They had too much hope they could win the game still, even with the home run taken away an' a third-string catcher up there pinch-hitting for the Big T. You're always hopin' somehow there will be justice in this game, even when you know there won't.

Al The Fade finished off the pinch hitter with three straight fadeaways that Spock Feeley was callin' all the way, without even lookin' toward the bench. We ran off that field with fifty thousand fans on their feet, yellin' an' screamin' like we just clinched the pennant.

After the game, all the flies were around The Little Maniac's office, list'nin' to him tell 'bout The Home Run That Wasn't A Home Run—like it was some sort of brilliant strategy.

"You gotta know the rules of the game," he was sayin', an' they all nodded their heads.

"You gotta know the rulebook inside out," he said, an' they all wrote it down in their little notebooks.

John Barr had three hits plus his stolen base, made that nice catch in the first, an' threw some sucker out at second that probably saved us another run. But the only one over by his locker was Ellie Jay, makin' meaningful eyes at him an' tryna ask him serious questions about a baseball game.

"How did it feel to be in the number-five spot today?" she asked him.

"Fine," he said, lookin' at her like he didn't even know what she was talkin' about.

"Did it hurt your concentration?"

"Hitting's hitting. It don't matter where you do it."

"Do you think Charlie Stanzi's trying to send you a message with this move?"

Another shrug.

"He's the manager. He can do what he wants."

That was all she got. Barr just went about takin' hisself apart after the game as quick as he did puttin' hisself together. He always got out of his uniform right away and straight back into his street clothes. He never even showered in the clubhouse—just put his clothes on an' walked right out, like he couldn't wait to be out of the ballpark.

"Yeah, I think he's about to open right up," I told her. "How long this book gonna be, anyway?"

"I'm gonna get him talking yet, one way or the other," she said, lookin' after him.

"You don't think maybe he's just dumb, do you?"

"No, and you don't either," she said, her eyes flashin'. "He's got depth, and I'm going to dig it out, goddamm it."

I took my own time gettin' ready, figurin' maybe Wanda would get tired of waiting an' go home. She wasn't anywhere in sight when I picked Lisette up by the players' gate. I kept my head down as we eased past the autographers at the gate, just in case, but I thought we gave her the slip. We was almost past the crowd when there was a tapping on the passenger's side window.

There she was, smilin' underneath that official African cap, motioning real friendly for Lisette to roll down the window. Like she was a fan who just wanted to say somethin' nice.

"Don't touch it!" I yelled over to her, but it was too late. As soon as Lisette had that window down six inches, Wanda hit her with a straight jab, right in the face. I mean, she hit her with her *fist.*

"Come on out of there! Come on—the both of you!"

I braked the car an' tried to scramble across the seat. But Wanda already had the door open, an' she reached inside with one hand an' pulled Lisette out by her hair.

"Get your ass home, girl!" she said, an' gave Lisette a backhand an' then a good kick in the rear to get her on her way. The girl ran off whimpering toward the parkin' lot, an' she didn't look back.

"Whatta you doin'? That was just a family friend—"

"I told you not to bullshit me."

"All right. It's the wife of this new kid we got up. She needed a lift. I didn't want you to get the wrong idea."

"Uh-huh."

"It was only physical. I been spoiled by you for any other woman. That's the truth—"

But she just turned and started walkin' in the direction where Lisette had run off. Then I saw she wasn't walkin' after Lisette at all. That's when I started to get fearful. She was goin' toward where she had my antique Caddy parked. The green one with the old-style fins, which The Emp'ror had convinced me to buy as an investment an' keep stored away in the garage all the time.

"You take that out of here. That car's supposed to be home, appreciating," I told her.

She paid me no never mind, just slid in behind the wheel an' gunned the motor. She brought that old Caddy tearin' up over the curb an' I tried to get in front of her, but it's hard to play chicken with a car when you ain't got one yourself. She must've been goin' thirty already when she smashed into the side of my Japanese luxury car. With that big old Caddy she caved in both side doors, but she didn't stop there. She backed it right up an' hit the Jap car again, head on.

"You're wrecking my investment!" I yelled at her, bangin' on the trunk of the Caddy to get her attention.

She almost run me over when she backed up again. She hit that Japanese car in the front, then the back, then in the front again until you couldn't have got those two cars apart with an acetylene torch. She knocked out all the headlights on both of 'em, took out the rear windows, an' ripped the fenders off. She banged around on that car until it was a little Japanese lump, an' the Caddy wasn't much better.

Then she straightened her African cap, walked over to me like she was just back from pickin' up the groceries, an' handed me the decapitated steering wheel of the Caddy.

"A souvenir," she told me, an' kissed me on the cheek. "Let's see how your bimbos like driving around in a rented car." She walked off to get a cab, and some of the stadium cops came runnin' up to see what was goin' on.

"Somethin' the matter, Swiz?" one of 'em asked me.

"Nah," I said. "She just be that way."

I always hate Opening Day. You can't get anything right.

10

The Boy

It was during that spring, too, that Evan Barr finally decided to paint the house.

As usual, his decision was a mystery. His wife had pleaded with him for years to paint it. Each spring, the house emerged from the snow with more of its old white coat gone, until the exposed wood began to curl and rot from the soaking it took every winter. During the worst storms, the water would seep into the corners of the rooms in little puddles. Sometimes it even iced over, like the woods puddles, driving the boy's mother almost to despair.

Yet each spring Evan would shrug his shoulders and say there wasn't enough money. When his wife was most adamant, he would even agree to do it—and then do nothing at all. When all else failed, he would nod confidently and say that next year they would have enough money to hire painters. This was always outrageous enough to end the argument completely—to send her running back to the kitchen, and more frenzied scrubbing and sweeping.

But this windy, indecisive spring he decided to do it—though not in white again. Almost every other house in the town was white or brown or grey. Evan Barr picked out a bright shade of red from the thick color catalogue down at I. F. Mattson's hardware store, and insisted on it even though he had to place the color on two-week order.

"You sure you want red now, Mistah Bahr?" Old Man Mattson teased him in the store. "Don't always hold up so good in the weather, you know. Most folks like a good dahk brown—"

"That's just why I'm taking red," the boy's father cut him off proudly. He couldn't resist saying it, though the boy knew he was falling into a trap.

For Mattson was one of the bah-bah shop regulars—one of those men who sat around all day pleasantly condemning everyone else in town, their lips flapping like loose chicken skin around false teeth, mouths gaping in wicked smiles.

"Like a bunch a' goddamned sheep, ignorant as their daddies were before them," Evan Barr used to fume.

The day the paint arrived, they assembled one by one by his property fence, like seagulls gathering on the telephone lines when a storm blew in. They came openly, making no bones about their appearance, nodding and calling to Evan as he went about preparing for the big paint job.

"Why don't you wait until tomorrow?" his wife asked him when he stomped back inside, looking around wildly for something. "Let them rot!"

"Can't. Just be back tomorrow, anyways," he said, and the boy knew he was right. They would be back tomorrow and the day after, or any other day he would be painting his house bright red. And if he put it off long enough, they would start spreading the word that Evan Barr had bought paint, but never painted. That would be the new joke: that he had been scared off by a few old busybody men at the barbershop.

He couldn't even say anything to them, ask them what the hell they were doing leaning against his fence. He couldn't stand the thought of the cackling noise they would make then, shaking their heads as they slowly, insolently moved off, pretending to be surprised by such unneighborliness. Already, it was bad enough the way his neck was blushed bright red, veins bulging as they called to him:

"Afternoon, Evan."

"How are ya, Evan?"

"Hear you're gonna be paintin' the place, Evan."

Being that brazen about it, the laughter bubbling up just under their jocular hellos. Evan Barr nodded back as unconcernedly as he could manage, grimly going about his preparations. Trying to act like a man preoccupied with the job in front of him.

Everything was going wrong already, of course, since he never knew how to plan. The first thing was the brushes. They were rock-hard when he finally found them in a corner of the garage, stuck together with the paint from when he had last used them at the hotel, the season before. He had to soak them for a long time in a bucket of turpentine to get them limber, and of course it took him more time to find the old can of turpentine, buried in the cellar—

Then there was the ladder. It hadn't been used for nearly seven years, since he had climbed up to clean out the eaves—only to find them already rotted through by water and decayed leaves. It, too, had been left buried in a far corner of the garage, under-neath a pile of useless car parts, and it looked old and frail by the time he got the grease wiped off it. The boy noticed that there were long cracks running up the handrails.

His father squatted for a few minutes in the sanctuary of the garage, amid the sawdust and the metallic litter on the dirt floor, calculating whether he should go back to Mattson's for a new ladder. But he didn't have the money, and anyway he knew that would just become part of the tale. They would howl to see a man who planned things so slipshodly he didn't have a ladder ready before he bought his paint—

"You might have to give me a hand with this," he said a little ashamedly to the boy, his head half turned. His son nodded gravely back at him.

"Okay."

He squeezed the boy's shoulder, and went ahead and brought out the ladder. Laying it against the house, he could tell right away it was too rickety to hold him up. It swayed wildly before he had gone ten rungs up it, and he saw he would have to stand at the very top in order to reach the gable peaks of the second floor. There was an anticipatory rustle from over by the property fence, and he knew that the men from the bah-bah shop had realized his dilemma already. He climbed back down as nonchalantly as he could, as if making out that he had it planned it this way all along, and was just testing the ladder. He beckoned to his son.

The boy eyed the ladder warily himself. But he came to his father willingly.

"I'm too big for it," Evan told the boy quietly. "I'll hold it tight down heah, you go on up. It shouldn't move too much."

"Sure." The boy tried to smile at him reassuringly. He went up the ladder at once, as an act of faith.

He climbed slowly but determinedly, holding the open paint can in one hand, the brush handle between his teeth. He clutched the ladder with his free hand, and tried not to notice how it creaked and swayed beneath him. As he got higher, he even felt a little excitement. He was up as high as the tops of the trees, which he had only seen before from his bedroom window.

But there was no support beneath him. The ladder buckled and swayed widely despite his father's grip, and each rung bent under his footstep. He wondered if one rung gave out, would the others break too, one after another like in the cartoons, leaving him to tumble all the way to the bottom?

Still, he had to get higher to reach the roof peak. He had to climb until he had outstripped even the dubious security of the handrails, and then balance by the toes of his sneakers alone against the very top rung. He hugged the ladder, slowly sank his brush into the paint, and blindly smeared the first broad stroke of red across the old boards above his head.

"Attaboy!" he heard his father shout below. "Pour it on!"

He moved the brush back and forth, swaying out as far to each side as he dared, becoming steadier and more confident as he worked. Glancing below him, he could see his father grinning, triumphant and defiant, for the bah-bah shop gang was silent for now. It was an edgy, embarrassed silence, many of them looking down at the ground as if they recognized their own culpability in the reckless act now taking place before them. Misunderstanding as usual, Evan Barr was smiling fiercely to see them defeated.

The boy couldn't see much of what he was doing, but he tried to make smooth and careful brushstrokes, not wanting to give the crowd anything to censure. He tried to shut everything else out and paint by feel, despite the ache in his toes arching up on the top rung, the ludicrous plunking of an occasional paint drop on his head. He inched the brush up along the peeled and flaking wood so he wouldn't miss a streak between his strokes.

But even immersed in his concentration he could hear the sound from inside the house. A small, scratching sound, persistent and unsatisfied, barely audible above the sweep of his brush. At first he thought it was a squirrel, or some other small animal or bird that had crawled in through the ruined eaves. Ofttimes they had heard little feet scrambling above the first-floor ceiling, small wings fluttering inside the walls.

But he soon realized what it was: the scuttle of a broom across the floor downstairs. His mother sweeping, cleaning, trying to shut out what was happening. His stomach began to knot, but he tried to paint faster, undulating dangerously back and forth along the top rung.

Behind him, too, a murmur began to rise. It came from the bah-bah shop crowd, as they lost their inhibitions and pointed up at where the boy was painting. His father could hear them talking, too; the ladder shook a little as he looked nervously over his shoulder. A titter, barely restrained, ran through the crowd. It was followed by outright guffaws and mocking snorts. At first Evan Barr didn't believe it. His son could feel him grasp the ladder all the harder, determined to ignore them, the moral energy surging up through the handrails.

"They're cheating..." the boy could hear him whisper, and, crazy as it was, he knew what his father meant and sympathized. He thought it was some new mean trick they were playing, to make him *think* he was doing something wrong. But soon they could both make out the jubilant words drifting across the yard, spoken just loudly enough for them to hear. And they realized their mocking audience was right.

"He didn't scrape it. ... He didn't scrape the old paint off. ..."

"It'll ruin the new coat! It'll ruin it!"

The laughter swelled loud and open now, full of relief that Evan Barr's defiant new approach to painting was after all as devoid of common sense as they could have wished. Relief that they no longer needed to be ashamed of causing a man to risk his son's life on a high ladder. Evan Barr was obviously a damned fool anyway—

"Dammit, get down heah!" his father hissed at him.

The boy stumbled on down.

"I didn't know! I didn't know!" he whispered miserably to his father, close to tears.

"It's all right. It's not your fault."

His father spoke with martyred calm now. The boy had seen him like this a few times before, when reduced to absolute failure. He patted the boy on the head, and walked back toward the garage.

By the time he got back the crowd was quiet again, waiting with the anticipation of a golfing gallery watching a great pro approach the green. They were past all restraints, though, and the laughter and loud talk began to swell gradually as he approached. The boy began to fear that his father had made yet another dreadful mistake, or lost his mind altogether.

Evan Barr was carrying out an armful of assorted garage junk now. A hammer, a box of nails, several long pieces of lumber. And two huge white sheets of plastic, salvaged from some long-forgotten scheme.

But it was soon evident that he had a plan, and the crowd quieted again, each one hoping to be the first to discover what it was and denounce it. He ignored them and set to work furiously, directing his son to help him. The boy didn't see how they could get whatever it was done and still paint any considerable portion of the house before nightfall. He feared that his father was working so ardently just to get the mysterious device itself finished—so the bah-bah shop crowd would go away properly chastised by his brilliance. Gradually it came into shape: a platform of some kind, nailed sloppily together.

"Heah, help me get this up on the side of the house," his father said with his old-car confidence. "No, no. It goes underneath the ladder. Now take this."

His father handed the boy the great swath of white plastic sheeting.

"Tack it up as you go up. Heah, like this."

The boy tacked the white plastic sheets to the platform crossbar as he went back up the ladder. Then he pulled the whole thing up around his shoulders, until just his head and forearms stuck out, with only enough mobility to let him scrape.

His father's inventiveness gradually became clear to him. The plastic sheets all around him blocked off the section of the house that he had already painted from any old white paint chips he would scrape loose. But the boy soon began to suspect that this was another mistake. The chips fell off the plastic and into the new paint anyway. It would have been easier to just wait and scrape the new paint off as well, but that would have meant starting all over, he knew, and then the bah-bah shop men could tell the story about the time Evan Barr painted for a whole day and didn't get anything done.

"Looks like a damned turtle up there!" one of the men called out, and there was another laugh, but for the most part the bah-bah shop gang was quiet again. What was going on now was so convoluted that they seemed intrigued.

The boy glanced down at his father holding the ladder, and saw him grinning again: the same witless, gleeful grin with which he had battled the leaky gas tank. But the boy didn't flinch. He knew his father took the crowd's silence for victory, and he wanted him to have it.

Within a quarter of an hour, though, a light breeze had blown up. It was just a little wind, but it was enough to make the entire paint-scraping structure shake. The boy heard his father curse quietly at the foot of the ladder, and he began to scrape wildly, erratically, trying to get the job done.

There was another gust, still light and playful. But it was enough to billow out the white plastic sheets around the boy and the jerry-rigged platform. They puffed up like sails, pulling the whole canopy a little bit away from the house. Evan Barr staggered backward, trying desperately to steady the ladder and the platform.

But the canopy began to sway far off the house, swinging back and forth. The boy was forced to drop the scraper and clutch on with both hands. He was able to push the ladder temporarily back against the house with his weight, but the wind swung it out again. It pitched back and forth—once, twice—and a tortured shudder ran the length of the wood.

Below him, the boy's father was a skinny, jerking figure pushing impotently against the whole ramshackle structure he had put up. The bah-bah shop crowd stood a little awestruck at what they were seeing. And at that moment, too, he saw his mother run out on the lawn, hands going up to her open mouth—

The boy began to tear the plastic sheeting away from his neck and shoulders. He felt no real peril, but he was just in time. The wind took the white plastic dropcloth again. Ladder and canopy both swung out too far this time, and began to fall backward. With a decisive snapping noise, it all gave way—the plastic sheeting, the ladder, the sloppily nailed boards—and plunged toward the earth. The boy's mother let out a shriek.

But to the boy it seemed like it was all happening very slowly. The whole structure and he with it seemed to be floating to the ground. He had felt this way before, in games—everyone else reacting frantically, while he had the time to move calmly and deliberately. He poised himself on his remaining rung of the ladder, waiting patiently until the ladder was as close to the ground as he could risk, and jumped clear of it—

Years later, he would remember that feeling. He was playing right field in Yankee Stadium, during the World Series, and he climbed the wall to pull down a drive above the top railing in right field. The next day the sports pages would call it one of the greatest catches ever made, but it had seemed simple enough to him. It had just been a matter of gauging the jump, getting a hold on the plastic wall padding with his spikes, and launching himself up—

He landed easily in the high, wild grass of his father's lawn, and rolled over and over again through it. His jump had already propelled him well clear of the ladder, but he simply felt like rolling on through the new spring grass, his eyes closed, blotting out all the stupid staring faces of the crowd, the shock of his father, the terror of his mother—

Finally he reached the edge of the property, and the yard's slope, and flopped out on his back with his arms spread wide, feeling strangely contented and lightheaded. He opened his eyes and looked up into a sea of frightened old faces, and he could have laughed out loud. His fall had shut them up, all right. They had never thought Evan Barr capable of tragedy, and it would surely have given him the last laugh over them. They could practically hear their own disapprobation.

The boy smiled, and they began to laugh again. Laugh harder

than ever: a forced laugh—some of them actually doubling over to make sure Evan Barr saw they hadn't been fooled. The boy felt like he could have stayed lying on his back in the grass forever, but he dutifully stood up and began to walk away.

His mother was running full speed down the yard toward him. Her eyes were wide, her normally stolid Scandinavian jaw wobbling loosely in terror. She clutched him to her right there, in front of the suddenly re-embarrassed bah-bah shop men. Then she held him gingerly out at arm's length, afraid she might be aggravating some terrible internal injury.

"Are you all right? Do you feel all right, everywhere?" she demanded.

"Yes, Momma."

"Nothing hurts anywhere? Not even inside?"

"No, Momma."

She thrust her hard fingers abruptly up along his rib cage and into his stomach. Tremulously she ran her hands along the lengths of his arms and legs. He shied from this sudden search of his body, but she held him tight, until she was assured of his basic wholeness. Then she turned on his father, hovering a few feet away.

"You'll kill him," she said quietly, furiously. "You will kill him with your nonsense."

His father stood before her with his mouth still hanging, arms bent out in different directions. The boy looked over at the remnant of the scaffolding structure, where it had fallen like a wrecked airplane. It occurred to him absently, as if considering someone else's accident, how the plastic sheeting enmeshed in the wood could indeed have snapped his neck like a baby bird's.

His mother swung her arms up abruptly, landing awkward, straight-armed, woman's punches on his father. This time even he couldn't summon up his usual anger, but only cringed and put up his arms defensively. The bah-bah shop crowd began to move away. The boy's mother paid none of them any mind. She finally exhausted herself and strode back toward the house, spitting invective at her husband.

"But you *wanted* me to paint the house," he bleated after her, genuinely bewildered.

"I don't care about the house!" she had shrieked back at him.

"You think you know what you're doing. You can't do anything! You're a stupid, stupid man!"

She stopped again, in front of the kitchen door.

"You're a stupid *little* man!"

The boy stood where he was, stock-still in the yard. He didn't dare move, but his father turned slowly back toward him, as he was afraid he might. The boy thought his face looked as white as the clouds the wind had brought in from the sea, but he did manage to move his lips, and the boy could see to his horror that he was indeed saying something stupid.

"Her," he mouthed, trying to grin. "Hasn't she got a great temper on her?"

11

Anybody who doesn't wanna fuck can leave right now.

—BABE RUTH

Charlie Stanzi, The Little Maniac

You have to go ahead an' grab her pussy in the first ten minutes. If she doesn't do anything, then you know you're on. And if she slaps your face, you still got the whole night to try an' get laid. You might as well find out right away.

The Old Swizzlehead

It was the first big West Coast swing that got us in trouble. Up until then we were winnin', but we were winnin' lucky. We took thirty-five of fifty comin' out of the gate. We did it without even playin' partic'ly good ball, an' usually you don't mind winnin' like that. When you play bad an' still win, you're ahead of the game.

Still nobody could really get untracked. Except for John Barr, of course. He hit just the way he left off the year before, an' just like he did every season, year after year. Bein' moved down a spot didn't make no difference to him. By June he was leadin' the league in anything Dr. Roscoe T. Jones could scrape down on paper an' call a statistic.

But it broke up the lineup. Everybody could pitch around Barr

now, walk him an' leave him stranded at first with the bottom of
the order comin' up. There wasn't much behind him, an' there
was only the great rookie hope in front.

"That boy still can't get off the I-95," I said to Maximilian Duke,
just before the first big road trip.

"The I-95? Hell, he can't get out of the breakdown lane."

Every now an' then some swizzlehead would try to throw a
straight fastball by him an' he'd hit a great big parachute over the
leftfield fence. The Little Maniac would come runnin' out of the
dugout to shake his hand an' pound his can, an' the flies would
all write stories about his potential the next day.

"What's this potential they're always writing about?" The
Emp'ror asked me. "Is that his dog's name?"

"At least he's not lettin' his slump at the plate hurt his game
in the field," Stanzi would tell the flies, which was true, since
Terry White could not field to begin with.

And he never let any of it bother him. He'd go up there an'
overswing at every pitch, hit some little dribbler back to the
pitcher or a high pop-up to second base. Then he'd come on
back to the dugout with a smile on his face. Stanzi would try to
get him out to the park early to take extra cuts, field some grounders. But he would never do it.

"I just want to have some fun out there," he told Stanzi.

I thought The Little Maniac was gonna have a stroke. His face
turned that sick grey color, like you see on people in coffins.

"You think this game is goddamned *fun*?" he asked the boy.
"You think I spent my goddamned life at this because it's fun?"

But Stanzi had to stick with the rook, since his name was on
him. He still got most of the flies to write him up.

"Terry White's batting average not whole story. . ." Dickhead
Barry Busby would write. "White may not hit ball out of park every
time up. . . but he helps team in so many other ways. . . ."

After that we all started callin' him Not The Whole Story White,
or So Many Other Ways White. He just laughed about it. After all,
he was gettin' his money an' pussy on the side, he didn't care.
But it started to get to The Little Maniac.

One day in Chicago, Terry White takes a called third strike with
the bases loaded, cost us a game with the Cubs. We were on the
team bus, on the way back to the hotel, an' Stanzi made the driver

stop right in the middle of a bridge. He got out an' dragged White off with him, an' made him look over the side.

"Why don't you just kill yourself right now?" he asked the rook. "If you can't hit any better than that, you might as well jump off an' kill yourself right here."

White stared at him like he was crazy. So Stanzi whips his pecker right out of his pants and waves it at the kid.

"Jesus," he says, "I could hit better than that with my dick!"

It was The Emp'ror, in the number-three spot, who was hurtin' the most from Not The Whole Story White hittin' fourth. The pitchers knew they could work him real cute an' hit the corners. They knew if they walked him they could just pitch to White next, instead of John Barr. The Emp'ror's average went down an' his home runs dropped off, an' the fans started gettin' on him.

He started pressing at the plate, which was why he ran into trouble when we went on that first big trip. You can't ever listen to the fans out there, an' you sure as hell can't listen to the writers. But The Emp'ror would sit in the dugout thinkin' over an' over about how it wasn't fair.

"Let *him* look bad," he would tell me. "Let them see how that kid looks up there on his own."

"You ain't the swizzlehead who makes up the lineup," I told him. "You can't do nothin' about that, so don't worry about it. 'Sides, by the end of this trip, he'll have to drop that rook an' get Pippin to make a deal for a real third baseman. Then you'll be back in that sweet pussy spot, right in front of John Barr."

But I didn't count on what Charlie Stanzi could do with two weeks on the road. Most particul'y, I didn't count on what he could do to Maximilian Duke.

The Emp'ror, Maximilian Duke

My first year in pro ball, I almost got shot dead right in front of where my parents lived in Jersey City. When I came out of Stanford, the Mets gave me a big bonus to sign, and I went right out and bought a car. That was before I knew all about fine cars as an investment. I got the biggest, flashiest Cadillac I could find. That thing got five miles to the gallon if the wind was blowing right.

The night I got home, I drove straight over to where they lived, in the Greenville projects. I pulled up in front of their apartment house, and all of a sudden there's a blinding light in front of me and somebody I can't even see is pointing a gun at the side of my head and saying, "Get out nice and slow." I reached for the key to turn off the ignition, and next thing I know there's an arm around my neck and my head's being pulled out the window.

They pulled me out, then they shoved my face down on the backseat until my cheek burned against the nice new leather. I was sure I was being mugged, until I felt the handcuffs on my wrists. One cop was sitting on my back and another one had my legs spread and was running his hands up and down my legs. They went through the trunk, the glove compartment, looked under the mats on the front seat. When I asked what they wanted, they just told me to shut up.

It wasn't until they looked at my license that they recognized me. I was sort of a local hero—though I guess not enough. When they saw the name, though, one of them even asked me to sign a baseball he kept in his car. I signed it. I was willing to do anything by that time.

"Sorry about the frisk job," one of them said. "But you shoulda said who you was. You know how it is around here."

"Yeah," I said. "I know."

I signed his ball, then I got back in that Cadillac and drove it straight through the tunnel to New York. But they still write me, those cops. I get letters from them all the time, even after so many years, asking me for an autograph, free tickets. They even start the letters, "You probably don't remember me, but I pulled you over." Like it's a common bond.

The Old Swizzlehead

It all began with the double plays on that road trip. Bobby Roddy an' Lonnie Lee were lookin' shaky around second all season. They didn't have their timing down—probably because The Little Maniac spent so much time on his football drills in the spring.

Like most things in baseball, a double play is impossible,

though it may seem easy enough. The second baseman scoops up the ball an' flips it to the shortstop. He catches it, drags his right leg over second base like a martini drinker wavin' the vermouth bottle over the gin, an' makes the throw to first. Or the shortstop flips the ball to the second baseman, who's got to catch it, spin around, an' jump over the runner to make the throw.

But either way, it's got to happen just like that—in one continuous motion. Each part is simple by itself. A little toss of the ball. A foot on the bag. A throw ninety feet down to first base.

Trouble is, you can't get ahead of yourself. You got to have the ball before you can toss it. You got to make sure you touch second before you throw it to first.

On the other hand, you also got to know what you're gonna do next. You got to know where the other man is so you don't flip the ball wide. And you got to do everything with that runner from first base comin' down the line, set on knockin' you down or even tearin' your leg open with his spikes.

You have to think about what you're doin', an' what you're gonna do, both at once and the same time. Only you can't think. You got to *know.*

Bobby Roddy an' Lonnie Lee had been playin' together for ten years, an' when they were on, they were like one person out there. They just needed a little time to get their game back together. But that was when The Little Maniac decided he should make a few suggestions.

I saw the whole thing begin right before my eyes, like a slow-motion car crash. It was before the first game of the road trip, out in San Francisco. Bobby Roddy an' Lonnie Lee were takin' infield, workin' on the pivot, an' you could tell they were a little tense about it. Just then Charlie Stanzi walks out friendly as he can be an' tells 'em, "Maybe if you tried it this way. . ."

They were the magic words. "Maybe if you tried it this way." All he had to do was say those words an' nobody could do a goddamned thing.

Lonnie Lee just looked at him when he said it, an' Bobby Roddy grinned an' said, "Fuck you." But The Little Maniac wouldn't let it stop him.

"You know, I used to play the infield," he says, an' reaches out for Lonnie's glove at the same time. "I learned a few things. Now maybe if you tried it this way..."

He stood out there for half an hour, havin' Old Coach Plate hit grounders to him so he could show them. There was nothin' new about it, nothin' they didn't know already for years. Bobby Roddy just looked off into the stands, an' Lonnie Lee only paid attention out of his Christian forbearance.

But he got to them all the same. First ball hit to Bobby Roddy with a man on base, he flipped it right over Lonnie Lee's head. Then somebody hit a ball at Lonnie, an' he couldn't even dig it out of his glove.

From then on, they were hooked. It was just the simplest little motions they had to do. Pick the ball up. Flip it two feet. Throw it over to first. But they couldn't do it. They were thinkin' about it. The Little Maniac was in their heads, an' they couldn't get him out.

That was just the beginning. He got to everybody, one by one, the whole rest of the trip. In L.A., it was Spock Feeley. There was a passed ball that got away from him the last game against the Giants, cost us a run. Soon as we get to Los Angeles, Stanzi's showin' him the proper way to get down on low pitches, even though The Little Maniac never caught a game in his life.

"Maybe if you tried it this way..." he said.

Feeley looked at him like he would at some rookie pitcher who just shook off a sign. But from that night on it was like somebody dug the Lincoln Tunnel under him. No matter what he did, he couldn't keep the ball from goin' through his legs.

In San Diego The Little Maniac started talkin' to No-Hit Hitt about how to make the toss when the pitcher has to come over to cover first. It was another two-foot flip, simplest play in the game, but Hitt couldn't do it. Not after Stanzi started talkin' to him. Next night he ran into Moses Yellowhorse three times goin' for the bag, an' tossed a ball off Al The Fade Abramowitz's head.

"Maybe if you tried it this way..."

He tried it on me, too. He come over to me before the last game in San Diego an' started talkin' about how I catch the ball. It's a thing I do: snatch the ball out of the air the way you'd grab a coin if somebody flipped it at you. Most of the fans like it, though there's always some old white guys in the stands, sayin',

"He's gonna drop one of those someday, and it'll cost us a big game."

I never understood wantin' to go to a show an' not see a show. But white guys like Stanzi thought it was immoral to catch a ball that way. He came out when I was shaggin' flies before a game, an' he just stood there until I gave in an' snuck a glance over at him. I couldn't help myself, even though I knew what he wanted.

"You're gonna drop one of those," he said.

"Never did yet."

"Sure," he says. "But sooner or later. You're gonna drop one. Maybe in a big game."

I stopped then, an' looked him over good. My grandmother down in the South was a superstitious old Gullah woman from McIntosh County, Georgia, an' she used to say, "If you wanna know if you can trust a man, look for his skull behind the smile. If you can see that smilin' skull, you know he's an evil man." I never knew what the hell that meant. But I looked at The Little Maniac an' I thought I could see his white skull right behind the smile.

"Maybe if you tried it this way. . . ." he said, an' reached for my glove.

"Get behind me, Satan," I said, like she always did, an' snatched that glove away from him.

"Fine," he says then. And his smile snaps shut just like a skull all right, like crocodile jaws after a big fish, an' he slouches off in that way he had, with his mouth all scrunched up.

"Just don't be surprised when you drop one."

That night for the first time I bobbled a couple balls. I almost dropped one. It popped out of my glove an' I just did catch it with my bare hand before it hit the ground. It was that close, an' you know if I had dropped it, the flies never would've let anybody forget it. Stanzi'd see to that.

The only other ballplayer who Stanzi couldn't get to was John Barr. The only thing he could do was talk dirty to him, and then he would just move away. Barr kept up his hot streak on the road, just like he'd kept it up for the last twelve years in the major leagues and two years in the minors before that. I never once saw the man have a slump, even for two games in a row.

Naturally, that kind of consistency was an unbearable tempta-

tion for The Little Maniac. The trouble was, he didn't have the
excuse of a slump or even one misplay for his usual approach.
Barr hit a four-hundred-foot dinger into the wind off San Francisco Bay, threw three runners out at the plate in as many games
in L.A., and stole home with the winning run when the pitcher
forgot about him on our first night in San Diego.

It was hard to beat that, but Stanzi had to try. The very next
night, he was out at the ballpark early when John Barr was takin'
batting practice. He stood by the cage watching, the way he liked
to do until he made you notice him. But Barr just kept ripping
one pitch after another into the outfield, until after half an hour
Stanzi was forced to finally speak up.

"I see you got a little hitch in your swing there," he said. Barr
ignored him, and knocked the next pitch against the fence.

"It's not much. Just a tiny little bit. But who knows if you don't
correct it."

Barr kept whackin', an' The Little Maniac tried again:

"I know about these things. I got a lot of guys out of slumps.
Maybe if you tried it this way..."

"Bullshit," Barr said, without even lookin' at Stanzi behind
him.

"What?"

"Bullshit. I got no hitch. Nothing wrong with my swing. Go
away."

The Little Maniac's nostrils flared, but he wasn't put off that
easy. He still kept talkin' like sugar.

"Have it your way. But you really think you can get away with
that big a bat forever? And swingin' from the heels the way you
do—"

"I always carried this lumber," Barr told him, still not botherin'
to look around.

"Sure, but you're gettin' older now. How long you think you
can play this game?"

"Long as I want to."

Charlie Stanzi laughed a knowing little old man's laugh when
Barr said that.

"Oh, yeah. That's what I thought, too. I used to think I could
play on pure meanness and desire. I honestly didn't see how they
could ever get me out of the game.

"But it happens," he went on. "Happens to everybody. I was fortunate enough to develop a valuable second career. Whatta you think you'll do, Barr? Manager? Go up in the broadcast booth? Gotta get a little more loquacious for that."

Barr took a break for a minute to change bats. He stood outside the cage to rub the pine-tar rag over his new stick, and that was when he looked at Stanzi for the first time.

"What're you gettin' on about? I got years left."

"Maybe. Though I don't see how you'll do it with a bat that big. The reflexes get old, John. They get old whether you like it or not. Before you even realize it, most times. Then you have to make an adjustment. Or look for something else to do when you can't play anymore."

Barr just snorted at him and went back into the batting cage.

"You tell me if I can still play," he said, and then he ripped three straight line drives down the third-base line.

Stanzi never gave up, though. That's why he was dangerous to be around, even if you didn't want to listen to him. Little by little he was chippin' away at us, without even exactly meaning to. We couldn't do anything without thinkin' about it too much, an' when we did think we couldn't think straight—which is what happened with Maximilian Duke.

The Emp'ror never got along with the flies. They never knew what to think of me, an' they stayed away from John Barr. But they assumed Duke was arrogant because he had a college degree, an' because he used to walk around the locker room bangin' the end of his bat on the floor, sayin', "I'm the man, I'm the man." They were always writin' that he thought too much. They didn't like the way he used to follow the stock market, or collect fancy cars an' fine wines. There's nothin' a sportswriter likes less than a nigger in a big car.

Duke was sensitive to it, too, that was the trouble. He was always tryna control things, hang on to things. That's why he was always tryna to find the best deal for his money, find the very best investment when he was already set for life with what he made every year. Nobody in the game took better care of hisself than The Emp'ror, except for maybe John Barr. Duke would work out all through the off-season, an' come into spring training every year with his muscles bulgin' through his shirt.

"If you condition yourself, you can get three or four more years out of this game," he would say.

He studied the game, too. Not like Barr, nobody did, but he kept a good book on the pitchers. Always got to the park on time to take his cuts. Before every game he'd go around, studyin' his book an' tappin' that bat on the floor, sayin', "I'm the man, I'm the man."

We didn't mind it, not like the flies did. But he wasn't the most popular person in the clubhouse. Guys would get on him sometimes, it was just in fun, but he wouldn't take it. They would rag him about bein' so keyed up, about knowin' everything. But that's what baseball is all about, in between the couple hours you get to play. It's all personalities, an' Maximilian Duke took everything too personal, he had too much pride to be smart.

The Little Maniac got to him down in Houston, the next to last stop an' the last victim on the trip. We had this new kid, Dana Salo, on the mound to try to break up our bad streak, an' he was bringin' it. The Astros couldn't get around on his heat, but late in the game Duke started playin' back on their right-handed hitters anyway. We were only a run up, an' he knew once they started hittin' the kid, the ball was gonna travel.

But then their number-eight hitter dumps a broken-bat single in front of The Emp'ror, an' The Little Maniac starts wavin' from the dugout for him to move in. Stanzi hated to see anyone get a dump hit like that. It was typical of the man: he never understood the balance of the game. You can play your outfield right behind the shortstop an' maybe you will cut off every little dink Texas League hit. But then you're gonna give up the big hits over your outfielders' heads. There's always a tradeoff.

Maximilian Duke just ignored Stanzi when he saw him signalin' to move in, and The Little Maniac went right for him when we came back to the dugout after the inning.

"Didn't you see me wavin' out there?" he asked.

"Yeah, I saw you," The Emp'ror told him. "I thought maybe you were saying hello."

Stanzi was mad all at once, the way only he could be, the way he was with umpires.

"Listen, you son of a bitch, when I say come in, you come in!"

"They're gonna get to this kid," The Emp'ror told him.

"One ball gets by me, they have the tying run on second or third."

"You just do what I say," Stanzi told him. "If I see one more drop in front of you, I'm gonna fine your ass."

Duke ignored him. He went deep in left again the next inning, an' sure enough, they started gettin' to Salo. Of course, Stanzi can't figure to take him out in time. The 'Stros got men on first an' second, an' the next hitter slams one toward the wall.

The ball was hit on a line, just fair and right into the corner, an' The Emp'ror saw he had no chance to catch it or cut it off. He turned around and played it off the wall instead, one hop perfect, then whipped it home. The tying run was already in, but Duke's throw cuts the runner from first down at the plate. The game's still tied, an' John Barr hits one out in the top of the tenth to win it.

Stanzi didn't say a word after the play Duke made, but he was still mad about it. He knew if The Emp'ror was playin' where he wanted him, he couldn't have got to that ball in time, an' Houston would've won the game right then an' there. He knew that we knew, too, which was why he couldn't resist when the flies asked him about the play.

"It was a helluva throw he made," Stanzi says. "But maybe we wouldn't have needed it if my outfielder goes to the wall in the first place."

"Are you saying he could have caught that ball?" Ellie Jay asked him.

"I can't say that for sure," Stanzi says, holdin' out his hands, like he's only tryin' to give The Emp'ror the benefit of the doubt.

"Are you saying he was afraid to hit the wall?"

"All I'm sayin' is maybe his judgment would've been a little different if this wasn't the last year of his contract."

The next day it was all over the papers, even down in Houston. It was just one of those sportswriter controversies. The kind of thing they like to do when they can't think of a column on their own. It's usually about a black ballplayer, an' it's usually about him not hustlin' enough, or bein' afraid, or bein' a disruptive influence in the clubhouse. I never saw a sportswriter run into a wall so he could write a good sentence. It's just one of those bullshit things you got to take for granted in this game.

But Duke couldn't let it go. He went out an' bought all the papers the next day. He brought 'em back to our hotel room, where I was sittin' around watchin' the stories, an' kept readin' what Stanzi had to say over an' over again.

"The man's saying I was afraid. That's what he's saying, right here in black and white."

"It's just Whiff Dick," I told him. "Just forget it."

But The Emp'ror couldn't forget it. He went out to the Astrodome early the next night, an' confronted The Little Maniac in his office. Old Coach Plate Pasquale an' Spock Feeley had to hold him back from takin' a poke at Stanzi.

"You think I'm afraid?" he kept sayin'. "C'mon. C'mon, I'll show you who's afraid."

They finally got him calmed down, but he had a look about him before the game. Kind of a dead-ahead stare and a heroic fixed jaw—like a man who's gonna do somethin' very, very stupid.

"You gotta just leave that shit," I told him. "Play your game, don't let it bother you."

"I'm fine," he said, but he kept starin' straight ahead.

First inning, there was a long fly to left an' he went after it. He had no chance, but The Emp'ror threw himself right up against that wall, an' the ball hit five feet over his glove.

"You keep doin' that, you're gonna wind up in a hospital," I told him. "Charlie Stanzi's gonna come visit you with a bunch of flowers an' a box of chocolates. He might even say nice things about you in the papers."

"I have to do what I have to do, Swiz." An' when he said that, I knew the fool was done for.

It happened in the fifth inning. There wasn't any chance he could catch this one. It hit the wall at least ten feet over his head, but The Emp'ror never stopped running an' he never took his eye off it. He went headfirst into the wall. He didn't even slow down when his spikes touched the warning track.

By the time I got to him he was still on his back an' beginning to turn blue. I pried his jaws open an' pulled his tongue out of his throat. He opened his eyes then, an' in between gasps he was tryna say somethin'.

"Did . . . did I get it, Swiz?" he asked, like it was the end of a war movie.

"What you got was most likely a concussion," I told him. "Now lie still an' wait for the stretcher."

"I showed him," he breathed at me.

"Yeah, you showed him," I told him. "You showed him there's nothin' more stupid than a ballplayer."

They finally got the stretcher out there, an' I helped 'em haul The Emp'ror back in, and made sure they didn't bump him around too much. We were goin' through the dugout, when Stanzi leans over him on the stretcher an' claps his hands an' says, "Great effort out there, Duke."

I almost hit him. I would've popped him right there, in front of the whole stadium. But John Barr had come in, too, and he was right behind me. He grabbed my hand before I could punch The Little Maniac.

"You want somethin'?" Stanzi yelled across the dugout at me, back where he was bein' safely held by Old Coach Plate. His eyes were shinin' like they did when he was drunk.

"You did this, you son of a bitch," I told him.

"C'mon," he said, grinnin' at me. "C'mon, tough guy."

I had lost it by then. If I could've got free I would've hit him as hard as I could, no matter how much older an' smaller he was than me, and no matter who was watching. I would've been fined an' suspended by both The Great White Father an' Commissioner Woodrow Wilson Wannamaker. But I didn't get the chance. John Barr got a grip an' hauled me right back out to center field. By the time I got there I was calm again, or at least I had enough sense to see what I was up against.

"Thanks," I told Barr, but he didn't even blink, as usual.

"Make sure you work it out with Lary," was all he said, pointin' to Franklin Lary, the backup outfielder Stanzi had sent out to left.

"Make sure he knows what you're covering."

"You see? It's another clue," Ellie Jay said afterward when I told her about it.

"It does seem like he's changed a little this year."

"I got a new lead up in his hometown, too."

"How's that? After all that time?"

"I got this letter from Prides Crossing. No name, no story. Just an address, and a note from somebody who wants to meet with me about him. That's all."

"Prob'ly some crank who just wants money," I told her, but I didn't quite believe it myself. "You gonna check it out?"

"I'm going up the next day I have off, right after the All-Star Game. It's up in Boston this year, anyway."

"What're you gonna do if it turns out to be something really bad?"

"I can't picture that."

"Mysterious men ain't all they're cracked up to be. What if he did somethin' so terrible they don't wanna talk about it?"

"It can't be something that bad," she said, an' then she was speaking with real fervor, like it was some cause of hers.

"I can't believe he would do something truly terrible. Not seeing him play for so long. Maybe it sounds stupid, Swiz, but a man can't play like that out there and not have a soul."

"You might be surprised," I told her.

Nothin' would've surprised me by the end of that whole terrible road trip. When we finally pulled into Atlanta for the last stop on the road, we were a dog team. At least the news from Houston was The Emp'ror had a concussion but nothin' worse, and they were lettin' him out in a few days. By then we'd been on the road so long we almost didn't care.

You get slow, hangin' around in the hotel rooms watchin' TV an' orderin' up room service. You can go out an' walk around, but all the cities look the same. An' if you get recognized the fans'll come up an' shake your hand, or yell at you, spit at you, ask for your autograph.

I think that's how some guys get too deep into the blow. They want somethin' to keep 'em up while they sit in the rooms waiting for the games to start. That's why the flies an' the fans always think ballplayers look like they don't care. We can't care *that* much—not like they do. There's nobody alive can care that much, every day, about what they do for a livin'. You hear the fans on the talk radio sayin', "It's just a game. They get that kind of money to play a game." But it's less than that. It's just a job.

By the last Saturday night of the trip, everybody on the team who wasn't a Stiff-Leg or a Jeebee Jaycee was down in the hotel bar, lookin' over the talent. That was where Ol' Cal Rigby always liked us to be.

"It ain't the pussy that wears a ballplayer out," he always used to say. "It's chasin' it all over town."

He liked to have us stay in the hotel, where he an' the coaches could keep an eye on us an' make sure we could still stand when we left the bar. My second year, we had this big Canadian farmboy named Claude Broadhead up for a shot. He was all over the plate, but he could throw the red stuff. Big dumb kid from Moose Jaw, or someplace like that, who never could get over all the annies who were around. He couldn't pay any attention to the game after a while. He would spend all his time out in the bullpen checkin' out the stands with his binoculars, then get the ballboys to take notes to 'em.

"And it works!" he told me, like he never got laid before in his life, which maybe he hadn't.

"Once they find out you're a ballplayer, they'll go with you. When I leave the parking lot they press their breasts against the windshield. Honest to God! It's unbelievable. If I roll the window down, they throw in little pieces of paper with their phone number on it."

He couldn't get enough of it. He could barely pay attention for nine innings before he got out there again, after the pussy. Then one time in Chicago he took a fourteen-year-old girl up to his hotel room, an' her momma called the police. The next night they arrested him right in the dugout.

You shoulda seen his farmboy face. They come down an' cuffed him an' took him off the field in the middle of the seventh-inning stretch. Cal Rigby was furious, yellin' at the cops:

"Yeah, you gotta be sure to get this big criminal right away before he kills again."

But some DA wanted to make a point, an' they took Claude downtown an' charged him. The Great White Father was so mad about the negative publicity that he wouldn't even let the travelin' secretary bail him out. Some of us got the money together an' went down there as soon as the game ended, but that boy was already all busted up.

"I never knew she was that young," he kept blubberin', the

tears rollin' down his baby fat cheeks. "Not with all that make-up. She even had high heels on."

"Yeah, Claude, let's just get you out of here," we tried to tell him. But he wouldn't shut up about it.

"She told me she was eighteen. I didn't see any reason to doubt her. She acted like she was old enough."

"Shut up now, Claude. This ain't the goddamned church, an' you don't got to confess it all."

But he couldn't stop hisself. He knew he blew it. The girl's mother dropped the charges after Pippin gave her some money, but it was too late. The story was all over the news, an' The Great White Father traded Claude's ass out of the organization for a couple of bench splinters, and he never made it back.

He was a fool, but you couldn't always tell. That Saturday night in Atlanta there were a couple annies giggling across from me at the hotel bar. They didn't look to be much more than seventeen, eighteen, but there wasn't much else around. Some of us bought 'em drinks an' went over to sit with 'em. It turned out they were from New York, come down special on a charter trip to see us play.

"We make a trip like this every year. We love you guys!" one of 'em said, an' they both started gigglin' again.

They were wearin' knee socks an' butterfly pins in their hair an' button-down sweaters, the kind with little pink fuzz. I didn't think they could be out of the eleventh grade, but they told us they were secretaries.

"We never had the nerve to meet any of you before," the first one told us. "I made Tracy come over here tonight."

We told 'em to get anything they wanted on us, but they only ordered beers. Finally Spock Feeley got the one who wasn't Tracy to come up to his room with him for a nightcap.

"Vick-y!" Tracy hissed at her as she went off on his arm. "What are you *do-ing?*"

But Vicky was a little drunk. She just laughed an' went off with Feeley, sorta wobbly on her high heels an' holdin' on to his arm. She was in for a surprise, though. I knew No-Hit Hitt was upstairs, an' they were gonna pull a Sleeper on her.

That's when one roommate brings someone home and the other one pretends he's asleep in bed. When the girl gets inside an' sees the other roomie there, he tells her it's okay, he's a deep sleeper an' nothin' can bother him. Then they get into it, an' lo an' behold, the roomie wakes up an' joins in.

"What is she *doing*?" Tracy turned to me when they were gone, her eyes wide an' excited. "Do you know what she's doing?"

"I know. Why don't we go up to my room, get to know each other in private."

"I don't know," she breathed, like it was the most dangerous thing anybody ever said to her. "I don't know if I should."

"Sure, you should," I told her. "I'll order up a bottle of champagne from room service. We can talk real quiet up there."

'Course, there's risks. Stillwater Norman pulled a Sleeper one time an' the annie still refused to do it, no matter how loud his roommate tried to snore. She insisted they go into the bathroom an' lock the door.

"I spent half the night bangin' my head on the pipes under the sink," Stillwater told me later. "An' my roommate kept bangin' on the door to let him in."

That ain't even the worst. I know ballplayers who still do tendollar hookers in Cincinnati, lookin' for a bargain. I know guys who go to peep shows an' try to convince the girls to come on out.

It's just somethin' to do. We play three, four nights in each city at the most. Sometimes just two games. You get in early, play the first night, stay over, an' leave the next night after the game. One night in the hotel, an' then you're gone, an' you want somethin' to kill the time. Nothing seems real after a while.

I was about to reel in old Tracy, when I spotted John Barr a couple stools away, nursin' a beer. It surprised me, since it had been years since I seen him steppin' out. His first few seasons in the show, he would come out sometimes with the guys, but he never seemed to like it. He'd never drink much, or say anything. I never saw him go home with an annie. Sometimes it seemed like he really wanted to say something, an' join in, but then he'd just leave. I would watch him across a table, or a bar, an' see his face pull back, the way it did when he tensed to hit the ball.

Now here he was, down at the bar, like a regular human being. I figured even he got wore out by that horror road trip. Not that he was actually with anyone, of course, or that more than a third of his beer was gone, or that he was sayin' anything. I wondered what Ellie Jay woulda thought about her mystery man bein' down there, lookin' over the annies. It's hard for anybody to look too mysterious next to a bowl of peanuts in a hotel bar, an' John Barr was no exception.

I could tell he *was* sneakin' little looks over at me an' Tracy from time to time, which surprised me even more. I thought maybe he was interested in her, an' if he was, I was willin' to forgo the great romance of my life. I brought her right over an' introduced her to him, an' her eyes got wide an' she looked properly excited again. But he was quiet like usual, an' could barely even acknowledge her.

"Glad to make your acquaintance," was all he could mumble out. He snuck another look up and down her, but the whole time she was talkin' about what a great ballplayer he was, he couldn't do more than mumble an' look back at his beer. I wasn't sure whether I should give up or try leavin' 'em alone, when all of a sudden he bolted.

"Glad to make your acquaintance," he said again, an' threw down a few dollars for the bartender and ran right out of the room. I didn't know how to figure it.

"What's the matter with him?" Tracy asked me.

"Price a' greatness," I told her. "You wanna continue this party someplace more convivial?"

I got her up to my room, an' had them bring up the champagne. I never pulled a Sleeper myself, roomin' with The Emp'ror. He had too much class for that. But I mighta done it with somebody else, I have to admit that.

I ordered the cheapest bottle of champagne they had, 'cause I didn't think it would make any difference to her. It didn't, either. She sat halfway across the room from me, in a straightback chair. I sat on the bed an' poured us two glasses an' left one by the bedside table for her to come an' get it, like a stray cat to a saucer of milk.

"Come on an' have some of this, sugar."

"Are you married?" she asks. First damned thing out of her mouth. I looked over at her there with her knee socks an' her schoolgirl bangs hangin' in her eyes, an' I almost laughed.

"Yeah, I'm married," I told her up front. "But my wife an' me got an understanding."

"Does everybody on the team cheat on their wives?" she asked, an' I nearly spilled the champagne.

"We all sleep around sometimes, except for the Stiff-Legs an' the Jeebee Jaycees," I told her, decidin' to give it to her straight if that's how she wanted it. "That's the real family men, an' the religious ones. We're on the road half the year—"

"Do you do this a lot? I mean, do you have a regular girlfriend in every town?"

"Nah, baby. I hardly never do it. Just when I get real lonely. An' when I meet somebody nice like you."

I didn't expect her to believe it. But she came over then an' sipped a little champagne, an' looked at me with her big eyes.

"What's it like, bein' a superstar?" she actually asked me. She wanted to talk now. She asked me what the team was like, an' all the guys on it, an' what it was like bein' on the road. She wanted to know all about my life.

I told her some, too, though I was starting to lose my patience. I was startin' to get mad because I realized I was actually enjoyin' it, talkin' about all my troubles to some girl who barely made it out of high school.

It was gettin' weepy. I even started to ask her about her excitin' life. Bein' a secretary in Manhattan, takin' the express bus in from Queens every day— Finally I reached out an' took her by the shoulders an' gave her a kiss. She looked at me then with those child's eyes bigger than ever.

"I don't know if I want to do this," she said.

I kissed her again, an' she kissed me back then. We kissed for a while more an' then she hugged me. She just hung on to me, with my shirt balled up in her fist. Finally I held her back an' looked at her. She was wearin' too much rouge on her cheeks, an' too much liner on her eyes. But I kissed her again, an' then I asked her if she would spend the night with me.

"I don't know if I should stay here," she said.

"You just take your time, baby," I told her. "I'm gonna go ahead an' get ready for bed."

I went into the bathroom an' stripped down to my shorts. When I came back she was lyin' on top of the bed, but she still had her clothes on.

"I'm gonna get into bed now," I told her. "You're welcome."

I turned the lights off and slid into bed. She stayed on top of the covers, still lookin' at me but not sayin' anything.

"C'mon, baby. I like you. Didn't we have a good talk tonight? What've we got to hide from each other?"

I took off my shorts then, real slow, an' slid 'em out, over on top of the bed. She looked at them like I just slid a snake out there on the covers.

"Okay," she said, barely breathin'. "Okay. Lemme just go into the bathroom."

"Okay, baby. Anything you want."

She rummaged around in her purse for a while, then went into the bathroom. She took a long time in there, an' I assumed she was just gettin' ready, puttin' her diaphragm in. But then I heard some other strange noise, an' I thought maybe she was throwin' up.

I had an annie do that on me once. By the time I banged the door open the whole place was a mess, an' she was lyin' passed out by the toilet. I realized later she could've drowned in the toilet bowl before I got her out. Another time I walked in an' found some girl fixin' on me.

I started to panic a little. I went scrambling down from the bed after her pocketbook, bare-ass naked on my hands an' knees. Her license said she was twenty-three, an' I calmed down some. But you can imagine how much I felt like makin' it then. I thought of maybe knockin' on the door an' tellin' her I changed my mind, an' that I liked her an' all that, but I respected her too much to do anything with her.

Then she came out, stark naked, with her hands in front of her even though it was dark. She closed her eyes, too, like that would keep me from seein' her, an' stumbled a little an' hit the night table. I reached out to steady her by the hips, and I could feel then she was tremblin' a little. I lifted her right up on the bed. She slid under the covers an' I made love to her, my hesitation gone with all those words about respectin' her too much.

Much later on—after she got up an' dressed in a hurry in the bathroom, an' ran off a little embarrassed to find Vicky—the phone rang. I was half asleep by then, but I picked it up, half afraid it would be the hotel detective, or maybe The Great White Father.

"Richard," said a soft, warm voice over the line.

"Hmm? What's that?" But I knew who it was.

"Richard, I was just thinking about the old days," Wanda said, an' I thought if only she could know that the door had just clicked shut. But she didn't sound mad at all.

"What old days?" I asked, afraid it was some kind of trap.

"You know," she said. "That first year, after we were married. You used to call me every night after a road game."

"Yeah," I said, 'cause I didn't know what else to say.

"We couldn't even afford it then," she said, an' laughed a little, the way she used to do, too. "But you called anyway."

"Yeah, I did," I said, then I laughed too.

"You alone tonight?"

"Uh-huh. I'm alone."

"I heard about Maximilian. That's a shame."

"It is that, the fool."

We talked for a while more like that, me sittin' there in the dark, in a hotel room in Atlanta, just enjoyin' her voice come over the telephone, tired an' sultry like in the old days.

"Richard, you gotta face life one of these days," she said. "We have to settle this sometime."

"What's the matter?" I asked. "Isn't there anyone in the ANC you can help tonight?"

"You can't run away from it forever," she said. "You have to come home sooner or later."

"Yeah, well, maybe," I said, thinkin' about that Tracy girl, steppin' out from the bathroom like a scared virgin, holdin' her hands out in front of her.

"Good night, Richard."

I sat there for a while more in the dark, holdin' the phone an' thinkin'. I was thinkin' it had been a helluva road trip, an' I needed to go home all right.

12

He's going to leave writing dead on the floor.

—Ernest Hemingway

Ellie Jay

You have to be goddamned careful competing with men. Sometimes you end up where you don't want to be, just for the sake of winning.

The Color Commentary

The ballpark stretched out endlessly below him. Its center field flowed on and on, toward two distant staircases that ascended to a row of dark windows. Above the windows was a clock, so far away that you could not even read the hands.

The players' uniforms were baggy, thick, old-fashioned. But they still stood out sharp and clean against the bright green grass, and the ball still zipped between them as if it were on a string—

He had just finished typing the words, "... as if it were on a string," when the ball was hit out to the endless center field. The man out there drifted back toward the big clock, his feet gliding over the turf, coal black face turning toward the sky. He seemed to move effortlessly after the ball, and it looked as if it would soon be over his head, crashing against the clock.

But somehow the outfielder gained on it even as he watched, and began to unfurl one long, dark arm toward the ball tumbling down out of the sky. . . .

There was a ringing somewhere that wouldn't stop, and an unspeakable taste in his mouth. Dickhead Barry Busby felt a hand on his shoulder and bolted upright.

"I haven't got any money, but you can take the wristwatch!"

"It's me, Barry."

Ellie Jay's face loomed ironically before him.

"You ought to stop sleeping on the bar. It isn't sanitary."

"For your information, I have a column to write, and I'm not going anywhere before it's done," he said with great dignity. "Now where was I?"

He drew himself up and looked down blearily at his typewriter. There was a page already in it, damnably blank. The room began to dissolve again into the giant Leroy Niemann prints lining the wall. Orange athletes skied down blue and green mountains, swung pink and yellow bats, swam through red and lavender seas. . . . He felt dizzy, and closed his eyes.

"Here, shove over," Ellie Jay said, sitting down beside him and pulling the portable typewriter away.

"What're you doing?"

"Writing your column for you," she said, looking over his notes. "At this rate you'll be here all night."

"It'll be done when it's done," he said huffily, though he made no move to reclaim the typewriter. "Not just anyone can do my column, you know. This is goddamned inside stuff here."

"Yeah, yeah," she said, studying his notebook. "Jesus, didn't the nuns teach you penmanship?"

She folded his reporter's pad out to an item, and slowly began to type.

"Goddamn, it's been a long time since I used one of these," she said, shaking her head.

"Whatsa matter?" he slurred. "'Fraid of breaking a nail?"

"Only against your thick head. Now shut up and let me work, if you want us to get out of here tonight."

"It's this goddamned gutter brand scotch," he said, studying the remnant of brown liquid and two shrunken ice cubes in his glass. "I don't deserve scotch like this, you know. I've drunk scotch with the best of 'em."

"That right?"

"I remember back in 1966, I had a drink with Arnold Palmer in the clubhouse the day he blew a seven-stroke lead at Augusta. I said to him, 'Arnie, you blew it.' And you know what he said to me? He said, 'Barry, you're right.' That's the kind of guy he was, class all the way through."

"Uh-huh," she said. "Tell me how this looks."

He cast his one open eye over the typewriter and read:

" . . . Dodgers say Chuck 'Hammer' Martel no longer scourge of NL West . . . Martel can still come up with big hit from time to time, but those in know about L.A. situation question his work habits, real market value as heavy hitter . . . Despite past heroics, The Hammer might be looking at one-way ticket to Palookaville if he doesn't shape up . . ."

"Not bad," he said, nodding ponderously. "How the hell you'd ever get into this shithole, anyway?"

"Probably the same way you did," she said guardedly. "I was suckered in. I wanted to be a writer. I thought maybe I wanted to be a journalist."

"A journalist?" he said, wheezing with laughter. "You're a goddamned beat reporter, that's what you are."

"Hell, I thought I'd be a great foreign correspondent. Then I got on the college newspaper, and they had me cover sports. From that moment on I got so much shit from every man who ever lived that I decided I had to show 'em all."

She lit up a cigarette, and blew the smoke lazily toward the ceiling.

"Like I said, I got suckered in."

"Bullshit," he said, leering drunkenly.

She looked him over for a moment, then turned away from the typewriter.

"Bullshit," he repeated. "It wasn't only the challenge, 'cause that fades. And it wasn't the athletes, 'cause they'd always disappoint someone like you. It was the game, wasn't it?"

"You're right," she said, looking more closely at him. "I told myself for years it was worthwhile because the game had a grace unto itself, apart from all the assholes who run it and play it—"

"But now you're not sure."

"Barry, didn't you ever want to do anything besides this?"

"Sure I did. I wanted to be a novelist," he said, blinking solemnly at her.

"You really wanted to write novels?"

"You know this is the exact same model of typewriter Hemingway used to use when he reported from Africa? I dragged this typewriter all the way down to the goddamned White Horse Tavern in the Village once so he could give it his blessing. He tried to slug me because he thought I was drinking his whiskey, but we were best friends by the end of the night. It would've killed him to see what Cuba's like today."

"Why didn't you, Barry? Why didn't you ever write a book? Or anything besides this, the same stuff every day and every year?"

"Because I was part of a team," he said softly.

"You *covered* a team."

"No, no. You don't understand what it was like. You were always together. Sunday afternoon, you'd take your bag to the game with you and when it was over you'd send in your copy to the desk and hop a cab to Grand Central or Penn Station. You'd wait right there on the platform with them, listening to them talk, thinking of all the cities you were going to."

"That doesn't sound so different."

"You'd travel everywhere by train. On a western swing, you'd hit Philadelphia or Pittsburgh first, then Cincinnati, Chicago, St. Louis. If you were covering the Yankees, you'd go to Cleveland, Detroit. You'd have hours, days to kill—playing cards with them, eating with them, telling jokes, telling stories about women. You were part of the team."

He finished the last swallow in his glass, and a terrible despondency descended upon him.

"No, that's a lie, too," he said. "I take that back. You never were part of the team. You wanted to be, but you never were. Just when you thought maybe you were one of them after all, they'd make it clear you weren't."

He stared blindly across the bar, fingering his empty glass.

"I remember when I wrote something Leo Durocher didn't like. He started calling me a faggot, every time I walked into the clubhouse. He used to say stuff like 'What queer sold you that suit? That's a queer suit.' And one day he walked right up to me an' said, 'You know what we do with queers in this locker room? We flush their heads down the toilet bowl!'"

He swallowed deeply, as if he could still recall the fear of that moment, the little manager standing right up against him, face creased in a belligerent grin and his hot breath on Busby's face.

"They could've done it, too. All those big ballplayers standing around behind Leo in their towels, leering at me. I thought they might do something even more disgusting, like shit in the toilet first. I could just picture getting crap all over my nice new suit, my hair, everything."

He looked back at Ellie Jay, and smiled ruefully.

"It was just a big joke, after all. I couldn't get a word out when he said that, and Leo had his laugh and he walked away. And I stood there knowing I would never be one of them."

"Didn't you ever just get sick of them?" she asked. "Didn't you ever have a desire just to walk away from it?"

"Oh, no," he said, surprised. "They were a law unto themselves, and I wasn't one of them, but I still loved being around them. It was enough just to be part of it all, to see their grace and their skill on the field. To feel their confidence. I wouldn't have given that up for anything."

He yawned loudly and put his head on the table, still talking in a singsong voice.

"I tried writing that novel, after I met Hemingway. The next swing out to Chicago, I took notes on everything I saw, on and off the field. I was going to spare the reader nothing. It was going to be the great American baseball novel."

"So what stopped you?"

"The last night out, they went through my stuff and ripped up my first draft and all my notes, and scattered them out the window, all along the Pennsylvania countryside. It was a typical ballplayer joke, mean and childish and stupid."

"Didn't they like what you wrote?"

"No, that wasn't it. They didn't even read it. I just wish they had, that's all. I would have liked to know what they thought."

"I don't care what they think," she said, puffing on her cigarette and throwing her head back defiantly. "But I'd be happy just to do one thing, just to write one thing that would make it worthwhile.''

But Busby was already asleep again, his old, puffy red face ground into the bar. She looked at him for a long while, then snuffed out her cigarette and went back to finishing his article.

Deep in center field, the black man in the baggy white uniform turned his back on the ball. He ran straight ahead, toward the clock, as if he knew the exact, predestined spot where the ball was going to come down. He took one more long stride, thrust his glove out in front of him without looking up—and seized the ball in the webbing. In the same motion he whirled, fired the ball back toward the infield, the runners scrambling desperately back to their bases—

High above in the press box, Busby could feel hands pummeling his back, shaking him excitedly. It was the best, he knew. It was the best catch he had ever seen.

13

And in the midst of it, in the midst of chanting and cheering crowds, colors, noises, hot and cold weather, the glare of lights, or rain on my skin, there was only this noiseless, colorless, heatless void in which the pitcher and I together enacted our certain, preordained ritual of the home run.

—SADAHARU OH

The Old Swizzlehead

By that summer, I didn't know if I should get a divorce from Wanda or beg her forgiveness. Somehow I didn't think it was exactly my decision anymore.

I married Wanda when I was playin' Double-A ball for the Jacksonville Jukes. It was the same year that John Barr broke all the records and killed ol' Moose Maas. Or at least that's the way it seemed to me at the time. John Barr broke all the records, an' Moose Maas died, an' I think it was more than coincidence.

An' I sure as hell got married. I did it for no good reason, which is the usual ballplayer's story. She was a pretty thing, used to sit out in the centerfield bleachers every night wearin' a white dress with flowers embroidered into the sleeves by hand. I got to noticin' her when I was playin' the field. Then I started talkin' to her when I ran out to start the inning.

I didn't say much at first. I was still a skinny kid, an' even though I knew I was goin' to the major leagues, I wasn't so sure with the ladies. I'd say "Hey, there," or "How you doin'?," somethin' real smart like that. But she'd smile back and say very politely in her soft voice, "How are you tonight?"

She had a nice smile. She used to light up when I got a little bolder an' told her how pretty she was. She started to compliment me on my game. She'd say, "That was a nice catch you made" even on a routine fly ball, or, "That was a pretty hit last inning," when I maybe just beat out a single to the infield.

I'd get kinda stupid then, say to her, "That wasn't nothin'. You just watch the next time I'm up, I'm gonna get a good one for you, just because you're so pretty." She'd smile until her whole face, her whole body seemed to shine, and I would most likely go in an' strike out.

They used to rag me about it on the bench. They would look out at center before the game started an' say, "Uh-oh, Swiz is gonna be no good today. His sweetheart is out there." Ol' Cal Rigby used to say, "I can't wait till we get you on the road so we can get some goddamned hits out of you again." But he never interfered with it. I think he figured it was better for a ballplayer to have some silly crush in the stands than the usual temptations an' distractions.

Wanda wasn't like those annies who used to scream our names the whole game, an' wait outside the locker-room door with a few joints an' a six-pack. I had trouble just gettin' a date with her, an' she wouldn't even let me kiss her until the third time we went out. Her brothers used to go to the games with her, an' when I talked to her they would come to the rail an' stare down at me.

"They're overprotective of me," she would say. But the brothers wouldn't sit down.

"They don't like me to be out here alone. I think they're afraid I'll eat too many hot dogs."

An' I laughed an' said, "Yeah, you're probably right, yeah, that is somethin' to be afraid of, all right, an' don't forget the diet sodas, neither," an' I chuckled some more like an idiot while she smiled an' the brothers kept frownin' down at me with their arms crossed over their chests.

But I was impressed by her family. I was impressed by the size of it. It wasn't just the brothers an' sisters; she had all kinds of cousins an' nephews an' aunts an' uncles runnin' around. They all lived in the same town, the same neighborhood. I only had my cousin John Bell an' my two grandmothers growin' up: the one in the projects off 99th Street an' the other one down in Georgia where they sent me every summer. I envied after her family.

Her daddy had his own furniture store and was even a deacon in the Jacksonville First Abyssinian Baptist Church. He was a large man, with a voice like God, an' that's how he acted. When she invited me over for roast beef supper one Sunday after the game, he looked me up an' down from his chair at the head of the table and didn't say a word.

I was tryna do everything real polite, like not chew with my mouth open. I would ask him some kind of fool question about his church or somethin', an' he would keep his head down an' grunt a little in between mouthfuls of roast beef. Until finally he looked at me real close an' said, "So I understand you're a *ballplayer*, son? Is that right?" An' when I told him I was, he nodded his head an' pursed his lips like that was just the sort of trouble he expected all along.

Like the fool I was, that made me want to marry her all the more. I didn't know Wanda, an' I didn't know it wasn't really in my hands anymore. She was a stubborn woman, which I should've picked up on. After her father said no, that just set her mind on it, too. The next thing I know I'm walkin' up to the plate in a green ruffle shirt and a ivory tuxedo that Cal Rigby got me a deal on from one of the advertisers on our outfield fence.

We got married between games of a doubleheader. I remember the preacher stood in the right-hand batter's box, an' Wanda's relatives stood out by the pitcher's mound—includin' her daddy, who looked like he was about ready to crawl away an' hide somewhere to see his daughter married in a ballpark. But Wanda insisted on him bein' there, an' he was.

She looked beautiful herself, with another big smile on her face, an' another nice white dress that got a few grass stains from the field. They advertised the whole thing before the game, an' a couple of the fans even brought wedding presents. I remember there was a beater, an' some bowls, an' the club gave us a vacuum cleaner to help Wanda around the house. Cal Rigby was the best man, an' a band out in center field played "Take Me Out to the Ballgame."

It *smelled* hot in that ballpark—smelled like sweat an' stale beer an' bug juice. By the fifth inning your shirt would be soggy, just standin' in place in the outfield, and your legs felt like lead weights. It was down there I really learned to hit the breakin' stuff.

Any pitch they'd throw you would break all the way down around your ankles like a spitball, with just the natural perspiration hangin' off it. Some nights you didn't feel like even standin' up there in the box an' squintin' out through all the mosquitoes an' the giant flyin' cockroaches. It would use up all your energy to get the bat off your shoulders.

About the only people who came out regular were the kid hoodlums. They liked to sit out on top of the giant jukebox in center field an' diss us. That was the strangest thing about the park: the real imitation jukebox, risin' fifty feet straight out of the ground in dead center field, 450 feet from the plate. It was painted gold an' silver, with revolving red an' blue lights runnin' down both sides. And fastened up along the top of the jukebox, right under the local juvenile delinquents, were the records.

That was the most unbelievable thing of the whole unbelievable story. They were four gigantic fake plastic records. On the label of each one was written the names of the men who hit the four longest home runs in the history of the park, along with the dates they did it and how far they traveled.

Those kids used to go up to drink an' gamble behind the records, an' hang their feet off the edge. They yelled a lot of shit out to everybody and especially to me, personally, in center field 'cause I was there every night. They would toss their empty bottles at me, an' call me a stupid bobo, an' all kinds of Southern things.

"Hey, Falls, you never gonna make the major leagues," they'd yell. "You never gonna get out of Jacksonville, nigger!"

"You just wait an' see me get out of Jacksonville!" I'd yell back at 'em sometimes, to impress Wanda. Though that was the trouble with her bein' there: I didn't want to yell back anything too nasty. I couldn't even make fun of the town too much, seein' as how half the people in it were related to her by blood.

But they didn't appreciate my admirable restraint, even if Wanda did. They would just give me more shit when they spotted me walkin' over to her an' her frownin' brothers, to talk some honey an' blow kisses.

"You better take that pussy, 'cause that's the only thing you're takin' out of Jaxville!" they'd yell. "You ain't good enough to make the major leagues, nigger. You *know* you gonna be back in

some town like this on Saturday afternoon, mowin' the lawn for
that woman!''

It was fool talk, I know, just designed to make me doubt. But I
still did. Language like that is usually enough to spook any minor-
league ballplayer. Even when you know you're good enough for
the show, like I did, you still don't *know* if you can make it. There's
anything can go wrong. You can fall down an' break your ankle
that very night. It might not even be that dramatic. Just one thing
can lead to another, one slump at the wrong time an' you find
yourself ridin' the buses forever.

They were a hard crowd. They wouldn't even take their eyes
off their dice an' card games when we were up. Cal Rigby used to
complain, but the management couldn't afford not to let 'em in.
But one night we *made* 'em pay attention. Or, that is, John Barr
did. That night, he nearly tore down the park all by hisself. Not
to mention killin' Moose Maas.

It happened a couple weeks after I got married, when I was still
feelin' fat an' happy. We couldn't afford to go anywhere for the
honeymoon, not even for a day. I had a road trip to make. An'
we couldn't really afford to live anyplace, either. Wanda found us
a little house, not much more than a shotgun shack—like the
kind my old grandmother down in Georgia used to whistle at
when we walked by, 'cause she was afraid she would end up dyin'
in one.

But Wanda fixed it up real nice. She sewed curtains for it, an'
got leftover furniture from her daddy, an' picked flowers to put
in empty Coke bottles around the windowsills. I was gettin' fat on
her cookin', all sugar an' spice. She got free apples from one of
her relatives who owned a fruit business, an' she made apple pies
all that summer. The house would be like a steam bath afterward,
but it smelled nice.

I didn't have time for any of the annies anymore, except for
once when I walked out after callin' Wanda from the locker room
on the road an' there was one waiting for me an' I took her under
the stands an' did it right there. But I considered that to be a
tribute to her. I couldn't wait to get back, an' when I came back
to that house it smelled of apples an' brown sugar cooking, an'
when I came to her she smelled the same way, sweatin' an' grinnin' at me over that stove, wipin' one hand long an' slow over her

forehead. She was wearin' a old faded dress that I pulled down right past her shoulders, she was so skinny an' young that it slid right off, and we made love in the kitchen while the pie cooled. Then we sat around at the kitchen table, naked still, an' stuffed ourselves with pie an' vanilla ice cream that we melted over it just from the natural heat of that room.

It was that night, back from the road, that we started a big series with the Nashville Sounds. We always liked to beat Nashville since they were the Yankees' farm team, an' we thought it mattered up in New York. But it was still hard to get too excited, it was such a miserable night out there. It was even hotter than usual, an' the lights were so dim it looked like there was fog layin' over the whole outfield.

"We really gotta play tonight?" I asked Moose Maas, who was a coach down there. I could still feel that pie an' ice cream sloggin' around in my stomach. And Moose didn't even have the energy to cuss me casual. He barely had the strength to spit his tobacco, it was so hot.

"You get up to the major leagues, all they play in is air-conditioned houses," was the best he could wheeze out. "The ushers come bring you a mint julep between innings."

He always had a glad word like that, which was good, since I never learned anything from him. He fell asleep in the dugout every night, an' the only thing he did was sit around with Cal after every game an' help him write out the nightly report to Ellsworth Pippin. That's what The Great White Father required: a report on every game from his minor-league managers, written the same night, so their impressions would be fresh in their heads. Cal would write it out longhand, in pencil, with Moose Maas sittin' next to him to give him a few invaluable suggestions. Only not this night.

It started out simple enough. I hit a single to lead off the first. I was still there when Barr comes up with two outs an' this Nashville swizzlehead tries to put some smoke by him. Like most minor-league pitchers, smoke was all he had, an' like most of them it wasn't even all that fast.

It seemed from first base that Barr swung slow an' easy, like he was behind the pitch. But before I could turn my head all the way around, that ball was gone. It was hit on a line, like everything

else he connected with, but I figured the humidity would keep it
in the park. I started diggin' hard from first, but before I was
around second I looked out to center field, and I could see the
kids jumpin' down like leaves into the bleachers.

It tore into the first giant plastic record, just below where they'd
been sitting. Pieces of the black plastic fell like giant bats through
the night, swooping down after them. That distracted 'em from
their dicin' an' their card games for a few minutes. They were
yellin' about it for the next couple innings, an' tryna hit me with
their empty whiskey bottles.

But when Barr got up again in the third, they were quiet. There
was always somethin' about John Barr that chilled the fans. They
never really got on him, an' they never cheered him—not even
in Jacksonville, after that home run that broke the record. But
the punks up top the jukebox stopped their gamblin' operation,
just to see if he could do it again.

'Course, they didn't really *believe* it. They all knew a shot that
far an' that high was once in a season—maybe once in a career.
But just the fact that he made 'em stop an' *consider* it happenin'
again was respect enough.

The swizzlehead that Nashville still had out on the mound was
ready now, an' you could tell he was thinkin'. He was thinkin',
Hell, Barr hit his fastball the last time up, so now he's gonna throw
him nothin' but curves. Everybody on the field knew what was
comin'—though you could see the kid was proud of figuring it
all out, just like in the major leagues. He had a little smile on his
face when John Barr came up to the plate again.

It almost worked, if only because that boy had the worst curveball in the whole Southern League. Nobody in this game *but* John
Barr would've had the patience for that first fat curve that come
in. It broke so slow an' wide that most hitters would've busted
their bats in half swingin' ahead of it.

But Barr didn't. He timed it as perfect as he did the fastball the
first time around. 'Course, he had to do more of the work himself,
the ball was movin' so slow. He had to pop those shoulders back
a little more, took a wider cut at the ball, an' get a little more
trajectory into it.

But it went. This time it lingered up by the top of that gigantic
jukebox, up by the giant flying bugs. It hit the next record in the

line and shattered it just like the first one. The kids all jumped down again, and when he come up for the third time, there was even what you might call a little tribute from the top of the jukebox.

"Let's see him do it again!" they were shoutin'.

"Shit, bet he can't do that three times in a row!" And they would roll over laughin'.

But they were watching to see if he could. Everybody in the whole ballpark was, with the exception of Moose Maas. He was asleep in the dugout, arms crossed over his big gut, same as every night. Not even the clappin' an' the oohin' an' the aahin' was enough to wake him up.

By the time John Barr came up again, the fool who started for Nashville was departed for the night. The reliever they had in now was the second most common kind you see in the minors. He was a finesse man, without even a pretense at major-league heat. He got by with what passes for smarts in the game.

His strategy was never to actually put a pitch in the strike zone. He got a couple promotions out of throwin' bad pitches to swizzleheads right out of high school. They didn't have the patience to lay off the first two or three, an' make him come around with the slow, tasty stuff.

But John Barr did. He had more patience than God. He would always take a couple from a junkman like that, until usually the pitcher got too frightened an' just gave in an' walked him. They couldn't bear thinkin' 'bout the consequences of havin' to put their slow shit across to someone like that, once they got behind in the count.

But this time, right from the first pitch, Barr is stickin' his bat out at the ball, just gettin' a piece of it. We couldn't figure out what he was doin'. I thought he'd gone crazy to hit another home run, just tryin' to connect with anything.

He kept foulin' pitch after pitch off, barely gettin' the bat on each one an' nubbin' it foul. Then I understood it. He was lurin' that finesse pitcher the way you'd catch a bigmouth bass. He was givin' him a little bit of the line, inch by inch, until he was ready to go for the whole hook. Barr was lettin' the kid think he was foolin' him. Lettin' him think he was one pitch away from strikin' him out, gettin' him anxious for that strikeout.

But no matter where he put the ball, Barr would reach it. He had the bat speed an' the reach to get ahold of all the junk the kid could throw and just trickle it foul. That boy out there was frustrated after throwin' all those pitches exactly where he wanted 'em, each one an inch or two off the plate. Finally he broke down an' threw one a little bit on the money. Not much—just barely in the strike zone. But it was enough for Barr, who turned on any ball in there like radar.

The ball got out to the third record so fast the kids didn't have time to jump down. They just lay there an' covered their heads while it smashed all over the field.

When he came up for the last time, the crowd was huddled around the jukebox like refugees from a flood. They wanted to believe it. It was just the minor leagues, an' nobody would even remember it for long. But they still wanted to see it.

I was out on third base at the time, but I could hear the quiet all over the ballpark. The only sound was the giant flyin' cockroaches snapping an' popping as they flew into the lights. And Moose Maas, still snoring. You could hear him out on the field. The Nashville manager wasn't even yellin' anything out to his third pitcher of the night, who was also the most dangerous.

He was a vet'ran, who'd been up an' down between the majors for a few years an' was still lookin' to make it back. He had a little stuff left an' he knew what he was doing, which counts more'n anything. His was a slow release, with all kinds of jerks an' bumps to his movement to break a hitter's concentration. He doctored the ball if he could get away with it, an' he liked to come in with what you were least expecting.

I was takin' a couple steps off third, tryna distract him. But he ignored me an' paid attention to the batter, an' when he came in to the plate he pitched from a full windup. We were seven runs up, an' he knew I wasn't goin' anyplace.

At the plate now, Barr was pumpin' his bat and takin' the same short, quick swings he always did. Like he was measurin' the pitcher, measurin' the ballpark—measurin' the whole world for himself. The vet'ran out there let him wait. He watched Barr pump that bat and then put it back up over his shoulder, and he waited for him to let up an' move it again—just once more—so he could start into his motion right in the middle of Barr's practice swing an' catch him off balance.

But John Barr didn't swing. He didn't do anything but wait right back at the pitcher. After a long time the vet'ran went into his motion, herkin' an' jerkin'. Thinkin' maybe instead that he'd froze Barr's bat—that Barr would've lost his concentration waitin' so long in one position, an' would be just that extra half-second late with his swing.

It was a good pitch, too—a low curve just under the strike zone and inside. Exactly where the pitcher wanted it, and with enough motion to make a batter start for it, then pull up. It was a major-league curveball.

But it didn't fool John Barr. His bat didn't freeze and he didn't break it trying to check the swing. He flicked that bat out there quick as a lizard's tongue an' hit a golf shot.

At first it looked like it was gonna go straight up an' come straight down, a can a' corn for the second baseman. Then it looked like it was goin' all the way out—right over the jukebox an' clear out of the park. Which meant it would've had to travel at least six hundred feet, but it seemed to have the distance, the way he hit that ball, right on the fat end of the bat.

But it didn't go quite that far, neither. I don't know if it was the heavy air, or all the bugs, or the slowness of that old vet'ran pitcher's curve. But the ball started to come down just as it reached the giant jukebox in center field.

It couldn't be that he aimed it, of course. Not even John Barr could've aimed a ball that far, an' that exact, to where it was comin' down right now over the last record. I don't think he could have, anyway.

The Color Commentary

The fans watched it descend with their heads turned up and mouths open, as if to catch an apple falling from the sky. As the ball plummeted toward the thin edge of that giant record, there were only two figures moving on the frozen diorama of the field. One was the centerfielder, a mad white speck, running hard toward the fence as if he had any chance in the world to catch it.

Not even stopping when he reached the high, smooth wall, but trying to clamber over it, clutching at nothing on the cement— as if once he got over he could somehow rise up to the height of the ball, fifty feet above the playing field. He did get to the top of the wall, out of sheer force of will, to hang there by one arm, waving in frustration at the ball.

The other figure moving was John Barr, running quickly around the bases, head down as usual, not even watching the ball fall toward the last record. He didn't spare it a glance as it plummeted back toward the jukebox and nicked, just barely nicked, the record's edge.

The Old Swizzlehead

You could hear 'em go *Ahhh* out there. You could hear 'em go *Ooohhhh*. It's just as good as the miracle, I thought. It's just as good as actually knockin' down the last record, even if not quite. I started to trot on home, tryna hide the disappointment to myself, for after all it *was* almost as good.

Then I heard the shout. It was like a big footstep landed right behind me, all those voices goin' up at once. I looked back over my left shoulder an' I saw that last giant record, startin' to wobble.

It shook slowly back an' forth, buildin' up its own momentum. I stood still on the baseline, unaware of where I was on a ballfield for the first time in my life. I just watched that big black record, wigglin' an' wobblin' out there, gettin' looser an' looser. Until finally it bent nearly in half an' propelled itself right off the edge of the jukebox. It rolled right off, past all the openmouthed fans, and flew off the edge. It smashed up on the centerfield grass and fell into another thousand pieces.

For a moment it was silent again. The only thing you could hear was Moose Maas, snorin' away in the dugout. It was almost a terrible silence, like nobody could believe what happened.

Then the cheering started again, only it wasn't what you'd really call cheering. It was something different from what I ever heard in a ballpark anywhere, before or since. It started out like a regular cheer, but it rose higher an' higher. Like the crowd was *bayin'* at that home run, like a dog howling at the moon. Like they weren't victorious, or happy, but only astounded.

I guess I got caught up in it myself. I was yellin' somethin', too, though I don't remember what. An' then there was that sound again, like a big footstep landing right behind me. Only this time it *was* a foot.

"Go on!" I heard him say, right behind me on the base path between third base an' home plate. I nearly jumped in the air. I had no idea he was so close, that he came around the bases so fast, runnin' head down an' not even lookin' at his own miracle. It just never occurred to me where John Barr was in the ballpark— though I should've known he wouldn't stand around admirin' his own handiwork.

"What the hell are you waitin' for?"

He was waitin' for me to run, since if he'd passed me on the bases it wouldn't have been an official home run an' he officially would have been out. But his voice didn't sound cold like it usually did when he was impatient. It almost had a little fun in it.

"What— what—" was all I could get out.

An' then I got an even bigger shock. John Barr grinned at me. It was the only time I ever saw him smile, at me or at anyone else—at least until the end of that last, strange season that he ever played in organized baseball, when he wasn't exactly hisself anymore.

I still wasn't sure of what all I had seen out there. I'm still not sure today. I ran home all the way to tell Wanda after it was over, like a little kid comin' back from a playground game. When I ran in she was sittin' in the kitchen of that little house, readin' a book, an' I felt like a kid, all right. I started shoutin' all about it to her, an' she lowered her book an' looked at me, an' smiled, an' told me that sounded great, that she wished she was there to see it.

But I could see, even as excited as I was, that she had kind of a dazed expression on her face. Like I had just interrupted somethin' she was *really* interested in. I started noticin' that more an' more when I came in at night.

I tried to get her to go out to the park more, be with the other wives. When I was comin' up, the wives used to be like another team out there. They did everything together. They would sit in the stands together, keep scorecards, root for their man. They used to go shoppin' together, baby-sit each other's kids. Cry on each other's shoulders when they found a picture of some road annie in his wallet.

Most of 'em was high school sweethearts, married their man when he was back in Single-A ball, or the rookie leagues, an' nobody knew how'd he do. It was a gamble, takin' up with a ballplayer. They were right out of high school themselves, usually, an' just as stupid an' young as their husbands. But they put up with all the hard years, makin' it through the minors an' raisin' the kids on nothin'.

They hung on after their boy made it to the major leagues, keepin' their marriage together by threatening and ignoring. They turned a blind eye to some things their husbands did, an' made it clear they could get a divorce lawyer if he did others. They would stick together for the team, for each other. It kept 'em in line, if you wanna look at it that way.

Then it started to change. Most of 'em still sit together, but it's different. It's got more a threatening side to it. A couple years ago, two guys on Oakland dropped their wives for some young annies. They'd been married since high school, but they thought the two of 'em would just go away an' raise the kids an' leave 'em to some younger pussy.

But the wives didn't go away. They'd been takin' college courses in the summer, an' they knew what they were doin'. They hired a lawyer. They even wrote a book.

That whole summer, whenever you turned on a talk show, there they were, tellin' stories about somethin' stupid or nasty their ex-husbands did. You couldn't get around 'em. You'd turn on some local cable channel in Pittsburgh, an' there they'd be, talkin' all about the dumb things their husbands did. It got to be depressin'.

By the time I made it to the majors, Wanda didn't bother to go to the games at all anymore.

"That's your thing, and I respect it," she would tell me, still smilin' that sweet smile like back in Jaxville. Only now it seemed a little more superior.

"I don't expect you to go to Off-Broadway shows with me, do I?" she said, like it was the same thing.

"'Off-Broadway' *what*?" I asked her. "What the hell does that mean? This is my life we're talkin' here."

But it got worse. She started changin' fast. She'd wear designer clothes, an' her little African revolution hat. She got her hair cut all the time, an' her nails done. She even modulated her voice. You'd get home, it sounded like the public-address man came home with you.

"Who you talkin' to with that voice?" I'd ask her. "There somebody else here I don't see, you go around talkin' like that?"

"Just because I wish to sound like an educated woman is no reason for you to feel threatened," she'd say, roundin' out every word like she was bein' careful to touch each base on a home run.

It was like she was a different person, more sure of herself. She even got bigger. I don't think Wanda gained a pound from the time she was nineteen years old. But somehow, when you looked at her all done up in those serious clothes, with her African hat an' her modulated voice, she just seemed *larger.*

She started takin' classes, too. She took pottery classes, black history classes, feminist consciousness classes—like she weren't conscious enough already. Anything she could get her hands on. She was always goin' off to somethin' at the New School, goin' up to a lecture at the West Side Y. That was all she would talk about. She wouldn't barely mention how I did in the game.

"What do you think about the idea of establishing a separate black state in the South?" she would ask me, right after I walked in from a seven-hour doubleheader. She asked it all breathless an' eager, but not one word about the triple I had in the first game an' the three stolen bases in the second.

"Yeah, that's what I want," I told her. "To go back to goddamned Jaxville."

"Seriously, Richard," she would say, like I was her student. That's when I felt nasty, I couldn't help it.

"When they tell us what state they're gonna give us, that's when you know they decided where to put the national dump," I told her, an' she looked at me like I was puttin' my mouth on the most important thing in the world. Then I'd try to act cynical like I really meant it, an' we'd have a fight about it. We'd have a fight about the goddamned mythical black state in the South.

One night I got back at one in the morning after goin' oh-fer five against the Astros, an' all she wanted to talk about was Hannibal, an' how he pulled his elephants over a mountain.

"He was a proud black man," she would say, close to tears about the whole thing. "What a feat to accomplish."

"Yeah, that musta been somethin'. His soldiers musta loved walkin' over those mountains through that elephant shit."

She would say, "Don't you care? Don't you care about your heritage?" An' then I would just make it worse.

"You wanna see a proud black man, come out to the god-damned game sometime!"

Things like that, but I couldn't help it. An' then when I even looked sideways at some fine young thing she got mad. Like most of the wives, she couldn't see it that it was nothin' personal. That it was there, an' the hotel room was feelin' small, an' there didn't seem any good reason against it.

"How much reassurance do you need?" she would ask me, like I was her psychological patient. "How big does your penis need to be?"

"It's somethin' on the road," I would tell her.

"How old are you?"

The year before, she started talkin' about puttin' our relationship "on a more equal basis." That's how she talked now. She wanted us to move to some small town out in Oregon 'cause they had a good degree program, whatever the hell that was.

"What do you want me to do out there?" I told her. "You think they play big-league ball in some little piney town out in Oregon?"

"I've traveled to places because of your career," she said. "Now it's your turn."

"Honey, I don't even got a career if I move out there. Can't you understand that?"

"I know something about the big leagues, Richard," she said. "They have a team out in Seattle. You could play there."

"Sure. I love seventh place in the American League West. I'm not goin' out to play for the Seattle Mariners just so you can take some college courses."

"But in the meantime I'm supposed to get an inferior education," she snapped back, like I was imposin' on her. "Your contract is up in another year, and you could become a free agent and go play for Seattle."

"What you do? Go call their general manager?"

We started fightin' all the time, an' it was fightin' lazy. It wasn't even things we were so mad about. We just said stuff to get on each other, like a dog who can't leave an old piece of rope alone.

By the time that last, strange year started, we didn't live together most of the time. She had the big house out in New Jersey, an' I mostly tried to stay out of her way. She was always talkin' about gettin' a court order, gettin' my property tied up so I couldn't go blowin' money on the horseflesh or the annies.

"I know killer lawyers," I would tell her. "You won't get a thing."

"Richard," she would say, "when are you going to get a real life?"

For some reason we never got around to divorcin'. I didn't want to lose the money, an' I guess Jaxville was still in my head. I could still smell the smell of apples an' sugar melting all around that shotgun shack.

There was somethin' about Jacksonville that stuck, I think. It was like with Moose Maas, who was the point of the whole story in the first place. He was asleep there in the dugout, right through every home run John Barr hit that night. Asleep even when he touched home plate the last time an' the fans went wild, bayin' at the moon.

In fact, he never woke up. We played the last half-inning, set the Nashville Sounds down one-two-three, an' went back to the dugout still yellin' an' yippin' over Barr. Everybody was so excited that no one noticed Coach Maas didn't get up on cue. Not even Cal Rigby noticed. I guess when you just seen a miracle, wakin' up the dead tends to skip your mind. It wasn't till we got back to the locker room that Cal noticed he didn't come with us.

"Hey, Swiz, go back an' wake up Moose, willya?" he yells over to me, an' everybody has a big laugh over the idea of Moose Maas still sittin' there asleep.

By the time I got back up to the dugout, all the fans had gone an' the stadium lights were out. There was just one light way up on the giant jukebox to see by. The whole place was peaceful as if there had never been a game there, not to mention somethin' you would only see once in a lifetime.

An' Moose Maas was still asleep in the corner. I know he was alive then, 'cause I set an' watched him for a minute. He was still snorin' away, though now his breaths were comin' longer an' qui-

eter. A fat old white guy, with bugs hoppin' over the flabby folds
in his cheeks, and his arms still crossed over his stomach.

Then he stopped, just like that. He stopped breathin', an'
leaned over a little bit to one side. No warning, nothin'. His
breath just stopped comin' out. His arms didn't even unfold from
his chest. I saw it right in front of me. And of course I couldn't
believe it. I shook him an' pounded his heart, an' yelled for help.

But he was dead, just like that. Like he was content to fade off
in the corner of a dugout, not even caring if a rare an' miraculous
feat was goin' on in the same ballpark.

I thought then that it was John Barr who killed him. I thought
maybe those records he broke tilted the universe so much that it
sucked up whatever extra life force was keepin' Moose Maas alive.
The other guys on the team thought so, too, except for the Jeebee
Jaycees, who called the idea a sacrilege.

14

He's awful. In fact, he's worse than bad.

—TOM BOSWELL

The Boy

Sometimes in the summer he would go with his father to the hotel, to swim in the pool and follow him on his rounds. On these occasions his father would swing along, whistling aimlessly, hips broadly waggling and jangling his tool belt. He was proud to have him along, the boy knew—to play the experienced father before the other hotel employees, showing his son the ropes.

The boy liked the pool, at least. It had heated salt water, so the chlorine didn't sting his eyes, and it wasn't as cold as the real ocean, which was too frigid to swim in for most of the summer. But he realized it was an illusion, even as he cut through the water with long, easy strokes. From the pool he could see the real sea breaking at the foot of the cliff the hotel was situated on. The real ocean was like a live thing, dark and fathomless, constantly moving and tugging at you. The saltwater pool was an ocean with a bottom you could see and even touch. The illusion unsettled him, for it was such a nice one he could see how you could get used to it.

He heard his father call, distant and familiar, and he climbed obediently up out of the pool, and began to pat himself dry with the small white hotel towel.

The hotel itself was a sagging white wedding cake, with ante-bellum pillars across the front and grand wooden porches curling around each of the upper stories. It was over a hundred years old, and it had outlived all the other grand old hotels in Prides Crossing—its owner fervently believed—by offering old-fashioned New England charm. This meant no air conditioning and no TVs in the rooms. Thick, dusty rugs covered the stairs and all the corridors. On each of the landings were little tables and overstuffed couches, and locked glass cases in which old and un-interesting books were slowly falling to pieces. Everything was warped by the sea air, so that none of the room doors quite closed against the wood of their doorjambs.

This was where his father worked, and the boy knew he thought of it as his own. He knew it just from the way his father was stand-ing, leaning nonchalantly against a wall by the recreation room, his arms folded over his chest. The room was dark, and smelled heavily of mold. The only other people there were two guests batting a ping-pong ball around, and another plucking sluggishly at a piano.

"C'mon, I wanna show yah a little something about electricity," his father said when he reached him, enveloping the boy with a big arm around his shoulders, and moving him awkwardly for-ward through the hotel.

Everywhere the boy could see his father's shoddy handiwork: electrical wires sloppily enveloped in black tape, crooked wall-paper that was already puckering and peeling, nails driven into the walls at oblique angles, and cheap wooden slats shoved under the legs of wobbly dining room tables. Everything was either half-done, badly done, or not done at all. While his father walked obliviously by these daily proofs of his own incompetence, the boy wanted to stop at each one and smooth it over, make it right in order to hide his father's shame.

"Now let's see, where was that outlet?" He pretended to be searching for the right room, taking the opportunity to parade his son past as many of the other staff as possible. Not that they seemed to care. The boy noticed that they shunned his father. The chambermaids, clustering in the hallways to gab and smoke by their stalled linen carts, giggled and whispered among them-selves when he approached.

"Good morning, ladies," he called out loudly to them. "You know my son."

There would be more titters and occasionally a snort of derision. Sometimes they would call out hard things to him.

"You know that toilet's still backed up in 313."

"You know Mr. Squam's been looking for you."

"Hey, you gonna fix that plug in 56 this summer? The last people almost electrocuted themselves on it. It can burn down the whole place, you know."

"Sure, sure." He waved them off, the same way he waved off his wife's objections to his grandiose schemes, and anything else that got in the way of his view of things. He plucked a screwdriver from his belt, twirled it in his hand, and told the boy to watch.

"All you need's one of these to take care of this baby."

He wedged himself into the space between the wall and one of the arched twin beds of the room, and tugged at the wall socket. Because he did not want to look, the boy's eye wandered to the beds. They were set between warped wooden headboards, and covered with fine white lace bedspreads that matched the window curtains. The windows looked out over the sea and he stared through them, wondering what it was like to come and stay in a room like this for a night—to be a traveler free to come here and swim in the warm, salty pool, and do whatever he wanted, and then go home.

"Yeah, look at that baby."

His father was holding back the edge of the outlet, and pointing with the screwdriver at one of the frayed, multicolored wires behind it. Even as he pointed, the boy had the feeling that he hadn't ought to be doing it, that the screwdriver was too close to the wires.

"Careful, Dad—" he burst out involuntarily, instantly aware that his father might take this as a lack of faith, and be angry. But his father considered it instead a sign of filial devotion, and puffed merrily on.

"Don't worry," he said, inserting the screwdriver into one of the screws still half-securing the socket to the wall. "Your old man knows what he's doing. Just gotta take this off, do a little splicing—"

He turned the screwdriver once, and two thin blue rays of light raced across the tool and up his arm. His jaw dropped open even as his arm muscle jumped up, but he didn't drop the screwdriver. It was only the great reflexes of the boy, already anticipating trouble, that saved him, kicking the connecting tool across the room with his sneaker before more current could ground itself in his father.

His father sat pinned back against the little bed, his eyes closed, face grey, swollen tongue hanging loosely out of an open mouth. In that moment, all the boy could think of was how foolish he looked in death. He slapped his father's face once, then again. He had the urge to start pounding it hard, with his fists, over and over again.

Then his father's eyes opened. They rolled loosely around, like a cartoon character's, the boy thought. His mouth remained open, tongue still lolling out of one corner.

"Wake up!" the boy yelled at him.

But of course his father mistook that, too, for love—just as he took everything to somehow be an aid to his life and plans. He blinked and closed his mouth, slobbering his tongue slowly back inside.

"There, there," he lisped, stretching out an arm to wrap it consolingly around his son, and sending a row of tiny shocks down his spine. "I'm all right. Thath the dangerth of working with electrithity."

He didn't try to do anything more with the socket after that. He simply tugged his heavy work gloves on—as the boy knew he should have done in the first place—shoved the outlet back against the wall, and taped it there with heavy black swaths of electrical tape.

"There, that should hold it," he announced. "Oughta be a whole rewiring of the hotel, but that bastahd Squam's too cheap."

"That's all you have to do to it?" the boy questioned him, a little desperately. "Can't it start a fire in the walls?"

"Nah," he said, walking him out of the room with the two little beds, his arm still around his shoulders. "Once you do that, it'll be okay. You gotta know about electricity, son."

The boy looked back at the thin white lace curtains, now dancing a little on a sea breeze. He thought of a traveler staying in the room again. Looking out the open windows at the fake pool and the real ocean, lying back on one of the narrow, arched beds, unaware of the danger lurking inside the walls—

15

Your arm is all you are.

—JIM PALMER

Skeeter Mesquite

My old man always wanted to play in the Pacific Coast League, which was almost as good as the majors back then. He used to walk around saying the names of those teams like they were saints:

"The Hollywood Stars. The Oakland Oaks. The San Francisco Seals."

The trouble was, he didn't have any control. He had a lot of speed even when he was an old man, with his belly hanging over his belt. He'd take me out to play catch and my hand would hurt for days. But he could never put the ball where he wanted it. He tried out for the Chihuahua team in the Mexican League four or five times, but he never made it.

"I could never hit that catcher's mitt where he held it," he would say, and spit like the taste of the oilfield was in his mouth.

They used to make fun of him for it around the local fields. They would make it a sexual thing, like ballplayers do with everything:

"Hey, Chico, you can't put it where you want it? Your wife must be *hurting*!"

For a while he laughed it off. But after a few more tryouts he didn't think it was so funny anymore. When they would yell like that, he would try to cut off their ears with a pitch.

"Hey, Chico, what's the matter? You can't come *in?*"

When I was in high school he came back from the oilfields one weekend and took me to play catch. He was very serious about it. He marked off the regulation distance between the mound and home plate, sixty feet, six inches. Then he shoved a board into the ground, painted in the strike zone, and told me to pitch.

I couldn't hit it with one pitch in ten. And I had much less speed than he did. You could barely hear the ball against the board—just a tapping sound that was more embarrassing than missing it. When we went over and looked at it, there wasn't even a dent in the wood.

He watched me throw like that for fifteen minutes and didn't say one word. After we looked over the board, he shrugged and said, "I better get back to the oilfields. You're not going to make your living being a ballplayer, that's for sure."

The Old Swizzlehead

By the time The Emp'ror ran into his wall, we were floundering, like the flies like to say. There was nobody else in the division with our talent, but our lead kept dwindlin'. The Cards kept shearin' off a game or two a week, an' everybody was startin' to get nervous.

And we were sufferin' out there. Maximilian Duke was back in the lineup after a couple weeks, but he was still shy of the wall. That was the thing about Charlie Stanzi: he made players the opposite of what he said he wanted them to be. The Emp'ror couldn't go to the wall, Bobby Roddy an' Lonnie Lee could barely turn a double play, an' Spock Feeley couldn't stop a basketball. But the worst thing was what he did to Moses Yellowhorse.

Like most managers, The Little Maniac thought he knew everything there was to know about pitching. He stood up there in his cowboy hat an' his designer boots one night an' told the flies he was gonna get the staff to put out more.

"Pitchers have to pitch to get in a groove," he said, whatever that means, an' they all nodded their heads an' wrote it down.

He decided to start with Moses Yellowhorse. Best pitcher on the staff, in the major leagues ten years throwin' pure heat, an' The Little Maniac decided to give him tips on how to pitch.

"You know, if you just took a little bit off that pitch to Scatter-day, you might've had him," he'd tell Moses when he came back to the dugout after an inning.

"You'd have Whitaker fooled with a nice change-up," he'd say.

Just the usual manager's second-guessing. But it started to seep into Moses Yellowhorse's head.

Moses wasn't out there to fool anybody—he just blew the ball by you. The only time he ever threw a ball outside the strike zone was when you moved too close to the plate an' he aimed one at your head. That backed people off the plate in a hurry, since they knew how Moses drank.

His reputation for booze was exaggerated, of course, partly on purpose. It had to be, for him to still be alive. But he did like to absorb it. Cal Rigby used to watch him close, an' send some of us out to look after him when he thought Moses was ready to blow. He wasn't even tryna stop him. He just wanted somebody there in case anything happened.

There's all kinds of ballplayer drunks. There's what we call a Utah Yoo-Hoo, which is a mean drunk. You know—for that Robert De Niro movie where he keeps sayin', "You talkin' to me? Who you talkin' to?" Mean drunks always like to talk like that when they had a few, tryna seek out trouble.

They'd find it, too. We called the one who actually fought a Cock Biter, or a Headliner. They were the kind can't resist gettin' into bar fights an' endin' up with their names all over the papers. They were even more trouble than a Grabber, which is someone who likes to take a grab at any woman's ass when she walks by. A Grabber usually ends up bein' a Headliner or a Utah Yoo-Hoo just out of necessity.

Moses Yellowhorse wasn't that much trouble, but he was almost as bad. He was a Weeper, an' you never know what can come from one of those.

I never saw anybody happier to be drinkin' than when Moses walked into a bar. He'd line up shots an' beer chasers all around the table, an' then he would sit back an' laugh. He would laugh at everything anybody said. Anything with a passin' relationship to a joke, he would throw his head back an' roar till you could see every gold tooth in his mouth.

Then somethin' would happen an' he'd go into what Skeeter Mesquite called his tragic phase. It didn't take much to set it off. It could be anything. It might even be somethin' he was just thinkin' about to hisself. All of a sudden he'd be weeping. The first time I saw it was one night we were in some place down the Village. Somethin' came on the television over the bar about the Holocaust. I look over at Moses an' he's got tears runnin' down his face.

"It's so awful, Swiz," was all he could say when I asked him what was wrong. "It's so terrible what they did to those people."

I didn't think it was very nice or nothin', either. But he was weepin' like the Holocaust happened the day before out at Shea. At first I thought maybe it was because they were his people, at least on one side.

But it could be anything. The anniversary of John Lennon's death. A baby panda dyin' in the zoo. A plane crash. Whales stuck in the ice. Anything, great or small, and his big granite Indian face would crumple up.

Cal tried makin' a social work project out of him. He tried to get Moses to go into therapy, or AA, or at least get his teeth fixed. But Mose never liked to talk about it when he was sober.

"What do you do these things for?" Cal would ask him. "Is there anything you need? Money? Lawyers? *Anything*."

But Moses just put his head down an' was closemouthed as he ever was, away from a bar.

"No. Don't know. Won't do it again," was all he would say.

None of us knew why he got like that. Maybe we should have asked him when he was in the laughin' phase. Maybe you should ask a man why he drinks durin' each of his phases—when he's sober, when he's happy drunk, and when he's sad an' angry.

"Hell, when I was playin', they would've given him a bottle every time out," Cal Rigby told me. "Just to keep him happy."

It didn't seem to interfere with his game. Every year he was good for fifteen to twenty wins. He never missed a start, never gave you less than two hundred fifty innings. He was steady, at least out there on the mound.

But that wasn't enough for Stanzi.

"Great game," he would say, stoppin' by his locker to pat Moses on the shoulder. "You had your heater tonight."

Mose only grunted at him. He had his heater most nights, an' he didn't need to hear about it from Charlie Stanzi. But then The Little Maniac adds in:

"You know, one of these days they're gonna be waitin' for it."

He said it like he was half-kiddin', only he wasn't. It got Moses' attention, just like he knew it would.

"Let 'em wait for it. They still can't hit it," Moses said. But he looked up.

"Not right now," The Little Maniac says, an' shrugs his shoulders like it didn't matter that much to him. I knew that one, I was onto all his tricks by now. Moses was hooked.

"But they'll catch up to it. Maybe not this year. Maybe not even next year. But sooner or later they'll start timin' it. You oughta have another pitch already, for when that happens."

"They catch up to me, that's when I retire," Moses snorted at him, just like John Barr did. But he didn't want to retire. That's what got him listening to Stanzi. Moses Yellowhorse was a few years over thirty, an' when you're a ballplayer that's when everything changes.

"If you just had a good change, they couldn't touch you," Stanzi would tell him. And Moses would sit with his head down, knockin' the dirt out of his spikes an' actin' like he wasn't listenin'.

"All you need is one little out pitch. Somethin' to throw every now an' then so they can't wait on the heat or that big curve all the time."

Maybe he would've resisted The Little Maniac if things had gone right for a little while more. Maybe if he could've kept winning for a few more weeks with only his high heat—

But instead he had a couple poor starts in a row. Nothin' terrible. Couple losses where he hadda leave a little bit early, like a hundred other times in his career. But that's when he began to listen despite hisself. You could see it. He started to look up at the man all the time now when Charlie Stanzi talked. He'd come in after a bad inning an' Stanzi would give him a slap on the can an' shake his head like he was sympathetic.

"Don't matter how good a pitcher you are," he would tell Moses. "You can still be a better one."

Before long, Stanzi had him out there for special instruction.

"Stanzi said he spotted something in his motion," Skeeter Mesquite told me, an' made a face. "He told him that he just wants to correct it and get him back on the right track."

"Uh-huh."

I snuck out to the park early the next day myself, an' sure enough, there was Stanzi with him. He was tryna teach Moses Yellowhorse some kind of American League junk pitch.

"Just put your fingers there," he was tellin' Moses. "An' don't kick so far back—"

He was talkin' to him like he was some daddy out in the park on Sunday, teachin' his little boy how to play. But pitchers can go through their whole career tryna get their mechanics down. It looks easy, but it's not. All the parts got to work together, so a man don't rip hisself apart every time he throws a pitch. The arms, the legs, the feet, the knees—they all have to move coordinated. It's even more complicated than hitting. A pitcher's got to know how far to lean back, how high to kick up the front leg. How fast an' hard to pound forward to the plate. They even have to know how that ball should feel in their hands.

Moses Yellowhorse did. It came naturally to him, which is better than anything you can teach anybody in this game. He had pitched in the show for ten years without having to think hard about it. An' here was Charlie Stanzi, tryna teach it to him all over.

"You don't need this," I told Moses in the locker room later. "You don't need to have anything to do with that man."

But he looked away from me, kept holdin' an' twistin' the ball in his hand—in the grip Charlie Stanzi had just taught him.

"I wanna stay up, Swiz," was all he would say.

Skeeter Mesquite

When I came back to Chihuahua after my freshman year at UCLA, my old man set up the board again. He said he wanted to see what I had, to make a college team in the States. He measured out the exact distance with the yardstick, just like the last time, and set up the same board with the strike zone. And I didn't hit the target once.

Only this time, I didn't hit it in the same place, every time. I hit one exact spot, three inches low and to the left, with my first ten pitches. Then I hit another spot, three inches low and to the right, with the next ten. My father looked at that board and nodded his head. I still didn't have his speed, even as an old man. But he knew that I had something better.

"So you learned how to pitch," he said. "You can put it where you want it."

My whole career in pro ball, I don't think I put ten balls in the strike zone. But the goddamned fools never caught on like my father did.

The Old Swizzlehead

I remember the first time Moses threw one of those things in a game. He uncorked some big puffball that does a coupla dipsy-doodles an' a backflip on its way into the plate, then settles down into Spock Feeley's glove, easy as a feather. The batter let it go by for a strike, he was so surprised. But not Spock Feeley. He called time an' ran right out to the mound, where Moses Yellowhorse was lookin' pleased with hisself.

"What the fuck was that?" Feeley asked him. "I called for a goddamned fastball."

"That was my new out pitch," Moses told him, an' Feeley thought he sounded proud of it, which was the first time he ever heard Moses Yellowhorse sound proud about anything.

"Throw fucking strikes," Feeley counseled him.

But he wouldn't do it. Moses Yellowhorse fell in love with that new pitch, an' he wouldn't stop throwin' it even after they got smart an' knocked his ball all over the park.

"I gotta save my arm," he told Feeley when he came out to the mound again.

"Just throw the fuckin' ball an' save your ass," Feeley told him.

But it wasn't no use. He was hooked on that new puff stuff. The Little Maniac turned the hardest-throwin' starter in the National

League into a candy-ass American League junkman, an' there was no talkin' him out of it. He wouldn't even go out there an' throw his first couple warm-up tosses into the upper deck anymore.

"I gotta use my warm-up pitches to get my new stuff together," he told Feeley.

Days he wasn't pitchin', Moses spent all his time out in the bullpen, workin' on his new pitch. Pitchers like to throw some in between starts, but he wouldn't stop. He would stay out there the whole game sometimes. Three hours at a time, he'd be throwin' that foolish junk an' wearin' his arm down. Until that junk was the only thing he *could* throw in a game anymore. An' then he really was committed.

He won a game or two at first, before everybody figured out that it really was Moses Yellowhorse out there. Then it didn't fool anyone. The rumor got around that he musta blown his arm an' this was all he could throw. An' Stanzi wouldn't deny it, when the flies asked. He was too scared hisself to admit what he done. He would look away when they asked an' say, "I don't have anything to say about that."

"Like he's the martyr, holding back from knocking his own pitcher," Ellie Jay said.

"Even he's worryin' about this one," I told her. "He knows, he wrecks our pitchin', he ain't goin' to the Series."

"He doesn't care so much about that," she said. "He just wants to avoid the blame for it."

She was right. Now when Moses started comin' in at the end of an inning with his head down, Stanzi yelled at him about his pitch selection.

"What were you throwin' him that for when you were ahead of the count?" he'd second-guess him, in front of the whole team.

"I was throwin' him my new pitch," Moses would say.

"I didn't say you should throw that all the time," Stanzi told him now, like he had any more choice.

Stanzi would pull him out of the game, an' Moses would go down into the clubhouse an' wreck the place. He'd get knocked out earlier every start, an' by the time the game was over we'd find the whole place torn up and him gone. It kept gettin' worse. First he might knock over the water cooler or the postgame spread. Turn over the table an' leave the floor covered with salami an' cheese an' mayonnaise for the clubhouse boys to pick up in the international shitting order.

Then he started using bats to smash things. One time he broke up all the overhead lights an' the fans, until the whole floor was shiny with broken glass an' sharp bits of metal. Another time he smashed his own locker—just broke it into pieces—along with all his clothes an' his personal effects, scattered out over the carpet.

Guys were always throwing tantrums in the clubhouse. You even wanna see a little bit of it, to show they care. But we began to realize how much time it took Moses to do all that destruction. He was destroying things piece by piece, until the bat he was using broke or there wasn't anything left in front of him anymore. He'd show up the next day with his eyes red an' his hands swelled up big as hams. That started to hurt him, too; he couldn't barely hold the ball anymore, even in the way that Charlie Stanzi showed him.

There was no talkin' to him about it. There was no bein' with him even. He wouldn't let the old Cal Rigby protection squads go with him anymore to see that he kept out of trouble.

"You can't help me," he would say, an' swing his arm down in a peculiar cutting gesture, with his palm held flat toward the ground.

Soon he was pitchin' not to make a mistake, which is when a pitcher is near the end. He was tryin' to place the ball in there, like he was afraid of it bein' hit. An' the more he tried to do that, the less he could, of course.

"He's lost out there," Spock Feeley told me. "Like he's right back to the beginning of hisself."

"Are you going to send him down to work it out?" Ellie Jay asked Stanzi. That was in everybody's mind, though nobody liked to say it, not even the flies.

"I don't see any need for that," Stanzi said, since he never liked to admit one of his projects didn't work. But he took Moses out of the rotation and buried him in long relief. He pitched pure mop-up, in games we already had won or lost. But even then, with all the pressure off, the man couldn't throw strikes.

Moses did stop breakin' up the locker room, which I guess we should've seen was the first bad sign. He acted like he didn't care about it no more, sayin' nothin', starin' straight ahead. Shruggin' his shoulders when one of the flies asked about it. During the game he would sit on the bench and let his pitching arm hang down outside his jacket like a dead weight.

"Piece of shit!" he would hiss all of a sudden, an' pound at the arm with his other fist. "A piece of shit!"

He had one more bad outing against the Phillies. He went one an' two-thirds, gave up eight walks an' five runs, which got the fans at Shea not only booin' but also laughin' on every pitch. When Stanzi finally pulled him he ran right down the ramp into the clubhouse.

That's where we found him at the end of the game, two hours later, sittin' on the stool in front of his locker. He had his uniform on still, like he hadn't moved at all since he first came out of the game.

"You'd better get in the shower before that arm freezes up on you," Skeeter Mesquite suggested. But Moses didn't say anything, and he didn't move.

"Something's the matter with him," somebody said, in a nervous voice. But most of the guys didn't notice yet. They were sayin' when they walked by:

"Hey, buddy, get 'em next time."

"Big Chief, way to hum out there!"

"Okay, Mose. Good velocity today."

Baseball teaches you to say silly, encouragin' things, even when there's no reason to. They went by Moses Yellowhorse givin' him a tap on the knee or the shoulder and a kind word—but gettin' past him quick, with their eyes down. They knew somethin' was wrong, an' they wanted to cover it.

The whole time, Moses Yellowhorse didn't move. I mean, not at *all*. Not a single muscle on any part of his body, not even enough to twitch when a fly landed on him.

"His eyes aren't moving," Skeeter Mesquite said, lookin' close at his face. "He's not even blinking. Do you see?"

"Yeah, I see."

I looked right into Moses' face, an' I can tell you I never saw a human being look so blank before. Not even John Barr, with his drowned man's eyes, ever looked like that. Not even old Coach Moose Maas, dead on the bench in Jacksonville.

Skeeter was wavin' his hand back an' forth in front of him, slappin' him softly on the cheeks a couple times.

"Hey, big guy," he said. "Hey, big guy."

Everybody else was on the other side of the locker room by then, makin' a lot of noise horseplayin' in the shower, tellin' jokes an' snappin' their towels. Nobody wanted to notice what was goin' on.

Skeeter kept slappin' Moses' face, harder an' harder. When nothin' happened he took his pulse an' listened to his heart. Then he shrugged his shoulders.

"I can't be sure," he says, just like the doctors in the afternoon hospital stories. That was when a cold dread passed through me. You know it's trouble when people start talkin' like the stories on TV.

"I can't be sure, but I think it's serious," he said.

"I guessed that. By the fact he wasn't movin' an' all."

"I have some ideas," he said. "But I can't be sure."

"We don't want you to go on record, doc," I told him. "Is he still alive, anyway?"

"We'd better get an ambulance."

He went to get Doc Roberts an' Stanzi, an' the rest of us carried Moses into the trainer's room an' locked it off before the flies got there. Doc Roberts brought the ambulance 'round the back an' told the flies it was a sick fan, though we knew they'd find out soon enough. Skeeter covered his head with towels when they hauled him out. But he still didn't move, didn't speak.

"So nobody can see who it is," Skeeter explained, though I think he just didn't want to look at that face anymore himself.

They admitted him to Bellevue the next day. The papers were all full of respectfulness. The week before, they'd been callin' for him to take a drug test, an' sayin' he didn't have any guts. But mental illness was more respectable. It was okay to feel sorry for a ballplayer who had *that*. And it was the perfect way out for Charlie Stanzi.

"If we'd only known he was so sick," he told the flies, lookin' down at the ground like he might cry. An' sure enough, when he looked back up there was tears in his eyes. It was all over the front pages the next day, The Little Maniac with his dewy eyes.

They came by to get a few reaction shots from the team, too, an' everybody said the same things. We all talked about how Moses was a great competitor, an' how we was sure he'd be back soon. Everybody looked solemn, an' kept shruggin' their shoulders.

But five minutes after the cameras were out of the locker room, the first jokes started:

"All we need now is the cigar store," somebody said, an' that set it off.

"We could put him on third. He'd still have more range than So Many Other Ways White."

"Bend his head a little bit, he could be a surfboard."

"You put his arm up, he'd be the Statue of Liberty."

Somebody started laughin'. They couldn't help it, an' then the jokes kept comin'. One after another, each one cruder an' stupider than the last.

"He ain't schizo. That was just his world-famous imitation of a stiff dick!"

"Hell, he's never been *that* stiff in his life!"

We couldn't help ourselves. I know it don't make any sense, us sittin' there with the tears of laughter rollin' down our cheeks. But the time you have in the game is short, and it can come an' go for no good reason. It's why we're so scared an' superstitious all the time. It's why nobody likes to get too close to those rooks that Cookie Cochrane the bus driver used to finger-machine-gun every spring. And it's why nobody could take it serious when Moses Yellowhorse went out. We had to laugh. We couldn't afford to do anything else.

Except for John Barr. He didn't say a thing when we was all crackin' up over Moses, didn't even smile. I thought maybe he was offended, so I went over to him afterwards by his locker. But he was only gettin' suited up like he would for any other game.

"Terrible shit that happened to Moses," I said, thinkin' he would react one way or the other. But he didn't.

"Happens," he said, shruggin' on his shirt. "Can't be a fool an' take a fool's advice."

"It's still a goddamned shame."

He only shrugged again, an' rolled his stirrups down to precisely the inch he always wore 'em.

"Won't do him any good, us feelin' sorry for him." And he tugged on his cap an' set the brim just right.

"That's all he said?" Ellie Jay said when I told her.

"Uh-huh. He was that cold."

"Maybe he is just a hitting machine after all. Maybe there is nothing more to the man after all," she had to admit, an' I could tell she was angry. Sportswriters hate it when we disappoint 'em.

"We all kept our distance from that, one way or the other," I reminded her, but she just snorted at me.

"I don't know why I bother trying to find anything in you guys when there's nothing there to find," she said.

It was two nights later that we started the series against the Giants out at Shea. They were ridin' high, a couple games out in front of the Dodgers, an' they wanted us to prove they were for real. The first game they had Goog Fisher goin', so we knew they were serious.

Googer always had had a two-day shadow and a nasty inside fastball. He even plunked John Barr in the ribs a couple times when Barr wouldn't back off the plate, an' he never minded puttin' a fastball under my chin. His ball was hard to pick up, too, with the big windup he used. But I noticed that he forgot sometimes, an' used his big kick with men on base. I thought I could do somethin' with that.

First inning, I worked him for a walk an' took a good lead off first. Sure enough, he gave me one look an' went into that big kick of his again. I was into second base before the ball hit the catcher's mitt, an' Goog turned around an' tried to ice me out with his stare, but I just smiled back at him.

Second time up, I caught one of his fastballs an' slapped it back through the middle for a single. This time he threw over ten, twelve times, tryna keep me close. Then he forgot an' went into his full windup again. Their catcher didn't have a real shot at me, but he threw the ball anyway an' it bounced off into center field. I made a stand-up slide into second, an' jetted off again. By the time they got the ball back in, I'd come all the way around.

"You won't get to try that one again, you son of a bitch," Goog said to me when I crossed home plate.

I knew he meant it. Third time up, I expected to go down. Goog was steamin' now, an' he threw a low fastball that hit me right in the leg. Damn, he was fast. It stung some, but I was lucky, it only got me in the fat side of the thigh a few inches above the knee an' didn't do any real damage.

Thing was, Goog didn't know that, an' I made sure he was kept in ignorance. I went right down, clutchin' my knee in both hands, moanin' an' groanin'. I made it look so good that Doc Roberts even came runnin' out to take a look, an' when I finally managed to struggle to my feet an' limp up to first, I got a big hand from the fans.

Goog was out there on the mound, hidin' his smile behind his glove. When I went hobblin' up to first, he even held his hands out an' dropped his head to one side—like it was all a accident. I waved him off like that was okay, it was just between us men. And when I got to first, I stood right on the bag, like I was afraid to move a foot away with my wrecked knee. Goog went into his biggest windup yet—an' I stole second on the first pitch.

The crowd didn't stop hollerin' for ten minutes after that one. Goog stood on the mound with his arms crossed while they cheered, lookin' over at me again on second base. This time he didn't say a word—and I kept my head down, carefully wipin' all the dirt off my uniform an' tryin' not to laugh.

Next time up, I knew he'd be after me for real. Somethin' got ahold of me, though, an' I decided to let him use his fool's anger against himself. When I got into the batter's box, I didn't give the man the satisfaction of lookin' directly at him. I just kept my head down, kept pumpin' my bat, tryin' not to look at him except out of the corner of my eye.

Like I figured, he kept me waitin' a long time, tryna get me fearful about what he might throw at me. Finally he straightens up a little, an' makes like he's about to come to the plate. An' at that precise moment, I stepped back out of the batter's box an' called for time.

Googer was furious now. I'd pushed the boy too far, an' I shoulda known it. I don't even know what I was expectin' to get out of it, 'cept a pitch aimed straight for my head. I was ready for *that* when it came, the ball headed straight for my temple, an' I threw myself backwards almost as soon as it left Goog's hand.

That was my own fool mistake. When you *really* want to hit some- body, not just move 'em back from the plate, you don't throw at their head. You throw *behind* them. Anybody up at the plate, his first move when he sees the ball comin' in is to back up—an' when he does, he moves right into it.

I was still throwin' my body backwards, but the ball was movin' with me, an' I thought Oh, oh. I expected him to plunk me, but I never thought he'd try to kill me like that, an' all I could do was hope that my batting helmet would hold up.

When the ball hit, I could actually see the word *Zing!* go through my head. Just like that, in big orange letters with an exclamation point an' a line underneath. I remembered it clear as that. It was the last thing I remembered for some time.

The Color Commentary

The ball shattered the hard plastic helmet with a noise that could be heard around the ballpark. It threw the batter to the ground, leaving his body limp, long arms and legs splayed out.

There was a horrified "Oh!" from the crowd, which had just been eagerly anticipating this very confrontation. At first, everyone on the field was frozen, save for the pitcher walking back contentedly to the top of the mound. Then the umpires began to move, one of them running out toward the mound, the others jogging hurriedly toward the dugouts.

It was too late. First John Barr and the trainer burst out, running toward Falls where he lay motionless, feet still in the batter's box. Then the rest of the benches emptied, all the players running toward the mound or someone else to pair off against. Then the bullpens cleared, too, the pitchers and catchers running pell-mell toward the center of the diamond like circus clowns.

It was the typical major-league brawl: a real clown show, with one or two players actually mad and trying to hit each other, and the rest grappling and leaping about like little boys. Barr ignored them all. He stayed at home plate with the trainer, holding up Falls's head while the team doctor quickly ministered to him. When the stretcher came, Barr helped gently lift him up onto it, then followed it back to the clubhouse.

"How's he look?" he demanded, almost as soon as they had set the stretcher down on the trainer's table. The attendants ignored him, going quickly and expertly about their business, listening to the unconscious man's heart, taking his pulse, feeling the bruise along his head. After a little while his hands and feet began to twitch, and then his eyes opened, floating around uncertainly.

"Good," said one of the physicians, and that was the only word Barr needed. He ran at once out of the locker room and down the narrow corridor that led to the other team's clubhouse.

He waited there by the ramp that led down from the field, listening until he heard what he wanted: the faint metallic ring of cleats on the concrete floor. When they got close, he swung around the corner and brought his left fist up sharply. The big, shadow-faced man in front of him went down, rolling over on the concrete floor, all the wind let out of him.

"Sonofabitch!" he exclaimed, more surprised than angry.

He got back up off the floor, but Barr didn't give him another chance. He hit him in the pit of the stomach with a short right hand, then pushed him against the wall. He cracked the pitcher's head back against the concrete, then pounded his face with both hands until his cheeks were puffy and discolored.

"You . . . you . . . " the man sputtered, trying to hold up his hand against the sudden assault.

Barr hit him again, this time with a right hook he wound up on, then kneed him in the side as he fell. The pitcher lay face-down on the floor, breathing hard but not moving, and Barr started to walk away. Then he turned, pulled him halfway up by his hair, and hit him in the face one more time.

He left the man on the ground, and went straight back to the field, where it was his turn to hit just as he emerged from the dugout. He set himself at the plate, running his hands down his bat, tugging at his pants, digging in his feet in the exact same place he always did—every one of his rituals repeated as if it were any other at-bat. He looked for his pitch, and lined it cleanly up the middle. He ran quickly up the first-base line, his head up.

The Old Swizzlehead

The next night in the hospital, I still felt like I had a bruise the size of my head. I was sick to my stomach, an' everything was still blurry. An' come to look in on me was Ellie Jay with a smile on her face.

"What're you so goddamned happy about?"

"Did you hear?" she asked me in that whiskey voice of hers. "They had to pick Fisher up off the floor."

"I heard about it. They don't *know* if it was Barr—"

"It's gotta be him. You know it as well as I do. He was the only one not on the field. He even held your head up after you got hit."

"I guess it hadda be him," I said, rubbin' my neck, which felt like it had been transplanted for one of my bats. "Only he would do somethin' that crazy. I just hope I can get my batting eye back."

"Don't worry, the doctors said it didn't get the eye," she said, like my almost gettin' killed was a minor incidental. "I told you. He's the only ballplayer I ever met who wasn't completely transparent. No offense."

"None taken. I like transparent. Saves on the psychoanalysis bills."

"Right after the All-Star Game, I'm going to get to the bottom of him."

"It's funny, though," I told her. "Barr hittin' him like that— and then today, he didn't even come around."

Everybody else on the team, even The Little Maniac, came around to see me while I was in the hospital. Ellsworth Pippin sent a basket full of fruit an' English tea. There wasn't a sign of John Barr, though. An' when I got back to the team, he didn't even come over to my locker. Finally I went over myself an' thanked him for poppin' that son of a bitch, but he just shrugged it off, an' turned away.

"I would have done it anyway," was all he said.

16

I never called one wrong, in my heart.

—Bill Klem

The Phenom Turning Thirteen

The boy never understood why his mother liked the church, but he went with her anyway, every Sunday. He knew she wouldn't have forced him—not after he was a teenager, anyway—but he didn't want to disappoint her.

It was an unpretentious building, a small, white-paneled evangelical chapel, just back from the ocean. At first he attended the little Sunday school downstairs in the sparse concrete basement. He sat on folding metal chairs with a few other bored children and stared dully at an elderly woman telling Bible stories by moving cloth figures across a felt-covered board. Because he could sit still, he was allowed to go upstairs to the full church by the time he was ten. But this was only worse.

The church was a paragon of Protestant austerity. The boy had been with his Catholic friends to the cathedral in Granitetown a few times, and he had marveled at its lurid crucifixes, the bleeding statues of the saints, the gold tempera paint flecked all around the main altar. But in his mother's church there was only a simple wooden cross above the altar, and rows of plain wooden pews. The only adornments were a flat red carpet down the center aisle, and tranquil stained-glass windows depicting the acts—and not the sufferings—of the apostles.

The service was long and deliberate. The boy's mother would keep the Bible on her lap and the hymnal next to her. The hymnal she marked with little scraps of paper from her pocketbook, so she could turn to each hymn as it came up. During the sermon, she would look up each of the references the minister made to the Bible, nodding her head each time, gratified that she could indeed confirm them.

On those Sundays when they could get him out of bed, the boy's father still refused to take the church seriously. It was another way to deride the conventionality of the town. He would bellow out the hymns in his off-key bass, often singing a word or two behind the rest of the congregation. He made a big show of slapping a single dollar down when the collection plate came around, and he slurped the little glass thimble of grape juice that was passed around for the communion on the first Sunday of every month.

He tried to catch his son's eye when he was performing some of his high jinks, or when the minister said something that he considered particularly asinine. When he did get his attention, he would roll his eyes, or wink broadly. The boy tried to smile or avert his gaze when he did this, anything to get him to stop. He knew that his mother found it unbearable. At night she would scrub his head over the bathtub, and talk to him about the need to follow the Lord.

"It is the only salvation," she would say, as her fingers groped roughly up and down his scalp. "Without it, everything is meaningless."

She would tell him stories from the Old Testament, and try to get him to memorize the books of the Bible. He never could, and he didn't much see the point; they all had tables of contents. Throughout his life, he would think of the Good Book mostly with a sharp, tingling sensation along his hairline.

But she would laugh with him about almost everything else. When he came home from school, she would ask him about what he had learned and how he had done in the games afterwards. She would laugh when he told her some funny story, about a foolish teacher or another kid. It was an unexpected but not unpleasant sound when she laughed, like a hard rain falling suddenly through the leaves. She laughed most gleefully of all when he told her about something good he had done. "Oh, good for you!" she would burst out, and sometimes even put her hands together.

His exploits at sports thrilled her particularly. The boy was only an indifferent student, too bored by most of school to really concentrate on it. She kept after him about his studies, made him do his homework, but they both realized it was only for form's sake. It was already obvious that anything big he did would be on a playing field.

She soon realized that she didn't know enough about the different games to follow them, so she began to take books out of the library. He saw them in his parents' room, at the bedside: thin little primers on "How to Play Baseball," "How to Play Football," and so on. Whenever she attended a game, she asked him beforehand which one it was, and then she would refer to the appropriate book.

He glimpsed her sometimes in the stands, when he was running downcourt after a basket, or trotting in from the field. She would always be wearing a look of terrific concentration, her brow furrowed and her fierce eyes narrowed on the field. He got so he couldn't look at her if he was due to come up soon, or shoot a foul shot. It was too disconcerting, knowing that she cared that much.

He also came to realize that she liked it better when his father didn't come to the games with her. It was true that he actually knew the games and was therefore handy as a reference. But her husband's confident nonchalance bothered her. To him, his son's excellence was just another bragging point. Since so much of his world was full of illusions, it made her fear that this one might be an illusion, too.

After the games, she seemed so exhausted with relief that he was concerned for her. She breathed heavily, and wore a rather dazed smile—whereas his father simply thumped him on the back. The tension of the games often got the best of her, to the point where she could become nearly insufferable in the stands. She would not hesitate to shush anybody she felt was making unnecessary comments around her, or to upbraid them if they rooted against her son's team. By the end of the games there would often be a small but distinct circle of empty seats around her. It only increased the legend of her severity and the family's general craziness in town.

At home with him, she was almost soft. Even softer, he dared to think, than on those occasions when his father and mother were together alone. She could not force herself to be cross with the boy. Nor did she need to.

"You've always been so well behaved," she would say sometimes, with real delight, and it wouldn't give him a big head, or make him think about what he could get away with.

"You've always been a good boy," she would say, when absolutely carried away, and he would only grin and look aside.

She delighted in making things for him when he came home from school. All kinds of cookies: oatmeal, chocolate chip, soft, crumbly peanut butter cookies with the fork impressions in them, and large, round, green molasses cookies, coated in white flour. She would bring them to him while he studied as unsolicited little treats. Cookies, with a glass of milk, all served on a small tray. Or sometimes slices of apple dipped in sugar, or thick pieces of potato fudge.

"I just thought maybe you could use a little break," she would say, and smile at him inappropriately deeply for the occasion—but making him smile back in the same way.

Usually she would sit near him after approaching on this pretext, particularly if his father was out on one of his mad schemes. She would sew or knit, or read from the Bible, her murmuring, singsong reading a reassuring background to his dull studies. They would each be gratified by the quiet, affectionate presence of the other—and, by default, the absence of his father.

"Why did you marry him?" he got up the nerve to ask during one of these evenings that seemed especially close and sympathetic. She made a little sour face, the best commentary on the one unsensible thing she had done in her entire life.

"He had bright dreams," she told him. "He used to talk all the time, just like now. But what he said was so much brighter."

"What were they? What did he talk about?" He could not imagine anything his father could have said, then or now, that would have impressed his mother.

"All kinds of things," she said with a shrug. "All kinds of schemes, he was all over the place."

That seemed exactly like the father he knew, and the boy still couldn't see how she had gone for him. She saw that he was unsatisfied, and attempted to explain further.

"Bigger things, better things. He wanted to get an education. He wanted to build a big new house for us all to fit in. He wanted to be something real."

"Why did he need a big house?"

"Oh, didn't you know? He wanted to have a big family, back then. I did too," she said offhandedly, though it was the first inkling the boy had ever had that he was not their only intended.

"Why didn't you?"

"Hmm?"

"Why didn't you have more kids?"

"Oh, you can see how he is. It would take more money, more responsibility. Of course he wanted to, that was just like him. But I saw what he was already when you were young, and I put a stop to it. I wouldn't allow him to have another one. It wouldn't have been fair to any of us."

It dawned on the boy that his mother saw them both as unwitting sacrifices to his father's capricious nature. They were hostages of a sort, taken before the nature of the enemy had been detected. It was an idea that preoccupied him for some time.

"When did he first get like this?" he would ask his mother. "Did it happen all of a sudden?"

"I don't know," she would say anxiously, clearly reluctant to talk about it. "There were hints, signs earlier, I suppose, that I should have picked up."

She paused, overwhelmed herself by the memory of how he had been.

"But you should have seen how he was. Very earnest. Studying all the time, a book under his arm. Always reading about new things, inventions, other places. I thought he was ambitious."

She resumed sweeping, her old myopia resolved.

"But I should have seen, even then. Despite all his books, he was still not a good student. It was like he couldn't concentrate on anything for very long. I thought he just had to find his niche. And then he tried one thing, and then another, and he never did find it. Then he started to make it up, with the cars, the drinking, the get-rich-quick schemes—"

She broke off then, and looked at her son intently.

"If you have something, you should stick to it," she told him. "Set yourself on one thing, and do it. That's what counts."

A few days later the boy came across a stack of old books in the musty side room his father used as a study. They were a series of basic primers in one field after another, guides for aspiring lay-men that had been out of print for years: *Fundamentals of Account-ing. Basic Principles of the Law. A Guide to Mechanics. ABCs of Medicine.*

The boy could tell from the layers of dust that they hadn't been opened for a long time. But during bored moments in school or even in the outfield, he would think about that big house, full of his brothers and sisters, and of his father coming out the front door, a solid lawyer, doctor, accountant—

17

_My number suddenly rose toward the pitcher like a dark wave
just before I struck._

—SADAHARU OH

The Old Swizzlehead

After Moses Yellowhorse goin' stiff as a board, the only thing
kept us afloat was John Barr. He was playin' unconscious that
summer. At the All-Star break he was still hittin' over .400, and
leadin' the league in home runs an' ribbies.

But the stats don't tell the story—no matter what Ellsworth Pippin or Dr. Roscoe T. Jones like to say. John Barr was in one of
those grooves where it didn't matter what happened, he would
do something to win the game for us. No matter how many runs
the other team got, he would get us more.

He made the All-Star Game, of course, just like he had every
year in the major leagues. Usually he couldn't wait to get that
game over with. He hit those American League pitchers like he
hit everybody in the National, but it was just an exhibition, an'
John Barr always preferred to play for real. But this last year it was
different. The game was up in Boston, in Fenway Park, where the
Red Sox play, an' when he heard that, he almost smiled. I saw it
with my own two eyes.

"You sure?" he asked me. "I ain't played up there in years. I
used to go to that pahk, you know."

"That so?" I said, stunned at his running off at the mouth like that. I wanted to keep him talkin', but it was like a switch went off again.

"Yeah," was all he said. "When I was a kid."

I got picked as a reserve, so we went up there together, along with Big Bo Bigbee, who was supposed to start but came down with a superficial tear of his lower cretaceous tendon, or somethin' like that. Barr had his usual game, it didn't matter that he'd never seen most of the pitchers before. He knocked two balls over the big green fence in left, and in his last at-bat he went the other way an' hit the ball into the bullpen in right field.

There was somethin' else, though, that wasn't like him at all. When he crossed home plate after that last home run, he tipped his hat to the fans. Just a tiny little tip, rubbin' his fingers along the visor so you'd barely notice it. But it was a tip all right.

"I saw that," I told him afterwards in the locker room. "I saw you do that."

At first he acted like he didn't know what I was talkin' about. He looked like he was a kid who just got caught knockin' a ball through the neighbor's window.

"Why'd you do it now? Why here?"

He cleared his throat an' looked around the floor. It was just my idle curiosity that made me ask; I didn't mean to find out any big secret. But the more I pressed it, the more nervous it made him, and the more interested that got me.

"It's just—it's just—" he started to stammer out, like he was on his first date, about to ask for a kiss. Before he could say anything, though, a clubhouse boy comes up with a little white envelope for him. John Barr rips it open without lookin' at it, he's still so busy blushin' an' stammerin' an' tryna say why he tipped his cap. But then he looked down at what was in the envelope, an' his whole face changed. Right before my eyes, it hardened back into that game face he always wore. He never did get the words out.

"Whatsat?" I asked him. "Some old high school sweetheart up here, been admirin' your buns from the stands?"

He looked up with those drowned man's eyes, but like he didn't see me or nothin' else.

"My mother is dead," he said.

The Color Commentary

She finally found the address in the late afternoon. It was a skinny little house, at the end of a dirt road lined with oak trees and so pitted and strewn with rocks that she had parked her rental car along the side of the road, and walked the rest of the way in.

Even as she approached it, she felt sure that nobody lived there anymore. She banged hard on the front door and then the windows, but she didn't expect to get any response. The house's eaves had disintegrated, the front steps were rotting, and its red paint was badly peeled. The tall grass was littered with animal droppings and old cans and bottles.

She tried around the back, but it was no better. The yard was nearly overgrown with brambles and wild grass. The only signs of life were two strands of rope hanging from a tree branch, and a dilapidated garage nearly swallowed up by the woods. She peered inside and saw a huge brown and green station wagon, rusted down almost to its chassis. The only sound was the tidal sweep of the high oak branches against the roof shingles.

She knocked perfunctorily on the back door, and got no answer there, either. Yet she had begun to realize that someone *did* live in the house, or had until recently. None of the dusty window-panes were broken, and peering through them she was able to make out a few dull pieces of furniture, a rug, pots and pans in the kitchen. There was still a sense of order inside.

She contemplated trying to let herself in somehow, then decided against it. She had begun to walk back to her car, thinking of what to do next, when she saw him walking toward her down the pitted dirt road, his head down. He hesitated when he first noticed that someone was coming toward him from the house, and he stopped when he saw who it was.

She felt a little guilty, as if she had been caught red-handed at something. Still, she kept walking until she was standing right in front of him. She was going to say something, but then she realized that he was really looking at her for the first time, his face so solemn and uncertain that she wanted to laugh. Instead, she placed one hand along his cheek and gently, carefully raised herself up and kissed him on the mouth.

He returned her kiss for a long moment, without raising a hand or touching her. Then he broke away and stumbled back up the road, looking suspiciously back at her.

"Tell me—" she blurted out, but at that moment another strong breeze swept through the oaks along the road, brushing their heavy, leafy branches back and forth and swallowing her words. Soon he was a distant stick figure, struggling up the uneven road, still pausing to look back at her.

The Old Swizzlehead

It never really occurred to me John Barr still had a mother, despite all Ellie Jay's talk about investigating his past life. I knew something about the families of everyone I played with for any time, even the Dominicans who spoke only Spanish an' had their wives an' children down in Santo Domingo. At least you'd see a snapshot in their locker.

But not John Barr. His mother never came to any game that I knew of. He never mentioned her once, never kept a picture of her, or anyone else in his family. I didn't even know if he had brothers an' sisters.

When he got that piece of paper from the clubhouse boy, he looked like he was gonna fall over. He blurted out that she was dead like he couldn't help hisself, which was rare for John Barr, an' for a moment I thought maybe he was gonna say more. But five minutes later he was all business again, gettin' his gear ready, talkin' to the travel secretary about arrangements. It didn't seem to give him any more lasting grief or anger than a bad at-bat.

He did stay up there a couple more days for the funeral. I offered to go along with him, even though I knew it would raise hell with The Little Maniac. But John Barr told me no, he could handle it hisself, an' I let it lie.

He only missed one game. He flew back an' joined us for our first series after the All-Star break, which was in Cincinnati. He dropped his bag down in front of his locker an' started suitin' up, lookin' the same as ever.

"Don't you need any more time than that?" I asked him, even though he gave me a look that said it wasn't none of my business.

"Nope."

"I mean, don't you need to go through her stuff, look up the will—things like that?"

"Nope. The lawyer does that."

"Man, you can't trust no lawyers with that—"

"I don't want to see it," he said quickly, cuttin' off what you might charitably call future discussion.

It was only afterwards that I heard about the kiss from Ellie Jay. He never said anything, but she pulled me over near the stands while we were takin' infield.

"This is better than the afternoon stories," I told her. "You really kissed him? Just like that? Girl, you are lookin' for trouble."

"I've never done anything like that, kiss a ballplayer. It's god-damned embarrassing," she said, but I could tell she still liked it. There was that spark she had in her eye when she was grillin' somebody about a bad pitch, or standing up to Dickhead Barry Busby an' the other press-box boys.

"It was the moment," she said. "I was there, and he was there in the middle of the road, and there were all those great god-damned trees."

"Great trees? You kissed the man because of great trees?"

"He was just looking so damned pathetic. So I kissed him. And you know something, Swiz? He liked it—at least at first, before he got frightened. There is something in there—"

"What about the house? What about the mystery interview?"

"Nothing. I couldn't even find out who lived there. I think it might've been his place, maybe his mother's before she died. But I couldn't even find out if his father was still alive. The funeral was closed to the public, and nobody was talking. Those people are like some kind of hillbilly clan up there."

"That's somethin' for the boy," I had to chuckle. "I wonder if he's ever been kissed before."

It didn't seem to rattle him either way, not the kissing or the death. That night he hit three straight doubles in the gap, then he threw out the potential tyin' run at third. He was back, the same as ever—

The Color Commentary

John Barr looked out at the pitcher through the dust and the late-afternoon glare. He swung the bat, set his feet, and looked again—

See the ball.

A steady stream of paper airplane programs, hotdog rolls, and the round cardboard tops of Dixie cups fell onto the field. The big Sunday crowd was restless and irritable. It nearly overflowed the stands, shouting and screaming and overflowing with beer.

Charlie Stanzi had just worked them into a lather by disputing a close play at first base. He had bounced out of the dugout and gone into his full routine: stamping his feet, kicking dirt, pushing his chest up against the umpire's and screaming in his face.

The fans were ecstatic. Brawls had erupted throughout the stands as he stalked back to the dugout. Bare-chested, drunken young men flailed at each other in imitation, and the rest rose and sat, rose and sat, as they struggled to see each new fight.

Barr ignored them all, and narrowed his eyes on the pitcher. It was the late, dry stretch of the summer, and no matter how much the grounds crew hosed down the infield dirt, it kept sweeping up again from the base paths. The umpire and the catcher behind him both wiped their mouths free of grit, but Barr ignored it, just squinting to keep it out of his eyes.

See the ball. You can at least do that, can't you? You can at least see the ball in time—

The pitcher waited for him. He was a veteran, throwing a solid game, and his rhythm had already been disrupted by Stanzi's performance. He wasn't going to hurry now and throw some pitch that would end up in Barr's wheelhouse. Instead he went through his full array of motions designed to distract and divert. He touched his cap, hitched his pants, pulled his shoulders back, and brought both hands together at his belt—

See the ball—

Only then did the pitcher rock back, front leg kicking up and swinging hard down to earth, remaining leg and arms cartwheeling after it. His entire body was flung loosely forward, his right arm releasing the ball like a slingshot.

It made a good smack in the catcher's glove, pounded a small cloud of dust from the mitt. Barr took a step back from the batter's box, already thinking about the next pitch while the umpire grunted "Stee-rike!" behind him.

But he had seen what he wanted to see. He changed his grip on the bat almost imperceptibly and stepped back in, carefully planting his feet in the same place again, like they'd been painted there. Despite the bat's size he held it high, wiggling it slightly at the top as he waited.

The noise in the stands welled up. There were a few boos, though the umpire was comfortable in the knowledge that if John Barr had not protested, it was indeed a strike. Barr made a last sweep of everything before him: checking the fielders, checking the runner off second. He even checked the signs from the base coaches incessantly spitting, clapping, tugging at their uniforms— though the sign, as it had been every time for thirteen years without exception, was to hit away.

See it. See everything—

He turned his eyes back on the pitcher, who wiped sweat, peered in, checked back on the runner himself. Barr thought, Same thing as last time. Started off with the fastball. Then that big, slow curve—

The pitcher began his long, complicated motion again. The ball came in on a lazy trajectory toward his head, then—just as expected—cut wide and down. He followed it all the way in, waiting until a point that would have been too late for most ballplayers.. . .

The Old Swizzlehead

But there *was* something different. It wasn't much, but I knew it the next morning when he knocked at my hotel room door. It was kind of embarrassin', actually. I'd just ordered up some room service, an' I thought that was it. He surprised the hell out of me, standin' there in the doorway. All I could do was make motions toward the annie who was sittin' up in my bed, with her titties lyin' out over the bedcovers.

"Uh, this here is, uh, *Maybelline*," I told him, tryna sneak a peek in her purse for her driver's license.

"That's Juanita, you bastard!" she gently corrected me.

"You wanna go somewheres?" Barr said.

"Excuse me?"

It musta been three, four years since I even had a beer with the man in the clubhouse. And here he was, poppin' up like he was ready to go have a few an' reminisce about the old days at Yale.

"You wanna go somewheres, have breakfast? I gotta go out to Louisville."

I didn't know exactly what he was talkin' about, but I said okay, an' got dressed an' left the room-service meal all to the lovely Juanita. We went down to the hotel restaurant, where I got coffee an' he ordered up a whole exciting breakfast of a boiled egg an' a piece of plain toast. I expected some great big revelation out of him then, I guess, to explain his sudden sociability. But he didn't say nothin', just sat there munchin' on his toast an' spoonin' his boiled egg into his mouth, starin' straight ahead the whole time like he was concentratin' on a pitcher in front of him.

I didn't press the man until he put his dollars down and got up to leave.

"Where you goin'?"

"To Louisville, like I said," he said, soundin' perplexed. "It's just over the river."

"I know where it is."

"You wanna come?"

"All right," I said, givin' up. "Might as well be Louisville as anyplace else."

He had a rented car reserved, which surprised me, since I didn't think John Barr even knew what a credit card was. It was a luxury car, too—some big old Caddy, an' I thought, Could he have a woman someplace? But it was too hard to imagine—John Barr with both a woman an' a credit card—and if he did, I didn't know why he would take me along.

I thought maybe he was gonna finally break down and say something about his mother's dying, or maybe that kiss. I decided to wait, an' let him work up to it. But he didn't say one word about anything, and I finally gave in when we crossed the river into Kentucky.

"So why we goin' to Louisville?"

"For the bats."

"For the bats?"

"For the bats."

All ballplayers are fussy about their bats, but Barr was the worst. He wouldn't let anybody else touch 'em. I picked one up once, an' he was all over me. Some poor rook took one into the batting cage another time, an' I thought Barr was gonna hit him.

"That ain't yours," he said, an' took it right out of the kid's hands.

They were big black bats, with the number "B-99" written on the handle, which was his model number. Every player in the show has his own model. That was how you ordered 'em. The clubhouse boys would come around with the order forms first day of spring training, then again just before Openin' Day, an' you'd write down your model number and any changes an' specifications you wanted, an' the club would take care of it.

But not John Barr. The bats were the one thing he brought with him in the spring, in his duffel bag. He'd cart 'em away with him again at the end of the year, all that were left, an' during the season he wouldn't let anybody else use 'em for a single at-bat.

Not that anyone else much wanted to; they were too heavy. The biggest power hitters that ever lived don't use a bat that weighs much more than thirty-six ounces. But Barr's must've been at least forty. They were the biggest bats anybody ever seen. We could never figure out how he got around on a pitch with 'em. We didn't know where the hell he got them.

The bat factory looked like a airplane hangar. Inside there was a long line of men, all workin' some bat over a machine. You could taste the sawdust in the back of your throat, an' there was a screechin' an' hummin' sound in the air that never stopped. Nobody looked up when we come in. Each man had his head down over a saw or a sander, doin' each bat to specifications.

But soon a bald little cracker with a checkered shirt an' a cigarette danglin' from one corner of his mouth looks up an' sees us. He takes off his goggles an' comes over to shake John Barr's hand.

"I thought you'd be in," he shouts to him over all the saw screechin'. "I checked the schedule. Second trip to Cinci, same as always."

"This is Ricky Falls," Barr says, flippin' a thumb toward me.

"Uh-huh. Sure, I know him," the little cracker says, an' he shakes my hand. He held it a extra second, like he was tryna calculate somethin'.

"F-111," he shouts. "Light bat, like a buggy whip. You get around with it all right. You got small hands, I can see how that little knob is just right for you."

"You got my order ready?" Barr asked him.

"Sure do." The cracker grins over at me confidentially.

"Same bat every season, thirteen years in the major leagues. Black finish, large knob. Narrow grain, with as many knots as we can find in the wood. Forty ounces. A unique model."

"Uh-huh," says Barr.

The little cracker shook his head an' spat on the ground, but when he looked up he was still grinnin'.

"Goddammit, that's a large bat, son," he says to Barr. "One of these years, when you don't get around so good anymore, you're gonna come in here beggin' me for a smaller one."

"Nope," Barr told him. "That's the year I retire."

"Yeah," says the cracker, walkin' over to a cartload of bats. "That's what they all say."

He brought back the bats, already finished.

"I figured you'd be in," he says. "So I took the liberty."

Barr picked one up by the barrel and held it out carefully, testing the weight. A veteran ballplayer can tell the weight of a bat to a quarter-ounce, just by holdin' it. Then Barr started to swing it, over an' over, the way he did before each game. That cracker must've had fifty bats for him there, an' he swung each one twenty-five times, then handed two of 'em back.

"These are a little light," he says, an' the cracker nodded an' didn't even try to dispute him, just put them aside. Barr paid him in cash an' shook hands with the man.

"Pleasure doin' business with you," the cracker said. "See you next spring."

"What's the narrow grain for?" I asked Barr as I helped him haul those damned heavy bats back to his car.

"Makes the bat harder."

"I always thought a wide grain was harder."

"Nope. Narrow grain means the tree grew longer, got tougher. Just like the knots. Ted Williams always had a narrow-grain bat with lots of knots."

"But what about the black finish? What's that for?"

He almost grinned at me then, pullin' just his lips back from his teeth, like that night down in Jaxville.

"That makes the bat *look* harder," he says. "It ain't, but the pitchers think it is."

"Is that what makes you such a good hitter, then?" I ragged him as we went back to the car. "These big black bats?"

"It ain't the bats," was all he said, the whole way back to Cincinnati. There was nothin' else about his mother or his first kiss, an' I was beginning to wonder what meant more to him—those little things, or his bats.

The Color Commentary

He drove the ball far out into right field, in a perfect arc down the foul line. In one continuous motion he let the bat fall and began to sprint toward first base. Ahead of him, he could see the rightfielder racing to cut the ball off. He knew at once, He's in too far, it's by him. And he swung out wide as he reached first. The ball skipped off past the outfielder as he had foreseen, the man lunging futilely at the ball, short by inches.

Barr didn't even slow down at second. He took another perfect turn around the base, one foot skimming the bag, racing on toward third without breaking his stride. He ignored the frantic wavings of Old Coach Plate to stop, thinking only of the rightfielder. He thought, No way he can beat me with his arm. And kept running.

He was right, once again by seconds and inches. At the last moment he flung himself full length toward the base, arms extended. The throw from the rightfielder plopped into the dirt right behind him. But he was already sprawling into third, butting his head up into the third baseman's stomach and making him jump so far back that he was barely able to knock the ball down.

Barr got to his feet and called time, ignoring both the muttered curses of the third baseman and the cheers rolling through the stands. He brushed the dirt deliberately off his uniform, thinking about the pitcher's pick-off move, and how many steps he could take down the line.

There was a persistent tugging on his arm, and he turned to face Old Coach Plate, who was smiling shakily, relieved that he wouldn't be made the scapegoat after the game.

"Look up there, John," he was saying, pointing to the stadium message board in center field: THAT WAS HIT NUMBER 2,915 FOR JOHN BARR***ON THE ROAD TO 3,000! AND HIS 151ST CAREER TRIPLE!

"Wasn't a triple," he said. "Should have been a single and a two-base error."

"It was a tough bounce out there, Johnny—"

"Should've cut it off."

He turned back to the game and began to measure his lead off third. He took five purposeful strides down the line, daring the pitcher to throw over.

"That's enough now, Johnny. Get back some now, John," Old Coach Plate pleaded with him.

Barr paid no attention. He crouched on the balls of his feet, precisely balanced so that he could either dive back to third or take off for home. He kept one eye on the pitcher, the other open for the third baseman or the shortstop moving behind him for the pick-off.

The pitcher eyed him back, then unwound awkwardly, making an extra, crucial motion before he whipped the ball over to third. The hitch gave him all the time he needed to throw himself back, hooking one hand around to the base. The third baseman brought the tag down hard on his hand anyway, repaying Barr for his rough slide. He got up and stared at the fielder, expressionless, his eyes like a drowned man's eyes.

"Fuck you, man," the third baseman said.

Old Coach Plate moved quickly to get between them. But the third baseman was already backing off, moving sullenly to his position a few steps from the bag. And Barr made no move to go after him. Instead he called time and deliberately brushed his uniform down again, hand by hand. When he was done, he went right back down the line, the same five large strides. Within seconds he was back at the base, facedown in the dirt again.

"Take it easy now, Johnny," Old Coach Plate said again, eyes bulging like the Popeye tobacco chaw in his cheek. "That last one was too goddamned close."

Barr nodded, and walked back to the exact same place. Again and again he walked to the end of an invisible tether, measuring the distance he would need to get back safely. In repeating his motion toward the base, the pitcher had smoothed it out a little, cutting the margin a little more. But there was still enough left of that betraying flinch that gave Barr the fraction of a second he needed—

See everything—

He would dive back, hands spraying dirt up into his own mouth and eyes, the ball-weighted glove slamming down on him. Then there was the umpire's face, almost down to his own, judging the minuscule battle before him—that last indivisible fraction of time that was hand-on-base-glove-on-hand.

They did it again and again, until the fans began to boo from boredom. At first they had enjoyed Barr's audacity. But they were unable to see the finer points of this inside game: how close each apparently routine play actually was. They did not appreciate how any minutely wrong decision—by the pitcher, by Barr, by the umpire—would end it.

At the plate, the next batter fidgeted and fussed with his bat, his own concentration thrown off. Barr didn't care. He kept walking down the line, measuring it out. Finally the catcher called time and went out to talk to his pitcher. They started to say something to each other, but ended up just looking over at him. Barr stared back—and took five big strides down the line.

The home plate umpire broke up the conference on the mound with the pitcher still staring at him. Barr thought, *He doesn't like this—he will tire before I do.*

Finally he did. The pitcher let loose and delivered the ball to the plate. Barr, running down the line, now jumped past the hold of the invisible leash he had allotted himself—and from the corner of his eye, the pitcher saw him.

The distraction made him let the ball go too soon. Not by much; not by any discernible amount of time. But it was enough. The ball spun too far downward. It bounced in the dirt and away from the glove and the bare hand of the catcher, also distracted by the sudden leap of Barr past his tether. He had to run after the ball, cursing and throwing off his mask, while it rolled tauntingly back toward the stands.

Barr crossed the plate standing up. The fans howled and jeered at the pitcher, standing uselessly near the plate. He was furious enough to say something out loud for Barr to hear. But he was superfluous now, and Barr ignored him, trotting calmly and quickly back into the dugout, without raising his cap or acknowledging the fans in any way.

Already he was thinking about his next at-bat.

18

Keep your eye everlastingly on the ball while it is in play.
—*Complete Official Rules:* GENERAL INSTRUCTIONS TO
UMPIRES, 9.00

The Phenom at Sixteen

By that spring he was watching his mother. He felt ashamed
about it, even though it was just giving in to what his father had
always wanted. He couldn't get over the feeling that what he was
doing was wrong, obscene. And yet he couldn't help himself.

He hadn't noticed anything strange, though his father had im-
plied in their talks that he would. He watched her more closely
every day—and all he saw was how hard she worked, and how
much of her work was devoted simply to keeping the house
standing.

They lived in a small, old place; two cramped stories, built narrow and pointed sideways against the northeast and the storms,
like every other house in town. It was never a house that had been
bright or cheerful, but at least it had once been tight and strong
against the weather. Now it was beginning to fall apart, because
of what his father had and hadn't done. The eaves were gone, the
roof shingles were beginning to break loose—

Inside, his mother waged a relentless battle against the rot. He
could see that it was a hopeless fight, with the outside falling apart.
Water slipped in through the deteriorating roof and the leaky old
pipes that his father periodically took apart, examined, and

wrenched sloppily back together again. It crept down the walls, leaving brown stains on the yellow wallpaper. It dripped on their beds and floors in the upstairs bedrooms, and nearly drove his mother crazy.

Sometimes he would hear her wake, sputtering and screaming. Shouting at first that insects were running over her face, and then screaming even louder when she realized that it was water. She screamed until her husband held her and squeezed the breath out of her.

She absolutely refused to have guests (those few remaining people who would socialize with Evan Barr anyway) when the ceiling boards in the living room began to show through— the rotten bones of the house exposed at last. The plaster would not stay up on the ceiling. It flaked down continually, leaving a fine white covering on everything in the living room, no matter how many times a day she dusted it.

In fact, her dust rag only scattered it around more thoroughly. Most of her efforts only made things worse, the boy soon realized; just like his father's, they were locked into a symmetry of futility. For instance, she had put up the yellow wallpaper in a desperate bid to instill some cheeriness into the house. But in the end, the light color had only made the water stains look worse. There was no getting around her husband; the house made a mockery of any attempts at improvement.

No matter how often she washed the sheets and beat the rugs and flung open the windows to the mad spring air, the house still reeked of mold. Her efforts only left the rugs and the sheets that much more threadbare from washing, the furniture all the deeper sagging and lumpish and discolored. But she went on scrubbing and dusting and beating the house.

"Does she look, um, *red?* You know. In the face, or anything?" his father had asked him in one of their talks, sitting in the ruins of the brick barbecue that he had let fall apart in the backyard.

The boy hadn't answered. He hoped, somehow, that he wouldn't say anything more. But his father had persisted:

"Does she look out of breath?"

Yes, he had seen her face red, and panting for breath. She generally worked with the same concentration, the same skilled economy of motion he had seen in the major-league ballplayers at Fenway Park. She swept the kitchen floor with short, quick broom strokes. She beat the rugs hard and fast, folded the sheets and laundry with rapid, snappy motions. Even so, after a day of working around the house, she seemed exhausted.

"See if she'll look at you. See if she keeps tryin' to turn away from your eyes."

The boy looked at his father, confused again.

"See if she looks like she done somethin'—"

"What?"

It was the first time the boy had said anything, or looked up from the ground. The activities of ants had become impressed upon his mind. Now his father tried to turn *his* eyes away.

"You know. Like it's somethin' she's ashamed about. Or somethin' she's *afraid* about."

The boy stood up slowly, cautiously, then, and went into the house. He had never disobeyed or talked back to his father, but he could not discuss it anymore—what his father was groping toward; what he would, in his awful, stupid way, inevitably spell out. But still, he did watch her.

He kept track of her from when he was first sleepily aware of her stirrings at five o'clock in the morning. Sometimes he would call to her then, but she would only shush him affectionately, tell him to go back to sleep while she made breakfast. He would hear her down in the kitchen, starting the oven, running an iron over their shirts, packing their lunches. She would move quickly and efficiently about the darkened house while they slept, a thick robe wrapped around her, her hair already wrenched tightly back in braids.

By the time he came downstairs she would be buzzing around the kitchen. The eyes in her small, square Scandinavian face would glare at the task directly before her, even at inanimate objects like the toaster or the stove, as if challenging everything to try and stop her.

"You see, she's home that long," his father had said. "You see how fast she works. It doesn't make sense, she can do that much cleanin' in the morning, still have anything left to do in the afternoon."

But watching her closely, the boy only became more convinced that his father was a fool. He had no idea of the woman he had

married or the home he lived in. It would have been easy for ten
women like his mother to work on the house for a thousand years
and get nowhere. And the boy had never seen her look ashamed
or afraid of anything—except on those occasions when she was
confronted with another of her husband's schemes.

She never looked away from *him*—but rather looked at him
only with affection when he came home at night, from practice
at one sport or another, and the two of them had dinner together.
His father was usually away, working on some new plan. They were
alone, in the house set back nearly in the woods, surrounded on
three sides by tall trees. On those nights it felt like it was only the
two of them, isolated from the whole world. Eating together, sitting in the living room afterwards, he would do his homework,
she would sew or knit by the yellow light of the table lamp.

The boy would begin to drowse over his schoolwork, disturbed
only occasionally by the long whistle of a car on the abandoned
highway outside, lulled by the rhythmic click of her needles.
Sometimes she would read the Bible out loud, softly but distinctly,
believing that his mind could absorb Scripture at the same time
that he concentrated on geometry or chemistry. She ran her finger down the onionskin pages, tiny print smudged nearly illegible
by the oils from her fingers. That night during the warm, crazy
spring she was working her way through the Book of Matthew,
and Christ's visit to the tax collectors:

" 'Those who are well have no need of a physician, but those
who are sick,' " she read out word by word, with no inflection but
great feeling. Nearly asleep, his mind pawed over the words as
they were read, one by one, slowly shaping them into some sense
that he was not yet sure of:

" 'Go and learn what this means, "I desire mercy, and not sacrifice." For I came not to call the righteous, but sinners.' "

Then there was the sound. It was only a quiet bump, against
the back of the house. But it was clearly not one of the usual
sounds of the night: raccoons scuttling around the garbage cans,
the close branches sweeping over the roof shingles. He looked up
and saw his mother sitting stiffly, listening. When he opened his
mouth to ask her what it was, she shook her head and he remained silent, watching her.

She stood slowly up from her chair and moved into the shadows of the far wall. She signaled for him to turn off the lamp and follow her. He did so, and moved to her as slowly and quietly as he could, until both of them stood with their backs against the wall, waiting and listening.

He could hear her breathing beside him, could smell her body in the darkness. It was a strange smell to him, musky, like all the sweat he knew from hundreds of gyms and locker rooms and other boys, but also sweet. It smelled like an overgrown apple grove he had come upon in the woods one day in the late fall, after the apples had all fallen but still lay fragrant and decaying in the grass.

The smell would not have been important, but that it made him turn his head toward his mother, and in that instant he missed it. With the lights off, the night outside was brilliant. There was a full moon, and he could see the outline of the lawn and the silhouette of each tree through the windows. He should have been able to see anything that appeared there. Any face—

He should have been able to see what his mother saw.

But the scent distracted him. All he saw at the window was a vague form, out of the corner of his eye, and he heard his mother take in her breath. Then a large, dark shape moved quickly past the next window and around the end of the house.

Both of them hung back against the wall for another long moment, stunned. Despite the strange noise, he had still expected it to be a cat, a raccoon—some familiar animal from the woods. He had never expected it to be the size of a person, or to move in a way that was oddly familiar—

They both broke away from the wall, and ran to the windowsill, staring out into the backyard. There was nothing out there they could see, except the empty, moonlit yard.

He looked back at his mother again, just as he had been looking hard, for weeks now—and saw a look of terror on her face that he had not expected. And something that surprised him even more: a hard glint of hatred.

Then she was in motion again, coolly organizing everything:

"John, call the police. Now. Don't worry about the number, just dial the operator and tell her to put you through."

She was walking swiftly around the living room, pulling down all the shades. Then she went to the closet.

"Do as I tell you," she said to the boy, who still hadn't moved. "After you're finished, make sure that all the doors are locked. And stay away from the windows."

She was rummaging through the bottom of the closet, searching with a flashlight she always kept on hand for the winter blizzard blackouts. She plunged her arm down past the family's ragged collection of boots and galoshes, and delicately, slowly, pulled out an enormous shotgun. She steadied it carefully against the wall, then groped around in the closet again for the box of shells. The boy watched her break the gun, load it, and slide the safety off, all without a hitch or a moment of hesitation, the same way she folded the bedsheets.

"There, that will do," she said, propping two chairs against the wall, and settling back in one with the gun over her lap.

"You go on now and call the police," she told the boy, but she no longer sounded urgent. He went to the phone in the kitchen. His throat was dry, and he thought his voice sounded ridiculously small. He had no idea what to say.

"Please send a car," he got out, giving the address and fearing that he would hear some kind of knowing chuckle from the desk sergeant as he realized it was Evan Barr's place.

"There's a burglar, or something."

But what had it been, really, out there? A burglar in their small town? The boy had never heard of it; he had thought of the term from the TV.

He went back to his mother and they sat in the dark, waiting and listening. From time to time the wind would pick up, clattering the branches against the roof. The boy would start, but he noticed that his mother sat perfectly still, even seemed relaxed.

They heard a new needlepoint of sound: a high, whining noise that rose and fell but gradually became louder and louder, until it could be unmistakably identified as a police siren.

"The fools," his mother said. "The damned fools."

Outside, while the revolving lights on their car bathed the house and woods in blue and red, the police officers talked amiably about people who were supposed to be hiding up in the woods: hippies, lunatics, escaped criminals. The boy's mother finally lost her patience and sent them away. They looked sorry to leave so soon, before they could expound on all the threats they were sure awaited the family in the dark woods.

"Evan oughta be heah lookin' aftah his family," one of them had made sure to say loudly as they walked back to the car.

"The fools!" the boy's mother swore, as she strode back into the house. "Without all their noise, they might have caught him!"

They made sure again that the doors and windows downstairs were locked, but it felt like the danger had passed. Without saying anything else, they both went up to their bedrooms, the boy noticing that his mother nonetheless made sure to take the shotgun with her.

In bed, he scared himself a little more, thinking about who it might be lurking around the woods and the backyard. But then he remembered how that indistinct figure had moved across the pale, moonlit yard. It was impossible to really know it, that dark shape fleeing past the window, but there was something familiar about it. . . .

Just before he dropped off, he heard another noise. But he recognized this only as his father's step, moving slowly up the stairs, saying in his foolish voice, "I heard there was a commotion—" before the bedroom door closed behind him.

19

They were always telling him that if he kept screwing around he would lose his fastball. They claimed it would float right out of his dick.

—BILL LEE

Eileen the Bullpen Queen

I started goin' to Veterans Stadium to see the Phillies with my high-school girlfriends, Sharon Anastasia an' Ann Binder. Ann was in love with Steve Carlton, an' Sharon loved Mike Schmidt. In the winter we'd go see the Flyers at the Spectrum, and Sharon was in love with Bernie Parent an' Ann liked Bobby Clarke. They'd scream their names from the upper deck all game long. They made up posters on bedsheets sayin' WE LOVE YOU SCHMIDTY, with his face drawn in the middle of a heart an' a arrow stickin' out each end. They would walk around the stands with it, hopin' the TV cameras would pick 'em up.

We dressed up real hot for the games. We wore halter tops an' middies, an' cut-off jeans with ankle bracelets, an' pink ankle socks with lace on the top. Ann even wore leopard-spot panties, like Steve Carlton was really gonna get to see 'em. They would dance really wild to the PA music an' hope the cameras would put their picture up on the scoreboard.

"You never know," Ann would say. "Maybe they'll be lookin' up there for the out-of-town scores."

But the guys they loved were always the best players on the team. How realistic was that, even if they could see us? *Everybody* was in love with them. I think Ann an' Sharon really dressed like that to show off for guys in the stands. But when they said anything, they would pretend to ignore 'em an' look down at the field.

They'd cook lasagne an' brownies for their favorites, an' leave 'em with the clubhouse men. They would look at pictures of their wives in the yearbook, an' try to dress like 'em. They found out what their horoscope was, an' their favorite hobbies. Once Ann even sent Steve Carlton a picture of herself wearin' her pink polka-dot bikini.

But they never did anything.

The Old Swizzlehead

John Barr kept carryin' us all through August and into September. He was still playin' unconscious. And he never said another word about either his mother or Ellie Jay, even though I could see it was drivin' her to distraction.

"I feel like a goddamned virgin," she told me, "worrying so much over a boy I kissed once. I must be getting old, getting so damned pathetic like this."

She couldn't help herself. You could see it more than ever in the way she talked to him. Every question sounded like a caress, until Dickhead Barry Busby an' the other flies started laughin' about it behind her back. She just ignored 'em, but Barr still didn't even want to talk about his batting average.

"You have a chance to hit over .400," Ellie Jay tried. "No one's done that since Ted Williams in 1941."

John Barr just looked at her.

"Well? Do you think you can do it?"

"If I get enough hits."

"It's not a goal, then?"

"Nope."

"What is your goal? Another pennant?"

Barr just shrugged.

"See the ball," he said. "And hit it."

"All right, so he ain't a great interview," I told her. "Never was."

"He doesn't have a heart," she said.

"This is gettin' sad, girl," I told her. "Have some self-respect."

"But I can't give it up," she said. "I feel like I'm this close to him."

It didn't look like it to me. He came to the ballpark every day, did his job, an' went home. Not that we could complain. It was Barr who got us all the way to the climactic, division-clinchin' game in Philly, featuring Eileen's greatest performance and the loss of all my worldly possessions the same night.

It was The Little Maniac who got the credit for our success from most of the flies, of course. He would stand there in his boots an' his ten-gallon hat an' tell them he was responsible, an' they would write it down. They even started callin' it "Charlie Ball."

"I've got 'em playing hustling, aggressive baseball," Stanzi would tell 'em. From then on, everything was because of Charlie Ball. John Barr hit a ball four hundred feet, it was Charlie Ball. Al The Fade go in there an' punch out six hitters in a row, an' it was Charlie Ball the next day.

The fans lapped it up. They gave him a standing hand anytime he came out of the dugout at Shea, and he made sure to come out every excuse he had to rag the umps. His act got bigger all the time. He'd be out there for fifteen minutes, swearing, spitting, an' stomping around. They never got tired of it.

The Little Maniac had us on the run, too. Half the team was a wreck from simply followin' his suggestions. But he had no control over what happened to us when we went into Philly. Guys started three, four games in advance, just to be sure, workin' on those bad ankles, rubbin' sandpaper over their fingers to bring up the blisters. Except for John Barr, of course, nobody wanted to take a chance on havin' to start, or at least play the full game. The rest of us wanted to make sure we got in at least an inning with Eileen.

Eileen the Bullpen Queen

I liked all of 'em. The Phillies, the Flyers—I even liked the visiting teams. Sharon an' Ann were still takin' in brownies. But I wanted to meet 'em.

The first time, I got in to see the starting left wing on the Flyers when he was laid up in the hospital with a knee injury. I was only fifteen, but I told the nurses I was a reporter for the school paper, and I even brought along a little pad an' pencil. They kept lookin' at the short skirt I had on, but he said it was okay. I asked him two questions about his knee an' then I leaned over an' kissed him on the mouth.

He was wonderful. I was so nervous I was shaking like a leaf, but I kept kissing him all over, on his mouth an' eyes an' nose, an' he held me tight. We talked for two hours an' he called me up as soon as he got out of the hospital. We made love the first night we went out, and it was perfect. He tried to give me some money after it was over, but I wouldn't take it. He said I had the most beautiful breasts he had ever seen. He said I had an angel face, an' he could kiss it forever.

My parents were upset about it at first. My mother wanted to call the police when I got home, and my father hit me in the face with his open hand. But I told them I would run away if they did anything, an' they let me keep seein' him.

He was only a few years older than I was. In a lot of ways, I was really more mature, growin' up in the city. He was from western Canada, out by someplace called Saskatoon. A lot of his team-mates were from around there, too. I think they were lonely to be that far away from home. He introduced me, and I went out with a lot of them. I liked them all, an' they liked me, too.

The Old Swizzlehead

There were always annies around, willing to do anything, every city we went to. There's one-night stands, an' then there's the regulars, who like to be around famous ballplayers. They're characters, star-fuckers, weirdos, nymphomaniacs, drug addicts, giggly girls. Anything.

They like the fame through us, I guess. I don't know what else is in it for 'em, except a few bucks an' a little bit of blow. And ballplayers are cheap with their money an' their coke.

In L.A., there was this actress with a cheap blond wig, called herself Holly Wood. She was always outside in the parkin' lot, willin' to do anything for anybody she thought could get her a part. I don't know why she thought that. Ballplayers might know movie celebrities, but we wasn't about to talk to 'em for some annie in a bad wig. But there she was, every trip out there.

She got so popular after a while, she would bring along a friend, who we called Holly Wood II, the Sequel. They would drive a big green VW van right up to the players' entrance after the game, an' we'd pile as many ballplayers as it would hold in the back. We'd all get down on the floor, just to make sure Ellsworth Pippin or Cal Rigby wouldn't see us. We'd fit ten or twelve millionaire ballplayers, lyin' on the floor of the van an' gigglin' like school-kids.

Most of the wives knew about it, but they didn't ask. I remember one year, we had this rook pitcher up who was married to some college girl. They were havin' dinner with me an' the Emp'ror an' No-Hit Hitt one night, an' this girl started askin' what it was like to be on the road.

"Think of all the cultural opportunities!" she said. She wanted us to tell her about the museums an' concerts, an' zoos an' shit. We all avoided her eyes while somebody tried to think of one.

"I can't *believe* you guys never *explore* these cities," she said. "Just what is it you *do* on the road, anyway?" I think everybody agreed it was a good time to order dessert.

Eileen the Bullpen Queen

The guards got to know me after a few seasons. I would bake the brownies for *them*, instead of the ballplayers, and they would let me in when all the other girls would beg and plead. Sharon an' Ann stopped goin' to games an' got married. They started acting like I was weird an' slutty to still be at the ballpark.

I never hung around the hotel bars, or anything like that. I didn't want it to be like a one-night stand. I like to really get to know the guys. And it feels so dirty and secret in a hotel room, like you're doing something wrong.

I love bein' on the field. You can't imagine what it's like to be out there, with thousands of fans cheering. It feels like they're all cheering for me and loving me. One time I got so excited that I ran out onto the field and kissed the leftfielder. All I had on was a bra and a pair of hot pants, and I got a big hand from the crowd. The police took me off, but they were laughing about it. They didn't beat me up like they do with the drunks. I waved, an' the crowd cheered even louder.

The Old Swizzlehead

She walked into the bullpen dressed in her own Mets souvenir uniform. It was typical of Eileen to go all out like that, an' we thought it was a nice touch. Her uniform was made for ten-year-old kids, too, which played up her finer features, jutting out her big titties an' her big old ass. It had number zero on the back, which a couple of the guys said seemed appropriate.

"You guys are the best after today," she said, givin' each of us a big hug. "You deserve extra special treatment."

We couldn't hardly imagine what *that* was. It got us to tremblin', just thinkin' about it. Eileen would do almost anything, anywhere, an' she would do it without even being asked. The other ones, you might *persuade* them to do things, if you bought 'em a nice enough dinner, or told 'em you loved 'em, or that you could get them into the movies.

Eileen didn't need that sort of motivation. She *wanted* to do stuff for us. We'd already had some wild scenes with her over the years, right out there in the bullpen, on the little bench half-sheltered from the field and the stands. That's how we took to callin' her the Bullpen Queen. She would take on one guy after another, take on a bunch of guys at the same time, do us in her mouth, up her ass, straight-up fucking—anything we could desire, an' it was like she read it out of our minds before we thought it up ourselves.

This time, first thing she does is stand back an' strip off her cute little kid's uniform, right out there in the bullpen. She took off everything, down to her socks an' stirrups and cap, which she turned backwards like Charlie Stanzi so she could get closer. She didn't even go back by the covering over the bullpen bench. She just stood out there in pure daylight with a big smile on her face an' said, "All right, who's on first?"

Before the game started, the whole team found an excuse to sneak out by the pen. 'Course, we had to use some discretion. One year during a crucial Phillies game, some swizzlehead had the cameras pan the bullpen staff for the sight of their tense faces. They looked tense, all right. Only trouble was, they were all facin' away from the ballfield. There was a big stink, but Eileen kept gettin' in. She was what you'd call resourceful.

"Nothing could keep me from comin' out to see you guys," she said in that little girl's voice she had, runnin' her tongue over her cherry red lipstick an' battin' her eyelashes. I think she wore all the makeup to make herself look older, even though she wasn't that young anymore.

"Come on," she said. "Don't be shy. I love you guys."

Bobby Roddy walked up to her an' she reached down, unzipped his pants, and pulled his cock right out. She got down on her knees an' took him in her mouth, right there. Her pudgy little cheeks drew him in, then she took his cock back out and began to stroke it, runnin' her hand up and down its length until he came an' let fly with a big gob of it that fell an' damn near sizzled in the dirt track between the bullpen mound an' the imitation home plate.

"I like to watch it," she said. "I like to see your things, right out in the open."

"Fuck," said Bobby Roddy.

We could barely keep our pants on, watchin' that. There was so many ballplayers out there, Charlie Stanzi called up on the pen phone to Aurelio Macondo, our combination backup catcher an' bullpen coach, to try an' find out what the hell was goin' on.

"Uh, some of the guys, they forget their gloves, skeep," says Aurelio, who had a little trouble thinkin' on his feet.

"Christ, every time we come to Philly, it's like you guys leave your head up your ass," Stanzi said when we finally came back to the dugout.

"Nerves," I told him. "It's the thrill of being in a old, historic city like this. Gives us the gooseflesh, thinkin' 'bout the Constitution an' shit."

He just gave me a nasty look, an' got together enough guys for infield practice. The rest of us wandered back in the general direction of the bullpen. It was the rawest thing I ever saw out there, even for Philadelphia.

She was on her knees—still stark naked except for her socks, an' she had three peckers out in front of her. She had her eyes closed, an' she was moving her mouth back an' forth over one guy's cock, and her hands were circlin' an' strokin' the other two like they were fine big sticks she was getting a feel for. There was a old white-haired usher an' a kid shovelin' popcorn in his mouth in the stands above her, watchin' her every move like they was hypnotized. But she didn't seem to care.

I couldn't resist it then. I pulled myself right on up over the wall, an' took my place in line. She interrupted all the things she was busy with, an' smiled up at me.

"Take it out," she told me.

"What?"

"Go ahead an' take it out. I want you ready."

I went an' did what she said. There was already three or four other guys with theirs hangin' out, too. It felt funny to have it right out there, in the breeze an' all, so I could get pleasured by some poor tramp annie with the makeup of a thirteen-year old. And still, waitin' for it out there in the bullpen, I started to get larger, until by the time her warm little hand was on me I was stiff as a bone. It didn't take long before a couple licks, a couple pulls, an' her loving, appreciative glances and I was through, drained an' zipped back up an' strollin' back out on the ballfield like I'd just been shaggin' flies. It was over like that, an' still it was exciting, an' still I was thinkin' that I would like to go back for more.

It was no surprise, then, that when it came time for Stanzi to take the lineup card out, he barely had enough for a full nine.

"Philadelphia," he said in disgust. "What the hell gets into you guys, anyway?"

We ran all over the Phillies that day. Our hitters were goin' up there an' swingin' off their heels at the first pitch they saw, an' they wouldn't stop runnin' until they scored or were thrown out. Anything to get back to the bullpen. It got so Old Coach Plate wouldn't bother to put up his hands out at third base.

"Listen!" the Emp'ror said to me, pointin' toward the bullpen when we went to the outfield for the bottom of the first. "You can *hear* it out there."

And you could, or at least we thought we could: kind of a sigh-
ing and a rhythmic creaking sound. We could imagine all kinds
of things that were goin' on out there. It created a kind of electricity for us, like playing in the seventh game of the World Series.

"Hear it, hell!" I told him. "You can smell it!"

And it was true, too. There was such a carnal commotion
comin' from over there I couldn't understand how everybody in
the ballpark wasn't aware of it. It made my palms itch just to think
about it.

By the third inning we had eight stolen bases an' were up seven
runs. Stanzi didn't know what was goin' on. At first he was mad
nobody was payin' attention to his signs. But then he naturally
decided to take credit.

"Charlie Ball!" he started sayin' kinda hopeful, clappin' his
hands together. "Let's see some more Charlie Ball out there!"

"What drugs are you on?" Ike Mopes, the manager on the
Phils, bellowed at us like a wounded cow. "How can I get some
of that New York shit for my ball club?"

"Read my book!" Stanzi yelled over at him. "I'm gonna get a
book out of this next year. All about Charlie Ball!"

But he kept peekin' suspicious glances down at the bullpen.

"Whatta they have, goddamned cable TV out there?" he said,
which cracked up the whole bench.

No-Hit Hitt was the first one quick enough to fake a injury.
There was a bang-bang play at first where he took a little flip from
our starter, Big Bo Bigbee. Hitt crumpled over like he'd been
shot.

"Son of a bitch stepped on my heel," he told Stanzi an' Doc
Roberts. He was hoppin' around like a chicken, makin' it look
like what the flies called a game effort.

"I can stay in if you need me," he said, then made a extra little
grimace. No-Hit Hitt limped off, gettin' a nice hand from the
Phillies fans. Then he sprinted up the runway under the stands
all the way to the bullpen.

"It's unbelievable what she's doin'," he told us when he came
back an inning later. "You gotta get out of this game, Swiz."

I wanted to. The whole time I was out in center field, my eyes
kept wanderin' over to the pen, an' I thought maybe I'd try to
fake a sprained ankle on the next fly ball.

The only trouble was, the goddamned Phillies were mountin' a comeback. Big Bo Bigbee put in a good first six innings, then he started lookin' toward the pen, as usual. He figured he did enough for the win, now he wanted to get a little of the action. Big Bo walked a few guys to let it look like he was tirin'. But Charlie Stanzi never did believe in takin' his pitchers out while their arms was still actually attached.

"C'mon, Bo!" he said when he walked out to the mound, an' shook his fist. "Let's have some Charlie Ball out here!" Then he turned right around an' walked back to the dugout.

After that, Big Bo starts outright groovin' the ball. The Phillies are bangin' him around the park, an' Bo sneaks a look over to the dugout, where Stanzi is out on the top step.

"C'mon, Bo!" he's yellin', clappin' his hands an' whistlin'.

Bo stepped back up on the mound and spits on the ball right out there in the open, so the umps have to throw him out.

"What the hell you do that for?" Stanzi asks him when he walks into the dugout.

"Sorry, skip," he says. "I better go out to the bullpen right away an' work on it."

We were still up plenty after Big Bo Bigbee left the game, but now all the relievers looked a bit drained. We got down to the last inning still up three runs, an' just hopin' she could hold out. Stanzi was finally beginnin' to get nervous, an' he called on the bullpen phone to Aurelio Macondo.

"Abramowitz an' Mesquite," he said. "Lefty-righty. Get 'em up, let's go."

Aurelio went over to tell 'em, but Skeeter Mesquite was previously engaged in the crowd around Eileen.

"Stanzi wants the lefty and the righty up," Aurelio told him. "He wants Al an' you getting ready."

"The goddamned Phils don't have a righty who can hit his weight," Skeeter told him. "Why the hell's he think they're last?"

"That's what the man said."

"He said he wants a lefty and a righty," Skeeter says. "You're a righty. *You* warm up."

"No, I cain't do that," Aurelio says. "He will know it's not you."

"You go ahead and warm up," Skeeter told him. "He'll never notice."

"I don't know, Skeeter—"

"Trust me. He's not going to put in a right-hander now. Not even Stanzi could be that stupid."

"I don't know," Aurelio says again, but he went ahead and put on his glove an' started warmin', an' Stanzi never noticed.

We got the first two outs in the ninth, an' it looked like we wouldn't have to worry about another relief pitcher. I started edgin' in a few steps, waitin' to make a break for the dugout when we got the last out. But then there was a walk, an' a dink hit to left, an' Not The Whole Story White boots a gimme. The Phils got the bases loaded an' Shawon Kaesee comin' up to the plate, who can hit the ball out of the park with one hand. Charlie Stanzi starts walkin' out to the mound an' we all assume naturally Stanzi's gonna bring in the lefty, Al The Fade Abramowitz, to face another lefty.

"I want the right-hander," Stanzi says to the ump.

"Have you become a complete asshole?" Spock Feeley asks him on the mound. "I want to know. Have you become one giant, walking asshole from head to foot?"

"For your information, this guy has a .158 lifetime batting average against Skeeter," Stanzi tells him. "Against Abramowitz it's .173. That's Charlie Ball."

He waves his right arm, an' the umpire relays the signal out to the pen, and nothing happens. Stanzi waves his arm again, an' the third-base ump waves his. Still nothing happens. The third-base ump goes running out toward the pen to investigate.

I took a look over the wall myself then. There were all these ballplayers still standin' around her, oblivious to anything else. All I could see of them was their backs, an' their numbers. And in the middle was her pudgy little baby face, her hair slicked back, shiny with sweat an' jism an' who knew what else. Her eyes were still closed an' it looked like she was workin' as hard as she could.

"You have to go now," Aurelio says to Skeeter, but he was stuck.

"No way," he said. "She's got a death grip on me now. I don't care if they suspend me. I'm staying."

Meantime the umpire is gettin' closer an' closer, an' Stanzi's wavin' his right arm around like a helicopter. Just before the ump gets out there, the bullpen gate finally opens, an' out comes one of those little golf carts with the giant baseball cap on it. The cart drives all the way up to the infield, an' then it stops an' out pops fat old Aurelio Macondo, who runs up to the mound an' Stanzi there with his mouth open but not able to make a sound.

"Here I am, skip," Aurelio says.

The Little Maniac finally manages to get somethin' out, seein' his third-string catcher out to pitch crunch-time relief in a pennant-clinching game.

"You . . . what are you . . . ?"

"You wanted a righty," Aurelio says, an' tries to smile.

"What I want is for you to turn around and get off the field," Stanzi says. "I want you to go back into the clubhouse, and take off your uniform, and get out of the ballpark right now."

"He's gotta pitch," the home-plate ump says.

"What did you say?"

"He's on the roster," the umpire says. "He's gotta pitch to at least one batter. That's the rule."

"You throw the next four pitches five feet outside, then you get off the mound, do you understand me?" Stanzi says. "Don't even wait for me to come back out to the mound. You just put your glove down and walk off. And you keep right on going."

"Yes, skip."

"I don't want to see you out here after this batter. In fact, I don't ever want to see you again in my life."

Everybody in the ballpark saw Aurelio come out, but nobody could believe it when the PA announces he's gonna pitch. The Phils are all screamin' from the dugout. They thought somehow Stanzi was tryna show 'em up.

"I'll get you for this!" Ike Mopes is bleatin' at Stanzi. "I'll cut your goddamned pecker off, tryna show me up like this!"

Meanwhile, Shawon Kaesee's up there whippin' his bat around, with steam comin' out of his nose an' ears. I think it got to Aurelio. He takes a step back off the mound in the middle of his windup— an' next thing you know, the home-plate ump is runnin' out there, wavin' his hands an' yellin', "Balk! Balk!"

That brings in one run, an' now the Phils are only two runs down. The crowd is startin' to yell, Stanzi is kicking in the dugout water cooler—an' Aurelio stands out there on the mound and starts goin' through all the fixin's like he's a real pitcher. He peers in at Feeley like he's waitin' for the sign, and shakes his head a couple times, like he's actually shakin' off a pitch. Charlie Stanzi finally can't control hisself any longer in the dugout.

"Throw the goddamned ball already!" he screams, but that just shakes Aurelio up again. He sets, brings his hands down to his belt—an' drops the ball for another balk. Stanzi lets out a scream from the dugout, an' another run comes in. We're only up by one now, with the tyin' run on third, an' still nobody's thrown a pitch to Shawon Kaesee.

The crowd is pouring it on Aurelio now, an' Shawon is up there with a grin I could see from center field. I couldn't blame him— the man could break a bat just by checkin' his swing, an' now he's up against a old bullpen catcher. Spock Feeley is standin' about three feet to the left of the plate, holdin' his glove out as far as it'll go, just hopin' Aurelio will take the hint an' throw outside. All Stanzi can do is kneel on the top step, mumblin', "Charlie Ball, Charlie Ball now, let's go."

Aurelio was standin' out there now like he was afraid to even move. He moved back an' touched the rubber, then went real slowly into a windup, tryin' not to do anything wrong. He didn't balk this time, but when the runner on third saw how slow Aurelio was movin', he took off for home on his own. Stanzi tried to holler to him, but with all the crowd noise Aurelio couldn't hear him. The runner was more than halfway home with the tying run before Aurelio noticed him, an' he would've scored standing up— if Aurelio hadn't panicked and chucked the ball blindly down the middle, right into Shawon Kaesee's wheelhouse.

"NO!" Stanzi screamed from the dugout.

"NO!" screamed Spock Feeley, divin' back toward the plate.

Nobody could take back the pitch, though. Shawon took his full, fat swing, the bat blowin' air into the face of the runner racin' down from third an' sliding just under his bat. He knocked that ball deep to right field, and at first I thought it was long gone.

It was Barr out there, though, an' I knew it wasn't possible anything was gonna get past him, down the stretch. He took a step or two backwards, measurin' where that ball was goin', an' I began to pick up hope. He took another step back, then another, an' then he broke an' ran for the wall with that big easy stride he had. He stopped at the wall, put one hand on the padding, an' then lifted hisself up.

He took a grip on the padding an' vaulted himself up over the top of the wall. He caught that ball in a snow cone at the top of his trajectory, an' at that instant some fan of the game throws a full cup of beer right in his face. They scratched at his arms, an' tried to pull the ball out of the glove an' the glove off his hand. How John Barr hung on to that ball I'll never know, but he came tumblin' back down with his glove still held high for the umpires to see as they came runnin' out from the infield, an' both lift their thumbs up at the same time.

The fans jumped down after him, all around us, an' they ran out on the field, punchin' an' grabbin' at anything they could get their hands on. We were all runnin' for the dugout fast as we could, straight-arming the fans, even knockin' over the cops who ran out with their clubs. The bullpen gate opened and those guys in there ran out, too, with Skeeter Mesquite still zippin' up his fly.

I looked back in as I ran, an' saw Eileen strugglin' into her toy uniform again. She was wiping her hair down with her towel, still soaking wet with everything, an' her makeup was gone. She looked a little bit dazed, but she was still most concerned about us. The last thing I saw was her callin' to us, "Be careful! Oh, be careful!" as we ran back down into the long, dark clubhouse tunnel, with the cops formin' a solid line against the fans still tryna get to us.

We had won the pennant.

Eileen the Bullpen Queen

Sometimes I think it would be nice to marry a ballplayer and have two children, one boy and one girl. I would like to sit up in the section with the players' wives. I think it would be nice to know all of them, an' sit around talking about our husbands.

But the hardest thing would be giving up all the rest of them. I don't know if I could do that. Right now, I love them all, and they all get to love me.

The Old Swizzlehead

Somebody had a few bottles of champagne on hand back in the clubhouse, despite the express orders of Woodrow Wilson

Wannamaker. But most of us didn't feel that much like cele-bratin'. We'd been there before, an' besides, we were all feelin' a little bit worn out.

John Barr hadn't got close to the bullpen, of course, but he was pretty calm about the whole thing, too. He sat there in front of his locker, wipin' the beer from his face with a towel, and actin' like it was just one more game on the string.

"Yeah, I had it all the way," he said when the flies asked him. "The alcohol stung my eyes some, but I made sure to keep a grip on the ball."

"That was pure poetry," Ellie Jay said to me later, when we were all in the airport, waitin' for our quick hop back to New York.

"That was what makes it worthwhile, seeing a catch like that, Swiz. That's what makes this a beautiful game."

"Uh-huh." I was wonderin' what she might say if she coulda seen that scene out in the bullpen. She didn't have any idea what this game was really like, even after coverin' it for fifteen years. Then I spotted John Barr, over by the big window, watchin' the jets come an' go, looking contented as he ever did. It occurred to me that maybe I didn't know, either.

I do know that when I got back to my house that night, I thought there had been a fire. I was right, too. It just hadn't started yet.

All my stuff was out on the front lawn. My clothes, my music, my trophies from all the way back in high school—everything. Even my electric razor an' a bottle of cologne. I just stared at it for a couple minutes. I thought maybe I was bein' robbed. Just then somethin' else flew out the bedroom window an' landed on the ground, I looked up an' there was my devoted wife, Wanda.

"What the hell you doin', woman?" I asked her. "You get down here an' explain yourself."

"Uh-huh," she says, wipin' her hands. "I'll be *right* down."

She comes down with a gas can in one hand, an' a box in the other. I noticed she was wearin' her little African cap, too.

"What's all this about?"

"You know what it's about," she says. "The same old thing. I heard about that woman out in the bullpen. Are you going to tell me you had nothing to do with that?"

"Ah, that wasn't nothin'," I told her. "She's there for all the guys. She's just like a good-luck charm."

"A good-luck charm?"

"It didn't mean nothin'. She likes us, that's all. What's the matter with that?"

"Is that what you really believe?"

"Yeah, why not?" I asked her, tryna sound as calm an' reasonable as possible. I was beginnin' to get a little suspicious about that gas can. "Maybe she's just the kind of woman loves a lot of men."

"Are you serious? Do you really think this pathetic little white girl loves you all for who you are?"

"I guess so," I told her. "I mean, why else would she give everybody a blowjob out in the bullpen?"

"Oh, really? And what's that feel like? Getting a blowjob out in the bullpen?"

"I don't know," I said. I was frankly a little afraid of what she might be drivin' at, but I could be as stubborn as she could.

"It felt good, I guess. It felt a little, you know, *dangerous,* havin' my cock out in broad daylight. But that felt good, too. It made me feel fine, like I was gettin' away with somethin' over every other man who ever lived."

"And did it feel like love?" she asked me. "Did her mouth feel like she loved you out there?"

"I don't know," I shrugged at her.

"Well, it's time you learned," she said, unscrewing that can an' pointing it down toward my things.

"Does this mean you're throwin' me out?" I asked her, like a swizzlehead.

When I smelled what was comin' out of that can, I tried to grab it from her. But it was too late. She already had the match lit, an' she tossed it.

"You're crazy, woman!" I yelled, tryna pull out a few of my best suits.

"That's just for starters," she said. "You don't get out of here right now, I'm gonna do your new car."

She started to walk toward the car, an' I took off. I drove out of there fast as I could go. I could picture the headlines the next day.

"How you think this is gonna make me look?" I yelled at her as I screeched on out of there. "What the hell you think I am, a goddamned cartoon?"

"That's for you to decide," she yelled back. Whatever the hell that meant.

20

Swing the bat, for Christ's sake. You're not a statue until you have pigeon shit
on your shoulders.

—BILL LEE

The Old Swizzlehead

It was the day after Eileen's amazing performance that John
Barr forgot how to play the game. For a while I thought there
might be some kind of connection, but in fact he stopped playing
from the moment some kid messenger stepped into the clubhouse an' handed him a little envelope.

I should have seen it at the time, but we were all still hung over
from clinchin' the division and other things. The Little Maniac
insisted we come into Shea on our off-day an' have a workout. We
knew it was so Ellsworth Pippin could sit in the stands with the
flies around him, an' act like he was what they called a harsh
taskmaster.

We were all suitin' up, when some punk from a messenger service comes in with his bike chain wrapped around his arm, an' a
sealed white envelope addressed to Barr. We were talkin' about
who we was likely to see in the playoffs, an' he signed for it an'
tore it open without barely lookin' at the thing. I don't think he
expected it to be anything at all.

It wasn't no more than a couple pieces of paper. One of 'em
looked like somethin' legal and official. The other one was some-

thin' else again. I only saw it for a flash, but I remember it looked older, an' lined, like it had been folded for a long time.

It wasn't exactly like the color drained from his face when he saw it, or he fell back clutching his heart. I was sittin' right there watchin' him, an' he barely changed his expression. He just turned an' put it up in his locker like it was one more piece of fan mail. But from then on, John Barr stopped playing. Stopped cold dead, just like that.

The next night he came out an' went oh-fer five against the Cards. He struck out three times an' didn't hit a ball out of the infield. It didn't mean nothin' with the division wrapped, an' we thought it was just a real bad game. The kind that can happen in baseball to even the best players—even if it never did happen to John Barr before. We told ourselves maybe he was usin' the mean-nothing games to try out a new swing.

But the next day after that it was three weak ground-outs, and three left turns back to the dugout. He took the collar again the next night, an' lost the game with his glove when he overthrew third. One mistake followed another. It became undeniable, even with the games not meaning anything. John Barr was in a slump.

"Maybe he's old," Charlie Stanzi told Dickhead Barry Busby. "I've seen men get old all of a sudden."

The next day out at the batting cage, Barr was takin' his turn before the game, an' The Little Maniac tried to tell him how he could improve his swing.

"Thought you was gonna use that big bat forever," he said, when Barr took his usual cut at a ball from Old Coach Plate an' missed by a mile. "Thought you was never gonna get old. Now maybe if you did it this way . . ."

I thought Barr would ignore him, the way he done before. But instead he turned around on him hard, his eyes lookin' really angry. I was just behind Stanzi, waitin' my turn, an' I never seen him look like that before. This was pure frustration, like anyone else who's ever played the game an' got tangled up in it.

"Shut it," he says to Stanzi, real quiet, but with his mouth in a line. "Shut it right now, I don't wanna hear it."

Coach Plate throws another one, right down the pike, what John Barr can only dribble off his front foot like some rookie shortstop just up from the Carolina League.

"Oh, yeah, you don't need to change your game at all," The Little Maniac says, watchin' Barr hop around by the plate, tryna get over the pain in his toes. "What you say you were gonna do again when you retire? What was it you said you had lined up?"

That was when John Barr chucked the bat against the cage, so hard it rattled the wire with a sound you could hear around the ballpark. He came around the side of that cage faster than I ever seen him turn third, an' he woulda done some damage to Stanzi if he coulda got to him. I tackled him just in time, an' me an' Maximilian Duke managed to keep him down an' sit on him, until Stanzi could recover his composure enough to stop tremblin' an' make some tough-guy remark.

"Yeah, you better think about what you can do besides hit a baseball," he says to Barr, who was still writhin' around underneath us like a trapped water moccasin.

"I seen guys like you go just this fast."

He walked off an' Barr calmed down again. He went absolutely limp, an' got silent again, an' wouldn't tell us a thing about why Stanzi suddenly got to him.

"It's just this slump," he mumbled. "That's all."

"Well, no wonder," I told him. "You never had one before. It's about time you learned."

He didn't want to talk about it, though. He just gave me a look an' went back out to shag flies.

"There's something that's chewing him up from inside," Ellie Jay told me. "It's the same mystery."

"Maybe he *is* just getting old," I said to her. "Have you ever thought of that? He has to get old, too."

There didn't seem to be nothin' else to account for his slumpin' off like that, first time ever. I thought nothin' else could account for his strange behavior off the field, either. It seemed like all year he'd been tryna reach out to somethin', to tell somebody somethin'. I didn't know what, but I thought maybe he just got lonely after all these years roomin' alone, playin' alone, without one close friend on the team. I thought maybe *he* could sense he was slowin' down, losin' somethin', an' it was no great mystery like Ellie Jay thought, but just the usual fear.

The only thing was, I never saw anybody lose it this fast, even under Charlie Stanzi's influence. It wasn't just that John Barr lost a step, or was in a slump. It was like all of a sudden he couldn't play anymore.

Out in the field, he didn't seem to know where the ball was or what to do with it. He would throw to the wrong base, or chuck it in anywhere, in the general direction of the infield. He even began to drop fly balls. They banged right off the heel of his glove an' bounced out, like goddamned Charlie Brown.

But the worst was at the plate. I never thought it was possible for John Barr not to hit. But just like he'd been the best hitter who ever played the game, now he hit the worst slump I ever saw on anyone, majors or minors. It was worse than anything No-Hit Hitt or So Many Other Ways White ever got into. Overnight, John Barr didn't have a clue at the plate. He would stand up there like he was guessin' on every pitch. He would check his swing, take his cut late. He carried his bat loose off his hip now, like he didn't have the energy to hold it up anymore.

He didn't even have the feet right, which he used to position so perfect every time, it looked like they were painted out there for him. He didn't seem to care. After that first outbreak at Stanzi, he didn't seem mad anymore. The Little Maniac got behind the batting cage a few more times an' tried to get on him, but it didn't succeed in goading him, if that was Stanzi's intent. Nor did he want the man's advice.

John Barr didn't slam bats or break locker rooms like Moses Yellowhorse. He didn't run into any walls like The Emp'ror. He would just walk back to the bench after he had gone down again, an' slip his bat quietly back in the rack. The rest of the time, in the clubhouse an' out on the field, he would walk around listless, like he barely had enough energy left to keep hisself goin'.

The flies thought it was due to the pressure on him to hit .400 like Ted Williams. But the writers always like to give themselves too much credit. Only Ellie Jay remembered he'd already tore up five World Series in his career, when he didn't seem to be over-whelmed by the pressure.

"There's no pressure on a ballfield that could get to that man," she said, with that look in her eye that didn't allow any argument. "It's got to be something bigger."

I thought maybe he had a disease, from readin' *The Lou Gehrig Story* when I was in school. After all, it looked like he barely had the strength to hold up his bat anymore. But he wasn't wasting away, or turning color, or fallin' down a lot, doin' any of those mysterious sickly things.

Whatever it was, there wasn't no sign of it lettin' up by the time we had to go down to Atlanta and play the Braves in the National League playoffs. Before what happened to Barr, we all thought we could take Atlanta easy, an' win the privilege of takin' on California in the World Series.

The Angels had took the American League West by ten games, an' everybody was expectin' 'em to sweep right through the Red Sox an' make the World Series. The Rev. Jimmy Bumpley had started referrin' to it as "The Pennant Crusade," an' the Angels as "God's team." And of course Good Stuff Goodson had his face all over the national magazines, grinnin' his big plantation nigger grin.

"I can't say if we're God's team," he said with all modesty. "But I do know that we're America's team, and if America's team isn't God's team, then who is?"

We all thought we could whip *his* butt, too, but with Barr gettin' one hit in his last two weeks of play, the Braves didn't necessarily look like a pushover no more. They had a smart manager in Ollie Rawley, an' I was afraid of what he might do to Barr in the playoffs.

He was another one of the good ol' boys you always see runnin' around Florida in the spring, with a chaw in their mouth and a look behind 'em for their jobs. They usually catch on somewhere. Some manager hires 'em on as a coach, to talk about the old times, or tell 'em they're a genius late at night in the hotel bar after a five-game losin' streak.

Ollie looked like all the rest: big red face an' fifty extra pounds, all carried in his gut and his rear end. When he talked to you, he couldn't help belchin' every two or three words. He talked right around it, like it was punctuation.

Ollie had been one of Cal Rigby's coaches years ago, and he actually did know a thing or two about the game. He was even more superstitious than most ballplayers, but otherwise he had somethin' in his head. On road trips he always kept a bottle of bourbon an' some ice up in his room, an' he was happy to sit around in his underwear an' shoot the shit with you about the game or anything else. He stayed awake on the bench, an' he could pick up a thing or two that might help you, which qualified him as a managerial genius.

I went over to see him before the first playoff game, an' talk a little shit about the old days. But he was distracted by his bad luck.

"These goddamned dying fathers," he says. "Couldn't one of the bastards hold off for a couple weeks at least?"

"It's a tough break," I commiserated.

Day before, the father of his number-one starter had a heart attack an' fell over dead. Number-one starter goes home to bury the old man. That night the number-two starter calls up *his* daddy, tells him he's gonna be the new number-one starter, an' his old man gets so excited *he* has a heart attack. Ollie was already down to his number-three pitcher, a rookie.

"It's the goddamned evil eye," he said. "I must've stepped on a baseline last week."

He shrugged an' spat tobaccy juice. Then he looked up at me with a narrowed eye an' said all of sudden, "John Barr ain't been out today, has he?"

"What?" I said back to him, cleverly tryna stall for time.

I knew then the whole time he'd been talkin' to me he'd been keepin' track of every one of our hitters in the batting cage. Most of all, he'd been keepin' a eye out for Barr.

"What is it with him, Swiz?" he asked me with a shit-eating grin, like we were old buddies an' he just wanted a little favor, between him an' me.

"You know, I used to watch him hit every day, an' I can't believe anything can stop him short of a shotgun—"

"He's playin' possum for you, Ollie," I told him. "He's lettin' your pitchers get themselves overconfident."

"Yeah?" says Ollie Rawley, lookin' at me like he had seriously considered the possibility already. "Maybe so."

He went off then, back to his rook starter, but I didn't think he was convinced. I just hoped I was right, an' John Barr had got out of whatever temporary aberration he was in. Here it was his first slump ever in pro ball, an' the sharks was circlin' for him already.

But when he finally came out of the dugout, it didn't look encouraging. Barr was still draggin' hisself about like his shoes had concrete laces. He didn't even bother to take his usual cuts before the game, which I figured was the worst sign of all, except that at least that way Ollie Rawley an' the Braves didn't get to see him try to hit.

"What's wrong with you?" I asked him. "You don't even wanna hit now? You got a tapeworm, boy?"

But he just looked down an' away from me, almost like he was ashamed.

"Lea'me alone, I'm fine," he mumbled, an' I couldn't get nothin' else out of him.

Fortunately, when the game started, Ollie's rookie was too scared to go after anybody. It's natural to be scared to death the first time. I played in nine playoffs an' seven World Series, an' it still gets to me when they got a full house an' they call your name an' you go run out there an' line up along the foul lines. That Atlanta PA announcer spoke my name an' I ran out there an' looked up at all the people, an' the red, white, an' blue paper hangin' from the upper deck, an' the photographers snappin' my picture.

"Batting first . . . for the world champion New York Mets . . . Number one, Riiiiickey Falls!" the PA said, an' the Atlanta fans gave me a big, long boo, an' I stood out there an' waved to 'em an' dipped my cap an' gave 'em a little smile, an' the goosebumps ran all up an' down my arms. Even when you make the big money—and even when they boo you—it's still a thrill.

It's tougher on a rookie. Ollie's kid didn't have bad stuff, but he was all over the plate. He walked me an' Bobby Roddy, an' he didn't get a ball close to John Barr.

Barr looked just like he had for the last two weeks: standin' up there any old way, holdin' his bat like it was too heavy for him to handle. But the rook gave him a free pass, too, an' The Emp'ror came up an' hit a double for two runs, an' Spock Feeley hit one over the fence for three more. The big house got quiet in a hurry, an' the festivity went out of it.

Ollie pulled the rook, but we ran through their bullpen. Top of the eighth, we were up 11-4, and coastin' against some old junkballer they had out there called Bobo Zouave. He was the bottom of their staff, nothin' left in him but mop-up. An' Ollie Rawley decided he would be perfect to put John Barr to the test.

He still wasn't sure about Barr. He'd had three walks, flied out once, an' hit a grisly little seein'-eye single up the middle. Everybody in the dugout could tell there was somethin' missin'. But he'd been so good for so long that Ollie still couldn't altogether believe it. When Barr comes up again, he calls time right away an' runs his fat ass out to the mound.

The game was out of reach, an' the dreg end of his staff was on the mound. But Ollie was talkin' to him like he had to get the most important out of the season. Then it came. Just a straight, nothin' fastball with no deception to it. It tumbled in elbow-high, big and slow, with no dips or frills or anything else to fool anyone, an' you could see old Bobo actually cringe out there, expectin' that ball to come right back down his throat.

Instead, it floated across the plate untouched. The ump was so surprised he called it a ball, but everybody on the field knew different. That pitch sailed in like a ocean liner. It was just the kind of lame fastball John Barr would jump on without mercy, every time, no matter what the count or the score in the game.

But Barr didn't even swing. He only shuffled his feet a little bit after the ball was already by him. He could've been watchin' that pitch on TV, for all the attention he paid to it. Out on the mound, Bobo Zouave crossed hisself in thanks—and in the Braves dugout I could see Ollie Rawley watchin' the whole thing from the top step.

Our bench got quiet after that pitch. Everything was quiet by now: most of the fans gone home already in disappointment, an' the rest not havin' any idea what just went on. None of the flies or the TV people in their booth knew it, either. Only the players knew what was happenin', knew it was anything different from another meaningless pitch in a already decided game.

Bobo was workin' quickly out there now, throwin' as if he couldn't believe it would last. He threw another one straight down the middle, the ball barely even turning over. You could've counted the stitches on it. But John Barr only watched it go by again, an' this time the umpire's arm went up.

"Strike one!" he yelled, as if he was tryna wake Barr up. But Barr didn't even step out of the batter's box, didn't so much as pump his bat.

Bobo was so eager to get the ball over now he missed a couple, ran the count full. An' John Barr kept his bat on his shoulders the whole time. Zouave had to come in with the payoff pitch then, an' you could tell he was still afraid it was a trap, that's how much Barr could mess with your mind.

But he looked over at Ollie Rawley in the dugout, an' I saw Ollie give him a little nod. Bobo took another big breath an' threw one more of those outrageous fat pitches to the plate. It was right down the middle again. Barr followed it all the way in, an' at the last minute he took a half-swing at it, then pulled his bat back. It was strike three, an' the umpire couldn't help but punch him out. Barr simply turned around an' headed back to the dugout like he was goin' for the pine-tar rag.

"Do *something*!" I screamed at him.

"What?" he said, lookin' up at me with no kind of expression on his face at all.

"Goddammit, you got to at least look like he fooled you!" I was yellin'. "Go kick the water cooler, throw all the bats on the field. Do somethin' to make it look like a freak accident an' you're mad as hell!"

He only turned away an' sat back down on the bench like he didn't know what I was talkin' about.

We took that first game easy enough. But the next day it was just as bad as I expected. Every pitcher Ollie Rawley put out there came right at Barr. They challenged him like I'd never seen pitchers challenge him since his rookie season, when they were just findin' out what he had. They were feedin' him everything they could think of to throw. All their old hangin' curves. Their flat sliders, their slow fastballs—every old pitch they had used up an' wrung out of their arm. Like it was a clearance sale.

We were only saved by the dead fathers again. The guys Ollie was left with couldn't get anybody out *except* Barr, an' we scored at least one run in every inning. Goin' into the ninth, we were up by ten an' cruisin'. But the bench was as silent as if we were losin' the last game of the Series.

Barr had his last ups in the ninth, an' everybody wanted to see him get a hit. He was oh-fer on five pitiful strikeouts. Everybody on the bench was doin' what we could think of to help him. We tried all leaning forward on the bench together at the same time. We tried twisting our caps around. We even tried putting baseballs in our caps, which was the best good luck charm we knew.

Barr stood in there, an' this time he took a couple of those big, restless-cat flicks of his bat. This time he dug his feet in again, an' looked sharp at the pitcher. The rookie they had out there saw the change an' he was scared, he threw the first two pitches high. We were all clappin' an' talkin' on the bench now, hopin' he would get hold of one when the rook had to come in. But just before he began his windup, Barr shrugged his helmet off his head, dropped his bat, an' started for the Braves' dugout.

I thought, well, that was it, he finally snapped. I popped up out of the dugout an' ran after him. The Emp'ror an' No-Hit Hitt an' Bobby Roddy jumped out too, but even so, we woulda been too late. John Barr wasn't makin' a show. He meant to get there, an' it was only the home-plate ump, Ronnie Beluga, who stopped him by tacklin' him around the chest.

"Get him out of here," he told us, not even botherin' to throw Barr officially out of the game.

"They got no right to talk like that," he kept saying, when we finally got him back to the clubhouse.

"They got no right—"

"Talk like what?" I tried to get out of him. "What they say? Who said it?"

He shut up then an' wouldn't say nothin' more, but I remember his face was bright red. It musta been somethin' somebody said from the Atlanta dugout, but I never seen John Barr react to bench ridin' before. Nobody takes it too serious; after all, how much can you say to a millionaire? It's only when somebody's in a bad slump, an' his nerves is already ragged, that he lets that kind of thing get to him.

"Ain't you played this game before?" I asked him.

But I couldn't get nothin' more out of him. I hadda go back out to play the last half-inning in the field, and by the time I come back into the clubhouse, Barr's already changed an' left. It wasn't till later that night that I found out what it was set him off.

I was sittin' around the airport bar with Ollie Rawley while we were both waitin' for our flights to take us back to New York an' the next three games of the playoffs. John Barr was standin' right in front of us, lookin' out the window at the planes like he was a little boy. Ollie saw him an' gestured at his back.

"It was the damnedest thing," he tells me, tryna find out more, but at the same time genuinely astonished. "It was somebody down in the corner, just runnin' his mouth. He said somethin' about his mother, an' the next thing Barr's right over here."

"Do you know what it was he said?"

"I dunno. Nobody even remembered who said what exactly. It was just the usual bench-raggin' stuff. 'Your momma wears army boots.' Nobody thought nothin' would come from it."

"I know his momma died this year," I told him, hopin' I might get a little bit of mercy from the man. "Maybe he's more sensitive than he lets on. But that was back at the All-Star break."

"Uh-huh. Well, I'll put a end to it, then," Ollie Rawley says, real pious-like, dissin' my intelligence right to my face. "You know I would never try to win a game that way."

Barr couldn't hear us where he was, but I got the feeling it wouldn't have mattered. He was still glued to that window, like he could hardly keep himself from running out an' jumpin' on the first big jet he could find.

"He's mourning over his mother, that's obvious now," Ellie Jay said when I told her about it on the plane back to New York.

"But you saw how he played after he got back—"

"So it's a goddamned delayed reaction."

"I just wish I knew what was in that letter. That's when everything started."

Meantime, I didn't know what to do to get John Barr through the rest of the playoffs without comin' apart. I suspected Ollie was gonna try to run him off the field with it, an' I wished I could talk Barr about it, try to get him to chill. But the whole way back to New York, he just sat up in the front of the plane the way he always liked, starin' out the window at the darkness passing by.

Sure enough, first game back at Shea, Ollie Rawley's got his whole bench on John Barr's mother. They didn't know what it was all about any more than we did, but that didn't keep their mouth off her. They yelled anything they could think of out there. It was horseshit, mostly, just various statements questionin' the lady's breeding and birth an' sense of sexual etiquette.

It might've been funny in most situations. But it got to Barr, all right. He didn't get mad like he did the game before; he just drew into himself an' looked all sullen an' listless again. I don't think he got his bat on one ball. We took Ollie Rawley's number-three pitcher apart easy enough even without Barr, an' went up three games to nothin'. But it was clear to me an' Skeeter things couldn't go on this way.

"We've got to get him back for this," Skeeter said.

"Lemme take care of it," I told him. "I know Ollie an' his superstitions."

Next morning I got the biggest black cat I could find at the ASPCA. I put it in a bag and brought it over to Shea. One hour before the game started, I brought the bag over to the Braves' dugout and waited until I saw Ollie comin' up the runway from the locker room. I let that cat go right in front of him, an' it took one look at Ollie an' froze. It fattened its tail an' arched its back up an' hissed at him like it come straight up from hell.

Ollie tried to run back down to the clubhouse, his cleats scrapin' an' slidin' to get a grip on the cement floor. That cat kept sidin' toward him, still hunched up an' hissin'. Ollie Rawley could've shooed it away easy enough, but he didn't want to touch it. He didn't even want to look at the thing. He wound up in a corner behind the water cooler with his eyes averted.

"Get that thing outta here!" he sputtered, burpin' like a machine gun. "There's not supposed to be a cat here!"

But the damage was done, an' all Ollie could do was roll around, belchin' an' groanin'. He stayed on the bench, but the whole game he had no idea what he was doin'. We could see him walkin' back an' forth in the dugout, crossin' himself over an' over again.

We got a few runs early an' we beat the Braves goin' away, even with John Barr wanderin' around in his daze again. Nobody remembered to rag him about his mother or anything else, though. Ollie's ulcers gave out that night, an' he ended up in the hospital for a week.

"You know, I never set foot on a major-league field again," he told me a long time later on, when we met in an airport bar. "The next year they kicked me upstairs to general manager. Then we had a lousy season, and I got knocked down to scout. I was one step away, comin' out of that clubhouse, but after your goddamned cat I never set foot on a major-league field again."

I didn't know what to say to the man, 'cept to attribute it to his bad luck.

"You know, I finally got over my superstitions," he told me. "I even got a black cat myself now. I keep him around the house to remind me of you."

We still didn't know how we could beat the Angels without John Barr. Nobody even made any jokes, he was lookin' so bad. That last game he didn't take the bat off his shoulder, an' I thought maybe soon we'd have to point him toward home plate.

In his corner of the clubhouse, he was still half in his uniform, holdin' his head down. John Barr, who used to be in his streets ten minutes after the ump thumbed the final out and ready to go walkin' out to wherever it was he went walkin' alone out in the dark. He looked now like he was all used up. He was sittin' there like he could barely lift up his arms to get his shirt over his head.

But then I got distracted by all the flies an' the TV people for a few minutes. When I looked back I saw John Barr was gone, his uniform left crumpled up on the bottom of his stall an' even his bats flung around any which way. Like they didn't mean anything to him anymore.

21

He had to be a very graceful player, because he could slide without breaking the bottle on his hip.

—CASEY STENGEL

The Phenom at Sixteen

He betrayed her the day his father was fired, near the end of that warm and unsteady spring. His father told them about it while they were still at the dinner table. It was the first time he had been home in weeks for dinner, and he was in a rare amiable mood. He had said nothing the whole meal to set off his wife or put her on edge, and she and the boy had almost begun to relax.

"Well, yah," he announced casually, leaning back in his chair. "I been laid off."

"What are you talking about?" his mother asked, in evident disbelief. Then the full force of it came through. She spoke in a low and controlled voice as she moved toward the table, twisting a dish towel in her hands.

"You have been laid off? How can you have been laid off? You don't work."

"I mean at the hotel," he explained obligingly.

"You mean you've been fired!"

"If you want to call it that," he said defiantly. "I would've quit anyway, if I'd known what a cheap bastahd he is."

"Is he firing everybody at the hotel?" The boy had the feeling

she would rather the hotel had burned to the ground than find
out he had been fired for his own self.

"I asked him for a raise, that's all. I been there seven summers,
an' he still pays me the same thing."

"You asked him for a raise?"

They were both astonished. The idea of his father getting a raise
for what he did at the hotel was incomprehensible.

"Yah," his father continued calmly. "I figured I was good
enough for him to come through."

"You are not," his mother said, as sharply as she could manage
and still keep herself in check before the boy. "You are not good
enough, you are not anywhere near good enough. Don't you realize why you are there? Didn't you see his cheapness was the only
reason why he would hire somebody like you? You cannot even
paint your own house!"

His father looked surprised and hurt at this, as if her words
and her anger had been completely unexpected. That was what
amazed the boy most; the look of genuine surprise in his eyes.

"What do you intend to do now?" she demanded.

"I dunno. Somethin'll turn up."

"And what if it doesn't? Don't you *understand* that's not how
you are supposed to think? You have a family, a son. What if nothing turns up?"

"I dunno." His father shrugged, as if he honestly had not
thought it through, which the boy was sure he had not. "I guess
then I'll spend the summah swimmin' up in the quarry."

His mother drew back from the table, her voice no longer so
furious, but flat and knowing.

"You would, too. You would take the summer off and let everything go to the devil if you could."

"Oh, here, somethin'll turn up," he said with what was meant
to be a comforting grin, staggering up bandy-kneed from the table to try to hold her. He got his arms around her, but she held
hers up over her chest, as if trying to ward him off. He tried to
smooth her hair, and plant little kisses on her cheek.

"I'll get somethin' from my cahrs soon. Then I won't need any
other work—"

"Get away!" She shoved him back and he stumbled and landed
hard against the table, clutching at chairs. There was a commo-

tion of wooden legs scraping over the floor, and the boy shot up from his seat, thinking for a moment that they were finally going to kill one another right there. But his father only continued to look crestfallen.

"Your cars are *never* going to sell, do you know that?" she screamed at him. "You are never going to make any money. You are never going to have *anything*!"

"I know what I'm doin'," he insisted. "I don't got to go down on my knees to the owner of some crummy hotel—"

"No, you don't know what you're doing. Those cars are junk. Worthless, useless junk. *I* know that, but you don't."

She began to move around the kitchen with her usual freneticism, but this time with no real purpose. They watched nervously as she paced back and forth in front of the sink, wringing her hands.

"What are we going to do?" she asked, her voice rising wildly. "You don't even understand. You don't know anything. How are we going to live?"

"Look, I can get another job," he offered, frightened now by how she was acting.

"How can you get another job? You couldn't even do the one you had. You're known all over this town as a fool. Who is going to give you another job?"

"Somebody will," he said. "Or maybe you could get some kind of job. Typing again, like you used to do—"

She began to laugh, dreadfully and dramatically.

"Oh, that would be fine for you, wouldn't it?" she spat. "Work so you can spend the money tinkering on your junk cars."

The boy wanted her to stop, then. He wanted her to stop saying the truth. His father set his mouth, and strode into the hall to pick his hat and short brown jacket off the rack. This only brought more wild laughter from her.

"Oh, where are you going now?" she yelled after him. "To find more junk cars? To find all the junk in the world and bring it back here?"

"Nope," he said, planting the broken-down grey fedora on his head, and scrounging in one pocket of his jacket for his pipe.

"I'm going out to find a job," he said, gesturing at her with the pipe. "A position that's suited to my ability."

With that he swung out the door, fumbling with the matches and his pouch of tobacco. She screamed after him through the door, so loudly that the boy was sure he must have heard her:

"What will that be? Junkman? Town idiot? Ass? *Fool*?"

When he was gone she slumped at the table, crying into one hand. She held it over her mouth and nose, as if trying to gulp back in the sobs. She reached across with her other hand for his arm, and gripped him tightly.

"I'm sorry you had to see that," she said after a few long minutes. "You shouldn't have to go through this."

She let her hand drop from her proud head, revealing her face all red and streaked with tears, some strands of hair loose from her tight bun. He felt dirty, seeing her this way. He wanted to put her back together again.

"There may have to be some changes," she told him, patting his hand. "We might not be able to stay in this house anymore."

"That's all right," he said quickly.

"I don't know if your father can get unemployment. We might have to go on welfare. I might have to get a job. I've been avoiding it, but I knew the day would come."

He nodded, though he didn't see how it would change things much. It actually made him feel more secure to think of her at a job. Then, he knew, his father wouldn't have to think about her alone at home all day.

"I have some money saved up from the restaurant," he told her. "I could get more work somewhere, too, after school."

"You're a good boy." She tried to smile at him. "You keep your money for yourself."

She sat there quietly for a time, absently patting his hand.

"I might have to get a divorce," she said finally. "The Bible doesn't allow it. But I don't know."

This shocked him. He had never heard her talk about his father in any way but that she was attached to him for life. But after his initial surprise, the idea had its appeal: never to have to worry again about when he was going to come home and interrupt their evenings together—

"I'm tired," she said, getting slowly up from the table and trudging out of the room.

This was the most surprising thing of all to him this evening; she was leaving the dinner dishes behind in the sink, unfinished. He didn't think it could be true at first, but when she did not return he padded quietly upstairs and listened, out in the hall. There he could hear her, sobbing behind the closed door of his parents' room.

He went back downstairs and did the dishes, washing them slowly and carefully. He dried each one, and each piece of silverware, and put them all away. Then he ran a wet cloth across the top of the table, and swept the whole floor. When he thought it looked as clean as she usually left the room, he collected the table scraps and took them outside.

They threw their garbage in a canister built into the ground by the garage, so the raccoons couldn't get to it. There was a wind out, teasing around the boughs of the trees, but it was warm and he didn't bother to put on a coat. He went slowly, relishing the freedom of being able to walk in his shirt sleeves, and glad to be out of the house for a few minutes. He dumped the scraps and made sure to replace the heavy metal lid of the canister. The raccoons had claws like fingers that could pry open or tear apart anything not properly shut.

He was cutting back past the garage when he noticed the door was open. Inside was the green and brown behemoth; the massive station wagon looked as immobile as if it had been carved from stone. The boy wondered that they had ever been able to drive it anywhere, even with his father's lunatic strategy of replacing the gas as he went. The thought occurred to him that it would take just one match to send the whole thing up, but he knew it would only hurry the arrival of the next one.

He heard a small sound, and tried to tell himself that it was a raiding coon, or one of the cats that liked to visit the garage at night, leaving their paw prints on the roof and hood.

"Hey! Kid! C'mere."

There was his father, peering into the back window of the garage, rapping on the pane and motioning for him to come around. For a moment there was something unsettling to the boy about his face, bobbing up and down behind the window, trying to see in the darkness. He was tempted to pretend he hadn't heard, and run back into the house; he knew his father would be reluctant to follow so soon after his mother's rage. But instead he walked obediently around the garage.

His father had brought back not a job but a small square bottle of liquid, tinted rusty brown in the moonlight. He was grinning at him as if they were both out on a great lark, and the boy was sure that he had already put both the fight and losing the hotel job behind him.

"You shouldn't have done that," he blurted out suddenly to his father, surprising himself.

"What? Done what?" He seemed genuinely baffled.

"You shouldn't have quit your job." He stood defiantly before his father, clenching and unclenching his fists at his sides.

"But I didn't quit, I got fired," his father said, as if the boy hadn't heard right. "I asked for more money, like a man's got a right to do." He chuckled. "Got my ass handed to me, too. Hell, I would have done it anyway."

"You shouldn't have done that."

"C'mere," he gestured, doing a little dance with the bottle. "There's a nip still in the night, but it's okay with this."

He pointed the bottle at his son and inclined his head. Dumbfounded, the boy shook his head no.

"C'mon. Why not?"

"I'm not eighteen yet," the boy said ridiculously.

"I'm your father, you have my permission. Haven't you done any drinkin' yet?"

Hesitantly, but resenting the insinuation on his honor as a boy, he gripped the head of the proffered bottle, smelling the heavy, sour scent he had only smelled before on the breath of men.

"Go on!"

His father put a hand on the bottle and held it gingerly to his son's lips, then tilted it abruptly forward. The harsh liquor tumbled down his throat, and he got down one big gulp, then gagged, spraying the rest of it back out. His father laughed delightedly beside him, and whisked the bottle away.

"You don't got to take the whole thing in one swig. Yah, it was about time I taught you to drink!"

The boy needed to sit down. His eyes were tearing, his stomach felt weak, and his sure, fine control over his muscles seemed to have vanished. He plopped down on the ground, gazing stupidly out at the woods, now black and undecipherable. Then his head spun, and he had to fall back onto his elbows.

"Yeah-huh, that's good drinkin' whiskey," his father chuckled, stretching his long, thin body out beside him. "I don't usually get whiskey that good, but today's a special day."

"What, because you lost your job?" Again, the boy could not believe the words had come out of him. His father to his surprise took it philosophically enough.

"Yah, that's right. That's one thing you'll find out when you get older. You don't lose a job every day."

The boy laughed out loud, he was so startled by this response. For the first time he had some inkling of his father's feeling of freedom. What it must be like to break out of every routine—not just of time, and having to be where when, but also out of everyone's expectations of you. He lay grinning now in the grass beside him, one hand tucked under his dilapidated hat, the other holding out the whiskey bottle again—without a thought in his head, the boy realized, about what he was going to do next, or even what could happen *to* him.

"Go on, have another one. Big athlete like you."

The boy wasn't sure there wasn't some goading in his father's words, but he took the bottle anyway. This time he held it to his lips himself, and sucked slowly and carefully at the rim. The liquor trickled down his throat, still harsh, but controllable now. He was not sure how long he had been sucking at the bottle, but his father said something, and it seemed like hours had passed.

"Whoa! Mother's milk."

He heard his father's foolish cackling laugh, but found himself laughing as well. It was funny, he thought. It was all ridiculous. He took a bolder swig and handed the bottle back.

"You see, son, that's what goes into bein' a man," his father said, pulling himself closer and talking confidentially. "You have to take that risk sometimes. You got to stand up for yourself. For your dreams."

"That's your dreams? A raise at the hotel?" The boy began to laugh again. His father just grinned and handed him the bottle. He drank sloppily now, not really bothering to sit up, letting some of the liquor spill down over his shirt front.

"It's all part of it," his father said soothingly.

He moved even closer—and then, to the boy's horror, put his arm around his shoulders and drew him to his own chest, so that the boy's face now was drawn up right against his father and into the smell of him. From a distance he felt unspeakably defiled, but he could not muster the strength to fight him off, to push him away. He submitted to it, even felt comfortable and burrowed further into his father's chest.

"That's the way it is with men," his father went on, carefully enunciating each word. "You have to take the chances if you're not going to end up like the rest of them in this town, going nowhere. You see what I mean, son?"

"Yes," he felt compelled to answer, the one word slipping thickly off his tongue.

"But women don't understand that," he went on. "They have to think about things like keeping the house together. Your mother doesn't understand it. Now another woman, maybe—but that's all water under the bridge. I married your mother for better or worse. You see what I mean?"

"Yes," he said again.

"I knew you would." He pressed his arm against the boy's neck, pulling him more tightly to him. "You're a man now. Men can understand. Your mother, well, she's too nervous, am I right?"

He tugged again on the boy's neck.

"Huh? Am I right?"

"You're right," he said, and gave a short laugh, and in that moment he knew he had betrayed her.

"That's my boy." His father chuckled delightedly, the boy's head still crooked in his arm. "I knew you'd understand." He offered the bottle. "Here, you want to finish it?" His father offered the bottle again. "There's just a sip left."

He leaned over clumsily to drink, and managed to spill the remainder of the bottle in a small, dark streak down his father's chest. Automatically he leaned forward and tried to lick it up. It was when his tongue touched the rough cloth of his father's shirt that he realized everything he had done. He felt nauseated, and degraded beyond what he could have believed possible. He bolted up and ran for the back door, ignoring his father's cry.

He was barely able to make it back upstairs and into the bathroom. He retched as quietly as he could manage into the toilet, but the noise of him clomping up the stairs had brought his mother out of her bedroom. She rapped on the door.

"Are you all right in there?"

"Yes—"

"Dearest?"

"Yes, go away! Go away, go away, I'm fine!"

This silenced her, but of course she did not go away. He could sense her hovering out in the hall while he tried to clean up as best he could. It wasn't easy. He could not seem to keep his stomach from convulsing, even after it had passed up everything inside. Finally, when there was a stable interval, he staggered across the hall and into his bed, shutting the door behind him.

"Honey—" his mother called from out in the hall.

"I'm all right!" he shouted, though he knew she had seen him, must know what the bathroom smelled like. He threw off his clothes—his clothes that now stank like his father's—and flung himself into bed. Shivering despite the warm wind, he pulled the covers high up to his chin. He wanted to shout out to her, *I'm not like him, I'm not like him at all—*

22

Every day is Mardi Gras. And every fan's a king.

—Bill Veeck

The Old Swizzlehead

We could hear the Big A for miles before we could see it. By the time we got past Disneyland, the voice of the Rev. Jimmy Bumpley was hummin' an' reverberatin' all through the team bus:

"The Lord showed me a sea that shined an' shimmied with unnatural light, breaking upon the first letter, and surrounded by a host of angels—"

That is, the California Angels. He took it as a vision, or at least a good tax move. After all, the ballpark was surrounded by a sea of shining L.A. chrome in the parking lot. And out past deep center field of the ballpark was the first letter of the alphabet—a giant red *A* that stood for Angels, or Anaheim, or the Almighty, All-Seeing, and All-Forgiving, as the Reverend Bumpley preferred. When he bought the team, he had the big red letter *A* hooked up to his "Salvation Radio" show, so that all through the game it would crackle an' pop and send out the Word.

"I got no trouble with that," The Rev said when some fly accused the whole operation of bein' a shill for his ministry.

"I see no better purpose than to be a big, shiny neon sign for the Lord. I see no higher calling than to be even a lowly flier sheet for Jesus. Every word we say, every song we sing should be a jingle for Christ—"

When we got within sight of the park we could see the posters, pasted twenty feet up the stadium walls: the Rev. Bumpley, his backup Hallelujah Chorus, an' last but not least Jesus Christ. All smilin', everyone, includin' Christ on the cross, though you understand it was a somewhat more restrained smile. Underneath the nail through the feet it said "Jesus Died for Your Sins— Have a Nice Day!" And "Jesus and Baseball—A Winning Combination!"

The Angels *were* as heavenly as ballplayers got. Even when they *lost* a game they would chalk it up to what Jesus Christ wanted. They would tell anyone with a pencil or a microphone how *He* wanted them to play baseball, an' not only baseball, but to play for the Angels. An' not only for the Angels, but in particular at third base, or in left field. I think they thought of the Son of Man as a big general manager in the sky.

But the Rev. Bumpley also used his money to make sure the most pious team was coincidentally the best team he could get on the field.

"The American family is a *winning* family," was how he put it. The Angels won mainly because of Good Stuff Goodson an' The Big'Un, Cloyd Kooble, both of whose spiritual defects was forgivable.

Good Stuff Goodson was the fastest outfielder in the American League—for what *that's* worth—an' the hottest thing in Southern California since drive-by shooting. He could hit for power an' average, an' he played flashy in the field. But he always made sure to give the credit to Jesus.

Good Stuff even let them make up some cute little nigger story about his nickname. Everybody in the major leagues except the writers knew he got the name for bein' the best coke source in the American League, which don't compare to National League blow, anyway. But he let them put out the story that it came from bein' the best turkey stuffer on his granpa's turkey farm back in South Carolina. The flies lived on *that* one so long they built a house.

We thought we could handle Good Stuff. But we didn't know what we'd do with Cloyd. He was their closer, the top reliever in

the American League, an' the only man I ever feared on a ballfield. The rumor was they signed him off a chain gang from the
hill country in Tennessee, out near where they still see Bigfoot a
lot. Nobody knew for sure, since you didn't ask Cloyd Kooble a
lot of questions. He didn't communicate on that level.

The Angels liked to call him "The Big'Un." He looked like
he'd been shoveled into his uniform like a sack an' they used to
bring him into games on the back of a pickup truck. He had long
red hair and a red beard an' moustache that was always full of
leftover food. At least the face hair covered his mouth and his
rotted-out little stumps of teeth. You only saw those teeth when
he smiled. And when you were in the batter's box an' saw that
smile, you knew you were in trouble.

Cloyd just liked to throw the ball—across the plate, at people,
anywhere. He never said anything about Jesus. He stood out there
an' smiled that evil, black-toothed grin at you and then he threw
the first pitch a hundred an' ten miles an hour at your head. He
saved or won every game he pitched in for two years, an' I never
heard the Reverend Bumpley object to his religious observances.

"He lets his physical prowess serve as his offering to the Lord,"
the Rev said.

Turned out the Angels didn't need Cloyd or Good Stuff or even
God for the first game. We were done about five minutes after
the national anthem. The Rev. Jimmy Bumpley sang it himself, of
course. That is, he kind of *talked* through the song in front of the
Hallelujah Chorus and a Marine band—with a few words thrown
in for effect, the same way he liked to read the Gospel:

"Oh, say, *brethren* / Can *you*, personally, see / By the dawn's
best, early light / What so proudly we all did hail / By the twi-
light's last, terrible gleaming..."

Believe it or not, after that it got even worse. Good Stuff Goodson led off for them an' hit a soft fly ball out to John Barr in right
field. Barr circled under that ball like he was dizzy from the sun,
and it fell down an' hit him right in the head. He just looked at
the ball in a daze for a minute, an' then he threw it back in.

Good Stuff Goodson was already sittin' on third, an' the crowd
went crazy—all except a few Met fans who sat over in left field
chantin' "Angels suck! Angels suck!" They had three runs before
we got anybody out, but we wasn't concerned so much about that.

Me an' No-Hit Hitt both went over to Barr to make sure he was okay.

"What happened?" I asked him, but he looked at me like we hadn't been properly introduced.

"Sun's pretty bad out here already," No-Hit Hitt said, even though we both knew it wouldn't be a bad sun field for two hours.

But John Barr didn't bother to say anything to either one of us. He wasn't hurt—it was worse than that. He only sat down on the bench an' stared straight ahead at the infield.

Without him, we couldn't get anything going at the plate. We kept startin' little rallies—one, two men on base every inning. But it seemed like John Barr was always up next. In the old days he woulda broke your heart with chances like that. But now he went up there with those big blank eyes, danglin' his bat, shufflin' his feet loosely in the batter's box. Even without Ollie Rawley around, the Angels' starter began to notice. He threw everything down the middle, an' Barr didn't even offer at 'em.

The crowd ate it up. They would sing along with the hymns the Rev. Jimmy Bumpley flashed up on the Vision Replay Board, an' when it flashed MAKE A JOYFUL NOISE UNTO THE LORD! they would all yell. The final score was 14–4, an' the scoreboard flashed a big final message saying THANK YOU—AND THANK JESUS! and the crowd began singin', "Amen, Amen!"

"I think the Lord wants us to make it a four-game sweep," Good Stuff Goodson told the flies, an' his usual fool grin was on the cover of the local papers the next day, under the captions all reading the same: HIS WILL BE DONE!

Even with that to motivate us, we couldn't get it goin'. The next day was Sunday, after all, which was prob'ly bad for us. John Barr still couldn't even catch the ball, an' it was beginnin' to get to us now, knowin' for the first time in thirteen years he wasn't out there to back things up.

Lonnie Lee made a bad relay to first on what shoulda been a double-play ball. Then Spock Feeley dropped a foul tip, an' I even let a ball get by me in the outfield to give goddamned Good Stuff Goodson three more bases. We opened the door for them an' they kicked it in, scored seven runs in one inning, and that was that. The final was 16–3, even worse than the day before. Our fans out in left field were chantin' "Mets suck! Mets suck!" by the time we made the last out.

"These pious sons of bitches are embarrassin' the fuck out of us," No-Hit Hitt said, an' we all felt the same way.

"I don't think this is the Lord's will at all," Lonnie Lee said, after givin' a good beating to his locker. "This looks to me like Satan's doing, or a whole big pile of horseshit."

The only one in the locker room who didn't seem that pissed off was Charlie Stanzi. Before most of us could get our socks off, he was all dressed up in a brand-new dude outfit from a store called Rodeo At Rodeo, tellin' the flies why he wasn't worried.

"I got a secret weapon," he said, an' winked at 'em.

"What's that?" Ellie Jay asked him.

"Charlie Ball," he told her, an' gave everybody a significant look. "That's how we'll beat 'em. We'll play Charlie Ball."

Which meant another goddamned workout when we got back to New York, to make it look like he was really doin' somethin'. We didn't get in from L.A. until two in the mornin', but we had to be back out to Shea by ten, workin' on Charlie Ball in a steady drizzlin' rain. We played almost two hundred games, countin' spring training, and we were in the goddamned World Series. If there was anything we hadn't learned, we weren't gonna learn it now.

The flies all approved, of course. They took our bad play personal, an' though they would never admit it, they were happy to watch us get our punishment. Dickhead Barry Busby was out there almost applaudin'.

"The way you guys played the last two games, Stengel or Durocher would've had you practicing for a *week*!" he told The Emp'ror. "You ballplayers today have no goddamned fundamentals!"

What we needed wasn't fundamentals but some way to get John Barr functioning again. I thought maybe I'd try to talk to him direct on the flight home, but he made it clear he didn't want to be bothered. He just sat way up front as usual, lookin' out the window at the darkness.

"He's dying out there," Ellie Jay said to me, watchin' him up there. "We've got to do something."

"Can't *you* think of nothin'?"

"I tried kissing him already. What the hell else do you want?"

"All right," I told her. "I got a plan. Maybe it'll turn up somethin'."

Actually, I didn't have any good idea. All I could think was for us to follow Barr again, the way I did that time in the minors. Since we were at home, I figured he would lead me to his place. I didn't have any idea what I was gonna do then.

"You really think this is going to work?" Ellie Jay whispered to me after the workout, watchin' Barr get ready to go.

"Oh, yeah," I told her. "In all my years trackin' people, I never knew it to fail."

"What the hell," she said, givin' me a swift kick. "The worst we can find is that he has a wife and three kids somewhere."

Barr left the dressing room after that workout like a man who didn't have any wind left. His head was down, his arms spread out from his sides—his whole body sort of caved in on itself. He walked so slow Ellie Jay an' I could barely keep behind him.

Not that he was lookin' for anyone to follow him. He used to be like a cat in the clubhouse. Any sudden movement an' you could see his eyes follow it, even if his head didn't move. He was alert to everything. But now I coulda stepped on his heels. He never looked behind himself, never looked up from the pavement.

He didn't go far, only trudged a few blocks over to a little, trashy apartment buildin', across the street from one of the junkyards that are all around Shea Stadium. There was graffiti all over the building, an' a big metal fence around the front courtyard.

"*This* is it? This is where he lives?" Ellie Jay whispered to me.

"And this is what you wanted to come home to."

We waited until I saw the light go on in a window upstairs, but even with all the private-dick shows I seen I didn't know what to do next. A few minutes later the light went out an' he came back downstairs again, still walkin' with his head down. We watched him go into a greasy spoon down the street.

"Now what?" Ellie Jay asked me.

"That's it, baby," I told her. "You got me."

"Let's break in."

"Say what now?"

"Let's go up the fire escape and see if we can get into his apartment."

"You brought your burglary tools along with you?"

"C'mon, let's just see! If there's any clue to the man, it's got to be in the apartment."

My whole life, pretty women been able to talk me into things against my better judgment, an' this was just another sad example of the phenomenon. We went around the back of the building, an' with a good jump I boosted myself up on that fence an' got ahold of the fire-escape ladder.

"You stay down here, keep a lookout," I told Ellie Jay, but she wasn't havin' any of it.

"The hell you say. I'm in this all the way."

"Girl, it's a wonder you don't got a Pulitzer Prize already."

I pulled her on up after me, an' we tiptoed up the rest of the fire escape to where she was sure she saw the light. It was a crazy plan in New York, I know, an' I was prayin' there wasn't a trigger-happy super around somewhere. The fire escape itself wasn't too stable, either, an' Ellie Jay put her foot on a rusted-out bar an' almost fell right through. But when I grabbed her arm to steady her, she just started to laugh.

"You know I must be getting old," she said. "Climbing up on fire escapes to get myself a man and a story."

I had to laugh then myself. We were both standin' outside a tenement window on a fire escape, gigglin' like schoolkids.

"I was just thinkin' of the column Dickhead Barry Busby would write if we got ourselves killed," I told her. "It would be the greatest moment of his life."

Fortunately, John Barr didn't have a window gate, an' he didn't even bother to keep his window over the fire escape closed. We just lifted it up an' walked right in.

Neither one of us knew what we were lookin' for, exactly, but soon as I got in the window I knew it wasn't there. There was nothing in the man's room. That's all it was: a small, dirty studio apartment. With a single bed, a chest of drawers, a few clothes hangin' in a closet—an' a bat. There was also a full-length mirror, which, judgin' from his clothes, was mostly for workin' on his swing.

There was nothin' personal. No pictures, nothin' on top of the drawers except an alarm clock. No entertainment I could see: no TV, no stereo, no books. One little room with nothin' at all a normal human being could use to keep himself occupied for more than thirty seconds at a time. We both got quiet looking it over.

"What does he do up here?" Ellie Jay asked, an' it was a good question. "What does he do, when he's through swinging that bat over and over again in front of the mirror? Does he just lie on the bed? Does he look up at the ceiling, and wait for it to be time to get up and walk over to the ballpark?"

"It gives me the creeps," I told her. "It's like in the movies, when they track Dracula to his coffin in the middle of the day."

There sure as hell wasn't any clue to the man lyin' around, like Ellie Jay suggested. But now that we was illegally broken into his apartment, I figured we hadda find *something*. We looked through all his drawers. I thought if there was anything we would find it there. A letter, maybe, or a photo of John Barr with the Wild Caged Girl from the Relaxation Lounge.

But there was no privacy of the man to violate. Nothin' at all in those drawers but his socks an' his underwear. Nothin' under the bed, or the pillow.

"Not a goddamned thing about his mother," Ellie Jay pointed out. "Nothing on any family. Not even a picture."

The only interesting thing I turned up was in one corner of his bottom drawer, under his socks: his notebooks. I'd seen 'em before, when he brought 'em into the clubhouse.

"What're those?" Ellie Jay asked.

"His book."

"You mean on pitchers?"

"You could say that."

A lot of ballplayers kept books on the pitchers around the league—what they threw in certain situations, what their best pitch was. But Barr's book was somethin' else again.

"These have got *everything*," I told her. "It's the book on every other player in the league, period. The book on everybody he ever played with or against in the major leagues. Pitchers, hitters, fielders—*everybody*. What every other player does in every other possible situation."

"What's this in the back?" she pointed out, leafin' through his latest notebook.

It was one page, with only a few words written on it. An' unlike everything else in the room, it didn't seem to have nothin' to do with baseball.

"I should have seen," was what he had wrote. An' then: "I deserve it." That was all.

"Jesus, what the hell could that be?"

Just then, there was a footstep on the stairs, an' I rushed to put the books back.

"Wait a minute," says Ellie Jay, grabbin' at them, an' when she did, somethin' else slipped out of that book. I saw when it hit the floor it was the same envelope the messenger handed to Barr in the clubhouse, right before he started into his slump. I wanted to just shove it back in an' get the hell out of there, but Ellie Jay scooped it up first.

"Lemme see it!"

"We got to get out! Whatta you think, we can hide in the closet?"

"I've come this far—" she said, an' whipped out the two pieces of paper inside. They were the same two I'd seen: one typewritten piece of lawyer's talk, an' another little folded-over old sheet. The lawyer paper was somethin' about this bein' the last part of the estate of Barr's mother, signed over to him now. The steps outside were slow, but they were gettin' closer an' I snatched it away from Ellie Jay an' shoved it back into the envelope.

"Wait!" she said, holdin' on to the little folded piece of paper. There was hardly anything on it anyway, an' we were both able to read it in a glance before I got that away from her, too, shoved it all back into the book, and got us both back out the window an' clamberin' down the fire escape. By the time we got to the bottom, her eyes were shining. She thought she had done it.

"Did you *see* it? Did you see it?" she asked me, as we walked away from that tenement house in a hurry.

"Yeah, I seen it."

"I *knew* it!" she exclaimed. "I knew it was something to do with the mother all along!"

"Sure," I said. "But what, exactly?"

For that whole mysterious message from his mother had been just one line, written in ink an' faded now. It said:

"I would have done it anyway."

23

The quietness my mother had brought me surrounded me like a spell.

—SADAHARU OH

The Phenom at Sixteen

The evening had been guided carefully through its stations by his mother. The two of them ate silently together, then he did his homework while she sewed and patched and read from the Bible.

Above all, it was quiet. The meal was the first respite for her since the day had begun, and she had risen and braided her hair, and gone downstairs to light the stove. He knew she liked it quiet, so that even the clanking of plates and pots and pans was muffled. The boy understood it on his own; he knew the occasion didn't lend itself to clamor. Throughout dinner they held between them a careful tension of hope and relief and fear; his father had not come home yet.

They smiled conspiratorially at each other when they had finished dessert and he still wasn't home, as if they had put one over on him. The worst was to have him arrive in the middle of dinner, loud and ridiculous, disturbing the careful meal. But their apprehension only increased as they did the dishes. The longer he was away, the more certain it was that he would be home soon.

Their unspoken desire was that—somehow—he wouldn't come home again, ever. There was always that faint hope. But he was unpredictable, and might be back soon after all, and in a worse mood than ever, bullying and quarrelsome, demanding to eat his reheated dinner, to know what they had done with their day—looking to pick a fight.

He would shadow-box with the boy, pretending to play. But in fact his open hands would slap faster and harder against his son's cheeks. The boy would simply try to defend himself. He kept his hands out and his head down, peeking up at his father's perpetual grin. He would pretend to be enjoying himself; it didn't really hurt, but he was afraid at how loud the slaps sounded, wondering how long it would be before his mother felt obliged to intervene, and then there would be a real fight.

It did no good to anticipate the fear; it would arrive soon enough. The boy went back to his homework; his mother darned and sewed, hands whirring around needles and pins and cloth. He snuck glances at her work sometimes and was fascinated: she produced one miraculously whole garment after another, and laid it over to the side without looking, rushing on to the next one.

A warm spring breeze blew in through the window screen; he would find it harder to concentrate on his schoolwork. Outside, the woods were full of sounds. It seemed again like the whole world was alive and that everything, even down to the rocks, was shifting restlessly about in the dark.

He found himself nodding over his math book until a sudden, disharmonious noise made him start awake. But it was only the scrape his mother's chair made as she got up to "shut down the kitchen," as she called it.

She kept it "open" all evening, in case his father returned. She had to wait for bedtime before she could go in and bolt the back door, check all the pilot lights on the gas range, and turn off the coiled fluorescent light on the ceiling. The boy watched it hum and crackle and blink, then turn brown and flash out.

He looked at a few more equations, moving his pencil sluggishly across the fuzzy yellow paper. His mother read another passage from the Bible, murmuring just loud enough so he could hear— "soak it in your mind," she called it—without disturbing him. In fact he could concentrate on neither the math nor the Scriptures. " 'I desire mercy, and not sacrifice . . . for I am gentle and lowly in heart, and you will find rest for your souls. For my yoke is easy, and my burden is light. . . .' ''

When she was through she gathered her sewing, and he closed his book. They both stood up, and she leaned over to turn off the living room lamp before they started upstairs.

That was when they saw the face at the window.

24

They don't drop too many fly balls in this league, do they?
—WHITEY HERZOG

The Old Swizzlehead

It was still rainin' an' cold by the time I got out to Shea for the next game, but I liked it. I was in the mood for rain after all those goddamned sunny Angels.

I don't think they were much in the mood to play in that weather. And we had our crowd behind us now, too. They shook up Good Stuff Goodson in particular. He went out to warm up in left field with that big grin, an' the fans out there started chantin', "Jesus sucks! Jesus sucks!"

The only trouble was Stanzi. The Little Maniac began to believe his own press. The fact that the rain only let up right before game time an' left the field muddy an' slow didn't make no never-mind to him.

"We're gonna surprise 'em," he told us, cockin' his cowboy hat. "We're gonna surprise 'em with Charlie Ball."

Comin' out aggressive *did* throw the Angels off. I led off the bottom of the first with a single, an' when Bobby Roddy laid down a fine bunt I kept goin' right past second. I beat the throw to third by the length of my hand, an' when The Emp'ror laid down a perfect squeeze on the very next pitch, I came across standing up. Nobody'd ever seen The Emp'ror lay one down like that. Our fans were standin' in the aisles chantin' at the Angels, "Duh-duh-duh-da, duh-duh-duh-da . . . Hey, faggots, good-bye!"

We got another run on a double steal, an' then one more on a hit-an'-run when Bobby Roddy came all the way around from first on a single. The Angels were talkin' to themselves, an' The Little Maniac was already workin' on his postgame speech for the flies.

"You have to force the play," he was sayin' to nobody in particular in the dugout. "You have to give them the opportunity to make mistakes."

But the rains turned around an' got us. There was a full gale blowin' off Flushing Bay, an' the wind got so bad the pitchers could barely keep their feet on the mound. There was an hour delay, an' when we got back out they had to dump so much sand on the base paths you couldn't get any kind of jump. That shoulda been the end of Charlie Ball for the day. But The Little Maniac's reputation wasn't built on doin' anything sensible.

Our feet sunk down into that old swamp an' garbage dump Shea was built on, but it didn't make no difference. Stanzi kept runnin'. He had Spock Feeley, the slowest man on the team, try to steal third, which took us out of one big inning. He had No-Hit Hitt try to score on a safety squeeze, an' Hitt got halfway down the line an' fell flat on his face in the mud.

"That was pretty good," the Angels' catcher said when he strolled up to put the tag on No-Hit. "You could join the circus an' be the dog-face boy."

That started a little fight, but gettin' mad didn't do us no good. We didn't finish the Angels, an' they chipped away a run at a time, until they had tied it up goin' into the eighth. Then they brought in The Big'Un.

He was like a force of nature out there hisself. He punched out our last six hitters for us, every one of 'em strikeouts. He threw two strikes past me, an' then the son of a bitch gave me a big smile with his rotted-out little teeth an' whipped in the third one. Cloyd didn't much care for a waste pitch, 'less he could waste it on your head.

By the top of the ninth it stopped rainin' an' the sun was out. There was even a rainbow spread out over right field. I remember starin' over at John Barr who was standing behind it, lookin' kinda wavery behind all the different colors. I didn't like that. It made me think he wasn't really there at all.

Stanzi had brought in Al The Fade, but his ball wasn't doin' any fadin'. If anything, it was magnifyin'. The Angels got a couple men on, an' then he bore down an' got two outs. But the next batter hits a little dyin' quail out at Barr.

The Color Commentary

The sudden surge in the crowd noise alerted him that he should look up. He lifted his eyes, but in his confusion he had no idea what he was looking for. Then he picked it out: the small white ball rising quickly in a high arc before him, then just as quickly descending. He watched the infielders rushing furiously out after it, the batter pounding up toward first—

He began to run toward the ball, too, slowly at first, and then faster as he realized that he was supposed to catch it. But his fine eye told him it was too late already—

The Old Swizzlehead

"Yours, yours, yours!" I was screamin' at him. I knew I had no chance at it, but I kept runnin' anyway, thinkin' maybe I could make him move. Bobby Roddy an' No-Hit Hitt were racin' out from the infield, but I could see they weren't gonna catch up either. It was John Barr's ball, but he was runnin' like a drunken man. He froze up at first, then took one slow step, then another—

At the last minute he took a couple big strides and he almost made it. But it was that extra second he had missed that you can't give up. The ball hit the ground six inches in front of him an' stayed there in the soggy turf. Two runs were in, an' the Angels were up 5–3 now.

I expected the boos to come, an' they did. Out in right field some fans even started to chant, "Barr sucks! Barr sucks!" It was only a few of them, but they were loud, an' nobody tried to shut 'em up. Me an' Bobby Roddy an' No-Hit Hitt had all ended up there, out by Barr, an' we tried to look away an' make out like we didn't hear it.

"Fuck 'em, if that's what they think," said Hitt.

"Fuck you," added Bobby Roddy.

"All right, we can still get this one," I said. I just wanted to break up the wake, so I tapped John Barr on the back with my glove an' started back to my position.

"Get the next one," I said, even though I didn't think he would get it, or much of anything else. He stood out there limp an' still, lookin' ahead like he wasn't sure what was goin' on. But that wasn't even the main problem. There was this little figure walkin' slowly out of the dugout toward us.

I told myself it was the batboy comin' out for some reason. But I knew who it was, right from the start. He was walkin' hunched over as usual, moving very, very slowly. All the way out to right field.

"That son of a bitch," No-Hit Hitt spat. "He's really gonna do this."

"Hit him when he gets out here," I told John Barr. "I mean it. Unload on the son of a bitch. I'll back you up. At least you can get that in for yourself."

But Barr didn't say a thing. He didn't even look at me. And he didn't punch Stanzi when he finally got out there with a big smirk on his face, an' hooked a thumb back toward the dugout an' said, "You're out of here." He just took it an' went runnin' slowly toward the dugout the same way he had gone runnin' around the ballpark when Stanzi told him to, back in spring trainin'.

Cloyd Kooble finished us off in the bottom of the inning. We were down three games to none, an' the Series was all but officially over. Nobody had ever come back to win after bein' that far behind.

Everybody dressed as fast as they could an' got out of there, so they wouldn't have to talk to the flies 'bout havin' our butts whipped, or about John Barr bein' pulled. Barr hisself was already gone. But of course they found one swizzlehead to talk to.

"What's the matter with John Barr?"

"You tell me," The Little Maniac said, an' shrugged his shoulders an' tried to look a little sad.

"What's the matter with him?"

"I dunno. Best player in the game—all of a sudden he can't do a goddamned thing."

"Are you saying he's not giving a hundred percent?" one of them asked. Stanzi hesitated to answer him just for a moment—his timing was perfect—an' then they were all over it.

"No comment."

"Are you saying he may be on drugs?" Dickhead Barry Busby asked.

That was when Ellie Jay hit him. She was standin' next to him, holdin' up her tape recorder mike toward The Little Maniac, an' when Busby asked that she hauled off an' whacked him across the head with the machine. She just about broke that thing over him, an' it took four other flies to pull her off him.

"They're going to run him right out of this game, Swiz," she told me later. "He's the best thing in it, and they're going to take him down."

"I don't see what else we can do about it."

"It's got to be that letter from his mother," she said again. " 'I would have done it anyway.' But what did she do?"

"I don't think we'll ever find out," I told her. "Unless he wants to say."

But John Barr didn't have a thing to say about anything, not even Dickhead Barry Busby's drug charges. He came in late again the next day, an' sat in front of his locker not sayin' a word. He didn't even look up when Stanzi come in an' told him he wasn't gonna be starting—the first time ever he didn't start a World Series game.

Everybody else was already talkin' 'bout where they were goin' huntin' an' fishin' in the off-season, an' which golf courses they wanted to play.

"What's the difference for the loser's share?" So Many Other Ways White asked. "Fifty thousand? Hell, dudes, we make that in a week."

But then somebody got to talkin' 'bout how we should have won the day before. We started talkin' 'bout that goddamned fly ball, an' all the runners thrown out in the mud. We were talkin' 'bout how the Angels' starting pitching wasn't *that* good, an' how

Good Stuff Goodson hadn't shown us anything. Finally, Spock Feeley jumped up off his stool and shoved his hand through the shaving mirror.

"Fuck that," he said. "I'll be damned if we can't at least win two games an' make those pious sons of bitches go back to Los Angeles with us."

He was standin' on a stool with blood drippin' from his hand, makin' a speech to a bunch a' millionaires like he was a college football coach. But it got us goin'. Everybody was yellin' then, an' bangin' on the walls. We went out yellin' all the way to the field, like we were goddamned Notre Dame.

I know it was silly—a bunch of rich grown men, mad about losin' a ballgame. It didn't make any sense for us to be mad about anything at all. It didn't make sense for us to want to put off our vacation for even one more day, just to win a game.

But we did care. It mattered more than the money, or the pussy, or everything else put together. Maybe it was just sheer spite toward Stanzi, or the Angels, or every other fool we had to put up with. But we wanted to win.

"We better get Aurelio warmed up," somebody said, lookin' at Feeley's hand drippin'. But he grabbed a towel an' wrapped it around the blood.

"I'm startin' the goddamned game," he said. "An' I'm not leavin' until they have to cut it off."

'Course, once we got out there, we still had to actually play the game. That's the thing about baseball: inspiration only goes so far. Buddy Lucas gave us a strong game, he was doctorin' the ball any way he could. But we were still down 1–0 goin' into the ninth. We still weren't hittin', an' The Little Maniac erased every threat we had with his Charlie Ball ideas, runnin' into one out after another.

It came down to the ninth inning, with the Angels just three outs away from wrappin' up the World Series. The Emp'ror led off with a little dink single into left field. But Not The Whole Story White an' No-Hit Hitt both fanned. It was almost sunset, an' quiet out on the field. Our faithful had left to beat the traffic back to Long Island, and we could hear the Angels laughin' an' jokin', their voices carryin' across the field in the silence. We could see the TV people settin' up over by their dugout, an' Good Stuff

Goodson takin' off his sunglasses so he'd look good for the run out to the mound.

The only thing we had left was bein' angry. Angry at this whole goddamned weird season, about to end now without us even knowin' what hit us. And angriest of all was Spock Feeley, up there now with his hand so swollen he could barely get it around a bat.

"You better tell your manager," the California catcher said when he saw how red that hand was, right through the bandages.

"You can't hit with your hand like that."

We thought the same thing, too, but nobody could keep him from goin' up there. Feeley didn't even look back at the catcher. He just took a couple swings an' said, "You can shove it up the Lord's own pussy."

Then he hit the first pitch he saw over the rightfield wall to win the game.

It had nothin' to do with reality. We were on our feet the moment that ball went over the wall, but even we were too surprised to whoop or clap or anything. Feeley was runnin' around the bases pumpin' his bloody hand in the air, an' we were yellin' then, an' the few fans we had left were yellin', too.

The Angels tried to act cool, tell their pitcher it was okay. But it was in their head now, an' we knew it. We were still down three games to one, all they had to do was win one more. But you lose a game like that after you come so close to winnin' the whole World Series, an' it sticks with you. You keep thinkin' about all the little things you could've done. You lose a game like that and you begin to think you can lose anytime, any way.

I still didn't know how far we could go without John Barr. He sat down the end of the bench the whole game, with his head down, lookin' at the ground. And by the time we settled down from greetin' Spock Feeley, he was already in the clubhouse, and I suppose he woulda been gone right back to that empty vampire apartment of his, if it hadn't been that Ellie Jay was lookin' out for him. She spotted him as he slipped away, out of the locker room, and she went runnin' right out after him.

"Just tell me!" she called after him, an' he was so surprised he stopped in his tracks an' looked back at her.

"Just tell me what it is, and maybe we can help you," she said,

an' by now some of the clubhouse attendants and even some of
the other flies had turned to watch, but it didn't stop her.

"Can't you see I care about you? I can help. Dammit to hell,
Barr, how bad can it be?"

"What the hell do you know?" he said to her, his face all twisted
up, and turned away again.

"Is it your mother? Is that it?" she asked him quietly now, so
the rest couldn't hear. He just ran on out the player's entrance,
an' Ellie Jay turned back to the clubhouse, cussin' herself.

"Damn, I think I blew it!" she told me. "I couldn't help myself,
and now he'll never talk."

"He wouldn't anyway," I told her.

We talked about me stoppin' by his place again, tryna get him
to see us, but we concluded it was prob'ly useless. Instead, I got
in my car, but I didn't know exactly where I was goin'. I just started
drivin', an' pretty soon I found myself makin' my way over to
Jersey, an' Wanda.

I don't know what I missed in the woman, exactly. I thought
maybe it was that brown sugar apple smell from the first summer
I was lookin' for. Maybe it was the shape of her ass when she bent
over. Whatever it was, I just felt like talkin' to her.

"What're you back here for?" she said, the moment she saw
me at the front door.

"For you, baby," I said, an' held out my hands. "Ain't nothin'
else here for me. You made sure of that."

"You're just feelin' bad," she accused me. "About your friend.
About your silly ballgame. You just want me to say it'll be all right,
so you can go out there an' win tomorrow."

"How'd you know we won today?"

She looked evasive, an' tried to move away from me. But I put
my arms around her waist, an' smoothed my hands over her hips.

"You watched it, didn't you? You watched the whole game."

"I did not!" she said, but when she turned to look at me her
lips were tremblin' with laughter. "I listened to it on the radio.
While I was reading."

I told her about John Barr, an' how silly it was that we got so
pumped for the game, an' how good it felt to win it. I told her
about everything, right off the top of my head.

Then I kissed her, long an' slow. She kissed me back, too. Just like I never been away. God, she could feel good, just in her mouth alone. But when I moved to her lips again, she held a hand against my chest an' looked at me sharp.

"Hold on, lover," she said. "You think you can just come in here and use me like a pillow to cry on? We have to establish if we have a future."

"Let's negotiate the future," I said, an' slipped my face down to her cool neck.

25

No, I'm not sober. But I sure as hell can strike this guy out anyway.
—GROVER CLEVELAND ALEXANDER

The Old Swizzlehead

Everybody was looser when we got to the ballpark the next day. The guys were foolin' around, playin' clubhouse jokes like throwin' water on each other, or rippin' their suits apart. It was Maximilian Duke's birthday, an' No-Hit Hitt takes off all his clothes an' dives right in the middle of his birthday cake.

John Barr still looked like a zombie. Spock Feeley's hand was still big as his catcher's mitt, an' red as raw meat. But he insisted he was ready to go out there again. We all thought we could do anything after the day before. At least we did until The Little Maniac presented us with his latest brainstorm.

"Gentlemen, look who's back," he said, standin' right next to him to make sure the flies couldn't get the picture without his own face in it.

It was Moses Yellowhorse. Standin' there still starin' straight ahead like a cigar-store Indian.

"He's back from Bellevue, and officially decertified," Stanzi says.

"What the hell's he doing this for?" The Emp'ror said to me, but we all knew why before he said it.

"He still looks a little glassy-eyed around the edges," Ellie Jay said, noticin' that the man hadn't said anything, or moved or blinked yet.

"The doctors say he can play, an' I say he can play," The Little Maniac said. "You watch. He's gonna be the winning edge."

That was it. Stanzi had seen how all the flies gathered around Spock Feeley the day before; he wasn't gonna take a risk on anyone else gettin' credit for the Series. So he dressed up Moses Yellowhorse in his spikes an' uniform again, an' got Woodrow Wilson Wannamaker to put him back on the active roster.

"You can't be serious," Spock Feeley told him.

Skeeter Mesquite had to lead him out to the mound by hand. And when he gave him the ball so Stanzi could show him off for the flies, Moses dropped it.

"This is grotesque," Ellie Jay said, watchin' it. "The man belongs in a hospital."

"Hey, he's throwin' hard again," said Stanzi.

And we had to admit he was. When we finally got the ball to stick in his hand, he started throwin' the big red, just like he used to. Solid heat on nearly every pitch.

"If his location is any good, he might be able to get some people out," Stanzi said.

The Little Maniac had Moses taken out to the bullpen, and I knew he really would try to use him if he got any kind of chance. It was already strange enough, with John Barr still down at the end of the bench, starin' at his shoes. Now we had a bona fide schizophrenic who might actually come into the game.

Whether Moses was gonna come in or not, we knew we had to get out on top early with Cloyd Kooble in their pen. It helped that the Angels were still in a daze from the surprise ending the day before. I built us a run in the first when I singled up the middle, stole second, an' came around on Bobby Roddy's single. We got three more in the fifth when they made two errors an' The Emp'ror put one into the seats. We were up 4–1 by the seventh an' gettin' into bullpen time. No matter who they had, we knew they couldn't get three runs back against Al The Fade an' Skeeter.

They got a run in the eighth off our starter, an' when he walked the first man leading off the ninth, The Little Maniac started the walk out to the mound. I thought, Thank God, for once the man is showin' a little sense, pullin' the pitcher before it's too late. He made the sign for the right-hander, an' I looked over at the bull-pen an' expected to see Skeeter comin' in on the cart. But out in left The Emp'ror just shook his head at me.

"Whiff Dick," he says, like he could read what I was thinkin'. "Take another look."

It wasn't Skeeter Mesquite in the cart—it was Moses Yellow-horse. Aurelio Macondo was puttin' his jacket on for him, or at least kinda drapin' it around his shoulders an' over his arms while Moses sat there stiff as the steerin' wheel.

"He wouldn't," I said. "Not even he would do that."

But it was true. The Little Maniac was willin' to put the whole Series on the line, just to make hisself look like a genius. It was one for Dr. Roscoe T. Jones's book: Most Appearances by Delu-sional Mental Hospital Outpatient, World Series.

"I tried to go over the signs when he got out to the mound," Spock Feeley told me. "I held up one finger an' said,'That's a fastball,' an' he looked at me. Then I held up two fingers an' said, 'That's a curveball, an' three fingers is a change.'

"Then I went back behind the plate, held up two fingers—an' he threw a fastball right down the pike. I kept wigglin' my fingers at him under the glove, an' he kept throwin' fastballs."

Which was almost enough anyhow. That's what Moses did best, an' that's what he shoulda been doin' all along: just rear back an' bring it. He mowed down the next two hitters without either of 'em able to get wood on his stuff. I thought just maybe we'd be able to get out of this one after all, an' The Little Maniac can call hisself a goddamned genius all he wants.

But then Squeak Pfeffer came up for the Angels. Squeak could pick 'em at shortstop, but he could barely hit his weight. He wasn't five-six, an' he'd just seen Moses Yellowhorse blow away the last two batters an' figured he didn't have a chance to get a swinging hit. So instead he squared away an' popped up a pathetic little American League bunt that landed at the foot of the mound.

That bunt was a revelation to the Angels. Squeak dug head down for first, his little legs movin' fast as they could, but it shouldn't have made any difference. It was a bad bunt, an' all Moses Yellowhorse had to do was pick up the ball at his leisure an' lob it over to first for the last out.

He didn't touch it. He didn't even move for it. He stood there lookin' at the ball like it was the first butterfly of spring. That's when we knew we were in trouble.

The Little Maniac was so convinced he was about to win the great manager award of all time, he hadn't got anybody else up. He called down to the pen now for Skeeter an' Al The Fade to start throwin', but it was too late. They couldn't get ready that fast, an' in the meantime Moses was gonna have to stay out there.

"Stall it," Spock Feeley told him. "Take your time between pitches."

Moses looked at him an' smiled an' nodded. Then he threw the next pitch as soon as Feeley got back behind the plate.

It didn't take the Angels long to catch on. The next batter bunted too, an' it was a lousy bunt off Moses' high heat—but it went right back at him, an' that was enough. The bases were loaded, an' when the next hitter laid one down they had another run. They were only down 4–3 now. An' Good Stuff Goodson was comin' up with the bases loaded.

"Not this asshole," I heard Maximilian Duke mutter over in left field. "Please, God, not this asshole now."

The Little Maniac trudged out to the mound, and dug around it with his toe for a few minutes and pretended he was talkin' it over with Moses Yellowhorse an' Spock Feeley.

"He's gotta go," Feeley said. "They're onto it now."

Stanzi squatted down an' picked up some of the dirt from the mound an' rubbed it around in his fingers like he was a farmer. Then he stood up an' gave Feeley that slightly crazy look he gets whenever he gets himself worked up over a bad call.

"No," he said. "Moses stays."

"What? All Good Stuff has to do is lay down a bunt—"

"He ain't gonna bunt here. He's gonna go for all the endorsements in the world. An' Moses can take him."

Feeley stood out there an' argued with him until his face turned as red as his cut-up hand, but it wasn't no use. The umps came out to break up the mound conference, an' Stanzi just said, "He's my man," an' flipped the ball back to our mental-patient pitcher.

Good Stuff stood in with that big grin on his face, 'cause he knew he had us. He was far an' away the fastest man on the Angels. We knew if he could get any piece of the bat on the ball, he could nudge another bunt back at Moses an' be sittin' on first base before we could turn around. We didn't have any choice. We had to send So Many Other Ways White an' No-Hit Hitt racin' in full speed from third an' first, to try an' cut off the bunt in time.

But Good Stuff was also their best hitter. All he had to do was step back an' swing away at the last minute, an' if he could connect White or Hitt was gonna sacrifice some valuable part of their anatomy. Or even worse, he'd knock the ball right through the holes they left in the infield.

"Here, hold the ball like this," Feeley told Moses when they all went to talk it over out at the mound, reshapin' his hand around the ball like he would to throw a curve. "I wanna get out of this one with a win."

"I wanna get out of this one with all my parts," No-Hit Hitt said. "I'd settle for that, the hell with the goddamned win."

Moses Yellowhorse looked at 'em all an' kept grinnin'. Then when Feeley went back behind the plate he wound up an' threw another fastball, right over the middle.

Good Stuff had squared away to bunt, but he took the first pitch. That way he got to see No-Hit Hitt an' Not The Whole Story White chargin' straight for the plate. An' then, Spock Feeley told us, his magazine-cover grin got wider than ever.

"Oh, baby," he said. "I hope they can pray while they run."

He squared away again, an' the pitch was straight an' fat over the plate, just like before. White an' Hitt came runnin' in again, screamin' at the top of their lungs, every step of the way. They were anticipating the pain already. When they saw Good Stuff Goodson take a step back an' pull that bat up they weren't five feet from the plate. Both of 'em hit the ground, with their hands up over their heads an' their knees curled up over their balls. And Good Stuff sure enough took as big and full a rip at that ball as he ever had in his life, just picturing all the commercials he was gonna get for wrappin' up the World Series.

But he didn't get much of it. He put his whole body into that swing, but Moses Yellowhorse was still too fast for him, power against power. All he could do was hit a pop-up that went two miles high but didn't get out of the infield. He broke his bat on the play, an' ran cursin' up toward first base, holdin' the splintered handle in one hand still. The other Angels began to run around the bases, just in case somethin' unbelievable happened. And I saw right away we were in trouble.

The whole play was in front of me. It was a lousy little pop-up, but it was comin' down right on top of Moses Yellowhorse, an' nobody was sure what the hell to do. I started to run in hard from center field myself, but of course I knew there was no way I could get to it in time. All I could do was shout incoherently, which I thought was helpful enough in the situation.

No-Hit Hitt an' Not The Whole Story White were still lyin' crumpled up in the fetal position in front of home plate. Bobby Roddy was coverin' first an' Lonnie Lee was over at third, like they were supposed to be. Spock Feeley was runnin' out toward the mound, screamin' for Moses, but I could see he wouldn't get there in time, with all his catcher's gear on.

It was the pitcher's ball. Nobody else had a real shot. It was hit directly above Moses Yellowhorse's head—an' he was standin' there on the mound with his head tilted back an' his mouth open, an' his glove hangin' at his side.

The Angels didn't know what was goin' on. Good Stuff Goodson was runnin' by first base, still cursin' hisself. They all thought the game was over an' they weren't runnin' hard. But even so, one of them had already crossed the plate, another one was a couple feet away, an' the third one was already around third base. If that ball dropped we'd be down two runs, an' all they had to do was bring The Big'Un on to wrap up the World Series.

"Yours, yours, yours!" Feeley was screamin' at Moses, pointin' up at the sky.

Moses Yellowhorse *did* have his eye on the ball. It just didn't appear that he intended to catch it. He kept standin' there with his mouth open an' his glove by his side, like it was a pretty sight. At the last second he put up the glove a little bit, an' then only like a man stickin' his hand out to see if it was rainin'.

That was when a blur came movin' across the infield. Bobby Rodriguez was makin' a run for the ball from first. He was runnin' full speed an' wavin' his arms at Moses Yellowhorse to move out. He was even yellin', "I got it! I got it! Get out of the way, you son of a bitch!"—which were the first words anybody ever heard him say on a major-league ballfield besides *fuck* and *you*. By now two

of the three Angel runners are across the plate, an' the third one
is approachin'.

"Get out of the way!" Bobby Roddy screamed at Moses again
when he reached the mound, but the Indian didn't move a muscle. Bobby slammed on the brakes, but it was too late. He ran
right into Moses Yellowhorse, bounced off him, an' fell at his feet.

Moses still didn't move, like he never even felt Bobby Roddy
bouncin' off him. He stayed there with that hand stuck out like
he was feelin' for rain, an' when the ball came down it dropped
right into the center of his glove—an' then bounced right out,
with Moses still smilin' at it. It plopped right back out of his
glove—and fell three feet into the bare hand of Bobby Roddy,
lyin' prostrate on the mound.

After that, of course, we were as excited as little kids. We
mobbed Bobby Roddy an' Moses Yellowhorse—still standin' there
smilin' pleasantly. I threw my hat up into the crowd as I was
comin' off the field, an' I even waved an' grinned at the goddamned fool fans like I was some kind of Stiff-Leg.

I went on down to the clubhouse, where Charlie Stanzi was
tryna tell the flies all about his genius move to bring Moses Yellowhorse in. But everybody, even the writers, was too excited to
pay attention. They couldn't get quotes out of Moses, of course,
so most of 'em were around Bobby Roddy's locker. But he was
back to sayin' nothin' in English except "Fuck you."

"He says that it was no big deal," Skeeter told the flies. "He
says he's made that play dozens of times before."

"Dozens of times?" Ellie Jay asked.

"Sure. Back in the Dominican Republic, they even practice it.
It's called 'the pitcher pop-up-back-up play.' At least one infielder
lies at the pitcher's feet on a play like that."

"Uh-huh. You sure he's saying all this?" she asked.

But nobody much cared. Even Dickhead Barry Busby was excited, I noticed. He was goin' around from one ballplayer to another, poundin' him on the back, poundin' the locker an' sayin',
"Now that was a game! Now that was a goddamned game for
men!"

Now all we had to do was go back to the Big A an' win two
more. Barr was still in a coma, but I knew we could do it. After
this game, it almost seemed easy.

26

I don't know how fast I'm throwing, 'cause I haven't run alongside one of my fastballs yet.

—J. R. RICHARD

The Old Swizzlehead

The Rev. Jimmy Bumpley was set on whippin' us out at God's Ballpark. He even held a mass faith-healing before the sixth game, with a platform set up by home plate, and an aisle down the third-base line for those with enough faith to walk the last ninety feet.

"They're scared," Ellie Jay told me, after she got back from their locker room. "They think their God has deserted them."

"Uh-huh."

She looked over at John Barr, sittin' by the corner locker with his head down like usual. He had half his uniform on an' looked like he got stuck figurin' out the other half.

"You figure out anything yet?" she asked me.

"Nope. You?"

"Not a goddamned thing," she sighed. "I think it's gotta be that letter, but who knows? Maybe 'I would've done it anyway' refers to a change-up he hit in the gap last year. It could be anything."

I couldn't think about it anymore. Much as I was worried about him, I thought we could beat the Angels anyway, and I had to concentrate on that first. Ellie Jay was right—they were scared, havin' lost two straight they had almost won. They were nervous an' skittery, you could see that even when they took infield. We

knew we could take 'em. Even our starter, Big Bo Bigbee, was
motivated to get out there.

"I was getting a little fluish on the plane out," he told me. "But
nothing's going to stop me now!"

It was a great day for the pitchers. It was a Saturday-afternoon
game, hot as hell, an' everybody in the stands was wearin' a white
shirt. Woodrow Wilson Wannamaker had the game start late, so
it wouldn't interfere with the college football games on TV. When
the sun started goin' down you could barely see at all. We were
goin' up there just worried about not gettin' hit in the head.

By the bottom of the eighth inning nobody had scored, but you
could see the Angels was more worried. They had only two hits
all day off Big Bo, who was paintin' the corners like Bo Van Gogh.
They were gettin' into the late innings, when strange things kept
happenin' to 'em. Their fans an' their bench was quiet, an' you
could tell they didn't believe the Angels could do it. One run an'
we could take the game, an' leave 'em dead the next day.

But all at once, everything changed. The sun went down.

It disappeared behind the centerfield wall—and now the ball
wasn't comin' out of the shadow around the pitcher's mound and
into the sunlight. The lights were on, an' all those white shirts
were faded into the dark background. It happened just as the
Angels came up to bat in the bottom of the eighth inning.

"Goddamned change of seasons," No-Hit Hitt cursed.

Big Bo got a lot less enthusiastic about pitchin' all of a sudden.
He stopped throwin' in the middle of his warm-up pitches, an'
signaled for Spock Feeley to come out an' see him.

"You know, my arm's feelin' a little tight—"

"Forget it, Bo," Feeley told him. "You don't need the sun, or
the shirts. You can get 'em out anyway."

"I think I have a blister on my finger, too—"

"Just throw the fucking ball an' forget about it!"

But Bo's confidence was gone. He was tryna spot his pitches
now, tryna get 'em too fine an' takin' something off. He was
pitchin' like a scared man. He got one out, but then he got
behind on Good Stuff an' threw him a curve that broke too
slow. Goodson hit it out of the park an' ran around the bases
grinnin' like a son of a bitch the whole way. He knew he had
all his commercials.

The Angels finally had us where they wanted us. Soon as we get the last out in the bottom of the eighth, their bullpen gate opens an' out comes The Big'Un in his pickup truck.

His catcher didn't even try to stop the warm-up pitches; he just let them slam against the back wall. Cloyd hadn't pitched in nearly a week, an' he had a extra five feet on his ball.

"You think I should wait on his curveball?" Lonnie Lee asked me in the on-deck circle.

"You be waitin' a long time."

"I was afraid of that," said Lonnie.

He went on up there an' dug in an' waggled his bat some. The Big'Un threw an inside fastball that put him on his ass so fast he didn't even have time to back up, just fall. When he got up, he stood away from the plate a little, like maybe in Albuquerque. Cloyd put three fastballs on the outside corner that he didn't come close to. We were two outs away from losin', but Lonnie came back with a look of gratitude on his face.

"Praise Jesus," he said. "He missed me."

"He ain't God, man," Spock Feeley grumbled.

"No, that's true," Lonnie said. "God would've thrown a waste pitch."

I didn't see any way we could win with The Big'Un throwin' the way he was. I racked my brain for a brilliant way 'round it, but I was all out of 'em. Unless he happened to tear out his rotator cuff on the next few pitches, we were done for the year.

Feeley was swizzlehead enough to go up there an' dig in the same way Lonnie Lee had. The Big'Un didn't like that any more than before, an' he wound up an' threw one straight at his knees.

Feeley barely got out of the way in time. The Angels' catcher couldn't even stop this one, an' it bounced up off his shin guards an' had so much speed left that it rolled all the way into our dugout. Which was when I had my brilliant inspiration that saved the day an' the whole World Series for us, in my humble opinion.

It was the timing that was the trick. It was a brilliant piece a' thinkin' on my part, but it wouldn't have done no good if I didn't act on it right then an' there. I was standin' on the top step next to The Little Maniac, waitin' to take my turn in the on-deck circle, when that ball rolled right to my feet.

I looked at the ball. I looked at Spock Feeley, still doin' the little dance he did in the batter's box to get out of the way. I looked at Charlie Stanzi's brand-new shiny cowboy boots right next to me, an' that's when the inspiration seized ahold of me.

With one motion, I grabbed that ball, ran it over the side of Stanzi's new shined boot, an' ran out onto the field yellin' to the home-plate umpire.

"It hit him! It hit him!"

The ump looks over to where I'm holdin' up the ball an' point-in' to the shoe-polish stain on the ball. Feeley had come up from the ground with every bit of the blood drained from his face, but he caught on quick. By the time the ump looks around again, he's limpin' up a show, holdin' on to his foot an' cussin'. Even The Little Maniac caught on, an' he's out on the field after me, leapin' around, yellin' about the ball hittin' Feeley.

'Course, half the Angel dugout is arguin' the other way, an' Cloyd Kooble is makin' dangerous growling noises out on the mound. But there's that big black shoe-polish stain on the ball, an' by the time the umps chased everybody back off the field Feeley was on first an' we were still alive.

That is, more like we were in the oxygen tent, gaspin' for breath. There was the pitcher, Big Bo Bigbee, to hit, an' then myself due up. I didn't know who the hell we could send up to hit for Bigbee, an' I had no idea how I could hit The Big'Un.

But I didn't count on Charlie Stanzi, once again. He looked down to the end of the bench where John Barr was still sittin' with his head down, an' hooked a thumb toward the field.

"Barr!" he barked out. "Get a bat. You're up next!"

John Barr looked up like he wasn't sure he heard right. Then he started gropin' around for a bat, any bat. He couldn't even find his own special big black ones, still piled up in a separate slot in the bat rack. Lonnie Lee finally thrust one of his own in his hands, just to end the embarrassment. By this time the home-plate ump was screamin' for a hitter an' the fans were booin', an' Barr walks out to the plate takin' short, jerky little swings like he barely remembered how.

"What the hell're you doin'?" I said to Stanzi, who was standin' there with that satisfied look on his face again.

"I gotta send somebody up to hit for Bigbee," he said, shruggin' his shoulders. "John Barr's still the best hitter on this team, on paper."

The Color Commentary

He tried to pump the bat, but it felt heavy in his hands. Everything was unnatural. In the back of his head somewhere, there was that admonition again. See the ball. But he wasn't sure what it meant.

The Old Swizzlehead

The Big'Un gave John Barr a whipping out there. He watched him come out all the way from the dugout, like an animal sniffin' out a wound. An' when he was satisfied that Barr didn't really look the same after all, he went to work.

He busted the first pitch right down the middle, an' Barr didn't take the bat off his shoulder. He gave that evil little pointy-toothed grin, an' threw the next one right at his head.

The Color Commentary

The ball came in, and he couldn't see it. He couldn't see anything but a blur, and he held his bat rigidly back. The umpire's hand jerked up behind him, then thrust out to the right. It was happening too fast.

See the ball—

It exploded out of the pitcher's hand and he tried to follow it in. It kept coming toward his head, and he just barely ducked out of the way—dropped straight down, then stood up with his legs weak, while the crowd whistled and hooted around him.

The Old Swizzlehead

I wanted to go after The Big'Un when Barr went down for the second time. I thought what the hell, why not start a fight now?

But the umpires got in front of the dugout quick an' they wouldn't let anybody out. They issued a real serious warning to Cloyd Kooble, too, which he didn't bother to nod at.

Barr got up again, movin' back to the plate like he was in slow motion. The Big'Un grinned over at our bench now with his little sharp teeth, an' busted one back down the middle. This time Barr at least took his bat off his shoulder, if only for a little half-swing. The umpire called strike two.

Cloyd wasn't even tryna hide his grin out there now. He saw John Barr was helpless as a baby, an' he was ready to finish him off. He leaned back as far as his big gut would let him, an' threw the meanest, nastiest pitch he had ever directed toward any batter.

It was a change-up.

It must've been the first time The Big'Un ever took anything off a pitch. That was the real witty part. He made out like he was gonna try to throw it through a brick wall, then let this big floater sail in there, thirty miles an hour slower than anything he ever threw before in his life.

Barr was out ahead of it by fifteen minutes. He could've swung twice, he was so far ahead of that ball. He tied himself into a pretzel tryna hit it. The Big'Un had dissed him as good as I ever saw one ballplayer do another.

"Strike three," the umpire said. I nearly broke my bat poundin' it on the on-deck circle.

"Son of a bitch!"

I was too mad now at all of 'em. I was mad at The Little Maniac, when I looked back an' saw him standin' in the dugout with his arms crossed an' that satisfied look still on his face. And I was mad at The Big'Un, standin' out there grinnin' with his little pointy teeth-nubs, makin' a laughing noise that sounded like a drunk wheezin' through a paper bag.

But most of all I was mad at John Barr, leavin' me to make the last out of the World Series. I was mad watchin' him make that terrible swing—like a poor joke on that long, hard-dick stroke he used to take. I slung him around by the arm when he came back past the on-deck circle, but the moment I did it an' looked in his face, I knew it wouldn't make any difference.

"What's the matter with you?" I shouted at him anyway, over

the crowd's rhythm chantin' an' stompin'. But he still looked like he was in a daze.

"I didn't see it," he said, an' then he looked almost fearful.

I didn't know what the hell he was talkin' about. I let him go an' he was gone, back to the dugout, out of my life, leavin' me to be the last out of the World Series.

That was what I hated most of all. It's a terrible feelin', left to be the last man out on the whole season. They show it over an' over again on the highlight films, along with the celebration by the other team. Over an' over, on the local news an' the national news, an' in the year's highlights, an' on the nostalgia shows. There's you poppin' out, or takin' a called third strike, an' there's everyone else jumpin' up an' down an' goin' nuts, now that you screwed up.

I didn't know what the hell to do. That's why I started sniffin' around when I got up there, because I was just mad at The Big'Un an' everything else. I went up there with my nose wigglin' like a hound dog. I just kept sniffin' all around the home plate. I sniffed all around the catcher. I sniffed all around the umpire until he nearly threw me out. I sniffed until the crowd got quiet an' even The Big'Un stopped his grinnin' an' stared in at me, tryna figure out what I was doin'.

"Do you smell somethin'?" I asked the Angels' catcher.

"Huh?" He just looked at me.

"Do you smell somethin'?" I asked the home-plate umpire.

"Get in there an' play ball!"

But I kept sniffin'. I got to admit, I didn't plan it like I did with the brilliant inspiration of the shoeshine ball. I was just so mad I started doin' it to get at The Big'Un. But the more I kept doin' it, the more I thought maybe I could use it.

"You sure you don't smell nothin'?" I asked again.

"Get in there!"

I stood in, an' The Big'Un delivered. The smile was gone now, an' so was the change-up. He could smell the seltzer-water champagne, an' he was throwin' nothin' but pure, high heat.

"Strike one!" the ump said.

I backed out, and started my nose twitchin' again.

"What the hell is that?" I asked the catcher. "Smell like somethin' died."

"I don't smell nothin'," the catcher said, lookin' suspicious at me now. Out on the mound, The Big'Un was gettin' restless, scratchin' his big-toed feet around, tryna figure out what I was doin'.

"All right," I told the catcher. "If you can stand it, I guess I can."

The express train came in again, high an' tight for strike two. I was one strike away from bein' the last out of the World Series. The crowd was all clappin' their hands together, tryna will that very last strike of the year in there.

But I took my time. I had a plan now. I began sniffin' again. Up an' down the base line a little this time, then out toward the pitcher's mound.

The crowd started to boo. Even Spock Feeley, leanin' off first base, didn't know what I was doin'. I think the umpire an' the catcher thought I lost my mind. But I sniffed out a few more steps toward the mound, until I could see Cloyd's little red eyes an' his pointy teeth through all his facial hair. Then I straightened up an' let my mouth hang open.

"Oh," I said, lookin' out directly at The Big'Un. "It's you!"

From the look on his red face, I knew the next pitch was comin' straight at my head. The Angels' catcher knew it too, an' he was tryna sweet-talk The Big'Un out of it.

"Just forget it, Cloyd baby," he was sayin'. "Strikeout's the best revenge. We got the World Series, right here."

But I knew it was no use. I thought he might not actually try to hit me, but I knew he was gonna make me eat dirt. Not that I wanted to get hit, either. That wasn't part of the plan. I didn't know if I could survive a full heater from The Big'Un.

What was the plan, then? I guess you couldn't even call it a real strategy. I just figured they were in control of the game with The Big'Un out there. I thought with his fastball, they could control everything. So I wanted to get everything out of control.

I knew there was no way I could get on unless I missed that pitch. I knew I couldn't make it unless I struck out. The ball was headed straight for my head; that's how mad he was after my sniffin' around. All I hadda do was stand there long enough to block the catcher. It came in so hard an' so far inside I knew there was no way he was gonna get it.

I waited until the last second, an' then I got out of the way an' took my cut at the ball, makin' sure I missed it. It was strike three, but the catcher couldn't catch the ball. I could hear him say "Oh, shit!" as he tried to get around my legs. Then I was on my way to first, an' everything was out of control.

It still wouldn't have worked if they'd played it smart. Their catcher shoulda known there was no way he could get me at first, with that pitch by The Big'Un sailin' all the way to the backstop. When he recovered it, he should've just hung on to the ball, an' let Cloyd try to get Bobby Roddy out with men on first an' second.

But that's the point of creating a little chaos. This game is held together by such a thin edge that once you unravel it, anything can happen.

The catcher should've held on to the ball. You ought never try to retrieve an out that's gone by. But with the last strike in the World Series goin' by him, he got rattled. He made a desperation throw from the backstop to try an' get me at first.

The first basemen never had a chance. It went five feet over his head an' all the way down into the rightfield corner. By the time the rightfielder had it hunted down, Feeley was across the plate with the tyin' run, an' I was on my way to third.

The rightfielder should've held on to the ball, too. But that's what happens when you lose control. Once you start throwin' the ball around, it's hard to stop. He was tryna make things right again, somehow, an' he took a chance peg toward third. It was too late to get me anyway, an' instead it bounced right past their third baseman. And then past the shortstop backin' up the play, an' on into the Angels dugout. I crossed the plate standin' up, an' the Angels had to haul The Big'Un off the field to keep him away from me.

I never saw a crowd go quiet so fast after that play. The Angels were in shock themselves. It was the worst kind of play to lose a game on—even worse than a home run or a lucky catch. It was the kind of play you wish you could reach out an' pull back to keep it from happenin'.

'Course, we still had to get the goddamned Angels out in the ninth. An' there's no such thing as momentum in baseball. It's just one batter at a time against the pitcher. Stanzi at least didn't put Moses Yellowhorse out there, but Al The Fade still didn't have his best invisible Kabbalah stuff. He got two outs, but he walked a batter, an' that brought up Good Stuff Goodson, all set up to win it for the Angels again.

The flies like to write that the best players *want* the ball hit to them in the field. Especially in the real clutch situations, with the game on the line. That's all lies, of course. Nobody I ever played with ever wanted a tough chance or even an easy one with a big game on the line. I was out there in center field myself, prayin' I wouldn't have to handle anything. An' then Good Stuff Goodson hit Al The Fade's next pitch over four hundred feet to deepest center.

The Color Commentary

The noise from the crowd jerked Dickhead Barry Busby's head up to stare blearily out at the field. Everyone was yelling, everyone was standing in the press box around him.

He could see the black man in a white uniform, racing out under the ball, back and back—

The Old Swizzlehead

Good Stuff Goodson got all of that pitch—but not every bit all. He got just a little under it—not so you'd even notice, but enough to hang up there and give me my chance.

I got a good jump on the ball. It was hit right over my head, but I knew from the sound of the bat that it was hit hard, and I turned an' ran back toward the wall. Five strides more and I whipped a look back over my left shoulder an' saw I had it lined up. Now all I had to do was catch up to it. I turned my head back toward the fence an' ran like hell—

The Color Commentary

He was almost sure it was the same player as in the dream. There were so many young men in his mind now, their fine bodies jumping or running or twisting, like a long, circular dance.

But he knew this one. The young black man, running and running, in long, fluid strides. Looking back over his shoulder once, twice, at the ball that was surely falling too far ahead of him to intercept.

Then he flew through the air. He shot out one arm and, magically, his body followed. He flung himself out over the lush green grass and reached one hand out. It fell into the webbing of his gaping glove, and he somersaulted over and skidded along the ground, into the warning track, stopping just short of the wall. Then, without even looking back, he lifted up the glove turned backward to show the ball nestled in its pocket to the umpire—

The Old Swizzlehead

I had to gamble on it. If I'd hung back, played that ball on the bounce, only one run would've scored, an' we would still have been tied. But if I tried to make the catch an' missed it, Good Stuff would've come all the way around, an' we lose the game an' the Series right there.

I went for the catch. It was sailin' past me, an' I just flung myself flat out through the air after it. I stuck out my arm as far as it would go, an' it fell in the webbing. I looked down then and saw myself three feet in the air and completely horizontal to the ground. And I thought, *Hey, this is a hell of a catch.*

The Color Commentary

He stood up in the press box, his knees trembling. In the general pandemonium, he was aware that Ellie Jay had a hammerlock around his neck and was jumping up and down, threatening to choke him to death.

He didn't care. He was glad they were all ecstatic, for lifting his hand to his face, he found that his cheeks were wet. Something better had actually happened.

27

Go very light on the vices, such as carrying on in society. The social ramble ain't restful.

—SATCHEL PAIGE

The Old Swizzlehead

I ran back the length of the field with the ball in my glove, and fifty thousand people watching me in total silence. It was the best moment I ever had out of a bed.

"The flies don't understand that," The Emp'ror Maximilian Duke liked to say. "They think the biggest thrill is a big home crowd, cheering you on. But it's even better when you can leave them dead quiet out there."

When I got back in the clubhouse, I sat myself down in the whirlpool an' eased my bones. From that vantage point I entertained the flies with all about how I made the miraculous catch, scored the winnin' run, an' won the ballgame. That's my idea of a postgame interview.

I was most impressed with the shoe-polish ball, myself. That took real brilliance, if you ask me, but the flies didn't want to hear about it. Too afraid it would damage the youth of America, I guess. They preferred to dwell on the last play of the game.

"When did you know you had the catch made, Swiz?" Ellie Jay asked me.

"Well, I had it lined up all the way," I told her. "I got a good jump on the ball the moment it left the bat, an' I saw it all the way in, so I never had any doubt in my mind I could get to it."

"Okay, but when did you really know you had the catch made?"

"When I got back to the locker room. I opened up my glove an' the ball was still there, so I knew I caught it."

The one who had to be most excited about it was Dickhead Barry Busby, of all people. That swizzlehead cornered me by my locker an' started talkin' some stuff 'bout Willie Mays an' the old Polo Grounds an' egg creams. I couldn't make out half of it, but he seemed to like the catch.

"It was better," he kept sayin'. "It was better than back then. It was!"

After a few dozen interviews, even I was tired of talkin' about it. I was ready to get back to the hotel an' do some celebratin' already. We all were. It didn't matter that we had another game. We knew we could whip their Jeebee Jaycee butts again, even if it never had been done before in the whole history of the World Series.

We knew we could do it even without John Barr, or Moses Yellowhorse, or anyone else. And we knew we had to. It looked obvious, after that whuppin' The Big'Un gave him, that Barr wasn't gonna be back on any ballfield again this year—an' maybe never again, ever. None of us had seen a ballplayer lose it so fast. It spooked us so much nobody even made jokes about it.

Who knows, maybe if what happened next didn't happen, it would have remained one of the great baseball mysteries of all time. If it hadn't happened, I don't think John Barr would've even come to spring training the next year. He might have disappeared as sudden as he showed up that day in Hell's Gate—gone back to his farm up at Prides Crossing, or vanished altogether somewhere in the whole wide country. And what's more, if it hadn't happened, he might still be alive today.

I almost missed it. I was headed into the hotel bar when I saw him. I had gone back to my room, put on some fine things an' a quart of good smell, an' was on my way to check out the local talent when I saw him. He was walkin' through the lobby like a whipped dog.

Even then I almost said the hell with it, let him go bury his own demons where he wants to. But Ellie Jay was down there, an' she

come right over to me an' told me I had to say something to the
man.

"You've got to try it, Swiz. I just scare him away," she said
miserably.

"Say what?"

"Anything you can think of. Look at him. He's all used up. I
really think he'll just disappear if he goes on like this."

"All right," I sighed. "But don't expect no faith healings. I ain't
the Rev. Jimmy Bumpley." It's a hard life bein' a saint.

"Hey, yo! Barr!" I called to him. But he kept on movin' like
he never heard me, right out the hotel lobby, walkin' fast, like he
was dead set on something. I might've given it up right there, but
Ellie Jay was still lookin' at me with that pleading look, so I went
after him.

He was already a block away before I could catch up. He was
standin' at the curb, studyin' the traffic like he never seen a car
before. It made me nervous just to watch him. I called his name
again, but he didn't look around. I started to run toward him.

He was already one foot out in traffic by the time I caught up
to him. He was walkin' straight out, never mind the cars whizzin'
at him from both directions. I reached out an' hauled him right
back on the curb.

"What the hell?" I shouted at him, but the swizzlehead only
tried to pull his arm free. I kept hung on to it.

"Nothin'," he said.

"Hell you say," I told him. "I wanna know about it. Now. I
wanna know what's got you."

"I didn't say anything. That's all!" he said, hard an' low, and
his face crumpled up all of a sudden, like I had dragged somethin'
shameful out of him.

"What're you talkin' about?"

"Nothin'! It's just that I saw it, an' I didn't say anything. It don't
matter anyway!"

"*What* don't matter? What thing could you do or not do that
was so terrible you want to die for it?"

It felt like somethin' was about to break loose in the man, but
he wouldn't let go. That straight sheet mask was back over his
face, complete with his drowned man's eyes.

"It's nothin'! Leave me alone—"

"Listen, it's this slump, ain't it?" I lied to him. Another brilliant plan was formulatin' in my head. He watched me, suspicious, an' didn't say anything.

"You want to get out of this slump, don't you?" I persisted.

"Yeah, sure."

"You want to get back out there tomorrow an' stick it to The Little Maniac, don't you?"

"Yeah, I guess."

"Uh-huh. Then you come with me. I know how to get you out of it."

I started to walk away, hopin' he would follow. I didn't know for sure until I heard his step behind me.

"Where we goin'?"

"You'll see."

"You really know somethin'?"

"Uh-huh. It's a whole technique. First we got to relax the muscles. We got to relax your mind, 'fore you can hit."

I took him to a dark bar nearby, where nobody would bother us. I sat him down an' ordered us two beers, which I figured would be a good enough start to clear his head.

"I don't drink," he said, when they put the beers down.

"Just one. You got to drink just this one, to relax the mind. Then we can begin."

"Begin what?" he asked, but he took a sip from the beer.

"Begin my technique," I told him. "You'll see. I never knowed it to fail."

"How come I don't know about it?"

"You never been in a slump before. All these years in this game, this is your first slump. Now you know what it feels like."

"It was that goddamned Stanzi," he said, takin' another sip. "That's what did it. That's what must've did it."

"He was messin' with your head."

"It was his talkin' about what I was gonna do when I was through with the game. Like I was old. Like I couldn't play another ten years if I wanted to."

"Uh-huh. He got to you, just like he got to everybody else," I said, an' ordered up another beer for him. He had almost gone through the first one, an' I had never heard him put so many words in a row together.

"Not that it was any of his goddamned business anyway, what I did after I was through. Like I couldn't play another ten years, then go to Japan, or Mexico. Play five, ten years *more*!"

"That's right."

"I can still hit, you know, Swiz," he said, leanin' confidentially across the table at me. "I got my timing still. I know I do. It was just that goddamned Stanzi, screwin' me up."

"I know you can. Let's go prove it." The second beer was gone now, he was slurrin' his consonants, an' I figured he was just about ready.

"Let's go work out that slump now. You can still do it."

"Goddamned right. Where we goin'?"

"Out to the ballpark."

"Right now?"

It was a pure chance on my part. I didn't know if I could even get into the Big A, that time of the night. It was just somethin' I thought up on the moment. When things aren't goin' the way you want them to, you got to create a little chaos an' see what happens. We got a cab out to Anaheim, an' then all I had to do was talk my way past some young Christian guard at the gate.

"I am very sorry, sir, but you cannot come in under any circumstances whatsoever," he told us with the same precise politeness of his boss when he proved how the Scriptures specifically forbade federal funding for day care.

"Believe me, I don't want to be out here in the middle of the night," I told him. "I'd rather be back at the hotel, readin' the Bible an' restin' up for the game tomorrow. It's just that the Lord wants us to."

"Are you gentlemen Christians?" he asked, as if he was surprised—though *I* didn't know what looked so goddamned unholy about us.

"That's right. And the Lord wanted us to come down here tonight."

"What for?"

"I did not question the revealed word of the Lord," I told him, gettin' a little snippity. "I come down here like He commanded. I presume He will make His will known to us, now that we're here. 'S called faith."

"And you're sure that it was really a calling from the Lord?"

"Yessir. Otherwise I would not bother you tonight."

"I guess in that case it's all right. If the Lord says so."

"Whatta we do now?" John Barr asked me, once we were through the gate.

"Get a bat," I told him. "How else you going to get out of a slump?"

28

Once, dreaming with morphine after an operation, I believed the night climbed through the window and into my room like a second-story worker. . . . The night had the dirty color of sickness and had no face at all as it strolled in my brain.

—JIMMY CANNON

The Phenom at Sixteen

She dropped her sewing where she stood and went to the closet. While he stood staring at where the face had been, she strode back to the kitchen door, flicking on the dim backyard light, the gun in her arms. In another instant she had unbolted the door, broken the gun, and loaded and mounted it against her shoulder.

Frozen, the boy watched her from the living room. In the games he could react instantly, but now he had no idea what to do. He didn't feel afraid, but he was unable to move, to say or do anything. He made himself take two halting steps toward the kitchen, and watched his mother grip the doorknob with one hand, the gun still lodged against her shoulder. She didn't look back at him; her attention was riveted on the door and what was beyond it. She yanked it open in one swift motion, kicked out the flimsy screen door, and brought her other hand back up to the gun—

He raised one hand, as if to warn her, but then he stopped. There was a chance, maybe, that he could get to her in time, but he stopped, one stride away, while her fingers moved on the triggers. First one moved, then the other, and he heard the two reports, nearly deafening in the little house, and saw her shoulder jerk back twice, though she handled the big gun, and kept it up, and aimed. And still he stood there—

Then he yelled. He jumped forward, as if released, and threw himself at her, going for the gun. She dodged his grasp easily and with surprising strength, holding the gun away from him and clasping his head to her, keeping her eyes firmly fixed on what was outside.

A high, extended wail came from the newly illuminated backyard. It was followed by a series of short screams that sounded like barking. The boy tried to run outside, toward the noise, but he found that his legs were heavy and mired, his coordination gone. He stumbled, and his mother ran easily ahead.

The boy's father lay against the large oak tree, where he had once hung a swing for the boy. The shotgun blasts had knocked him back perfectly against the trunk, so that he lay propped up already, without their aid. Even in the dark, the boy could see where the middle part of him bubbled up. His eyes stared straight ahead, and his mouth hung open, trying to suck in the air that kept escaping from his torn belly. When she got to him, Evan Barr raised himself up a little, holding out one arm and moving his lips as if to say something.

"Don't speak!" the boy's mother commanded him, though it was not necessary. His lips kept moving, but nothing came out.

"Don't say anything! John!" She waved for the boy, where he had fallen to his knees in the yard.

When he was able to come close, he could see that his father looked completely surprised. His gaze swung back and forth between the two of them, until he lowered his eyes and then his hand back toward the ground. Now the breath came in shorter, wheezing bursts. And even though he was deeply ashamed of it later and forever, the boy could not help thinking that his father still looked foolish.

"Call the hospital." His mother was giving him instructions in a firm, urgent voice. "John, listen to me. *Do exactly as I tell you.* Go inside. Call the operator. Tell her it's an emergency and tell her to put you through to the hospital. Tell them to send an ambulance. Do you understand, John?"

She grabbed his shoulders and looked into his eyes to make sure he understood. "Be sure to tell them the address. Tell them there's a man dying. Do you understand? Tell them, then come back out here and help me lift him."

The boy moved in rote obedience to her words, as she had meant for him to do. It was actually easy to do it all, he found, in the order she had commanded. He felt as though he were listening to himself on a tape recording, but he was sure he got everything right. Then he went back outside.

His mother had one hand behind his father's head, and she was wiping the blood away from his stomach with her free hand. She was trying to find the wound and staunch it, but every time she touched it, however lightly, he made little wheezing screams of pain.

"We have to get him in the good light," she said, and the boy nodded, though he didn't know what seeing more could do now.

"We have got to move him. Take his legs."

She gripped his father under the neck and the shoulders, and waited for the boy to take his end. He hesitated at first, then slowly grasped his father's ankles. He thought how skinny and bumpy they were, like stick legs.

"Now when I say, we lift. Do you understand? We have to do this together."

The boy nodded.

"All right. Now lift."

He lifted his father's ankles slowly upward—and almost dropped him when the movement brought a high-pitched screech. It was a surprising weight, a dead weight, much more than the skinny ankles had promised, and he was forced to pull and heave and readjust the load until he thought from the screams they were tearing his father apart.

"We have to get him into the house," his mother warned him, and he hung on. The boy led the way, backing up slowly and looking over his shoulder. From time to time his gaze swung over his mother, and he saw that she wore the same expression she had when she cleaned the incorrigible house.

They were lucky that the wooden main door was still open; his mother had kicked the screen door so hard that it now lay to one side, partially off its hinges. Still, the boy moved a little too suddenly taking the body of his father up the one back step. He jolted him against the doorjamb, and he gave another sudden, high scream. But the boy hung on, and moved him slowly, slowly around the corner and back into the house.

In the kitchen they propped him against a wall, and the boy's mother flicked on the overhead kitchen light. He watched it snapping and flickering again until it ignited into a halo that flooded the kitchen with harsh white light. He blinked and choked when he looked down at his father.

The bright new light had changed the amorphous ooze at his midsection to something appallingly red, splattered with distinct bits of blue and white and brown. He made himself not be sick, he choked it in his throat. His mother had already gone to work, and he knew she needed him. She wet down a cloth in the sink and began to swab gingerly again at the new streams of redness welling up over his father's stomach.

The blood kept coming, pooling out over the kitchen linoleum. The boy could see now that dark red smears covered his own shirt, tossed away on the floor—covered the dress that his mother still wore, like the paint left on the house— He shivered, and his mother looked up and sent him upstairs to get a new shirt for himself and more fresh towels for his father, every towel he could find. When he came back, she set him to work wringing out the old ones.

But she couldn't stop the bleeding. She knew that you could tie off a limb at the pressure point above the wound, but she didn't know what to do about a shotgun wound in the gut. Except maybe to stopper it with a cloth directly, but when she had tried to do this—as gingerly, as cautiously as possible—the boy's father made sounds like a dog baying. She was reduced to leaving towels, cloths, anything she could find, draped loosely over the wound. The boy watched now as his father's blood slowly seeped through one layer of white cloth after another, gentle tentacles of it at first creeping through, then inexorably soaking each layer in red.

"We will have to wait for the ambulance," she told the boy, slumping wearily back against the wall. She pulled her son over to her and held his head against her own, whole stomach.

His face was nestled in her, but still only two feet or so from his father's torn-up belly. It kept laboriously pumping out blood, but his eyes were closed now, his breath subsiding. From outside, the boy caught an unexpected whiff of new clay, of the wild spring smell drifting in through the door. But it was quickly expunged by the putrid odor coming from his father.

The boy felt himself grow sleepy. He was ashamed, but the feeling was irresistible. Deep in the warmth of his mother, he felt himself drifting. She was murmuring something, but he couldn't make out the words. There was just the warm feel of her stomach, her hand on his hair—

He was awakened by the whistling. He looked straight into his father's eyes, which were open now, staring back at him, glazed with pain. There was a steady, tuneless, high-pitched whistling sound filling the room, like a kettle, or a piece of metal machinery. Gradually, the boy understood that the sound came from his father.

The boy knew that he was dying. He felt that he should say something to comfort him, to help him with the pain, at least, but his mind was blank. He looked up at his mother, but she kept her eyes closed, only turning her head from time to time, as if she were having a bad dream. The whistling went on and on. The boy lifted his head, and felt a thick moistness on his cheek: his father's blood, wet from his mother's dress.

He stood up and backed away, thinking wildly that they must take his father to the hospital themselves, in the terrible joke of a car. But then he heard the siren, far off, sounding like no more than a tiny mosquito whine. It rose and fell, rose and fell—up and down the hills, along the smooth, tidy streets, almost indistinguishable from his father's whistling, until it became an urgent scream in front of their house.

29

There are three ways to get rid of a slump. One is to drink and change the feeling you are walking around with. Another one is to get involved
in some sort of hobby so you can forget for a while. The third is
just to practice and practice again. . . .The last way sometimes
deepens the feeling of uneasiness.

—SADAHARU OH

The Old Swizzlehead

Inside the stadium, there was only a little patch of light over
the infield. The stands were all dark and deserted, of course, an'
even the outfield was dark. I had never seen a ballpark look or
feel like that before. The only sound was the ground crew testin'
the loudspeakers for the Rev. Jimmy Bumpley the next day. You
could hear his fine voice boomin' out bits of his sermon, over and
over again, an' cracklin' up the giant A-frame radio transmitter
outside like lightnin'.

"AND THE LOR-UD SAID UNTO ABRAHAM—"

"Cut! Take it back to the beginning."

"AND THE LOR-UD SAID—"

"Cut! Again, from the top."

"AND THE LOR-UD—"

"Again!"

"AND THE LOR-UD—"

"AND THE LOR-UD—"

"AND THE LOR-UD—"

We didn't bother to suit up. It was just like that first day back
in Hell's Gate, sixteen years before, with John Barr hittin' in his

street shoes. Barr got a bat, an' I grabbed the batting-practice pitcher's screen an' a bucketful of balls, an' we were ready.

"All right, what's your system?" he asked me.

"You know it," I told him. "Just let your mind relax, an' try to hit the ball back at me. Try to hit everything straight back at the mound."

"That's it? That's your whole system? Feed me a couple beers an' tell me to hit line drives back at you?"

"Let's just see if you can do it."

The Color Commentary

In the spectral ballpark, the slim man spotlighted on the mound threw home, and the batter swung hard and missed. In the darkness, it seemed a pantomime game. An observer would have had trouble making out the ball at all inside their little yellow square of light. The pitcher wound up and shot his arm out toward the plate, the batter swung hard and awkwardly—and then a small white dot materialized momentarily behind him, before disappearing into the greater blackness. It was as if the man pitching were hurling spots of light.

The Old Swizzlehead

I don't throw much like a big-league pitcher to begin with, an' I was layin' 'em in there as slow as I could. I figured between the beers an' the dark, I would get him if I lobbed the ball in, wrecked what was left of his timing. And it worked. He couldn't touch my slow shit.

"Goddammit!" he yelled out, after I left him flailin'. He nearly wrecked his big black bat, poundin' it on the plate. I never seen him get so mad before, an' I thought so far, so good.

"Too fast for you?" I asked him, an' he gave me a look, but I could barely hear what he said over the voice of the Rev. Bumpley.

"THE LOR-UD SAID—"

"Goddamn me, I can't hit anymore! I can't!"

"Just like Stanzi said."

"Goddamn him!"

"Think of that. After all these years, Charlie Stanzi's able to get you out, just with a few words. You *sure* that's all it was?"

"Yes, dammit!"

I threw the next pitch in, a little faster, and he swung right through it.

"Just try that son of a bitch again!"

I took my time, an' gave a kick so big I nearly split my suit pants. He was ready to swing before I finished my windup.

"Damn you!"

"Whatsa matter? Can't hit my change?"

"Throw it again, goddammit!"

"I don't know, man. You look pretty screwed up. You *sure* it was only Stanzi?"

"Throw the ball. I want to hit it back down your throat!"

I threw him a curveball, an' he missed it an' almost fell over backwards.

"Throw it straight!"

"Uh-huh. Just tell me one thing first. You sure it wasn't nothin' somebody else said to you?"

He stood there an' looked at me for a moment, lettin' the bat hang down by his side. Then he got set in the box again.

"Throw the ball!"

"You sure it wasn't somethin' like 'I would have done it anyway'?"

"What did you say?"

But he could hear me fine. The loudspeaker crew had folded up for the night now, an' there wasn't another sound in the whole ballpark. It was just the two of us out there, under that little patch of light over the infield.

"You heard what I said."

"You don't know what the hell you're talkin' about."

Which was true, actually. It was just a blind guess on my part.

"You sure now? You sure it has nothin' to do with somebody writin' you a one-line letter that says, 'I would have done it anyway'?"

"Throw the ball!"

He looked mean and sober too, now. He stood up at the plate like he knew what he was doin', in that old pit-bull stance, feet planted like they were painted in the box for him. I threw the next pitch straight at his head.

He ran for the mound, throwin' the bat ahead of him, but I was ready. When he cocked his arm back, I ducked behind the pitcher's screen. Still, it surprised me how far he was able to drive his hand through that screen. It hit me hard enough to knock me off my feet.

"What did you say? What did you say?"

He was wild to get at me again. But his fist was all tangled up in the screen, an' when I got back on my feet it was easy enough to kick the thing over on him. I sat on top of it an' he struggled an' squirmed like a half-squashed bug, but he couldn't get out from under.

"Whats it mean?" I asked him again.

"Nothin'! It don't mean nothin'!"

"Whats it mean, 'I would have done it anyway'?"

"None of your business! None of your goddamned business, you lousy nigger bastard banjo hitter!"

I didn't pay him any mind. Fact was, I had to keep hard from laughin' at how he thought 'banjo hitter' was just as bad as 'nigger bastard.' I sat tight an' let him squirm around some more.

"You can't fool me," I told him. "I know you like me all right. That's why you popped Goog Fisher after that beanball."

"He just had it comin'. I just *felt* like poppin' him!"

"An' you can't fool me about Charlie Stanzi, either. That's not why you went into the only slump you ever had—just because that Little Maniac said somethin' to you about retirin'."

"Damn you, let me up! I would've hit Fisher anyway!"

"'I would have done it anyway'? *Who* would have done it? Done *what?*"

"She shot him!" he yelled almost as loud as the Rev. Jimmy Bumpley, in a voice so full of pain an' rage I thought for a second I was physically hurting the man.

"She shot him, goddamn you!"

"Who shot who?"

"My *mother*! She shot him!"

"Shot *who?*"

"My father, *goddammit*! He was lookin' in the windows, tryna catch her cheating on him. But she wasn't, she was with me, and she shot him with the shotgun. I saw it was him, and I didn't say anything, and she shot him dead, the poor fool son of a bitch!''

"Only . . ." I said, slowly an' delicately-like: "Only it's not true what you're sayin'. You couldn't have stopped her, could you?"

"No! It *has* to be true—" An' now he was almost pleading, like he didn't want me to say it. But I did anyway.

"But it isn't. That's what the letter means, doesn't it? She would have shot him anyway."

"No—"

"That's what you found out. That's what threw you off so that Charlie Stanzi or anybody else could've messed with your mind."

"You're wrong. I don't know for sure—"

"Yes, you do. That note you got in the clubhouse was from your mother. They found it in her stuff when she died, didn't they? And you know what it means. 'I would have done it anyway.' She would have, too. You know it now. No matter what you saw, or what you said. She still would have shot him."

"Yes. Yes, she would have."

He went quiet, weepin' an' snifflin', an' I thought it was okay to get off the screen an' let him up. He sat there, out by the pitcher's mound, an' started talkin'. After all those years of not sayin' a thing, he couldn't stop.

"I thought *I* let it happen. I thought I must've let it happen, because I could always move quicker than anybody else. I could always see things first, an' I saw it all right. I saw it was him, an' I didn't stop her."

"How could you stop her? You were a kid."

"I didn't say anything. I always thought maybe that she knew— that she saw who it really was, peekin' in the windows. But I thought if at least I said somethin', if at least I let her know that *I* knew, she wouldn't have done it."

"But she would have."

"I know, I know. But I thought I had control over it. I thought *that* one got by me, somehow, an' I was gonna be goddamned if I ever let another one get by. Nobody or nothing was gonna get anything by me, ever again."

"But you quit playin' ball. That's why nobody ever heard of you."

"You can't imagine how bad it was, in a town like that. They had the inquest, an' they let her off. But we lived off by ourselves, in that house in the woods. It was bad enough just goin' to school. People talked all the time—and I was still with her. I quit the team, and every day after school I came straight home to her for two years. Until the day after I graduated, I left that house an' headed for West Virginia."

"You never went back?"

"No. I never wanted to see the place again. I never wanted to see her. I knew I could still hit. I just wanted to get out of there an' go play. I wanted to go hit the ball over an' over again, until I got it right. I just wanted to see the ball and hit it."

"But you were wrong. She would have done it anyway."

"Yes. Ain't that the goddamnest thing?" John Barr put his head down in his hands, an' his shoulders shook. I was almost tempted to put an arm around him, kind of comforting-like.

But when he lifted his face up, he wasn't cryin' at all. He was laughin' so hard he could barely talk.

"Oh, goddamn! The poor goddamned fool!!"

I thought maybe he was startin' to have a breakdown, like Moses Yellowhorse. But it was the first time I ever seen him look happy.

"My father, the poor goddamned fool. That's the thing, don't you see? We *both* wanted to shoot him!"

I started to chuckle with him, though I wasn't sure why.

"Sneakin' around outside every night by the hedges, staring into the windows and tryna catch her lover. Oh, God. An' never even figurin' out that his son was in the house, too. Unless he thought we were all in it together against him."

He shook his head. "And you know what else? He deserved it! Oh, God, he did! Nobody should die like that, but he walked right into it. Oh, the poor goddamned fool!"

I think he woulda told me everything his father an' mother ever did. He woulda told me his whole life story, right then an' there. But I didn't know if it was right to take it from him, all at once. Instead, I tapped him on the knee an' pointed toward the clubhouse.

"C'mon, let's get you inside. You're gettin' overexcited out here. Besides, you got a game to play tomorrow."

Inside, we went into the sauna room an' just sat around for a while. He was still in a talkin' mood like I'd never seen him.

"I was afraid of that slump," he told me. "I was never afraid of anything like that. Not since my father. I was afraid I was gonna have to retire."

"You got years to go still," I tried to reassure him. "There's always some swizzlehead give you a couple hundred thousand just to go out there an' screw up. That's what makes this a great game."

"I used to feel like I had a hard core, an' it would never break. I used to think I could play forever, long as I had that core. Other guys would get old and retire. But I could make my body do anything I wanted."

"Oh, yeah. Heart of the lion, Maximilian Duke used to call it. Lets you cut out everything else."

"But the last couple seasons, I could feel it slippin'. I'd come down to Florida in the spring, notice I'd lost half a step, and that hard core would shrink a little more. I'd get a little more fearful."

"It don't look to me like you lost anything."

"I could feel it. An' when I got that letter, I really began to be afraid. It made me think there never was any hard core there to start with. It made me think I didn't have control over anything. Not even the power to do something terrible."

"You can hit. That's about as much control as you can ask."

"Did I ever tell you how much I love playing this game?" he asked me all of a sudden, an' I began to feel uncomfortable.

"No, I don't think you ever got around to that."

"I love just comin' to the ballpark, Swiz. I love to run in the outfield. Hell, I love to go out there and smell the grass sometimes."

"Yeah, it smells nice. Even when it's real."

"I love you, too, Swiz—"

"Stop that. Makes me nervous when a naked man tells me he loves me."

"I love you. I love all the guys on the team. I even love Stanzi and Pippin, and the fans. They're all part of it—"

"Next thing, you're gonna tell me you love Dickhead Barry Busby, too."

"I love the traveling most of all. I love waiting at the airports, and then flying up above everything. I love coming into a new town. I love the smell of the hotel rooms, and the players and the annies sittin' around the bar, tryna strike somethin' up. I love standing out there in right field, hearin' the fans, and seeing the whole game open up in front of me—''

"You sure you ain't a Jeebee Jaycee?" I asked him. "Next thing, you're gonna be tellin' me how God wanted you to play right field."

When we left the park, the Christian guard was still there.

"Did the Lord explain His purpose to you?" he asked us.

"Oh, yeah," I told him. "He said to take two an' hit to left, play for the tie at home an' the win on the road, don't run until you bunt the ball, an' never put the winning run on base."

"Oh," he said. "The Lord told you all that?"

"At least we *thought* it was the Lord. Turned out just to be a sportswriter."

I wanted to get John Barr calmed down an' back to his room for a good night's rest. But when we got back to the hotel, there was Ellie Jay, asleep on one of the lobby couches. He hesitated when he saw her there, then started to the elevators again, then came to a full stop. I'd never seen the man so uncertain, not even in the middle of his one an' only slump.

"You know how she feels about you," I said to him. "She been worryin' about you all year. She was the one wanted me to go after you."

"Yah, I know," he says, but he still stood there by the elevators, shufflin' his feet like he was goin' to a prom date.

"Whatta you think, Swiz?" he asks me. "I don't know much about it—"

"You faced everything else tonight," I shrugged. "You might as well go for the cycle."

The Color Commentary

She opened her eyes when he touched her shoulder and was instantly alert and ready to defend herself. When she saw who it was, though, she gravely smoothed her skirt, and stood up to face him. They were only inches apart, and he was so aware of her presence that he found himself struggling for words.

"Did you wait up for me?" he asked, and she nodded.

"Thanks," he said. "Thanks for everything."

He looked embarrassed and made as if to turn away, but she grabbed him by the elbow.

"Is that all you have to say?"

"Look, I don't know if you really want me," he said, barely able to look at her. "I don't know how much I have left, any way you look at it. Hell, I don't even know if I can hit anymore."

"Yeah, well, I don't know what you'd be getting either," she said. "I drink too much, and I smoke, and I don't know how many brain cells are left after trailing you guys around the country for the last fifteen years. But if you're interested—"

They both laughed then, and he put his hands on her arms, surprising even himself.

"You know, I liked it when you kissed me," he said quietly. "It scared me, but I liked it. I can still remember what it felt like."

"Here's a refresher," she said, and kissed him gently, tentatively on the lips. He took a breath as if gearing up, and kissed her back.

"I feel so tired," he said. "But I feel so good."

"Don't worry about it," she said, guiding him toward the elevator, arm-in-arm. "We'll get you up to your room and you can just sleep. I'll just lie down beside you, to make sure no one disturbs you. 'Course, I might have to get very close for that. . . ."

The elevator came, and they entered and went up.

30

Baseball defies an orderly process.

—RAY EISENHARDT

The Old Swizzlehead

John Barr came an' woke me up first thing in the morning the
day of the seventh game. I wasn't really positive it was light out
yet, but he assured me it was, an' dragged me on downstairs to a
big breakfast in the hotel dining room. He ate everything they
had on the menu down there, an' still wanted more.

"Damn, I feel like playing today," he told me. "You wanna go
on out to the ballpark right now?"

"I take it things went all right last night," I yawned at him over
my coffee.

He just smiled at that an' got all bashful as a virgin. I let him
drag me on out to the Big A. We were ready to play by ten in the
morning. I tried to get him to settle down, play a little cards, but
he wouldn't do it. He just wanted to walk around the clubhouse
with a bat in his hand, like a long-lost friend.

"I think I'm out of it, Swiz," he said.

"We'll see," I told him, tryna calm the boy down. "Slumps can
be funny. Sometimes even after you feel comfortable up there
again, you don't start to hit for a few games."

But there was a change in him, it seemed to me. Even The Little

Maniac noticed it when he came in. He squinted over at Barr pacin' around with that bat—an' Barr gave him a big wave and called out, "Hi, skip!" But when it came time to put up the lineup, Barr wasn't in it.

"I can hit now," Barr said, goin' up to him real earnest an' everything. But Stanzi just laughed at him.

"You been walkin' around here for the past month like a goddamned zombie."

"No, skip," he told him, perfectly serious. "I can hit again now. I got it worked out. I know I can."

"I can't take a chance like that. I gotta responsibility to this team, an' to Mr. Pippin. I gotta responsibility to New York."

"What the fuck're you talkin' about?" I pointed out gently.

"I can't take a risk on him droppin' another fly ball off his head. Maybe he can pinch-hit later—"

"He's the best goddamned hitter in the game," Spock Feeley joined in. "I can take the risk."

"It's not your goddamned decision."

"How're you so sure we can win it without him?" I asked, but that only made him cross his arms over his chest an' give us one of his Little Maniac smiles.

"We can win this thing with Charlie Ball," he said.

"You can't take this game away from us," Feeley told him.

"If you don't like it, you can sit, too," Stanzi said, raisin' his chin a little. "You an' Falls both."

"They don't play, I don't play," Maximilian Duke said, gettin' up off his stool an' comin' over to us.

"I don't care how many guys I have to bench—"

"If they don't play, nobody plays," Skeeter Mesquite told him. But The Little Maniac wouldn't back down.

"Suit yourselves," he said. "You wanna forfeit this game, it's up to you. I'm still the manager."

What happened next was sort of a spontaneous inspiration. The same thought just seemed to come to everybody at the same time. The Little Maniac must've seen it in our eyes, because he tried to make a run for it. He was a slippery one, too, an' he almost got out underneath Maximilian Duke's arm.

But The Emp'ror grabbed him with one hand, then everybody else joined in. In seconds we had him hog-tied naked to a chair with trainer's tape an' his own uniform. We shoved a towel in his mouth an' taped that around his head, just to make sure.

"Whatta we do with him now?" somebody asked.

"Take him to the trainer's room. Shove him in the equipment closet," Spock Feeley suggested.

We had him up in the chair an' on the way, when the door of the clubhouse opened an' in walked Woodrow Wilson Wannamaker, Commissioner of Baseball. He had come down with a couple bottles of a new, fizzly grape juice that he wanted us to drink after the game. When he saw what we were doin', he had to clear his throat a few times before he could give us any words of wisdom.

"Oh, my," he said.

"He was going to bench the whole team," Skeeter told him. "If he goes out there, nobody plays. It's a forfeit. Think of what that will do to the TV revenues next year."

"Right," said Wannamaker. "I'll tell the crew no close-ups on the bench. If there are any questions, he has a stomach flu."

He made a sign sort of like he was crossin' hisself. "It's for the good of the game," he says, and runs out the door. We finished tucking The Little Maniac away, an' Skeeter Mesquite turned to Old Coach Plate.

"You're the manager. If you want it."

Old Coach Plate stood there for a couple chews, shiftin' his chaw from cheek to cheek while he thought about it. Then his big melon head split wide open with a grin.

"It'll cost me my paycheck with Pippin next year," he said. "Maybe I'll never work in the game again. But what the fuck."

The Color Commentary

The little yellow numbers began to flicker down the main beam of the cross-shaped scoreboard. Ellsworth Pippin watched them from high up in the luxury press box and began to frown.

"He's playing John Barr," he said out loud to no one in particular, although his assistant and secretary both grunted meaningfully. "Why's he playing Barr?"

He put down the flute of champagne he'd been holding, and reached for the line that connected him directly with the dugout.

"Hello," came a laconic voice on the other end.

"What do you mean, 'Hello'?" he snapped. "Get me my manager."

"He's not here right now," the voice replied, and Ellsworth Pippin was under the distinct impression that he heard giggling in the background.

The Old Swizzlehead

Old Coach Plate wrote out the lineup card just the way it used to be. John Barr was hitting in the number-four hole again. And he had Moses Yellowhorse pitchin', even on short rest an' despite the bunts.

"Besides, the way he is now, he'll never know if he's tired," he explained.

We stood out on the baseline to listen to the Rev. Jimmy Bumpley talk through the national anthem again, only this time the really funny part was that John Barr sang along. He had his hat over his heart the whole time an' he was singin' at the top of his cracky New England voice, like some kind of rook playin' his first game in the show.

"You know, that's a beautiful song," he said when he got back to the bench. "And this is a great ballpark, Swiz. What a great place to play. Did I tell you how much I love to play this game?"

"You did, bo," I told him.

The Color Commentary

"I have reason to believe that my manager is being forcibly kept out of the dugout!" Ellsworth Pippin shouted into the receiver.

"I'm not saying you're wrong," came back the placating voice of Woodrow Wilson Wannamaker, Commissioner of Baseball. "But after all, you do have a fine lineup out there. Why don't we just leave it at that for now?"

"*What?*"

"Maybe we can have an inquiry after the winter meetings. You know—kind of a quiet, internal sort of thing."

The Great White Father let the receiver fall back into its cradle and picked up his drink. He watched the Angels below him run out on the field, and took a stiff gulp.

"Jesus Christ," he said to himself, shaking his head. "The inmates really are running the asylum."

31

The box score doesn't tell the story. It only tells the numbers.

—BOBBY VALENTINE

The Old Swizzlehead

The last game of his life was the greatest one John Barr ever played. I know the flies will tell you that for pure statistics, he had better ones. There were games when he got more hits, drove in more runs.

But I was there from the very beginning of John Barr in the game, an' I never saw him do so many impossible things. Never saw anyone do so many. An' what's more, it was the first time I ever saw him really enjoy hisself on a ballfield.

He was a little shaky at first. They didn't come back all at once, skills like that, after all those weeks of playin' in a stupor. He struck out swingin' on his first at-bat, but at least they were three good swings. He got beat on a fine slider, an' he actually came back to the dugout grinnin' an' shakin' his head.

"Swiz, you ever think how incredible that is?" he said. "How a good slider drops straight down like that?"

"Uh-huh."

"You sure he's over it?" No-Hit Hitt whispered to me. "You sure this ain't just the terminal stage?"

But the next inning Good Stuff Goodson hit a sinking line drive down the rightfield corner, an' Barr took off after that ball the moment it hit the wood. He snatched it off his shoetops, an' when he saw he couldn't stop hisself, he leaped on into the stands an' went halfway up the aisle with the ball in his glove. He ran all the way back into the dugout with a big grin on his face.

"God, I love to play this game!" he said when he got back into the dugout.

"I don't know if I can deal with this," Maximilian Duke said, shakin' his head.

Next inning I hit a little looper to right an' hustled it into a double. There was two outs an' nobody on first when Barr got up, but they decided to pitch to him anyway. He hit a rope into center field to score me, an' stole second base by ten feet on the next pitch. When The Emp'ror bounced a single into center field, he came in standin' up, and the whole dugout was on its feet to greet him.

We were rollin' now, an' the Big A got quieter an' quieter as the game went on. Next time around, Barr whacked a double to deep center, an' we scored two more. We were up 4–0, goin' into the bottom of the eighth.

"I'm just sorry this is the last game of the year," Barr told me before we went out to the field again. "I'd like to go on playin'. I'd like to play all year."

"Two more innings," I told him. "That's all. Then you can go down an' play winter ball in the Caribbean if you want to."

"Maybe I will," he said. "I just want to keep playin'."

It was gettin' late for the Angels, an' they knew we had control. You could see it in the way they went runnin' on an' off the field with their heads down, not sayin' much to each other. But they weren't finished. Not when they caught on to the secret of our pitchin' success.

Moses had been throwin' strange stuff all day. It was almost like the junk The Little Maniac had wanted him to throw, only with a difference. Now his stuff *looked* like fastballs, but they would break an' dip an' sail just before they got to the plate.

The Angels' manager, Gussie Lasagne, figured out Moses must be loadin' up the ball somehow. He kept bitchin' at the umps about it, but he couldn't catch him. And that was because Moses didn't know he was doin' it.

It was Feeley who was doctorin' the ball, sneakin' a little Vaseline from underneath his cap visor every few pitches, or cutting it on his shin guard. Moses got the ball an' threw it back in with no idea what was goin' on. He was the only truly innocent man in the history of the game ever accused of throwin' a spitball.

But the bottom of the eighth, the first batter up for the Angels took a swing from the heels an' missed the ball by five feet when it broke down by his ankles. Right away, Gussie Lasagne was runnin' out on the field, hollerin' for the umps to call time.

"Search him *now*! Check the ball *now*!" he yelled, pointin' out at Moses Yellowhorse.

Moses looked so innocent, the umps didn't think he could really be doin' anything. But Gussie kept walkin' out to the mound hisself, so Ronnie Beluga starts to walk out, too. That was when No-Hit Hitt over at first base started callin' at Moses to throw him the ball, as quiet an' inconspicuous as he could.

"Hey, Mose. Hey, Mose. Throw the ball over. Throw the ball over here now," he said, tryna make it sound like pepper talk.

But Moses doesn't pay him any attention. He just stands there on the mound with the doctored-up ball in his hand, smilin' at the Angels' manager an' the umpire as they walk out to him.

"Throw it! Throw me the ball!" No-Hit Hitt started yellin', not even caring anymore if Ronnie Beluga could hear him.

"Goddammit, throw me the ball! *Now*!"

Moses Yellowhorse just stood there, smilin' at everybody. Just when the umpire was reachin' for his glove, he dropped his wrist a little bit an' let the ball go. It dropped out, rolled down the mound, an' trickled over to first base.

No-Hit Hitt was on the ball before anyone else could see it. Ronnie Beluga waved for him to throw it over, but the ball dropped out of Hitt's glove, too. He reached down to pick it up an' accidentally kicked it over to Bobby Roddy at second base. Bobby swatted at the ball with his glove, an' knocked it through the dirt to Lonnie Lee. Lonnie picked it up and flipped it over to Not The Whole Story White. He picked up the ball, looked over at the umpire screaming for it on the mound—and rolled it slowly back across the grass.

The ball came rollin' all the way back to Moses, and stopped at his feet. With that same pleasant smile on his face, he picked it up, and handed it back to the ump. It must've been dry as a stone when he handed it over to Ronnie, an' he took it, smiled right back, an' told Moses, "You're out of here."

Spock Feeley and Old Coach Plate spat an' kicked, an' tried to get good an' angry after Ronnie ejected Moses Yellowhorse. But it was no use.

"After that stunt, either he goes or I toss your whole infield," he told Feeley.

"He ain't responsible for his actions," Old Coach Plate said.

"He didn't shoot the goddamned President," Ronnie Beluga told him. "He threw a spitball. I say he goes."

We had to bring in Skeeter Mesquite then, but he hadn't started warmin' up yet. Skeeter got one out right away, but he was wild an' loaded the bases with Angels on a couple walks an' a base hit. The crowd was back in the game now, yellin' on every pitch. The Angels was still alive, somehow, an' the whole game had just turned. The scoreboard was flashin' WE WANT A MIRACLE—an' Good Stuff Goodson was comin' to the plate. I swore I could see his agent in the stands, holdin' his fingers crossed.

Feeley went out to the mound an' told Skeeter to forget about his slider an' throw him a high fastball.

"Have you turned into The Little Fucking Maniac all of a sudden?" Skeeter asks him. "That's Good Stuff's favorite pitch."

"Don't worry about it," Feeley reassured him. "I know what I'm doin'."

Good Stuff stands in there, an' right away Feeley starts talkin' to him in a friendly kind of way.

"Big situation. Big at-bat," Feeley tells him.

"Uh-huh."

"Big hit here, you can get all kinds of endorsements. Beer commercials. Condoms. Maybe even the Wheaties box. It'll really enhance your goddamned portfolio."

"You say so," says Good Stuff.

Soon as that pitch from Skeeter Mesquite comes in—straight an' letter-high, just the way he likes 'em—Spock Feeley lets go with a great big gob of spit, right on Good Stuff Goodson's ankle.

"It was a good one, too," Feeley told Ellie Jay later on. "Lots of green, and some of my tobacco chaw. You know, spitting is really an overlooked part of this game."

There Good Stuff was, about to swing at the biggest pitch of his life, comin' in perfect an' true—an' all of a sudden he feels another man's spit oozin' through his sock. It made him twitch, it made him lose concentration just enough so that he swung wild, over the ball, an' tapped it out to Lonnie Lee at shortstop. There it was, a perfect double-play ball, an' that should've been the end of Good Stuff Goodson an' the Angels for the season.

We just didn't count on God's Groundskeeper. The ball rolled out to Lonnie Lee as nice an' easy as a St. Louis annie—and at the last second it hit a pebble in the infield an' exploded on him. The ball jumped up an' hit him right in the throat. Lonnie went down, an' before So Many Other Ways White could get ahold of the ball, there was two runs in an' Good Stuff was sittin' on second base, grinnin' his ass off.

Everybody ran over to Lonnie, who was still sittin' on the ground, holdin' his throat—though to tell you the truth, we were all kind of mad at him for not makin' the play. Doc Roberts asked him if he felt okay, an' Lonnie just nodded his head.

"What's the matter? Can't you talk?"

Lonnie shook his head.

"That's okay. We don't need him to talk," Spock Feeley said. "Just so long as he can still field."

"I don't know about this."

"Look, it's his own goddamned fault. If he made that play, this wouldn't have happened."

"Ba' bounce," Lonnie managed to croak out.

"This ain't a goddamned pool table," Feeley told him. "I hate to tell you, but that was a double play, tailor-made."

"Tail'-ma' yo' ass—"

Lonnie stayed in the game, but the damage was done. The next batter knocked in two more runs with a single, tying the game. The Angels had Cloyd Kooble all warmed up an' ready again—and I was the first batter up in the top of the ninth.

"Watch out up there," Maximilian Duke told me. "I think he's out for payback."

"No, you think so?" I said. The Big'Un was lookin' at me with his mouth open. In the best interests of sportsmanship, I went up there an' tried to get a friendly rapport goin'.

"Hey, tough loss yesterday!" I called out to him when I got set in the batter's box.

The first pitch came for me. I think he wouldn't a' minded hitting every batter he faced. In the head.

"Look a little wild today!" I yelled when I got back up. But The Big'Un meant business now, an' he wasn't gonna get tempted out of it by no fool words. He pumped three straight pitches by me, an' I felt good that I actually fouled one of 'em off.

Bobby Roddy was up next, an' The Big'Un put three more pitches past him, too. Bobby walked back to the dugout with the bat still up there against his collarbone, like he couldn't quite remember how to get it off. Two out, top of the ninth, an' that left only John Barr before the Angels got last crack in the bottom of the ninth.

"You think this is a good spot for him, so soon?" Maximilian Duke asked me. We were all a little nervous about it, especially after what happened the last time against The Big'Un. Barr went up with a grin on his face, like he couldn't wait to hit against that killer out on the mound.

"This is great," he told me. "What a great situation, huh, Swiz? What a great at-bat this'll be for the fans."

I didn't know if he was ready for The Big'Un, but Gussie Lasagne did. He'd seen Barr's last two at-bats, an' he didn't want to take any chances. He started out to the mound to tell The Big'Un to go ahead an' put Barr on intentionally. He got about halfway there before Cloyd noticed him.

"What the fuck are you doing out here?"

Gussie was only just across the first-base line. His mouth hung open for a moment like he was about to say somethin', then he took another look at Cloyd. He closed his mouth, turned around, an' walked back to the dugout without sayin' a word.

I guess it was supposed to be. It was the big finish that Ellie Jay needed for her book. The last inning of the last game of the World Series. The fastest, meanest pitcher against the best hitter in the game. There was no way you could avoid it in any good story—though I would just as soon we still had the four-run lead, an' the game wrapped up.

The Big'Un leaned back so far on the first pitch that his knuckles were scrapin' the ground behind him. It came in fast an' hard an' right at Barr's head, just like the day before. Barr dropped straight back in the dirt again and got up slow. He stayed out of the batter's box while he brushed every bit of the dirt off his uniform with his hands. Then he picked his bat up, stood in there just as close to the plate as before—an' grinned back out at The Big'Un.

Cloyd got serious. I guess he could tell somethin' was different. Barr was back in his old stance: feet planted so perfect it was like they'd been painted in the box, bat held high an' circlin' around a little at the top like a cat's tail. He saw he wasn't gonna back Barr off the plate, so he came right down the middle. Barr expected it—everybody in the ballpark expected it—an' he took a big swing an' sent something flying end over end back toward the dugout.

It was the top of Barr's big black bat. The Big'Un sawed it right in half with that pitch. It went spinnin' up over the dugout and into the stands so fast it was a miracle nobody was killed. That was some pitching, but Barr just trotted back to the bench, an' picked hisself up another bat.

"I think he's throwin' some heat," he told us, an' actually laughed.

He went back out there again, an' The Big'Un threw another that nearly grazed the end of his nose. You could tell this one wasn't intentional, which was even more frightening. The Big'Un was airin' it out now, he was leanin' back an' throwin' so hard he didn't have control of the ball anymore.

But John Barr didn't back out of the box after that pitch. He waved for The Big'Un to throw another one in—he actually waved for it with his hand.

Cloyd threw high an' inside again, an' now Barr was up three-one on the count. The Big'Un made hisself calm down a little; you could see he didn't wanna walk John Barr. That woulda been the smart move. But neither wanted it to work out that way.

He scraped a couple times at the mound with his foot, and took a moment to let the blood run. He wound up full again, but this time he kept control an' put another seed right across the plate. John Barr was waitin' for it, and he took a full swing. An' then there was another snappin' sound, an' John Barr is walkin' back to the dugout with another sawed-off bat in his hand.

Now he had a problem. John Barr was out of bats. He'd used up the last one of the big black monster sticks, with all his knots an' the narrow grain. It was gone—the last B-99 special.

"That's all," I told him when he went searchin' through the bat rack. "You ain't been orderin' 'em."

"That's all right. I'll take one of your little whippety bats," he said.

"You gonna hit The Big'Un with *that*?"

He looked back at me. "I told you," he said. "It ain't the bat."

Still, The Big'Un realized he had a smaller bat now. Cloyd let him wait, thinkin' he had got Barr to back down an' use a smaller bat, an' now he had the whip hand. The fans got hushed up, they had to wait so long, but then they started to send up a little clappin' noise, eggin' him on for that strike-out. On the bench we all tied towels around our right legs, hopin' for the big hit.

Nobody had to guess what The Big'Un's next pitch was. It was turned-up heat, high an' heavy, as good a high fastball as Cloyd Kooble ever threw: comin' into Barr waist high, then rising up to his shoulders, tight inside. You could not throw a pitch that was harder to see, much less hit, an' the catcher almost got his fingers knocked off stretchin' out his hand to grab it—he was so sure that ball would blow by John Barr.

But it never got there. From the moment The Big'Un went into his motion, Barr was moving. His shoulders were already goin' back, his bat comin' forward—like he knew, already, before it left The Big'Un's hand, exactly where it was gonna be. He had timed it before the ball was there to be timed.

He got the sweet part of my bat on it, but it still bent against The Big'Un's high speed—it bent almost all the way back against the sheer velocity of the ball. But it didn't break. He crushed that ball, propelled it out of here so fast that Good Stuff Goodson only barely had time to turn around an' watch it go out in center field.

It was a shot, all right, sailin' all the way out of the park an' on past the cracklin' Big A radio. Though most amazin' of all was that John Barr didn't do his usual quick hustle, his head-down home-run trot around the bases. Instead, he just dropped his bat an' watched, like any normal human being, while the ball sailed out of the park.

The Color Commentary

Dickhead Barry Busby remembered the rows of men in dark coats and jackets, dark hats and caps, peering into the afternoon shadows that stretched across the field. They would become quieter, more nervous as the game wound down, edging closer to the end of their seats. They knew that this was the last game of the season, and that it could all end suddenly.

But this was almost as good as those days. It was too bright and there were too many colors, but the last game of the year was almost the same. He peered forward into the Southern California sunlight, watching the man trot around the bases while the crowd was unable to contain itself.

He noticed Ellie Jay smiling at him from across the room, over the heads of the other writers.

"Is it as good?" she called softly to him. He smiled back at her.

"It'll do," he said, and rolled another sheet imperiously into his typewriter. Slowly, reverently, he began to write:

"These were men," he tapped out.

The Old Swizzlehead

Of course, the game should've ended right there. The hero hits the big home run, an' everybody goes home happy. That would've been fine with us.

But the Angels still had last ups. Old Coach Plate had pulled Skeeter Mesquite for Al The Fade Abramowitz, but he wasn't havin' much more success puttin' the goddamned Angels away. He let up a single right off, then a walk, an' the crowd started to holler again. Their Angels were miraculously comin' back from the dead. That was when Spock Feeley decided to make a trip to the mound to encourage his pitcher.

"What the fuck are you doin' out here?" he asked Al The Fade.

"I can't get it to move," Al said. "It must be the Kabbalah."

"Jesus Christ, it's the middle of the goddamned World Series. Will you stop with that horseshit?"

That seemed to get the Kabbalah movin' okay again. Al The Fade struck out one batter, then he popped up the next. We were one out from taking the Series—and the only trouble was Good Stuff Goodson was up again. I thought to myself he must be due for an out after all that trouble he caused with the double-play ball that hit Lonnie Lee in the throat. But the more I looked at him, the less I really believed it. He was pumpin' his bat around, standin' in right over the plate, pleased to get his big second chance to be the hero—though he did give a dirty look at Spock Feeley.

I kept thinkin', one more. One more, one more, one more—that's what you're always thinkin' in this game. One more strike to get ahead on the batter. One more out to get out of the inning. The whole year goes by like that, an' then you're down to the last one more of the season.

Al The Fade got ahead on Good Stuff Goodson, one ball an' two strikes, an' then it was down to that one more strike. Al The Fade was on top of Good Stuff, an' he was workin' him good. I thought we couldn't lose.

Good Stuff lined the next pitch into the gap in right center. You got to give that American League swizzlehead credit—it was a good pitch, endin' up down an' away about ankle-high, an' Good Stuff went down an' got it. He muscled it to the outfield, an' when I saw that ball spring out there, I knew we were in trouble.

At first I thought the best we could do was cut the ball off an' hold the Angels to the tying run. But that ball seemed to keep acceleratin'. I got a decent jump on it, but I could see right away that I couldn't catch up to it. John Barr was the same distance away in right field, an' I was always faster than he was. That ball looked like it was gonna roll all the way to the wall an' bring in two runs an' the game for the goddamned Angels.

I started to dig for the wall, hopin' I could make a strong throw, somehow keep that second run from crossin'. But then I saw Barr wasn't givin' up on it. He was tryna cut it off, an' movin' faster than I ever seen him. He was running to a point on the field, like he knew where the ball was gonna be.

The Color Commentary

He couldn't have said exactly which sense it was—sight, hearing, something else—but he knew from the moment the bat made contact exactly where it would go. It was hit well, and bounced high off the turf to his right without seeming to slow down at all. Exactly where he had expected it—

The Old Swizzlehead

It should've been by him. That was the most impossible thing, if you ask me. It was by *me*, an' I was the faster man. He had that ball lined up to the inch, an' he just headed for the spot. But even so, it should've been by him.

I don't know how he made up the ground, but he reached it. He grabbed it in the tip of his glove with his arm extended as far as it could go. He hung on to it, stopped hisself short in two steps, then set to throw. I was thinkin' maybe we had a chance after all to stop the second run from scoring, at least keep the game tied an' take it into extra innings.

The Color Commentary

He snatched at the ball shooting up off the outfield grass and grabbed it on the tip of his glove, the white showing. He still had to halt himself immediately, he knew, to have any chance at the runner. He had calculated it already, automatically, during his run toward the ball. He would have to stop so short that he knew he might tear all the cartilage and muscles out of his leg—end his career maybe right there, on one play. He had to jam his spikes into the turf and hope that they held, and that his leg held as well.

They did. He stopped and turned, spreading his arms like an archer as he pulled the ball back from the glove. He drew back his right arm, then let the bowstring go, and the ball shot to that spot on the diamond where every line intersected—

The Old Swizzlehead

It was even more impossible than the home run. A home run is a home run, no matter how far you hit it. But I still don't see how he made that throw.

You could see it in the centerfold photo they ran in the paper the next day. There was a white dotted line tracing the throw all the way in—but the writers all said it was wrong, it was an optical illusion.

He should have had to sacrifice some of the altitude to get that much speed on the ball. Or he should've had to sacrifice the speed for the altitude. He was too far away, an' the first runner was too close to home, for Barr to possibly get him. It would've taken a good throw just to get the second runner an' keep the game tied. The lead runner was already around third base by the time he caught up to that ball in deep center field. With the time Barr had to take to brake hisself, then throw it in, he should've been home easy, even with a great throw.

Barr threw that ball over three hundred fifty feet, and it landed in the middle of Spock Feeley's glove, held ankle high in front of home plate. Feeley didn't even have to move his glove. The impact of the ball itself pulled it right down on the runner's foot as he slid in.

Ronnie Beluga put up his thumb like he didn't quite understand it. The Angels walked out onto the field, toward home plate, like they didn't believe it. But they didn't protest. The lead runner was out, everybody could see it. And the game was over.

That throw was the last thing John Barr ever did on a baseball field. And it was perfect.

John Barr

I knew I had it all the way. It was just a question of timing.

32

Don't look back. Something might be gaining on you.

—SATCHEL PAIGE

The Old Swizzlehead

I know what they say. That it was bound to happen, and that it was only a little tremor anyway. That it was just sheer coincidence it came when it did.

But it was still enough to knock down the Big A radio frame out in the parkin' lot, an' rattle every seat, an' shake all the numbers an' lights off the cross-shaped scoreboard, so it was left standin' there pure an' simple with nothin' on it—an' so there was never any final, official record of John Barr's last play.

But I still think that earthquake happened because John Barr's throw violated a law of nature. It was too much, that's all.

We could feel the earth shake beneath our feet when we came back off the field, world champions again. It knocked out all the TV cables, too, so they couldn't show the postgame celebration, an' we got to drink real champagne. We even took Charlie Stanzi out of the closet an' carried him around the clubhouse a few times in his chair before we let him loose.

Of course, the flies didn't write up anything about it, which is why you're hearin' it here first. They said it was for the integrity of the game.

The Great White Father did let Old Coach Plate Pasquale go

right away. But Old Coach Plate was an old fat white guy, which guaranteed him a future in this game. His managerial prowess was so impressive in winnin' that one game by one run that the Giants signed him right away. He won the division by ten an' a half games, an' now he gets to tell all the flies how he became such a genius.

"I let 'em play ball," he says, an' winks, an' spits, an' they all write it down. "And I owe everything to Mr. Pippin."

Pippin was determined to get back at the rest of us, too, but everything he did turned to dust. He traded off Maximilian Duke to the Dodgers for a couple kids, an' The Emp'ror led the league in home runs. He let Skeeter Mesquite go to the Padres as a free agent, an' he became Fireman of the Year. Even No-Hit Hitt ended up hittin' over .300 for the Red Sox, bangin' one pop fly after another off the big green wall they got in left. The Mets haven't got above fifth place since everybody left.

I was gonna be one of the first The Great White Father got rid of, but I beat him to it. I signed as a free agent with the Seattle Mariners, an' now I play in the American League, in a indoor stadium. Ten games into my first season, I tore my knee up on the artificial turf, an' I stole five bases all year after that.

That was all right. I got the big dollars, an' Wanda got to go to her college in Oregon an' study early Zimbabwean archaeology, or somethin' like that. I grew me a pot belly, an' got a big bat like John Barr's old monster, an' now I get to pop the ball out of those dinky American League parks, an' stand at the plate an' admire 'em.

The flies like to write about me adjustin' my game to age, but I wonder why I was too much of a swizzlehead to do this in the first place. You don't have to run around all the time, an' you get more respect from the annies bein' a big home-run man. Not that I fool around anymore. Unh-uh. Never. Me an' Wanda even been thinkin' 'bout havin' a kid. She says it's our duty to have a few, for the future. I suppose somebody's got to spend my money when I'm gone.

I finally got out that book Ellie Jay talked me into, an' it's what you're readin'. It's my own true words complete, with a little editorial commentin' an' fixin' up by her, so it may or may not be exactly what I said. Whichever.

She got the dramatic ending for it, too—even more dramatic than the last game of the World Series. People's lives don't usually end that dramatically, but John Barr's did.

The last time I saw him was a few weeks after the World Series. He'd come down from his farm at Prides Crossing with Ellie Jay, an' the two of 'em was so cutey-pie together I was kinda missin' their old, miserable selves.

"He's wearin' me out," she said, but she looked happy enough about it. "It's like he wants to do everything at once now. We go mountain climbing, skiing, biking. I had to give up the cigarettes, just to keep up. And now he's learning to fly."

Barr had got religion, too, which was a shame. Not like a real Jeebee Jaycee, mind you, but he was always talkin' about giving something back. He'd put a Little League field in on his property up home, an' was givin' away all his money to the homeless an' savin' the whales an' shit. It seemed like the man couldn't keep his wallet in his pants pocket anymore.

That time he stopped into New York, he was on his way down to Peru, where he was gonna drop off medical supplies for a charity down there. That little tremor we got was the start of a big quake down there, an' now he'd signed up for some group called Athletes for Hope that No-Hit Hitt was always pushin'.

"Besides, it's a chance to fly," he said to me, lookin' a little embarrassed about the whole thing. "You know I always did love to fly."

"You be careful down there," I told him.

"That's okay," he said. "I don't think I'm afraid of anything anymore."

If you follow the game at all, or even if you don't, you know what happened next. How they lost radio contact with his plane somewhere off the coast of Colombia, an' they never did find the thing. Not one piece of it. It just vanished, an' with it John Barr hisself, greatest hitter in the history of the game—lost somewhere in the sea, or the jungles.

"It figures when I finally get a good man, I'd lose him into thin air," Ellie Jay said when I saw her at the memorial service. She looked like she'd been crying, but she was all right.

"At least it was something worthwhile," she told me. "Even if it was only for a short time, it made up for all those years."

She got the book out of it after all, an' she quit covering us. Instead, she moved up to some big New England house with lots of cats an' plants an' became a real writer after all. I still hear from her sometimes, an' she says she still follows the game. We always get to talkin' about John Barr, an' how we miss him.

"Poor John," she says. "He sure as hell didn't see that one coming."

Like I said, though, they never did find the plane. Who knows? Maybe in twenty years or so, some Indian kid with a hard New England face an' those drowned man's eyes will come out of the jungle to try out for a semipro team. An' then the super scouts sent out by The Great White Father's computer will be amazed to see he can run an' throw an' hit the ball better than anybody's ever seen.

But they still won't believe it.

The Color Commentary

He was half asleep when he felt it: the plane's engine half-catch, then resume, then catch again. After that it was peaceful in the starry Caribbean night. They glided in silently over the glimmering sea and the thick, dark forests.

At first he was tense, hope-listening like the rest of them for the motor to start again. But then he thought of that night, gliding back home in the silent car with his father, and he relaxed.

Whatever happened, he thought gratefully, he didn't have any control over it now.

■ Perennial   ■ HarperCollins*Publishers*

Books by Kevin Baker:

PARADISE ALLEY
A Novel
ISBN 0-06-019582-7 (hardcover from HarperCollins*Publishers*)

The bestselling story of three very different Irish immigrant women trapped together in the midst of events that would come to be known as the Draft Riots— perhaps the bloodiest, most destructive riots in American history. Baker captures the Irish immigrant experience—and the African-American experience—in the crucible of nineteenth-century New York.

"Keven Baker is quickly altering the landscape of American historical fiction."
—*Christian Science Monitor*

DREAMLAND
A Novel
ISBN 0-06-093480-8 (paperback)

A mesmerizing portrait of immigrant New York in the early part of this century, in which its characters confront both the glowing promise and the harsh reality of the American dream. Baker delivers both a masterful, sweeping chronicle of an era of American history and an intimate, heart-wrenching portrait of the lives of its characters.

"An epic re-creation of an era. . . . A boisterous, rollicking carnival." —*People*

SOMETIMES YOU SEE IT COMING
A Novel
ISBN 0-06-053597-0 (paperback)

Based in part on the life of baseball legend Ty Cobb, *Sometimes You See It Coming*— Kevin Baker's first novel—tells the story of John Barr. An all-around superstar, Barr plays the game with a single-minded ferocity that makes his New York Mets team all but invincible. Barr himself is a mystery, with no past, no friends, no women, and no interests outside of hitting a baseball as hard and as far as he can.

"Put this one on the shelf with Bernard Malamud's *The Natural.*" —*Time*

Want to receive notice of author events and new books by Kevin Baker?
Sign up for Kevin Baker's AuthorTracker at www.AuthorTracker.com

Available wherever books are sold, or call 1-800-331-3761 to order.